AF271119

FIRIAN RISING

CARLY STEVENS

Copyright © 2019 by Carly Stevens

All rights reserved.

No part of this book may be reproduced in any form or by any electronic or mechanical means, including information storage and retrieval systems, without written permission from the author, except for the use of brief quotations in a book review.

For information about permission to reproduce selections from this book, write to carly@carly-stevens.com

https://www.carly-stevens.com

To my parents, who have always loved me and supported my dreams

PART I

LEARNER (AGE 11)

1

___

FIRIAN

FIRIAN INCHED FORWARD on his elbows to see over the ridge. Rocks cut into his arms, but he barely noticed the pain. When he reached the edge, he crouched down in the moon-shadow of a large tree to his right. Scanning the dark valley carefully, he saw what he had been hunting: a mountain-ghost. It glimmered faintly under the shadow of another tree. Then it drifted on across an open field, unaware of his presence.

His stomach flipped. The ghost was huge and tall, with fierce fire in its eyes. Firian squared his shoulders. Maybe others would be afraid. Not him.

He moved his eyes a fraction to the left, expecting to find his friend Caedmon lying flat on the tough grasses beside him. But no one was there.

Wait, where was he?

Firian spun his head around, only to see Caedmon standing sullenly a little way down the hill.

"What are you doing?" Firian whispered.

"I don't feel like doing this," he said in his normal speaking voice.

"But right over there," he hissed, "I found the—"

Caedmon idly picked up a rock and chucked it at the tree where Firian was hiding. The rock pinged above him as he ducked. Chunks of bark pattered on his head.

He turned back to the ghost. To his horror he found that it had discovered their position and was rushing toward them, faster than any man could run. The edges of its shimmering cloak now burned with a bright light.

"Idiot!" he screamed as he jumped up and ran back down the hill, dragging Caedmon along with him.

They couldn't outrun it this way. They'd be killed.

"Firian! Firian, stop! I don't want to play this game anymore. Let me go!" Caedmon wrenched Firian's hand off his arm and jogged to a halt.

The night and the mountains melted away, transforming into the bright, stark dirt that hurt Firian's eyes. Low brown buildings sprang up here and there, the nearest one facing the clearing where a group of children played. He was back at the trade schools of Raewhith.

"I don't feel like playing this anymore. I don't feel like doing anything," he repeated.

"Are you sick?" asked Firian. After all, Caedmon hadn't come to school the day before.

Looking irritated and tired, he scrunched his forehead down. "Maybe. I don't know."

"Is that why you weren't here yesterday?"

Caedmon shot him a black look and stalked away to be by himself.

It was just a question.

Firian was alone again, and fighting a mountain-ghost wasn't as fun by himself. He imagined other adventures all the time at home. Here at least, he could play with other people. Sure, sometimes he got hurt when he imagined battles, but it was still more fun than trade school. He just couldn't let his father see his scars.

One of his teachers, Mr. Harlenn, stepped out of the small school building. "Come on," he cried, clapping his hands. "Break is over. It's time for lesson."

With many groans and derogatory remarks, all the children followed him inside. Firian only realized that he had forgotten to eat lunch after he had been swept inside. Somewhere out in the little dirt clearing there was some bread and cheese and even a cookie that his mother had made. Now ants were probably eating it and he wouldn't be allowed to have anything else until later that night. If only he'd stowed the cookie away in his pocket.

Sighing, he slid down to his section of the long, pockmarked bench. The rough-hewn bench had never been comfortable, but he suspected that that was all part of Mr. Harlenn's plan to get them to pay attention.

His teacher walked slowly up the aisle between benches, inspecting the boys. His eyes rested a little longer on Firian than on the rest. Firian didn't look back, and instead reached under the seat and took out his lead piece and something to write on. Some drawings were left from the last time he'd sat in that class, so he scratched them out before anyone could see. The teachers thought he had an unhealthy imagination, but he thought it was much more enjoyable than the real world of overbearing teachers.

"We're going to continue talking about multiplication today," Mr. Harlenn said.

This information would probably be important when Firian made glass like his father, but now it was unbearably boring. After all, he was only eleven and his apprenticeship was a year away.

"If you sell seven items for three tokens each, how many tokens have you earned?"

Mr. Harlenn called on another student for the answer, so Firian focused instead on the globes. Once he had seen his teacher blowing through a long tube with a glowing glob of glass on the end. Slowly, the glob expanded like a soap bubble until it looked like an eggplant. Before that, he had thought glass was always solid, like a sort of rock that his father cut into windows. But it could change and morph into all kinds of shapes. Sometimes he felt like asking if he could try shaping the fiery glass in a new way. But no one would let him do that. The globes were for the palace of Brithnem, the capital of the Western Kingdom. Raewhith, on the very outskirts of the Kingdom, separated from Brithnem by mountains, still had to do their part to support the huge nation.

Next to him, Ewin was drawing squares, triangles, swirls, eyes. Firian leaned over to him. "Do you know where Caedmon was yesterday?" he breathed.

"He was being tested," came the quiet reply.

"Why?"

"To see if he was good enough to be a Tanyu, stupid."

"A *Tanyu*?"

Ewin nodded slightly. "Before he left, he made it sound like he was a Tanyu already. Everyone wanted to slug him by the end of the day." A smug smile flashed across his mouth. "He didn't make it. He won't even talk about it."

"I know *that*," said Firian. "You stay if you're accepted."

"Aw, he deserved it, after talking that way yesterday."

"Have you ever been tested, Ewin?"

"No."

Caedmon hit him on the back of the head. "Yes, you have, you liar!"

Ewin turned very red.

"Sorry," Firian said.

"Shut up," Ewin replied.

"Ewin!" Mr. Harlenn said next. "If you've earned twenty-one tokens, how many coins does that equal? And how many coins will you need to earn to create the same amount of stock?"

Firian bit his lip and looked down. The first question was easy, but the second was ridiculous. Did Mr. Harlenn ever say how much the items cost to make in the first place? He didn't think so.

There was a short pause. "I think Firian should answer that question, sir," Ewin said.

"Why is that?"

"Because he was making me talk in your class, Mr. Harlenn."

"Is that so, Firian?"

"He thinks it is, sir," he replied, tight-lipped. He clamped his jaw tight and looked down. The room felt hot, and he twirled the lead piece in his fingers.

The teacher peered down at him. "Well. Same question."

"Two coins, one token, sir." He took a breath and felt anger choke him. He knew he should stop there, but he couldn't. "You never said how much the items cost to make so there's no way I can answer the second part. Make your questions clearer next time, sir. Most of the time you don't even teach us the answer before you ask. You just assume we weren't listening to anything you were saying, sir."

A few boys giggled under their breath at his boldness.

Mr. Harlenn set his mouth in a hard line and lifted an eyebrow. His eyes became flecks of black stone and his rigid body was framed starkly against the wall of globes. "I believe that you want to leave this room as much as we want you to," he said coldly, pointing toward the door. "You may go now."

Everyone watched Firian as he deliberately set his things back under the bench and left, closing the door behind him.

The air was colder and less musty outside. With calculated breathing, he marched to the nearest tree and punched it as hard as he could. The bark scraped the skin off his knuckles but the pain helped to soothe his rage.

It wasn't fair. He'd told the truth. But his teachers never wanted the truth.

He looked around. He couldn't go home early again. So he found his lunch in a little grove of trees. The bread was a little dirty but ants weren't swarming it. Even the cookie was still there. He stuffed it in his mouth whole. A few crumbs spilled from his open mouth as he chewed. His mother would have been angry with him for eating his sweets first, but he didn't care.

Gripping the rest of his lunch, he took everything past his trade school and across the dirt road. Several shops where real tradesmen worked lined the street. He kept his face aimed straight ahead toward his sister's school, but he still felt the eyes of Rhys, the town's rope and basket maker, following him. Sometimes he told on him, the sneak.

Finally out of sight of the road, he found a stump where he could eat the rest of his food in peace.

Several hours later, boys and girls started pouring out of the school buildings, most of them eager to be gone. Firian stopped sucking his stinging knuckles and perked his ears for the sound of his sister's voice. He stood up, dusting off the seat of his pants, and ran to entrance of the girls' school.

There she was, saying goodbye to a few friends. Brett was always surrounded by friends. He didn't like them. Brett had been his best friend for a long time when they were younger, but now she was almost thirteen and had other friends.

He ran up to her, ignoring the other girls. "Come on, Brett. Time to go home," he said as he began to lead her away.

"You're out early," she replied, pacing after him. She waved backward to a girl with short black hair, and then jogged up to match his fierce pace.

"I walked fast," he said, irritated that she would mention it.

Her soft brown eyes filled with concern. He had her full attention now. "Is something wrong, Firian?"

"No. I'm fine."

"Did you get out early again?"

How does she always know? "It's not your business what I do," said Firian sullenly.

Pursing her lips, Brett tossed her long glossy hair back over her shoulder. "That's the third time this month. Mother and Father won't be happy about that."

"They won't learn about it."

A strain passed over her fine features and Firian knew she was torn between siding with her him or their parents.

"I'll let you have all the rest of the cookies if you won't say anything about this one time," he said.

"Well... all right," she conceded, breaking into a smile. "But if you do it again, you'll be in trouble. What do you do to get the teachers so mad all the time?"

He shrugged. "I don't know. They just don't like me."

"Sometimes I think that Miss Dasa doesn't like me, but she never throws me out of her class."

Brett didn't understand. Firian shook his head, wishing he could get angry with her, but... he loved her too much. Just like everybody else.

"You just don't understand," he told her. "I don't like trade school and they don't like me there either. I wish I could be twelve now and get away from all those people." But then he would have to be Father's apprentice for six years before he'd be considered a man and could start his own shop. He squinted down at the road. *Awful choices.*

"I'm sorry, Firian," she said, and she meant it.

Cresting the top of the hill, a horse and rider clomped toward them, pulling a cart behind. Firian grabbed Brett's hand and dragged her to the side of the road. Her face twisted in an amused grimace, but she went with him anyway. Firian put himself between her and the rider as it passed.

From the top of that hill, they could see their little cottage. It sat back from the road, but part of the roof peeked out from the trees. Small, with a wooden roof and a wooden door, it was just like all the others in the little town of Raewhith. Behind it was a small garden where they grew vegetables and herbs.

Firian bustled inside and kicked off his dusty shoes.

Mother set down the rag she had been running over the furniture and gave them both a wan smile. She wasn't an emotional woman, didn't hug them as his friends' mothers did. Instead, she stayed careful and still. She glanced at Brett and then at Firian a moment. Seeming preoccupied, she picked up the cloth again. A hint of pink colored her gray cheeks. "You better start dinner, Brett. Your father will be home soon."

Brett dashed through to the second room, toward the food pantry and the stove. Firian tromped after her. She busied herself with the food and he headed toward the small pile of firewood in the corner. It wasn't very cold, but Father always liked to have a fire going.

He stacked the wood in one arm, a piece at a time. Clonk, clonk. How much could he carry? One time he had carried seven pieces at once. Maybe he could do better. The load grew until it reached eye level. His muscles strained and he finally had to use the other arm to stop all the wood from dropping.

He spun around, just able to see over the top log. The knife Brett was holding stopped in midair above a handful of spring onions. Her eyes widened, exasperated, but a smile spread across her face as she turned to chopping again.

The door creaked open. Father was home.

Firian only hesitated a moment before hefting his load of firewood into the front room. He chanced a look at Father. His tough, thin frame looked bent like a spring. He rarely smiled, but today his lips were pursed. A bad sign.

Mother smiled politely and looked around the room a little as if to present it to him. Father followed her eyes and apparently found everything in his house satisfactory.

"How was your day at the shop, dear?" Mother asked, moving some of her ashy hair away from her face.

At the fireplace, Firian tried to set down his load quietly, but the freshly cut wood went tumbling, crashing out of his arms. He cringed and caught his breath. Not daring to look up, he started putting the pieces gently into the fireplace, his stomach in knots.

"Not very good," Father said with gritted teeth. More of his materials must have been stolen by thieves from Archer's Point again. Coke for the furnace, molds, cooling windowpanes.... He knew his family couldn't afford to lose any more. And whenever there was trouble at the shop, they felt it at home.

Firian braced himself.

"Hello, Father!" Brett's voice.

"Hello, darling." Father's voice softened just a little as he greeted his favorite child. Sweet Brett never contradicted him. Ever since Firian could remember, Father had never acted like he hated her.

With Brett in the room, Firian could stand up and turn around.

Father's tired gaze strayed over to him.

"Yanon," Mother said quietly, "I have—"

"What is that, Firian?"

Father was looking at Firian's scabbed knuckles. One of them was bleeding again. Firian put his hands behind his back, but it was too late.

"How have you hurt yourself? Come here. Let me see," Father said, coming forward and gesturing with a finger.

Firian's pounding heart hurt against his ribcage. Having no other choice, he presented his hands to his father.

Mother sucked in a startled gasp. "Oh, Yanon, I'm sorry! How could I have missed...?"

Father hummed, like the low growl of an animal. "How did this happen, Firian?"

Firian's blood was pumping. "I..." – he felt the attention of all his family – "I fell," he said.

"And only scraped your hands?" Father raised a dark eyebrow. "You didn't get in a fight again, did you? You didn't hurt anyone?"

He always seemed to get into fights with his schoolmates. And he would win, which got him into more trouble. That wasn't the case this time, but how could he tell them that he had punched a tree? It sounded stupid now. Besides, then they would find out why he was so angry and he couldn't let that happen.

"Brett, darling? Do *you* know why he is hurt?" Father asked, turning to her.

All the cookies, Brett. Firian put as much meaning in his look as he could muster without drawing attention to himself. It was a large sacrifice for him for her silence. He knew she could easily assume why he had bloody knuckles.

"Brett?"

Seeing the indecision on his sister's face, Mother turned back to Firian, her face drawn with disappointment. "You didn't get dismissed from school again, did you?"

"Did you?" pressed his father.

Firian hesitated.

Striking him hard across the face, Father snapped, "Answer me, Firian. Did you?"

"Yes, I did, sir," he mumbled.

Both his parents rolled their eyes in disbelief. "Firian!" Even Brett seemed amazed that he confessed.

He planned on taking at least a few cookies now.

Father seized one of his injured hands, and tossed it away in disgust. "What did you do?"

"I answered a question correctly, sir."

"Firian! No one asked you to leave for answering a question correctly. I've had enough of this. What did you do to your hands?"

"I hit something, sir."

"What did you hit?"

"A... tree."

"A tree?"

"I was angry, sir."

Father huffed out a disgusted breath. "Firian, quit talking back or I'll pull you out of the school!"

"I would like that, sir," Firian murmured.

"That's *enough*!" Father roared, grabbing him roughly and dragging him across the room. His fingers dug deep into his thin shoulder. "No dinner tonight!"

He hurled Firian away in exasperation. When Firian glanced back over his shoulder, he saw Mother backing away from Father as he stalked toward their room.

"How did I get such a scut for a son?" he growled, disappearing into the room.

"Firian, go to your room," Mother said quietly, picking up the rag and starting to clean once again.

2

—————

FIRIAN

"FIRIAN! COME DOWN HERE!"

Firian jolted awake. Wiping the drool from his face, he ran out of his room.

He found his parents eating at the table with Brett. The room smelled like cabbage and cumin, which set his mouth watering. Mother gestured for him to sit down. Could he have dinner after all? That never happened once he was sent to his room. He glanced at Father, who regarded him with an undefinable emotion.

What's going on?

"Something came for you today," he said, edging a piece of paper across the table with a finger. His mouth pinched in what might have been a smile as he looked up from his meal.

Firian eyed them all as he took the note.

To FIRIAN KESS, son of Yanon and Lithia Kess.

Firian shall come to the watchtower in Raewhith tomorrow afternoon. From there, he will be taken to the Tanyuin Academy to be tested for Ability. The presence of both Yanon and Lithia shall be required as well.

 Sias Jairon
 Tanyuin Head

FIRIAN CLUTCHED the paper until it crumpled. Tested for the Academy. With his greatest dream in front of him, he felt suddenly terrified. This chance could be taken away as easily as it was given. His face went hot, then clammy. He looked up, barely breathing.

His family was all smiling—Brett biggest of all. She knew what this meant to him.

"You are going to be tested to become a Tanyu, Firian. Do you know what that means?" asked Father, matter-of-fact.

He nodded. It was everyone's dream to live the exciting life of a Tanyuin warrior, someone who mattered. It was the highest honor that anyone could get, so it was no wonder that the boys who were not chosen—like Caedmon—were somber and moody when they had to face their friends.

Tanyu. The word tasted like adrenaline. *Is it... possible?*

"We'll take you," Father said, "but don't get your hopes up. The Tanyu are warriors. Disciplined. Respected. They don't take boys like you."

Mother had tears in her eyes, happy despite his Father's negativity. She rarely showed this much emotion. At least she believed a little in his chances.

"If" – Father scoffed the word – "they let you in, you'd have to leave everything." He took a thoughtful bite of cabbage. Firian guessed he was weighing the merits of that idea. Father would lose a worker but also rid himself of a burden. Having a son in the Tanyuin Academy would also be a reason to be proud of Firian, maybe for the first time.

Father looked at Brett and Mother, giving them leave to speak.

"Oh, Firian!" Brett cried. "It's wonderful. You could do what you've always wanted—fighting for us and flying and everyone, everyone in the Kingdom would love you..."

"Now Brett, darling, flying is only a rumor," said Mother. "But this is amazing! Not everyone gets asked to come! They must think you're very special."

Firian nodded. "We're going tomorrow, sir?"

"Of course," Father answered. "Remember, not everyone gets chosen. But for some reason you got an invitation, so do everything you can to get in."

Brett sniffed and kept clearing her throat. "It's wonderful. I'm so happy for you, Firian," she said, a slight break in her voice. She wiped her shadowed eyes. "I hope they choose you."

"We all do," said Mother, holding Father's hand on the table.

FIRIAN COULD HAVE SAID a thousand things as he walked to the watchtower with his parents, but he kept quiet, glancing occasionally at Father.

Had the watchtower always been so far?

No one knew anything about the Tanyuin arts, really, even though the others in trade school pretended to know sometimes. He grew up hearing vague stories of battles, flying, and other worlds he could reach only by closing his eyes. Sometimes he imagined that he was in a world like that, but those were just his games.

He closed his eyes to calm down. *A Tanyu!* The possibility was real!

Now he just needed to be brilliant enough, strong enough, *and* have the Talent. He had no idea how they would figure out those things, since he wasn't sure exactly what the Talent was, but it didn't matter. He would die if he had to go back to his schoolmates dejected like Caedmon.

He *would* pass, no matter what he had to do.

They turned a corner and the tall stone outpost slid slowly into view through the trees. Firian sucked in a breath.

The building grew as they approached, getting taller and taller. *You?* it laughed. *But you're that little boy who's failing trade school. How can you hope to become a Tanyu if you can't even do that?*

Firian stuck out his chest as they came to the guard-flanked double doors. The walls seemed to loom not straight upward but over him as he passed through.

Even your parents like your sister better than they like you.

At that, his eyes stung, but only for a moment. He couldn't have the Tanyu see him cry. After all, he was far too old to be crying over silly little things. He closed his eyes and imagined that he was already a Tanyu, the very best. He saw himself walking through the same corridor, except now it was filled with people, all giving him respect. *They* thought he was worth something. He smiled in his vision and nodded to the people right and left of him as they stopped going about their business to bow and touch their foreheads in admiration.

Then one older man looked up. Straight into his eyes. "Firian?" he asked, an amazed smile forming on his lips.

Firian's eyes shot open and the vision fled. *What was that?* His imagination never talked back to him before. He had to calm down. He was far too nervous.

"Watch where you're going," said his father softly. The hard-edged sound of a voice connected to blood and flesh made him aware that he had strayed toward the left-hand wall.

"Yes, sir," he replied, correcting his error.

A tall man in a long black coat stepped soundlessly out of

the stairwell right in front of them. Mother jumped, her hand fluttering to her chest.

"Firian?" the man asked.

His deep voice resonated and the very word seemed to make Firian the best and most significant person in the room. The man's features were severe, but his manner held something like kindness behind it. His eyes and skin were very dark, like a polished stone, both soft and hard. He wore a close-fitted black shirt and looser pants tucked into black boots. When he shifted his weight, Firian saw a sheathed knife on his belt. Even without the weapon, power seemed to flow around this deadly man.

A Tanyu. Firian would have smiled if he hadn't been so nervous. All he managed was a nod.

Without another word, the man headed back up the narrow winding stairs, his boots barely making a sound. Firian followed, his parents trailing behind him. Up and up he climbed until they reached a room off to one side of a landing.

In the small room sat two black chairs and a desk with no one behind it. *Wouldn't it be fun to sit there...* Wordlessly, the Tanyu strode to his seat behind the desk. He seemed more comfortable standing than sitting, but he still felt dangerous, sitting poised and ready to strike at the desk.

"Sit," the man said to his parents, flicking his wrist carelessly toward the other chairs.

The man gave Firian courage simply by being in the same room. *He* was not afraid of his parents.

Father flexed his hand open and closed. No one ever told him what to do. Still, his parents obeyed and sat. A smile flickered over Firian's face.

The Tanyu's gaze shifted to him, and he remembered that this man had come for *him*. Would the man see through him? Judge him instantly?

"Firian," he confirmed again.

He swallowed. "Yes, sir."

The man stared at him a moment before turning to his parents. "We don't know how long the Test will take," he said, turning to his parents, "and we do not know what effects it may produce in your son, nor the outcome."

The blood drained from Firian's head and hands. He swallowed, his throat suddenly dry.

"You must understand—many are chosen for testing, but very few actually succeed in advancing."

Father's lips pursed knowingly.

"I hope you have not planted false hopes in this boy. More than likely he will be sent home tonight or tomorrow. A messenger will bring him home when he is finished, or, if he passes, he will stay at the Academy. If he advances, you may not ask about him or try to contact him. Your failure to comply may have dangerous results."

Firian shuddered. He realized he was holding his breath.

"Do you agree to these terms?"

His mother's eyes shifted to his father nervously and even his father seemed surprised by the intensity of the terms. He shot a hard glance at Firian, and nodded.

"Yes or no?" the man asked sharply.

"Yes," they replied, somewhat taken aback.

"Very well," said the Tanyu. "Come with me." He stood quickly and walked out of the room, not looking back to see if Firian followed.

"Goodbye, Firian," his mother said, suddenly animated now that he was leaving. She reached for his scabbed hand and pulled him in for a hug. It was paper-light, as though she would break or anger him. Firian mostly felt impatience rather than love or sadness. When she pulled away, the flyaways around her face gave her the breathless look of someone returning from a fast wagon ride. Sadness and pride flickered like light and shadow in her eyes. The end result was confusion, as though she couldn't fully comprehend what was happening.

Father stood and looked down at him, his light blue eyes narrowing. "Make sure you pass, son." He put a strong hand on his mother's arm to lead them out.

"Say goodbye to Brett for me," he replied. Then he swiftly walked out of the room. His parents would not miss him. Brett would miss him though.

Once out the door, he couldn't see the man. How could he fail already? Then—there!—he caught a ripple of black out of the corner of his eye and rushed after it down a hall on his right.

Never breaking his stride, the Tanyu looked back at him for a moment. "Quicker than most," he said.

He couldn't tell whether that was good or bad. The inflection offered no clue.

Questions boiled in his mind, but he kept silent as they walked, walked, walked down the hallway, upstairs, down a different set of stairs—seeming to get no place at all.

"Will your parents leave soon, boy?"

He jerked his head up. "Yes, sir. They've probably already left." An oddly desolate feeling swept over him at the thought.

"Down the street by now?"

"Probably, sir."

"Good. Precautions, you know."

He didn't know, but he didn't ask. They took a sharp turn around a corner, down another winding staircase, and then out a side door into the open air. He hadn't realized how stuffy it had been inside. He savored the breath of freshness in his lungs. It made him want to take off running.

They kept walking deeper into Esmeroth, the pine forest that surrounded Raewhith. The Tanyu led, swift and silent, and Firian followed.

Tree shadows began to lengthen. How much longer would it

take to get there? If he asked, that might show weakness, and every move he made was important now. So he said nothing.

The little winding paths through the thick woods finally took them to a stream. The Tanyu halted and refilled a flask that had lain inside his coat. At a motion from the warrior, Firian drank some of the water out of cupped hands, not knowing how long it would be before he would get another drink. He had to keep up his strength for as long as possible. Still the man said nothing, but he seemed to be thinking hard about something.

Firian's burning adrenaline began to cool inside him. He needed that adrenaline—it would help him focus. Maybe all of this was just part of the test. Could he keep up, keep going, not complain, do... something right?

The shadows deepened into pools of darkness and the sky grew dim. They only stopped once the trees turned black. The Tanyu didn't make any sort of camp. "Only one night," he explained, as he stretched himself out on the ground to sleep.

As Firian lay down at a respectful distance, rocks and sticks dug into his back. He twitched and rolled over. This side was a little more comfortable. Underneath him, something squirmed.

He shot to his feet, electrified with disgust, and stamped the place where he'd been lying. In a frenzy, he crushed the pine needles and dirt until he was sure nothing could have survived.

A single laugh made him remember the Tanyu, who had seen it all. Firian's insides chilled with embarrassment and fear, but he thought he saw a slight smile on his dark face. At least he wasn't angry. "Get some sleep," the man said.

WHEN FIRIAN WOKE up the next morning, nothing looked familiar. The stream wasn't there, and the pine trees looked taller. He shook himself and looked around, and still had no idea how he had gotten to this part of the forest. The sensation was like dizziness. "Where are we?" he asked the dark man, who had crouched down to get something out of his pack. His long black coat draped over the ground around his feet.

The man smiled grimly and tossed him some food, a piece of dried meat and a plum. Firian took and ate it gratefully as they began to walk again, but he still felt uneasy.

They walked through the fir trees for a very long time—into the afternoon.

Firian had started to wiggle his toes to stop his feet from aching when he caught a glimpse of a huge stone structure jutting out ahead of them. It filled the spaces between the pines; battlements rose dimly into the air.

The tree line stopped abruptly and the two of them came to a clearing. In front of them stood what looked like a castle, a barracks, a fortress without banners. *The Academy.* Even the building seemed proud. It had none of the airy quality of castles in pictures. This was rooted to the earth like a mountain. The walls, made of solid dark stone, looked as though they had been carved with a giant's knife, sheer sides and massive rounded battlements. For such an enormous building, there weren't many windows. Firian was glad they had come to it in daylight.

They hiked around the left side, which must have been the main entrance. The Tanyu tugged the iron handle, and the massive double doors swung open silently toward them.

The dark man gave Firian a knowing look as they entered. Firian could never tell anyone where the Academy really was, not his family, not his school friends... He gazed reverently at the worn wooden doors. Who else had touched them?

His mouth fell open as he looked inside. Men and women in black—many of them in their teens—walked around a massive indoor courtyard with a fountain in the middle. The high ceiling drew his eyes upward. A chandelier hung from an inverted dome high above, and a railed-in second story looked down at the open area. Most of the Tanyu in the courtyard walked with purpose, like his guide, but there didn't seem to be a rule about where they were going. A couple girls sat on the lip of the fountain, talking. Overall, the atmosphere was hushed and business-like, as though they had better things to do than socialize.

Many of the Tanyu noticed Firian. It was no more than a piercing glance, but even that was something. They almost all looked severe, focused, but not aggressive—Firian knew the difference. Their eyes burned with so much awareness that he was sure they would remember him. He was only eleven and now Tanyuin warriors knew his face. He would make sure they knew more of it. One day he would be famous, even among them, maybe even feared. He stood taller and tried to walk stealthily like one of them. The dark man led him down a hallway off to the side.

"In here," said the man, leading him through the last door at the end. The space was large with one long table in the middle of the room. Eight Tanyu sat around it. All of them looked at him intently. His throat closed tight.

The man closed the door behind him.

"Master Jairon," he said, acknowledging the man at the head of the table.

Firian paled at the name. *The Tanyuin Head.*

Master Jairon looked a little familiar. He had short graying hair, now with an iron circle over it like some kind of crown. His face was more good-natured than the man who'd brought him, but, unlike his guide, there was not kindness beneath the surface, but someone precise and dangerous. "Thank you, Master Makai," he said. "So this is Firian."

"Yes, sir," he replied. His voice sounded loud and high and empty.

"Firian," Master Jairon said again, lowering his head confidentially as if trying to spark his memory.

Then Firian remembered. "You're the man who—!" For fear of looking foolish, he allowed the statement to drift away. Better to be silent than ruin his chances.

"Who what, Firian?"

Hesitantly, he answered. "You were the man in my... imagination."

The leader laughed and the others peered around at each other in muted astonishment. "Very good, boy! You're right. I saw you there as well."

"What do you mean?"

"Come, come!" he cried, not answering the question. "Sit down if you like."

All of chairs had armrests, a small luxury for someone who grew up poor. He chose the most comfortable-looking one close to the door and sat down. His guide sat opposite him.

Master Jairon leaned back in his chair.

"It is an honor to get so far," said a woman, who looked too young to have her short, wavy, white-gray hair.

"Quite an honor."

Firian nodded wisely, laying his arms on the rests. He noticed as he looked around that the others all wore dark rings each with a pinpoint red stone.

There was a pause.

The dark man, Master Makai, spoke. "Do you know how many people have come into this room thinking they would succeed?" he asked in his low voice. "Nine hundred and sixty-one in the last five years alone. You make nine hundred and sixty-two. And do you know how many stayed? Hmm? Ninety-five—ten of them were eleven years old at the time." He relaxed in his seat. "This age is beginning to lose the Talent, Firian. Years ago, there were many who were gifted enough to become warriors in the Tanyuin arts. Now there is a surprising lack."

Firian listened attentively. He'd known his chances were slim; the odds didn't deter him.

Master Jairon continued the explanation. "The Khelê founded the Tanyuin Academy when they were still new."

Firian knew about strange-looking Khelê—no two alike, and they usually had tattoos as well. They visited Raewhith sometimes. The white-haired woman was probably one of them.

He continued. "We were a branch of the Exmorei. You've heard of the Exmorei? They were the Khelê elite. Religious at first. Then over time they broke into factions. The Tanyu were the stronger branch, appointed for defense."

That sounded a little familiar. Exmorei... *Wasn't that a secret organization?*

"The Tanyu are the only ones who test those who wish to join, who *require* Talent. The Amir care only for the Sacred Scroll, for study. They are still loyal only to the Western Kingdom, but we have broken free of those constraints and help anyone in need of our great strength. The Tanyuin Academy is the greatest lasting organization of the Exmorei in the world."

There was a pause.

"Are you beginning to see what you're trying to do, boy?" the dark man asked. "Only the best have even been allowed to see this building, much less be tested. People know who we are, but no one knows what we do for them. *You* don't even know what we do."

Firian's stomach felt sour and he swallowed roughly. Master Jairon watched him closely. His face and neck felt hot.

The dark man continued, relentless. "Only the best. Only the best, Firian, get to know the secrets of the Tanyu. Every person who passes inspection must be deadly focused, extremely gifted, and willing to pledge their loyalty to the order. We are... almost like our own race. Not anyone can join us. Very few do—the chosen, you see. The best are usually trained for at least thirteen years. Are you able and willing to practice intensely, every day, until you are twenty-four years old?"

Twenty-four? That seemed very far away. But it still would be better than facing everyone at trade school again. At the end of those thirteen years, he would be a Tanyuin warrior. Yes, he could wait if he had to.

His guide watched him intently. Firian's hands shook and he could hardly breathe, but he managed to keep his face still. A deep silence covered the room and he suddenly wondered if he was supposed to answer the question.

"You must realize that you'll probably prove worthless like all the rest," said a large blond man to his left before he could give his answer. "Can you live with that?"

Firian was about to say *I already do,* but someone else spoke first. "Tests have broken people's minds before, boy."

"So what chance do you think you have?" finished Master Makai.

No face seemed especially friendly toward him, not even the leader, so he found no comfort there. There was no Brett to look at him with sympathy. All the warriors waited for him to speak. He felt horribly unqualified to say anything, but he knew he had to. All the warriors were now silent, waiting for him to speak.

"I think I should take the test before I decide that," Firian replied stoutly, dry-mouthed.

Master Jairon laughed. "And spirit too!" he cried suddenly. "Take him away!"

Immediately, the guide got up from his seat and jerked his head for Firian to follow. Again he was out the door following the man, bewildered. He could barely feel his legs as he hurried off.

Had they dismissed him without even testing him? His heart

thumped fast and heavy in his chest. Before, he had learned to deal with failure, but not this time. This was his one chance to get away, to get out and become something great. If they denied him his only chance for freedom without even testing him...

It was not a long walk this time. They came out into the hall, then up a large, curved set of stairs that led to the second-story hallway he had seen from the courtyard. Doors lined the left side and a short railing closed them in on the right. Below, students still meandered around the indoor stone courtyard.

Misty tears started to fill his eyes before he remembered to stand up tall.

They stopped. The man produced a key and unlocked one of the rooms. Inside the very small chamber was a bunk on the left, a dresser on the right, and a window. Firian turned to the guide. "What is this?"

"This is your room. Congratulations. You passed the test."

3
______

KIRIA

This was the night to try again.

A small painting crashed off the wall. "*Shhhh!*" Kiria hissed. It was probably Atty's fault; he was clumsier than his brother Jori even though he was two years older.

The three of them crouched low, hurrying through the wide corridors. Living in Brithnem's palace, Mon Párinath, had its advantages. They didn't need to see the grand sculptures and potted trees to know which way to turn next. Since Kiria lived on the opposite side from the Calthwaite brothers, in the royal wings that fanned back into the gardens toward the sea, they had met in the front section of the palace. In her excitement, Kiria had jogged the entire way from her chamber near her mother, the Second Keeper, all the way to the Main, where important official meetings took place during the day.

All they could see was darkness but they knew that they were approaching the huge doors. No one stood guard, as they had last week after reports that people were sneaking into the grand hall—running around, creating disturbances. Atty reached up and cracked the carved door open enough to admit the three of them.

Not so much as a lantern shone around the Main tonight.

"Jori? Did you bring a match?" Kiria whispered.

"Of course I did," he replied, and a bright light struck up and underlit his face. He went over to the nearest round lantern hanging from the wall. He wasn't tall enough to light the wick inside and the match burned close to his fingers. "Atty! Take it!" he said, reaching up.

"Here. Strike me another one," said his brother.

Jori shook out the first one and there was a moment of blackness before he fumbled and lit a second. Gingerly, Atty took the match and lit the lantern. It was still too dark to see most of the room, so he lit one more.

Now they could dimly see the entire space. Banners, light blue and deep purple, hung like clouds from the ceiling, each one marked with a laird flower, the symbol of peace. Where the wall met the high ceilings, verses from the Sacred Scroll had been etched into the stone. Kiria's mother said the words were there to remind them of their devotion to God. Three large carved thrones, one for each monarch, stood side by side on a raised platform in front of them.

Smooth stone tiles, the pattern broken by a large circular mosaic in the center, stretched across to a crowd of chairs. Set in the floor, the mosaic depicted Shane and Mari Calthwaite at the center and their four children in four quadrants around them. Three of the children began the lines of Keepers, but the fourth son died and was called the Father of the Lost Line. Kiria's favorite had always been her ancestor Maril, the only woman. She was depicted in blue and white, holding a knife and a sprig of lavender.

She knew that Atty and Jori preferred their own Line, the Third, which still carried the Calthwaite name. Only the Second Line, passed on from daughter to daughter, kept Maril's married name: Arioc. Calthwaite for the men, Arioc for the women.

Statues of four war heroes, including Shane and Mari, towered twelve feet high in their respective corners. In the light of the flickering lanterns, the figures appeared to smile and wink at the intruders.

Kiria ran over to the raised chairs and sat in the middle one, where her mother usually sat. Her feet barely touched the floor. "What do you think?" she asked grandly as she laid her arms on the armrests.

"Wait!" Atty cried as he jumped up and sat on her left. They both gazed imperiously down at Jori, who stood alone in the middle of the floor.

"That's not fair," he said.

"Well, *you* can't be Keeper!" said Atty. As the second-born, Jori wasn't in line for any of the three thrones.

"You wouldn't like it anyway," said Kiria, looking out over the group of smaller chairs facing them. *That's where the advisors sit. And there is the place for the Keepers' families...* "This is weird."

Atty nodded solemnly.

Jori huffed and strode over to the place where the First Keeper, Cúron, sat. "I'll sit *here*," he said.

"You can't sit there." Atty leaned over to see around Kiria. "Even if I died or something and you had to be a Keeper, you'd sit in *this* seat."

"I'll sit where I like."

Kiria kicked at the floor with her feet. "*Kader* will sit there before you do, Jori," she told him. Kader was Cúron's two-year-old son, the heir to the first throne, just as she and Atty were heirs to the second and third.

Jori rested his chin on his fist and sighed. "It doesn't matter. Keepers do boring things anyway. People say they do exciting stuff, but Dad does boring things all the time. Lucky you, *Atael.*"

"It's not that boring," Atty said. "Dad's been all the way out to the Pillars of Awel before. And he went to visit the Tanyuin Academy once, remember?"

"Oh yeah." A dreamy look stole over Jori's face. "I want to go to the Academy."

Kiria wasn't so sure she'd want to visit. Her mother said that the Tanyu protected the Kingdom, but they acted as though they were out for themselves, like a tiny kingdom of their own. Remembering the strong, stern men that came to the palace maybe once a year unsettled her. They didn't seem very nice. They looked like they were ready to hurt everybody who disagreed with them. Even though they were a little... terrifying, she liked watching them. It was like watching the large desert cats she had seen in the royal zoo when she visited the large neighboring kingdom of Charäkhnem a few years before.

Once, Jori dared her to stick her foot out and see if she could make a Tanyu trip. She tried it but he only adjusted his pace to step over her. He hadn't even glanced down.

"Why does every boy want to go to the Academy?" she asked. "We have the Amiran Academy right here."

They both looked shocked. "Are you serious?" Jori asked, sounding scandalized.

"Tanyu," said Atty. "They're amazing."

"They're really mean," she said.

"No, they're not!" Jori cried, leaping to his feet. "It's just that they can do all kinds of things that normal people can't. They're the best warriors in the world..."

Kiria stood up too. "I know people who don't like Tanyu—"

"They're jealous," said Atty, as though he was explaining something extremely simple. "They wish they were Tanyu too."

"Yeah," Jori agreed. "But they're stuck doing boring stuff and memorizing all of the Sacred Scroll."

"That's important for the Kingdom," Kiria protested, but they would hear none of it.

"Girls just don't understand," said Jori, knowing that that would bait her.

"What do you mean we don't understand?" she cried. "There are girls at the Academy!"

"How do you know?"

"Our advisor's sister goes there! And I heard she's better than a lot of the boys."

"Mm hm," said Jori. "Sure she is." He grinned evilly at her.

She narrowed her eyes. "Be quiet!" she hissed, leaping at him to cover his mouth. Jori stumbled backward.

Atty jumped up from the throne, offering to pin Jori's arms to his sides so Kiria could close his mouth. Jori couldn't beat both of them together. The scuffle afterward left all three of them on the floor, laughing.

Then they went back to exploring the huge forbidden room with the thrill of knowing that as long as they weren't too loud, they could stay up until their servants awoke at daybreak and no one would know.

Kiria smirked as she watched Atty, Jori, and their father through the window. The boys struggled to keep their whole bodies from drooping. Even from here, their eyes looked saggy with sleep as they trudged alongside their father and a handful of servants. They always missed their father when he traveled, so it surprised her that they had forgotten about their early morning hunting trip.

Their father Aylmor, the tallest man in the group, sported a trimmed brown beard and dark brown traveling cloak pinned with the royal insignia. He stopped on the path for a moment and turned to Atty, who—now that she noticed—carried nothing but the bow and quiver slung over his back. His father bent down kindly and handed him one of the rabbits he carried. Jori already held two by the feet, and stood a little straighter.

They wound their way up the path, past the curved walls of the Amiran Academy. She imagined her tutor was studying in one of the rooms, as usual. Everyone in the domed Amiran Academy acted much friendlier than they did in the Tanyuin one. At least the Amir weren't all about fighting.

Two servants opened the palace doors for the Third Keeper's family, where she stood waiting.

"Welcome back!" said a booming voice behind her.

Kiria whirled around to see Cúron, the oldest of the three Keepers, looking particularly regal in long purple and blue robes. *What's the special occasion?*

He spread his arms. "A successful trip, Aylmor?"

Kiria glanced at Atty. The boys' father nodded, slinging his bow off his shoulder and handing it to the nearest servant. "Yes, we all managed to make a few kills."

"I'm glad your boys are growing up so well. I'll let the kitchen know to prepare rabbit tonight." He cast a smile at the boys, but as he turned back to their father, his tone turned businesslike. "Aylmor, the ambassador from Charäkhnem has just arrived. He is still settling in, but you had better get ready."

The Charäkhni ambassador? That sounded important. "Should I tell my mother?" Kiria asked, ready to run down the hall.

Cúron smiled down at her. "If she wants to come, she certainly may."

Kiria knit her brows. Something about his tone didn't sit right with her. Shouldn't her mother be at the meeting? She ruled the Western Kingdom just as much as he did. Why did he make it sound as though she didn't need to come?

"I'll tell her," Kiria said, running off down the wide hallway.

Her parents' room was all the way at the end of the huge

palace wing. Not stopping to catch her breath, she knocked on the door, ignoring the two guards.

Her father answered the door, looking concerned. He and Aylmor had become friends in the army and they shared the same style of clipped beard, not like Cúron's longer gray one. He had the intense eyes of a general, deep-set and focused, even though he didn't campaign very often any more. He looked at eye level first, and then down at her. "Kiria, what's wrong?"

"Where's Mother?"

"Right here," came a softer voice from inside the room. "Is everything all right?"

"The ambassador from Charäkhnem has just arrived!" Kiria cried, projecting her voice past her father, hoping her mother would hear.

"Not so loud, honey," Father said. "Sometimes these things are secrets."

"She should be at the meeting."

Finally, Mother came to the door. "Hello, Kiria," she said kindly, soothingly.

Her mother's dress was all wrong for an official meeting. It was an everyday dress, Brithnem blue but made of rougher material. She ought to be wearing something flowing and gauzy, maybe with jewels... And where was her crown? "You should get ready to see the ambassador," Kiria said, and then realized that she had forgotten to greet either of her parents. "Hello."

"I'm sure Aylmor can handle that meeting," she replied, perfectly calm. "Is he back from his hunting trip?"

"But Cúron will be there, too," Kiria insisted.

"He likes to know what's going on."

"You should know, too."

"Kiria," Mom said, tampering down her enthusiasm with a word, "having three Keepers wouldn't work if we didn't trust each other. I trust the two of them. I'm sure they'll tell me if they come to an important agreement."

Kiria pursed her lips.

"You have to trust me. It'll be fine." Her mother smiled.

She tried, but she couldn't smile back.

4

———

FIRIAN

HE HAD PASSED THE TEST.

With a satisfied sigh Firian sat down on the edge of the lower bunk. No one was there to take the top one, but he decided that if anyone did come, he would rather have the bottom. He had more privacy down there and could get in and out without disturbing anyone.

He had passed the test and didn't even know how he had done it.

His mouth broke open in a smile and he jumped up, screaming. "Ha, *ha!*" he screamed, not caring who heard. "I'm free! I passed! *Ha!*" He fell back on the bed laughing and panting. He was going to be a Tanyu. A Tanyuin warrior. He took on the expression a fully trained Tanyu would have—utmost seriousness, of course—and attacked his pillow expertly.

The door opened.

"I'm sure it's not the pillow's fault," said a man Firian hadn't seen before.

He stopped beating it and stood.

"This is your room," said the new man to someone Firian couldn't see. Then from behind him came a boy who looked about his age, except that he was smaller and looked weaker. His strength wasn't in his muscles but in the energy gleaming bright from his large black eyes. His hair spiked wildly. The boy's eyebrows twitched down when he saw Firian standing there, but his curiosity gave way to a grin.

"I'll send for your things," the man said, closing them into the room.

A second of silence, then, "I'm Bard. Who are you?"

"Firian."

"How long have you been here?"

"I just got here. I passed the test," he added proudly.

"I did too... barely," said Bard, craning his head to look around the room. "Where are you from?"

"Raewhith." Bard's skin was a little darker than his and his features were smaller. And he spoke with a lilting accent. He certainly had never seen eyes like his back home.

"I'm from Enderin. You're lucky to have the Academy so close to your house."

Firian had no idea that people came from so far away. It had just never crossed his mind. Enderin was as far north as the capital city Brithnem was south. The Academy wanted the best, after all, and that meant from anywhere in the world, even Enderin. Tanyu weren't just connected to the Western Kingdom, but had all the world's best.

"So which bed is mine?" Bard asked.

"The top one. What do you mean you barely passed the test? They said I passed but they didn't even test me."

Bard was already trying to scramble up to his bunk. "They didn't even test you? They just let you in without all that mind stuff?"

"Mind stuff? I guess. They said the 'tests can break your mind,' but then they just took me here and said I passed."

"Weird."

"I thought the test was maybe seeing how I would react when they said I probably wouldn't get in, but that doesn't make any sense. What'd they do to you?"

Dragging himself noisily to the top, Bard reached his bed and sat down on the edge with his feet dangling. "They told me to close my eyes and think of different things. They said I wasn't thinking hard enough. Then they told me to stop thinking."

The Tanyu hadn't made Firian do any of those things. It didn't make sense. "Stop thinking? What do you mean? How do you do that?"

"Think of nothing. That part was easy."

Firian had never tried to think of nothing. His vivid imagination would always take over and sometimes he would have visions even in the daytime. *Nothing... nothing...* It wasn't black and it wasn't white. It was clear and there was nothing on the other side. It covered him and he ceased to exist...

"Firian!"

"Hmm. What'd you say?" The fuzz of nothing cleared and he saw Bard staring at him from his perch.

"You're not paying attention."

"Yes, I was."

"What did I just say?"

"You're not paying attention."

Bard swatted at him but Firian ducked and grabbed a dangling leg. Shrieking, Bard held onto the mattress as Firian tried to pull him off. The mattress lifted and bent upward as Firian dragged him from the bed, laughing and screaming. Bard fell sprawling on top of him.

"We're Tanyu!" Bard yelled, springing up again. He kicked Firian in the side as he attempted to get up again. "We're Tanyu!"

Firian thought his face would split with happiness.

It took Firian far too long to find Mr. Belik's room. He hated that he was late for his first lesson. When he finally found the right place, he knocked. Silence. He knocked again, harder this time.

"Not so loud, boy!" cried a voice. Firian's fist froze in the air, mid-knock. "Just come in."

He cracked open the door. The room was dim and tiny. A man—the only person in the room—sat in one of two chairs. Large and imposing, he looked too big for the room, as if he were caged. A hint of softness gleamed behind his intense eyes, but Firian knew better than to appeal to it. No man had ever shown him unearned kindness. So he would earn it.

Mr. Belik glanced at a piece of paper he held in his lap. "You are Firian Kess," he said deliberately, peering over his glasses as he waved for him to sit.

"Yes, I am," Firian said, sitting in the other chair.

"Very good. I hear you have some ability."

"I hope so, sir."

"You will call me Master Belik if you call me anything at all."

"Yes, s— I will." He hoped his habit of respect would die easily. He suspected it would.

"It says here you're eleven years old."

"Yes, I am."

"Why do you talk like that?"

"Like what, si... Master Belik?"

"Like *that*."

"My father, sir." He clamped his teeth shut when the word escaped.

Belik smiled grimly and looked at the paper again. "Do you know what we do here, Firian?"

He had an idea, but figured that it would be better not to answer.

"We *fight* here, boy. We don't curtsy. So cut out the nice stuff.

Your dad won't be here to tell you to shut up from now on. Now *I* tell you when to shut up. Got that?"

Firian nodded, pleased.

Belik dropped his paper on the floor beside him. "Close your eyes," he commanded.

Firian shut them tight.

"Pretend you are in your old house, in your old room..."

Firian instantly pictured the old board house nestled uncomfortably in the trees as if it wanted to shy away from the road. Then he stood in his little room, with the low bed pressed against the far wall, under the window. Grayish-yellow plaster above the paneling emphasized the dusty light coming in. Maybe that was one of the reasons his parents never thought it was clean enough, even if everything was put away...

"Now you are in the outpost with your parents..."

He saw it all again, as if he were reliving it.

"Now you're back in your room."

He was.

"Now in the outpost."

He was.

Belik's voice took a less commanding tone. "Your father is tall and thin, with short brown hair and a mustache, your mother is a hand shorter, with medium-length brown hair and blue eyes, just like yours, and there is a window above the bed in your room."

Firian opened his eyes. "How did you know that?" he whispered. Could everyone in this place read his mind? In his sudden fear, he instinctively thought of the worst thing he knew, then flushed hot as Belik laughed.

"I could see almost everything," said Belik. "Do you know how?"

"No."

"You have an imagination. I have an imagination. I just have to imagine that I see what you're imagining, see?"

Firian thought about it for a moment. "Not really, Master Belik."

"Close your eyes again. You'll see what I mean."

His lids lowered.

"Now, clear your thoughts and our minds can meet halfway in the Unreal."

He tried to empty his mind and figure out what the Master was thinking at the same time. It wasn't easy, but slowly he saw the trade school and his teachers there moving around and telling him to pay more attention.

"Explain," Belik demanded.

"What?" His eyes popped open, his stomach churning uncomfortably.

"What did you see?"

"My... trade school teachers."

Belik leaned forward with a sardonic look on his face. "Why would I think about them?"

"Maybe to show me the differences between you and them?"

"I don't even know your trade school teachers. I was thinking of something completely different." He paused. "When did you arrive here?" He asked the question as though he already knew the answer.

"Just yesterday."

"Ah," he said, nodding. "And they just let you in?"

Firian's throat constricted.

Belik narrowed his eyes. "The Head was there for your test, wasn't he? He doesn't bother with new recruits unless he has a reason. He went because he knew you had the Talent before you arrived. That's why you passed. So come on," he said, clapping his dry hands together, "try again. What am I picturing? It's just a picture so it won't be hard for you."

Again in darkness, Firian's heart pounded. Nothing came to him. He still had no idea what Belik was thinking. How could they all expect him to read minds on the first day? It wasn't as if he'd been practicing. He hadn't known it was possible until now.

Then something Bard had said came back to him. *Nothing. Think of nothing.*

Nothing... nothing...

Then... something! Just one image, unmoving, unwavering, came slowly into view in the clear mirror. It was a person, a woman that he'd never seen before. The image was so detailed that she could have been standing in front of him.

"What does she look like?" Belik's voice echoed.

"She has dark skin and big eyes," he answered, without opening his eyes, "some kind of ring in her nose, and short, reddish-brown hair and... she's wearing a green dress."

"Shoes?"

"Shoes are yellow."

"There you have it!" Belik shouted so loudly it made Firian jump. "Look at me."

He looked up and the image lingered a little before his mind before flickering out completely.

Belik seemed pleased. "That's Chetana."

"Who's she?"

"That doesn't matter. Do you understand now? Do you understand?" His large, rough hands twitched with anticipation.

Firian swallowed. For a moment, he'd really done it. "I think so."

"Could you do it again?"

Firian nodded vigorously and beamed with pride.

"Well then, do it. Now!"

For hours, they practiced techniques for meeting in the Unreal until Firian was sure it must be well past lunchtime.

Before Belik let him go, he told Firian the rest of his class schedule, which all sounded more interesting than anything he had learned at trade school.

After a quick meal, Strategy was next.

IT TOOK a moment for Firian's eyes to adjust to the darkness. Six students sat on chairs and a Master sat facing them, her hair slicked back in a braid and her eyes calmly closed. Firian silently moved toward the one empty seat.

No one shifted or made a noise. They almost seemed asleep. He wouldn't mind a class like that at all... But they couldn't be sleeping.

An energy buzzed under the surface of the room. All the students were sharing one thought. He dove in, drenching himself in nothing as he had done over and over with Master Belik.

A bright moving picture materialized. Two men, one dressed in red and the other in white, stood in a square, black room with gleaming sides. Their slick, colored images reflected in the floor.

"Success depends on creativity, on calmness in whatever situation," he heard a woman's voice say. "None of the battle-grounds should be so simple, but your lesson begins here. There are two men, endless possibilities. Most of the battles you will be engaged in—if you make it—will be between you and one other person. So we begin Strategy here."

Long, thin swords appeared in the hands of each man. "In the Unreal, you have everything, and nothing. Thought is your only restraint. Any weapon you can devise, any way you want to move, is possible if you have mastery. Mastery is key. Strength of mind."

The men ran at each other, blades raised, whirling their

swords expertly at each other, and clashed. The weapons gleamed deep white in the sheen of the floor.

"This is one method," said the female voice, as the fight continued before Firian's mind. "But this is too simple. If your opponent has any skill at all, you must use more advanced tactics."

All of a sudden, the red and white men left the ground and slid on a film of air like ice, gaining height as they fought harder. Someone gasped—a sound heard from underwater. Soon the two were flying through the air, rotating in every direction as though no one way could pull them down.

"Typical," the voice said. "Most warriors are advanced enough to fly. The next step is to change weapons, like this."

The red man's sword dissolved into smoke and a spear appeared in its place. The white man kept his sword, but gained a knife. The fight moved faster, faster. Firian gaped as he watched. If the fight got too close, could it hurt him? He flexed, steeling himself, and focused on the complicated moves. Tonight, he would try to remember every last step in detail.

Then everything went blank.

"That's enough for today. Remember all that for tomorrow."

Firian opened his eyes and peered cautiously around. The room seemed brighter now.

During the rest of the lesson, the Master (he hadn't caught her name) spoke and drew diagrams of strategies that worked or didn't work and why. Her long, thick braid swung with each measured movement. The Unreal fight was much easier to remember than the diagrams.

When the class ended, Firian followed everyone out the door.

One day down...

He found his way back to his upstairs room, hoping he could find more food.

No one was there, not even Bard. But on the lower bunk was a small, bulging knapsack. He worked open the leather strap at the top and found his winter boots from home. The Tanyu must have sent for his belongings immediately for them to arrive so quickly. Not even a day had passed since he arrived.

He pulled out the items one by one and laid them on the bed. A note or gesture of good-bye from his parents was not among the items he received. He didn't really expect one. But there was a scrap of paper from Brett. *Congratulations,* it said. *I knew you could do it! Now you'll be a warrior—a Tanyu—one of the bravest and smartest people in the world! I love you. I won't forget you.*

He wouldn't forget Brett either. Based on what Master Makai had said at the watchtower, it was unlikely that his family could come often. And *she is the only one who would want to.*

With a sewing needle, he tacked the paper to the wooden bedpost beside the bottom bunk pillow.

He put away all his other clothes and belongings quickly. Since he didn't own very much, he noticed that a couple items of clothing were missing, but he wasn't going to ask about them. Maybe the Academy would provide him with clothes.

When he was finished, he threw himself down on the bunk and began to pick at the bedpost, tossing the flakes away with his fingernail.

The door swung heavily on its hinges and Bard stepped in, looking very small, followed by a stream of yellow-white light. He shut the door behind him and opened a dresser drawer, bringing out two oranges and a small loaf of brown bread. Though he looked tired, he smiled. "Hungry?"

"Yeah!" Firian hopped off the bed.

"A last gift from my parents," he said, handing him an orange and breaking off a hunk of bread.

Firian didn't feel like responding to that, so he peeled the orange instead. Mist spritzed from the peel as he ripped it off.

After a while, Bard finally said, "Is there anything else planned for today?"

"I don't think so," Firian replied with his mouth full of orange slices.

"Then I'm going to bed," said Bard. At that, he undressed and climbed up into his bunk.

Firian didn't feel tired, so he just sat at the edge of his mattress, chewing thoughtfully, reviewing all that he had learned in his mind. He reviewed his lessons in the dark. He didn't intend to take thirteen years to learn how to fight. Already, the Tanyuin Head himself had let him in, and he'd gotten a Master's approval on the first day. Once he believed he could remember every detail of Belik's teaching and the Strategy lessons, he blew out the light and lay down.

The only light in the room came from the moon and stars peering in the small window. Bard softly started to cry. The sound was painful and left Firian at a loss. He angled up on his elbow, wanting to comfort Bard but not having the slightest idea where to begin. Bard probably just missed home—something Firian couldn't fully understand. Maybe it was better to give him his privacy.

He settled himself back down. Drowsiness overtook him and he fell slowly asleep to the sound of Bard sniffing and quietly choking on sobs.

5

———

KIRIA

"Kiria."

Her daydream vanished—something about leading a battle or dancing with a prince. Blinking in the sunlight streaming in from the window, she looked up at her tutor, Daelon. He smiled at her, crinkling his deep eyes. Though Daelon wore the same high-collared long robe of dark blue-gray that all other Amir wore, he wasn't intimidating like some of the others. "Where have you been?" he asked.

"Right here."

The study rooms in the Amiran Academy were traditionally small, and held only a copy of the Scroll or some other guide for meditation. Royalty and other noble families sent their children there for their whole education. Right now, the room only contained the two of them and a large map spread over a table.

Daelon sighed. "I'm trying my best to keep your attention, my Kepress."

She smiled defiantly at him. "Just say it again. I'll remember this time."

She obediently turned to the map. Only the right-hand side was well filled out. The left side consisted mostly of the Kheltor

Ocean, which she would be able to see if she could leave this lesson and go outside. Inlaid silver marked her city of Brithnem, the capital of the Western Kingdom, on the coast directly between two slanting mountain ranges.

Running his finger across the huge distance from the southern mountain range to the area just north of the second range, Daelon said, "The Western Kingdom stretches from the Somul Mountains in the south to Esmeroth Forest in the north."

A barely perceptible line of silver marked the country's boundaries. She followed the line with her eyes. It enclosed almost the whole space between the mountain ranges and beyond, like tea spilling from a cup. One day, she would help to rule that whole area. She could hardly suppress a grin at the thought.

"Now, my Kepress," he continued, "without looking, tell me what kingdom lies directly east of ours."

She met his eyes, aware of her peripheral vision as she tried to remember.

Of course. Her parents talked about this kingdom all the time. "Charäkhnem!" she cried. The kingdom of Charäkhnem held the pass where the mountains met.

Daelon looked as though he would ask another question, but he glanced at the sun first. "Speaking of Charäkhnem, we don't have much longer. You're supposed to meet the prince later."

"Oh!" That was good. If Mother wouldn't meet with the ambassador, at least she could meet with the prince. She wasn't a grown-up, but even an eleven-year-old could make a good impression, and maybe get some information that would be helpful to the other Keepers.

He opened the door for her and they both went out into the bright palace gardens. Gravel crunched beneath their feet as they strolled back to the castle.

The space wasn't very large, about as big and dark as the formal dining room, where her parents sometimes had meetings over dinner. This room had a table too and the walls were covered in wood paneling and tapestries.

Atty stood awkwardly by the big table. A look of relief crossed his face when she entered. Two Charäkhni guards in pointed helmets and embroidered uniforms stood in the corner of the room. Swords hung at their sides. Kiria glanced sideways at the door she had just come through and was happy to find Brithnem guards at the ready too. At the center of the room was a gangly boy, maybe eleven or twelve, with toughened desert skin and light red hair, wearing a formal outfit much too big on him. He looked lost.

"Prince Amrit?" Kiria began, addressing him.

"Yes," he replied in a thick accent. He touched the middle of his chest. "Prince Amrit."

"I'm Kiria Arioc, the Kepress of Brithnem," she said. She loved the way her title sounded. Technically, she was the Kepress of the whole Western Kingdom, but Brithnem was a prettier word.

"And I'm Atael Calthwaite," said Atty, stepping forward. "I'm —I'm a Kepron."

Amrit bowed a little from the waist, first to Atty, then to Kiria.

"I'm glad you have come to the palace," Kiria said, speaking slowly. Hopefully it wasn't too slowly.

"Yes." Amrit narrowed his eyes. "You are a leader?" he asked.

She knit her brows. "Yes, I'm the heir to the Second Line," she said. Atty nodded in confirmation.

"Oh."

Oh? What's that supposed to mean?

"Shall we sit?" she asked, gesturing to the table. It sounded like something her mother would say, and she wasn't sure what else to do.

She and the two boys sat around the table, the awkwardness getting thicker.

Finally, Amrit spoke to Atty, who kept looking nervously down at his hands. "My ambassador is here to talk about an alliance." It was clear that he had memorized just enough words in their language to get that sentence out.

Kiria nodded, prompting him to go on.

But Amrit's pained look meant he had already run out of words to say. He seemed caught between speaking and not speaking. He called one of his guards over and spoke to him rapidly over his shoulder in Charäkhni. The guard whispered back.

The chair dug into Kiria's back. *Will he ever get to the point?*

Amrit centered himself again, ready to perform another sentence.

He turned his eyes to her. "I don't think we should make an alliance."

She didn't know what she had expected, but it wasn't that. "What? Why not?" she burst out. An alliance was a good thing, wasn't it?

He made an unreadable face.

She continued. "I think our countries would make great allies." It was probably true. Daelon was always telling her about how allies helped in times of war. Just think of the War of the Kingdom Rebels. They couldn't have won without allies. Right now, there were no wars, but it was never bad to have more friends in other countries, just in case.

Amrit shook his head. This skinny boy was getting on her nerves.

Atty finally joined the conversation. "Yeah," he agreed. "It would be good to have peace with each other." A slight slur crept into his voice, as it did whenever he felt overwhelmed.

The door behind them opened. Relieved to have someone

else take the pressure off her, Kiria twisted to see who it was. Her mother.

"Hello," she said, "I'm Merian Arioc, Second Keeper."

Amrit stood in a gesture of respect, and bowed to her. At least he got that right.

"Thank you for meeting with my daughter and Kepron Atael," she continued. "But I must pull them away. I hope you have a pleasant stay, Prince Amrit."

Kiria and Atty got up and followed her mother out of the room.

"We were trying to make an alliance," Kiria whispered. Surely her mother would see how helpful that was.

Her mother smiled, almost amused. "Aylmor and Cúron have already negotiated that."

Kiria deflated. It was a little silly, in retrospect, to think that she would have that much power to make political decisions.

"Amrit was being rude," she said.

Mom laughed humorlessly. "His father suggested that he marry you to firm up the alliance. I thought it was well known that Second Keepers can't be married off like that..."

Amrit's disgusted face made more sense now. But why should he be disgusted? He would be lucky to marry Kiria. Well, she didn't want him either. He was a gross boy.

"They should have known," said Atty, chiming in.

"Yes," Mom replied, turning to him. "They should have. Still, the Keepers have managed to make the ambassador come around." She sighed, a tired sound.

"As long as I don't have to marry Amrit!" said Kiria, not caring if he heard.

6

FIRIAN

KNOCK, knock, knock!

"You're late for class! Report to Master Jovan immediately!"

Bard rolled over and nearly fell off the bed. Firian saw his arm flail into view above him.

How did I sleep late? Frantic, Firian grabbed yesterday's clothes from the floor and pulled them on. Running into the hall, he left Bard standing there, still muttering and blinking the sleep out of his eyes.

He ran past the other rooms, down the stairs, and out again into the common area. He didn't see any trace of the person who had knocked on his door. Still groggy, he approached the nearest Tanyu, a tall older girl. "Excuse me," he said. If he hadn't been so desperate, he would never have spoken to her like this. She turned and looked at him. "Excuse me, I'm looking for Master Jovan."

Almost imperceptibly, her eyes widened. "Down that hall." She pointed. "It's the third room on the left."

He rushed off, frantic, without a thank you, almost barreling into two more students. The hallway was longer than he expected. There it was—third door on the left! He burst in.

Twenty people stopped and stared at him.

He froze. Facing the door, Master Jovan stood in front of the class, an angry look on his face. His tanned skin looked tough like leather. The black shirt he wore showed off the gigantic muscles on his arms. The smooth stone room he commanded looked just like Master Belik's, except much bigger. This one had a window and no chairs. Across the large room, arranged in rows, students around his age stood at attention. It certainly looked like more than ten students. *Did Master Jairon lie about that number?* Every one of them wore a long-sleeved black shirt and black pants tucked into short black boots. Firian looked down at his dirty green and brown outfit.

"Who are you?" Jovan demanded.

"Fi... Firian Kess."

"Get in line, Firian Kess! Don't stand there like you're stupid. We have no time to wait for gory students who are late." The curse word knifed through him. Jovan's voice became dangerously low. "Meet me after."

Firian's face felt on fire as he scrambled into an empty spot in one of the rows with the others. He held his hands behind his back to keep them from trembling. One boy sniggered at him.

"Do you have something to add, Shiro?" the Master barked, turning on the boy who had laughed.

"No, Master Jovan."

The door behind them flung open and Bard ran in. His eyes widened and he stopped.

"And here's another," Jovan said.

Bard swallowed visibly. Unable to face him, Firian looked away.

"And who are you?"

He hesitated for several seconds. "Bardhon Tanery."

"Come here, Tanery."

Firian raised his eyes to Master Jovan, who pointed to the

floor beside him. His fierce gaze burned as he looked at Bard. Instinctively, Firian flexed, ready to take a blow. This man was so much bigger than Father. Whatever he did to Bard was bound to hurt.

Firian heard stumbling footsteps as Bard appeared beside the Master. Bard's dark eyes rounded, huge with fear. At the first sound of the Master's voice, Bard flinched.

"There are many ways to kill a man," Jovan cried, so the class could hear.

The blood seeped from Bard's face until it was ashen. Firian stopped breathing.

"But we don't want to kill someone unless it's necessary. More often it's a better idea to injure in order to get information, or distract to get away. There are many ways to do those as well." He turned back to Bard, whose breathing rasped in and out, shallow and rushed. "One easy thing to do" – he raised his leg before Bard could move away, and stamped hard on his foot, scraping his boot down across the bridge – "is to step on the person's foot like that."

Bard screamed and his anguish-lined face glistened with tears that didn't fall.

"Don't merely crush the toes, but stomp higher up. Some people can still run with crushed toes. This will slow them for a while."

Firian tasted blood and realized he had bit his tongue.

"You will all practice that later, but now we're working on the basics—go line up, Tanery—so get in position," said the Master.

Limping, Bard slid into line, avoiding everyone's eyes. His ragged breathing betrayed that he was crying.

All the other students spread their legs a little and put their hands behind their backs. Firian followed their example and so did Bard, wincing.

Meet me after... He had heard those words many times from

his trade school teachers, but they were harmless. Master Jovan could kill him if he wanted to.

During the rest of class, the Master showed them all basic strength techniques: three different kinds of push-ups, deliberate postures flexing the abdomen or the legs, crouching jumps... Jovan corrected every weak repetition or wrong angle, and mocked anyone who struggled to keep up. By the end, Firian's muscles quivered, completely strained. Bard had trouble matching the pace but he managed. Finally, Jovan announced a short break for breakfast. The children scattered quickly, eager to escape his watchful eyes.

Everyone left but Firian and the Master. The room felt huge and empty.

"Kess!" Jovan cried suddenly. The name reverberated around the room.

"Yes, sir!" he answered, forcing himself to look the Master in the eyes. "Yes, Master Jovan?"

He laughed loudly and began to walk out through a back door that Firian hadn't seen until then. "With me, Kess," he said, disappearing through the opening.

The door led to a dark, stone hallway covered in dust. Obviously, people didn't use it often. A door rimmed with yellow light blocked the other end of the corridor. With one hand, Jovan opened it and blinding light burst in.

After they walked outside, the Master closed the door behind them. Huge weathered pines grew close together all around the Academy. The wall behind him rose tall and impassible, made completely with rough stones fitted together without mortar. No way to escape.

"Run."

Firian looked up. Master Jovan cocked his head to the left. "Around the building. Now. Run. As fast as you can. Go!"

Firian took off sprinting. Dread faded away the farther he

went. He ran like a hunted thing, but his muscles already ached from the workout during class. He didn't know how far he'd gotten before he slowed to a jog. Around the building, Jovan had said. All the way around. So he stumbled forward as fast as he could, keeping close to the wall.

Finally, he rounded the corner to see Master Jovan waiting there for him. Firian stopped, panting.

"Very good," Jovan said. "But you were too slow. Do it again."

Again?

He peered back, completely stoic. "Faster. Go."

Firian had no choice but to follow orders. *Warrior... warrior...* It was all for the sake of becoming a Tanyu. He had to do anything they said or they could send him home. So he ran even faster than he had before, though it used up all of his remaining strength. His legs burned, his breathing rushed against raw, dry lungs. *Keep going... keep going... keep going...*

He ran now to send a message to the other Tanyuin warriors. Grown and strong, he wore all black, running. He ran for the safety of the other Tanyu still trapped in that battle. Slowly the enemy troops were advancing to the real location of the Academy. They all knew where it was. So Firian ran to take his message to... Master Jovan.

He snapped from his thoughts and realized that he could hardly breathe. He slowed, and his muscles recoiled. He twisted in pain, but had no breath to scream. Bent almost double, he began to go again. He never should have stopped. *Faster... faster... faster than the last time...* He began to feel lightheaded and the tendons in his legs tightened more with every step. *Faster...* His side began to ache. *Faster.* He could see Master Jovan now, leaning with his back against the wall, watching him.

"Faster!" Jovan yelled when he saw him stumbling toward him. "It's taken you just as long as last time! How will this teach you to get to class on time if you don't HURRY?"

Firian tried to straighten and run again.

"Faster!"

He ran faster, and though his nostrils were flared like a running horse, he couldn't breathe at all. Only a few more steps. The Master grew closer. Closer.

Firian collapsed at his feet and vomited.

Master Jovan looked unconcerned. "You'll get to class on time tomorrow?" he asked.

Firian nodded miserably.

"Good," he said, going back inside. "That's enough for today."

The door clicked into place and Firian still lay there, panting like a dog. Stabbing pain seared his legs and his side.

Once he had gathered enough breath, he stood up painfully, wiped his mouth, and went back inside. He had missed breakfast.

PART II

DEFENDER (AGE 15)

7

———

FIRIAN

Master Jovan laughed. "Run!" he yelled.

Determined to beat his record, Firian finished his second lap around the Academy. Although he had moved on to weapons training and more advanced techniques, Jovan still insisted on ending every session with the same laps around the building that had ended his initial lesson. Now, the new muscle Firian had gained over the past four years made him look bigger and more impressive than he had when he had first arrived.

He jogged to a halt. Master Jovan crossed his large arms as he looked down at Firian. "Well," he said slowly, "you're getting better."

Those were some of the first words of encouragement he had ever heard Jovan say. Firian nodded as he caught his breath.

"That means you can do better tomorrow," he said, disappearing again through the door back into the Academy. Firian followed at a respectful distance, smiling.

You're getting better.

Jovan's leaving always signaled the end of the lesson, so Firian was free to go back to his room.

Bard wasn't there. Probably in class.

Firian slipped into the Unreal, felt its power sizzle under his skin. How could he practice today? He was improving physically, but would his skill be enough to pass the hall test later today? Their hall master Erron tested the guys on his hall every year or so. Even though Erron, at eighteen, was a Defender, not a Master, he was in charge of making sure they were all keeping up with their training. At least, that's how the Masters had explained this to Firian the first time. Almost everyone treated these tests less like an exam than a competition. Firian had always been a standout among people his age, but today he wanted to show up Erron. And today he could do it. He felt powerful, ready.

He stood in a shapeless space, idly switching out weapons in his hands. Bow, knife, sword. He could only do so much by himself, but he could practice the latest technique Belik had taught him. Become something else—maybe something from a nightmare. He shrank and grew, feeling the wind rush by as he changed. What would be frightening? A ghost, the kind he used to imagine as a kid? That sounded like a challenge, so he let the thought of it consume him. Ghosts were partially transparent— at least the ones in his imagination. He wasn't sure whether or not they really existed. If the stories were true, they stood a head taller than a tall man, so he grew. Flowing robes. Flashing eyes. That felt right, but he couldn't be absolutely sure he was doing it right unless somebody checked for him.

As though on cue, he heard the faint sound of a door opening. Bard was back.

Firian swam up through the layers of his imagination and broke the surface of reality again. The room smelled like sweat.

"Hey, Fir!" said Bard, closing the door behind him.

"Bard, look at this," he called, his voice deeper now. It hadn't cracked in over a year. He sat on the edge of his bed and shut his eyes.

Bard hesitated. "I'm kind of tired."

"Come on!"

His friend gave a barely audible sigh. "Just don't practice attack moves on me, okay?"

Firian nodded impatiently.

Nothingness gave way to a meadow. Bard materialized a few feet away, looking around apprehensively. "What do you want me to see?" he asked.

Firian didn't answer, but called for the energy to become the ghost he had imagined.

Bard's large eyes got even bigger. "Gore, Firian!" he swore. "What are you trying to do?"

Firian subsided into himself again.

Suddenly sheepish, Bard took a deep breath. "Sorry," he said, apologizing for the language. "Are you going to use that during the hall test?"

"I was thinking about it." It depended on the rules Erron set up. Sometimes there were restrictions so that the boys could prove their skills without actually hurting each other. Other years, it was a free-for-all. Hopefully today he could do whatever he wanted.

It was almost time.

The two of them opened their eyes and headed out the door. More students than usual crowded the hallway. Tiev, Shiro, and Rian walked past in the same direction, with Erron leading the way to the room at the hall bend. Across the courtyard, in the girls' hallway, another group headed to their test. Rhea, a girl from the little town of King's Heights, glanced over at him as she went down the staircase leading to the main level, her long blonde hair waving on the air. He rubbed his lips together and shook his head. Today, he couldn't be distracted.

Erron held the door open for all of them to enter. It was another typical Academy classroom—bare of decoration, only a couple of chairs in a stone room. The boys filed in, filling almost the entire space. Erron was the last to come in and silently stand behind one of the two chairs facing each other.

The door creaked open again, and Firian spun around to see Master Belik limping into the room. *Why is he here?* He had never come to any of the other tests.

Bard smacked Firian's arm and nodded toward Belik.

Students made way for the Master, pressing out of the way. Despite the limp, he commanded respect. Once, with a sarcastic yet meaningful look, he'd told Firian, "Whatever hurts makes you work harder."

Belik's face remained impassive as he claimed a spot against the wall. Erron raised his eyebrows at him to give him the floor, but Belik held up a hand. He didn't want to speak. He was here to observe.

Erron continued with the test protocol. "Shiro and Firian!" he said.

Firian nodded confidently. Shiro came from the same desert city as Tiev, so they both had dusty tan skin, black hair, and thin green-brown eyes. They were both about as tall as Firian, but more compact. The two of them roomed together, but Tiev, though a better friend, was the bigger threat, both in person and in the Unreal. Shiro, by comparison, should be much easier to beat.

The chairs were so close Firian had to spread his knees so they didn't knock against Shiro's.

"No shots to the head or heart. Hall master's choice." Erron wasn't one to waste words.

The three of them—Firian, Shiro, and Erron—closed their eyes and waited for a moment in darkness. Master's choice meant that Erron would control the environment. Firian and Shiro could only control themselves.

Blue. Blue and black and white. The colors came into focus,

surging, waving. Firian's body heaved upward with the color and he realized. They were in the ocean. That was new.

Erron floated above the sea like a deity, watching from a distance. Firian and his opponent floated in the water. He had never seen the ocean, so he took in as many details as he could —the wet, heaving waves, cold on the surface, the salt in his mouth, the depths below, the sky reflecting hard like glass.

A wave raised them both up as high as the Academy walls. Shiro, rising mechanically instead of organically, was struggling to find the reality in the situation. Without that belief, he couldn't hope to win. Firian brought his hands out of the water and slicked back his hair, feeling the cool sea splash his face.

Time to go. If he couldn't attack Shiro's face, the only part of his body peeking up over the water, he would have to go below. So he sank down, heavy as a stone.

Blackout. Water pressed in heavy on him. Shiro had to be roughly in that direction...

A current forced him deeper. Had he turned around? The sunlight filtered dim above him. His limbs burned. He couldn't breathe. He flailed convulsively, lungs on fire.

Where are you? You're in the room. You're fine.

He still couldn't make himself breathe. But if he didn't, he would pass out. Out of options, he gasped. No water entered his lungs. He could still feel it on his face, but none in his body. Panting, he smiled. This was exactly as it was supposed to be— believe without believing.

There was Shiro, shooting silver darts from his feet as they dangled under the surface. They passed harmlessly through Firian as he approached.

Now he could have a bit of fun. He'd heard of sea creatures, some menacing and horrible. Thank goodness he had a good imagination as a kid. He didn't need to have seen something to visualize it.

A huge, gaping mouth, full of teeth. Bigger. He could make himself even bigger. He wouldn't need to worry about realistic gills and all that if he could just scare Shiro back to reality, like a person falling to wake up from a nightmare. Firian's rubbery skin stretched over his enormous body, tiny eyes squinting at his prey, gigantic mouth ready to open at the right moment. Looking around at the blackened deep, even Firian shuddered at the idea of a creature like him controlling the water.

Closer, closer... Shiro's body and legs looked frail now. The surface of the water turned red, ablaze with fire. Shiro's trap couldn't hurt him, he was sure. The knowledge buzzed in his mind like a strong drink from the pub.

He swam closer, Shiro getting larger. Soon... closer... now!

With a roar of air and water, five rows of teeth burst high above the surface, water streaming down the head and long throat. Below him, Shiro screamed like a lost soul and disappeared.

It took Firian a shaky moment to get back into his own skin.

When he opened his eyes, Shiro was glaring at him, beet red. He hurled a curse at him and left, passing Belik on the way out.

Bard, Erron, and the others looked at him aghast. Hardly anybody won so decisively.

"Wow, nice job!" said Bard, as though he couldn't keep the words in.

Firian smiled as Belik silently left the room.

THE NEXT DAY during their lesson, Master Belik opened his eyes and squinted. Then he hummed, a noncommittal sound.

Firian treated it as positive. Stiff from sitting too long in the chair, he nodded, ready for the next scenario. The Unreal was always better than reality. There, he could feel like he was flying or standing or rolling or running...

"How did you do?" Belik asked, staring intensely as though Firian's response was crucial.

Firian's hands fidgeted.

"How did you do today?"

"What do you mean?" Firian asked, cracking his knuckles.

"I mean, you did as well as any other student," he said slowly. "But you, Firian, are not any other student. Your work today has been mediocre. Have you even seen half of the things I've shown you?"

Firian began to shrug and thought better of it.

"No," Belik answered. "Where's your focus? If you can't work with everything you have, then leave!" His tone grated, worn out. Belik was a hard man, but his edges were crumbling today.

"There are all kinds of things..."

"Anything more important than this?" he snapped.

"I'm sorry. I'll work harder."

"Yes, you *will* work harder. Why do you think we let you into this Academy? Because we liked your smile? No" – emotion lifted him a little from his chair – "the moment you walked into my room, you swore to me you'd work as hard you needed to become the best!"

Firian's throat constricted enough to force his breathing. Adrenaline snaked like lightning through his body, and he gripped the armrests until his knuckles lost their blood. "Of course! Let's do it again."

"Not until you stop being so gory distracted!" Belik roared suddenly.

Firian's chest rose and fell with hurried breaths. He fought to keep his wide eyes from rolling.

Master Belik slowly raised an eyebrow high above his glasses. Besides that, the lines on his face seemed immovable.

"It's a *very* good thing you're as Talented as you are, and that I like you. People *die* in war, and you're dicking around like none of it matters. You're not finished yet."

"But we're not in a war now," Firian found himself saying.

"That you know of." Belik's eye twitched evasively, and he resettled his glasses on his nose with a finger. The Academy loved their secrets.

Maybe they have too many.

Firian bit the inside of his lip hard. Belik saw the fight with Shiro. Why was he giving him such a hard time? "I am Talented, though," he muttered, unable to hold back the words.

"So am I," Belik replied. He laughed humorlessly through his nose. "I was in line for the Headship, once. And look where I am now." He exhaled a deep breath, his anger deflating. "Trust me. I understand." His tone had completely changed into something almost fatherly. "I could go to the Second Level of the Unreal before I was twenty years old. No one goes to the Second Level."

Firian's eyes widened. He'd tried to get to the Second Level before but almost suffocated. It was the Unreal within the Unreal. It took a dangerous amount of belief to establish the first layer, the one they could all reach, in such a way that it was a stepping stone to a level further down.

Belik continued. "That's how Anewa got Lost, the idiot. But anybody who can..." His gaze shifted to the floor, as close to vulnerability as Firian had ever seen. "Those skills earn you high positions. Strategic positions."

"What position did you have?"

Belik blinked, becoming aware of the room again. His mouth hardened. "It doesn't matter now, does it?" He drew himself up in the chair, his dark ring digging into his finger as he gripped the armrests. "I should have given everything. Everything. And so should you."

Firian cleared his throat. "Show me that last one, Master Belik. I'm focusing now." He closed his eyes. Only darkness and nothingness appeared behind his lids. Seconds passed, but he refused to open them until something happened.

Slowly, he was in a strange gray-white room with many half-guessed suspended platforms above and below him. Maybe fifteen feet overhead, Master Belik appeared, standing on one of them. This wasn't what the last scenario had been, but at least he was out from under Belik's penetrating glare, so he jumped up and Belik jumped down until they met in the middle.

"The object of this exercise," the Master began, "is to... Come with me." Walking away, he said nothing more, so Firian followed him up and up onto new platforms only distinguishable by a darker gray outline of shadow. Up and up.

Climb up. Above him, the room soared neverendingly upward into a haze. Firian jumped to catch the next ledge. Up and up. Most of the landings came to about his waist and he would pull himself onto them, accepting Belik's unstated rule that whenever *he* acted like there was gravity, Firian acted the same way. No flying. No floating. No growing or shrinking. He was just himself. Something exceptionally human in Belik's movements let him know when the rule was in play. The only difference from real-life movement was that Belik's leg never hurt in the Unreal, as it did from a war injury that kept him cooped in the Academy.

Finally, on a large platform that took up half the space in the room, the Master halted.

Turning slow eyes upon him, Belik looked Firian quickly up and down as he hoisted himself up to stand. "Why are you out of breath?" he asked. "Where have you gone?"

Firian hadn't even thought about it. None of his muscles were really tired at all. He slowed his breathing to a normal pace. "Nowhere."

"Are you sure?"

Doubt—just one unreasonable moment—entered Firian's mind as he looked down into the formless depths, then back at his teacher... who rushed at him with a knife! Firian didn't have time to think before he was stabbed and hurled powerfully backward into nothing.

Fly! Just fly, you idiot! He jolted to a halt again in mid-air and settled lightly onto a platform. Jerking his head up, he saw Belik standing there, disapproving.

"Open your eyes," Belik's mind said impatiently.

They opened.

"What was that?" Belik cried. "You know better than to believe in the Unreal! I could have killed you. You could have been Lost."

Belief was reality. If he had believed he died, then he would be dead. "I didn't believe in it, Master Belik," Firian said, fighting the urge to dab his fingers to his chest to check for blood. He glanced down.

"But you doubted, Firian, you doubted!" He motioned to the thin line of blood welling up near Firian's collarbone. "We have lost many good soldiers because they doubted for an instant. It's a good thing I've at least taught you enough to stop yourself from falling."

Rage coursed through him, but he held his tongue. He'd done enough damage for one day.

"Firian, at your level, you need to know this. We can't afford to lose even one soldier to their own stupidity!"

Firian lowered his head. *How dare...*

No. Master Belik was a full Tanyu. Firian calmed himself.

"Do you want to end up useless like Anewa?"

Belik referenced Anewa almost every week, so Firian was sick of hearing about him. He had been Lost a year before Firian entered the Academy. He was the best, they said—so good that his Talent undid him. He went into the Unreal one day and never returned. Belik, being in Retrieval, had tried to rescue him, but failed. The other Tanyu waited months for him to come back to his right mind, but in the end, it became too costly to take care of his unconscious body and they were forced to kill him.

"No Unreal for five days!" pronounced Belik. "Starting tomorrow, I'll post Sentries to make sure."

No Unreal? None? The one time he had experienced Sentries was terrible. Master Asoka had appointed a Sentry over the entire strategy class so she could teach them what it felt like: a painful buzz, a net preventing entry to the Unreal. "As you would have it, Master Belik," he said, each rehearsed word tasting sour.

"You have to want it." The lines around Belik's eyes deepened slightly before his face became a mask harder than before. Even a tiny misgiving—a little doubt—was good to see. Maybe he would regret his decision. Firian's lips almost twisted into a bitter smile at the thought.

"That's all. Leave. Now! Mistakes like that can't happen again."

Firian closed the door behind him without a word. He went to the courtyard and sat on the edge of the fountain, but he knew that his lesson wasn't supposed to be over for a long time, so instead he went to his room and dozed. *That* would prevent him from slipping into the Unreal, because this certainly seemed like a good time to go there.

FIRIAN

Firian hadn't gone home in four years.

He practiced so much that thin white scars laced his torso from the times he had practiced too hard, been too focused in the Unreal. So how dare Belik tell him that he was distracted?

"Stop! Fir, what are you doing?" cried Bard.

Firian jumped back from the doorway to their room. "What?" he snapped.

Bard presented the broom in his hand. "Erron told me to sweep and you wrecked everything."

"Why do you have to clean?" he asked, amused now, stepping over the scattered pile of dust.

"Because we've hardly cleaned anything since we came."

Firian laughed. "If we don't mind, why should Erron care?"

Bard swept out Firian's footprints with gusto. "It's his job to tell us what to do," he grumbled.

Firian jumped onto his bed and sat cross-legged to avoid touching the floor. "It seems that way." He thought for a minute. "Bard?"

"Yeah?"

"How many times have you gone back to see your parents?"

He had just come back from his latest trip a few days ago, when he had returned earlier than Firian had expected. He picked at the wood on the top of the broomstick. "This was the third time."

"I've never gone home."

Bard squinted. "Haven't you?"

"No."

Bard leaned on the broom, his look puzzled as though he were trying to remember a time when Firian had left. "Why not?"

"They never said I could."

"It's been four years, and they haven't given you leave yet?"

"No." Firian reclined against the hard wall. "I think everybody's been able to leave but me. Even Rian's been able to go, and his parents hate him. And you. You live pretty far away."

"I don't know," said Bard. "I can't think of any reason they would keep you here. It's been a long time."

Firian scratched the back of his neck and searched for his family in his mind, but he couldn't find them. He had forgotten. None of them had the Talent. Not even Brett.

"Do you want to see them? You don't really talk about them at all."

Firian wouldn't mind if Brett visited, but he thought better of mentioning it and leaned back again, dull anger stirring in his gut. "No. I don't want to see them. I was just wondering why they would keep me locked up like some prisoner without the chance to go."

Bard leaned harder on the broom and almost lost his balance. Falling silent, he began sweeping again and didn't pry.

"They should let you go," said Bard finally. "You learn everything faster than anybody else, practically. You deserve to have a day or two to yourself."

Firian laughed, half from resentment and half from amusement. "Yeah, they should. I should just leave without permission..."

"They'd have your head," said Bard.

They both knew that he wouldn't leave the Academy's grounds unauthorized. It would jeopardize everything he'd worked for. Students had been dismissed for that, even though it had been a mistake. Everyone suspected the worst for anyone kicked out, but no one talked about it. In any case, the consequences were more than he was willing to risk.

Firian had known that he belonged to the Tanyu from the moment he passed the test. Until now, he hadn't minded. The organization could do what they liked, could push him, could work him to the bone. Loyalty until death was part of the Tanyuin code, and he was proud to be a part of it. Honestly, he was excited to become the one to whom others pledged their loyalty. And they would one day.

The Tanyu could train him until he almost dropped dead, but Firian wouldn't stand to be manipulated. If there was a reason that he wasn't given leave, he wanted to know it.

"I could ask Erron why I'm still here," said Firian. Masters seemed to tell hall masters extra information about their group.

"He'll make you do chores," replied Bard, finishing his cleaning. "He'll probably ask me to do something else too, if we aren't careful." He shook out the broom in the hallway, and then hastily closed the door. "I wish I could burn that thing," he said, staring contemptuously at the brush.

Making himself more comfortable, Firian laughed. "I would like to watch that, just because you'd dance around like a giddy girl."

"Erron never asks you to sweep," Bard muttered.

"That's because I'm stuck here forever."

"Then go find out why."

Firian slapped him on the shoulder and slipped out of the

room. Erron had earned everyone's respect. Students only became hall masters if they had done exceptionally well every year at the Academy and were at least seventeen years old. Because of Erron's reputation as a ruthless fighter in the Unreal, many boys on the hall feared him but not Firian.

The hall felt claustrophobic now, narrow and unchanging. The thought of having another free day in Tánuil didn't cheer him much. He knew almost everyone there and had done everything there was to do. He didn't even *have* to see his family. If he could even visit someplace else, like Brithnem—that was supposed to be a great city—or if he could go with Bard to see *his* family....

He knocked curtly on Erron's door.

"Yes? Who is it?"

"Firian."

"Is it important?" Erron didn't open up much and kept mostly to himself. Only his imagination was savage, apparently.

"...yes."

"Very important?"

"Yes."

"Come in. I don't feel like talking to anyone for very long."

Firian hurried in.

"Close the door, Kess," said Erron, seated in a chair with his name carved in both armrests. He'd threatened death to anyone who attempted to steal it from him. No one had, but the thought had crossed every boy's mind more than once. "What is it?"

"Why haven't I been allowed to leave the Academy?" Firian asked. Small talk was a waste of time.

Erron arched an eyebrow. "What do you mean?"

Firian looked into Erron's large eyes. All his features were large, especially his nose. "I mean I've been here for four years and have never been given leave to go."

"You've never been into Tánuil," he said dryly, blanking his eyes. With one large finger, he tapped the dark band of his Defender ring inlaid with a light blue stone against the armrest.

"You know what I mean."

"You want to see your family?"

Firian shrugged, avoiding the question. "That doesn't matter. I've never been allowed to leave the grounds since I've gotten here. Everyone else has been given permission to visit their homes at least once in the last four years. I never have."

"Why does that bother you?"

"Erron. Can you tell me or not? That's why I came. I want to know. *Do* you know?"

"I have no idea," he said. "You should ask someone else."

Firian pursed his lips. Belik would know, but they weren't on the best terms right now. "Okay." He headed back out of the room, leaving Erron to himself.

The question grew in Firian's mind. He paused, gnawing his lip. *Is there anyone else I can ask?*

No. Belik was the only one guaranteed to have the answer. The food he had eaten earlier that day sat heavy in his stomach as he contemplated going back to the Master's room.

Why haven't I been allowed to leave? It was a fair question. And he was afraid of nothing. At least, that's what he told himself. Sticking out his chest and huffing out a breath, he turned on his heel and headed back toward Belik's room. Hopefully he wasn't teaching or doing Retrieval right now.

Firian stepped lightly down the stairs and through the fountain courtyard to the hallway where Belik's room was. After only a second's worth of hesitation, he knocked on the door.

"Firian," came Belik's voice. A flat, knowing acknowledgment, almost as though he expected him.

Firian opened the door and leaned in. Master Belik was alone.

"Master Belik," he said, "I... have a question."

Belik's face was impassive. He didn't respond, but instead waited for Firian to continue.

Firian's face flushed hot with sudden embarrassment. "I was just thinking, why haven't I ever been allowed to leave?" He didn't mean that he wanted to really leave the Academy, so he rushed on. "I mean, other people have been able to visit their families, but I've never been given permission."

Master Belik dropped his eyes and he opened his mouth to take a breath. Apart from Master Jovan, Belik was the strongest person Firian had ever met. He was always in control. Something about his uncharacteristic hesitation made sickness slowly start to rise in Firian's belly. He waited while the Master looked around for words. *What could be so hard to explain?*

"We should have told you sooner," he began in a low voice. Careful, almost tender. Compared to earlier that day, the tone sounded like a different person, a kinder person.

Forcing breath in and out became a difficult task.

Belik sighed and raised his eyes to meet Firian's. "Firian, two years ago your family was killed in a fire."

Firian's face went cold and his hands started shaking. "No. I want the truth," he said faintly. *Why haven't you let me go? That's impossible.*

The sympathy in Belik's look deepened. Regret, too. "I'm sorry. We should have told you. You had a visit coming up when we got the news, and then we thought it was better that you stay here. Focus on your training."

Firian's tongue stuck to the roof of his mouth and he found no other words to say but an automatic "goodbye." His mind registered nothing but pain and confusion. Fighting for breath, he vaguely headed in the direction of his room. No one else was in the hallway and the courtyard beneath the railing grew darker, lost in shadows.

Brett...

At the thought of her name, her face, she was with him. She smiled sweetly. She looked so different now that she was seventeen.

"Down that hallway is Master Belik's room," Firian said, pointing over the railing.

"Who's he?" Brett asked.

"He's my personal trainer."

"Your personal trainer!" Impressed, her eyes lit up.

He took a long look at the face he hadn't seen in years. Her glossy hair had grown even longer; she was still as tall as he was, and her features were still delicate and innocent, but more mature somehow. "I'm glad you came to visit me, Brett."

"Me too," she said.

Suddenly, he bumped into Bard and realized that he had taken her to see his room. "Brett, this is Bard. Bardhon Tanery." He smiled as he related the full name. "He's my roommate."

Brett shook his limp hand politely, but Bard looked confused. "You have a beautiful sister," Bard said, but it seemed forced, as though he spoke against his will. His lips barely moved when he said it. Then he said "Firian" and it sounded clear, but far away... and somehow more real than his compliment to Brett.

Firian thought about answering the call, but decided against it. "This is where I've been living for the past four years. I've missed you."

"I've missed you too." She looked around the room. "This place is a mess," she teased.

Bard gave Firian a meaningful look.

"I know," said Firian.

"What?" said Bard, squinting like a deaf man.

"You don't mind living here?" she asked, looking around.

Firian shrugged with one shoulder. "I... I think I like it here. I like it here a lot. But it's hard. Not like Mother and Father, but... it's like it means something."

"Firian, what are you talking about?" said the small, muffled voice of Bard. Firian ignored him.

Brett kissed Firian on the cheek. "I wouldn't have the courage to do this," she said in a low voice. "It would be too hard to move away from everything and have personal trainers and... what else do you do?"

"I'm not supposed to tell you any of this but we run and do things like that for some of the day but most of the practice has to do with the Talent—the mind Talent we have," he said. *Or has she heard of that already?*

Bard gave him an admonishing look. Or maybe he was scared. Firian had forgotten he wasn't supposed to say so much to someone from outside the Academy.

Brett carefully changed the subject to something that she understood a little better. Firian didn't begrudge her for not understanding him. He was almost glad that she didn't. That way he could have something that even Brett couldn't touch, that he could know and she wouldn't. She was smart, he knew that, but she couldn't understand how hard he had worked to become what he was. "You've grown since I saw you last," she said.

"You too," he replied.

She felt his arms. "You're a lot stronger than that scrawny boy I remember," she said, smiling.

"I wasn't scrawny. I was strong then too," he said in his defense, but he was proud anyway.

"Fir!" He heard the far-off voice calling him again. "Firian!" The voice grew more insistent.

Then Brett let go of his hand and left the room. "I have to go, Firian," she said. "I love you and I'll tell Father and Mother you're doing well. I'll visit again as soon as I can. Goodbye!" And she was gone.

"Firian!"

"What?" he cried. Then it was as if the room settled into itself and he suddenly knew none of it had been real. The Sentries just hadn't been posted yet to bar him from the Unreal. Brett had never come.

"What's wrong, Firian?" asked Bard, who stood before him, tense, like he was ready to fight or run.

Heat flooded his face as he realized what a fool he must have looked just now. And that Brett never would come. "What was I saying?" he mumbled as he closed the door.

"You sounded like you were talking to someone," Bard said apprehensively. "Are you sure you're all right?"

"I'm fine!" he said, taking off his clothes and getting in bed.

Brett's note, yellow and stained, still curled away from the wooden bunk post. He had pinned and repinned it until it was barely legible. He rolled over and scrubbed his eyes so fiercely they hurt.

9

KIRIA

KIRIA LAY ON HER BED, crying. The closed curtains let in no light, so no one could see her, so she couldn't see herself. She had told her two serving girls to watch the door and not to let anyone in the room. She hardly ever cried. In fact, her parents always said that she kept her head about her and would make a great Keeper of Brithnem someday. They were proud that she was the heir to continue the Second Line.

But none of that was a comfort right now.

Someone had said she was ugly. And the worst part was that he meant it.

She squeezed her hands into fists.

Stupid boy! I've never liked people from Charäkhnem anyway. Ever since Prince Amrit had visited the first time four years ago, she knew she didn't like him. Her face burned with how much she hated that skinny, mean prince.

If only Jori could punch him, but she was never going to tell him what happened because... because what if... what if he *agreed*?

She felt the blood drain from her face and suddenly felt

cold. Everybody knew her as brave, and usually she was. She didn't mind standing up to the occasional person who told her that it was stupid to have her mother as a Keeper since she was a woman. She would even stand up to Cúron, the oldest and most experienced Keeper of the three, if she didn't agree with him.

But was she brave enough to face this truth? What if she *was* ugly?

She squeezed her eyes shut. It was a desolating thought. The heir to the Arioc throne was supposed to beautiful, like in the stories. Like the statue of Mari in the Main—strong and beautiful.

Violently, she jerked back the curtains around her bed and ran to the looking glass. She didn't really look at herself much. Action had always excited her more than looks. Her serving girls picked out her outfit in the morning and combed her hair when it got ratty. She'd always assumed that when she got older, she would be beautiful. She hadn't thought much about it, but now that she *was* older, already fifteen... she needed to know.

There she was.

Her dry and ash-colored hair hung limply around her face. The freckles on her nose weren't cute; they looked like a mistake. Pudge puffed around her light brown eyes and her mouth was small and thin. Her ears stuck out too much. She was short and had no figure at all. On anyone else it would have been average—she wouldn't have thought twice about it—but on herself it was unacceptable.

Ugly.

She stood in pain for a moment, staring at the creature in the glass. She had never thought that there was something wrong with her—maybe even thought that she was a little bit pretty. The girl that looked back at her wasn't pretty.

"She's sort of ugly, isn't she? I expected her to look different. Weren't the other Keepers beautiful...?"

His halting words hit her over and over again in different ways, in different places, like torture. *Stupid boy.* Her nose turned red as she started to cry again. She wouldn't bear to look at herself anymore. Gritting her teeth hard, she felt stuck in her own body. It couldn't ever change. She would look the same, just older, when she grew up. No one would look at her and think that she was beautiful. Men wouldn't want to marry her and Brithnem wouldn't be proud to have her lead them.

All because of something she couldn't control.

A wild, desperate idea came to her. What if she *could* change? She had heard of things like that happening in stories.

She closed her eyes and thought hard about it, picturing long glistening hair, perfect skin, a figure. She thought for a long time, until her eyelids tingled from being shut so tightly. The tingling in her eyelids spread over her whole body as she kept wishing.

Then she opened her eyes and looked into the glass.

And nearly choked.

After she finished coughing, she cautiously looked up again, afraid of what she might see. It was true! She had changed! She was the most beautiful girl she had ever seen.

It was hard to pinpoint the changes. Everything she had seen a moment ago remained, except now it was all perfect. She was *breathtaking.*

Looking at that gorgeous face, foreign but familiar, she couldn't breathe. How was this possible? She didn't have time to think it through before the beauty faded into her average reflection.

What... what did I do? What was that?

Gingerly, she touched her face. After she convinced herself that she wasn't crazy, she tore out of the room with her maids jogging after her.

"I need to see my parents," she told the guards when she was outside her parents' room, panting from the run. "Let me in."

She didn't have to convince them.

Another fit of sobs rose up in her throat as she crossed the thick maroon carpet to the window where her parents sat talking.

Alarmed, her mother jumped up and rushed over to her daughter. "Kiria!" she said, taking her into her arms. "What's the matter?"

"I..." She realized that she didn't know how to begin, so she just cried until she didn't have any tears left.

By the time she looked up, both of her parents were looking down at her, extremely concerned.

"You have to tell us what happened, Kiria," said her father. Sternness and fear shone in his eyes. "Did something happen to you?"

"Well..." She took a deep breath, suddenly not wanting to tell them her story since she knew by now they were expecting something much worse. Once they found out what she was really crying about, it would seem so small. "I... I was looking at myself in the glass and..." – she felt her mother's arms relax around her – "and I don't know what happened. I *changed*. Does that happen?" she finished in a small voice. In the arms of her mother, she felt like a child.

"What do you mean, you 'changed?'" her mother asked her.

"I was... I turned... beautiful..."

"Beautiful?"

"I was the prettiest girl I'd ever seen," she whispered, feeling stupid for saying it, but it was true.

"Kiria!" her mother cried, excited. "You have an Ability!" She grabbed her shoulders gently and held her at arm's length.

Through her tears, Kiria saw her mother smile. "Ability?"

"The gift," her mother said.

In her shock, Kiria had forgotten all about them. They were so rare. Of course she knew about Abilities.

Her mother still continued. "Abilities show us our original state before men started worshiping other gods. Some people are given Original Knowledge, which allows them to know something without having heard it or seen it for themselves, and others were given Original Harmony, that deals with nature. Those people can walk out into a storm and none of the elements hurt them. My sister had that one. Other people can speak the Original Language. Tanyu have the Original Talent, allowing them access to imagination and the Unreal. And the last Ability is Original Beauty. Those people can make themselves appear like they were originally intended to look, before the world fell. Is that what happened to you?"

"I guess so." *Original Beauty.* It was real. She could *become* beautiful. Her mind flashed to Tanis, the new guard in training.

"You have Beauty! What a gift!" her mother cried, delighted. "But Kiria, listen to me." She became much more serious. "Now that you've found out your Ability, guard it. Abilities are dangerous gifts. Don't show your Beauty to anyone yet."

Kiria's mouth fell open. Just as joy began to well inside her, her mother had to dampen it.

"She's right," her father added. "Beauty is one of the most dangerous gifts. You need to be careful."

Kiria screwed her brows together. This seemed to be getting out of hand. Surely it couldn't be that dangerous to look one way instead of another.

"Yes," her mother continued, "never change unless you have a reason."

"But... why can't I?" Kiria asked, feeling as though the biggest discovery of her life was going to be swept out of sight in a drawer somewhere.

Her mother smiled more weakly now. "For now, only show

your Beauty to those you can absolutely trust. We'll discuss a time when you can reveal yourself to the people."

"Why?" Kiria thought of the look on Prince Amrit's face if she walked up to him in all her beauty. He would choke on his horrible words.

"Beauty is powerful," her father answered. It wasn't a good enough answer to her question.

Her mother stepped in again. "You need to learn how to deal with this gift before you reveal it to other people," she said. "Many will treat you differently when you're Beautiful. Some of the attention can be good, but" – her eyes flashed to Father – "some can also be harmful. There are many benefits to staying just as you are."

"Why would I—"

"You don't have to make a decision right now, but you'll eventually have to choose which appearance to use when you're a leader. Once you decide, you'll have to remain consistent."

Seeing the look on her face, her father added, "We're only thinking of you."

She didn't have to think about it. She would use her Beauty all the time as Keeper. She would have so much more confidence. There was no point in staying ugly.

"Of course," her mother agreed. "What you have is a more perfect beauty than this world knows right now, so guard it for now."

Kiria nodded. She would be careful, but she would change as often as she could get away with it. Scenarios whirled in her head. She wanted to change again right now. "Can I show Jori and Atty?" *And Tanis.*

For one maddening second, her parents hesitated. It seemed her father was about to protest when her mother said, "I think they've proven themselves. Yes. You may."

Kiria didn't need more encouragement. "Thank you!" she said, and rushed out of the room.

———

FOR A TERRIFYING SECOND, Kiria felt nothing. Could she only change once? Had it been her imagination after all? Her forehead furrowed with intensity as she tightly shut her eyes.

Finally, a tingle. She kept her eyes closed for a while, just in case. Shivers ran over her body, crackling like her leg did when it fell asleep.

She popped her eyes open and checked her hand, holding it close to her face. There was something elegant about it. *Perfect.*

Staying mostly hidden behind the palace wall, she peered across the open green field, beaten yellow in the center, to where a crowd of guards, warriors, and trainees gathered. She would be careful not to let all of them see her, and then she'd go to Atty and Jori. For now, Tanis' training session was almost finished.

A month ago, she had seen him accompany her mother's guards. He had been dressed in full uniform, though he was still in training. His long blond hair falling to his square jawline revealed him to be a Khelê. Every Kingdom Dweller had darker hair than that. She didn't know how old he was—seventeen? She just knew that he had made her stomach drop when she looked at him. At first she thought she might be sick, but then thoughts of him intruded in her mind all day. The smallest thing reminded her of him. It had been this way for weeks.

This is stupid. She was a Kepress, and was going to be a great leader. She didn't have time to go running after boys. Jori and Atty would laugh. Well, Jori would laugh. They both knew that Atty fell hard for almost every kitchen maid. As far as she knew, not many looked back at *him* either.

She peeked around the corner. Back by the well where the

trainees crowded around, strong arms pulled a helmet off a blond head, the long strands settling down separately. Her heart suddenly beat in her throat.

Maybe it wasn't stupid. Maybe he would think of *her* all day.

Tanis shot back a cup of water and broke free from the others as he headed back to the gate leading out of the palace grounds. Toward where she hid waiting for him. Kiria watched him, suddenly clammy. What to say? Every option she played out sounded idiotic. She was better than this—more elegant, brave, intelligent...

"Oh, hello!" His tone revealed that she had caught him off guard.

She looked up from her shoes to his blue eyes. He was very close. No, it was a normal distance, but closer than she had ever been to him. How had he come up so quickly? Her heart pounded.

"Hello."

His eyes rounded as he stared at her. He closed his mouth and cleared his throat. "Did you come to watch the practice?" He shifted the metal helmet under his arm, where it reflected the sun into her eyes.

"Mm hm." She nodded and swallowed. "Yes, you all are doing very well out there."

He gave a lopsided smile. "Thank you." When he lowered his head to meet her gaze, her arms felt a little weaker. "You are?"

"Oh yes. I'm Kiria. Arioc. The Kepress."

When she spoke her name, his roving eyes widened even further. He blinked a couple times. Bowing a little from the waist, he said, "My name is Tanis, at your service. You... look very nice today. Is it okay to say that?"

For a split second, she thought this was a joke. Had someone told him to say that? Everything was happening too perfectly. "Yeah, yes," she corrected. *You look good too. That uniform...*

"Are you going to come see us again tomorrow?" he asked.

Her face flushed hot with surprise. *He wants to see me again!*

She recovered her dignity as quickly as she could. "I'll try. I'll see what I can do. You have a good evening, Tanis." A pleasant churning in her stomach made her smile as she walked away.

10

FIRIAN

The more Firian's arms shook, the more the water in the buckets rippled. He tried to tighten his core, his chest, anything to take the pressure off his arms as he held them straight out.

Master Jovan watched impassively.

Firian huffed out a breath, fighting the urge to glare at him. At least this was physical pain, not mental pain. This was only the second day without the Unreal and he felt parched, like a man dying of thirst. He could do anything there, in that semi-actual imaginary space. Here, he was too weak.

He rolled his shoulders and adjusted his grip on the wooden handle. *Mind over body.* Like falling down a slide, his mind descended to the comfort of the Unreal. He could endure so much more that way.

Red pain exploded behind his eyes. Yelling, he vaguely heard water slosh out of the buckets as they tumbled to the ground. Sentries. His brain ached from the aftershock.

"Firian!" Jovan cried, scooping up the bucket handles. The sun glinted on his bald head as he bent down. "You did better last time."

Alarmed by the warmth of embarrassment creeping up his

neck, Firian muttered, "I'll do better next time, Master Jovan." His eyes felt prickly, so he rotated his shoulders, twisting at the waist away from Jovan's gaze.

"Yes, you will. That's all for today."

"As you would have it." Firian practically ran back inside before he finished the phrase. He hurried down the stone corridor out into the courtyard, dodging the fountain on the way to the stairs. Movement helped him stay out of his thoughts.

A swish of brown hair caught his peripheral vision and a hard lump lodged in his throat. When he swallowed over and over, it didn't budge. *Mind over body.* He always had somewhere to go when he was in pain, but not now. For the past two days, he'd felt the dull buzz of Sentries, like madness, press against his skull. If he tried to pass the barrier, to reach the Unreal, pain would incapacitate him as it did in front of Jovan. And that hadn't been the only time. Desperate to find relief, he'd hurled himself against the barrier at first. Almost missed his strategy class.

He wasn't as rash as he had been, but he also hadn't resigned himself to three more days of this torture. Those Sentries were experts. They had been Tanyu who deserved the terrible punishment of focusing on nothing, creating a painful, disembodied barrier to the Unreal. At least, that's what the stories said. The threat of becoming a Sentry cowed even strong Tanyu. It was a horrific fate, even worse than a Master ordering a Sentry to temporarily block the Unreal.

Firian had been punished before, but not like this. He felt cut off from air.

He flung the door open to his room to find Bard and their friend Tiev Gelir sitting on the ground around an Indisfate board. Tiev raised his knee to avoid the door, tipping over a Falcon. The tiny click of the wooden figure falling echoed in the little room. Firian let out a breath. Had Bard said anything about company?

"Hey, Fir!" Bard waved for Firian to take a seat, so he lowered himself cross-legged beside the board. It was an even game.

"You can play after Tawn and me," Tiev said, squinting his green eyes as he contemplated his next move. Everyone had started calling Bard that after someone had made fun of his accent—"tawn-yoo." Now, whenever he said the word, somebody laughed. Firian still called him by his name, but he was one of the last.

Firian had better things to do than watch two people play a game, but he didn't have the energy to leave.

Tiev moved the Man, a larger piece than the others on the board. "Ha!" he said under his breath. A smile crept onto his face.

Firian sucked the inside of his lip. It was a good move. Hopefully Bard could counteract it.

He glanced back at Tiev. Tiev often acted as though he were much older than Firian, even though the age difference was only a year. Besides that, his hair was always perfect. Every guy on the floor envied it.

Firian drew his aching arm across his chest, holding it at the elbow to stretch it, while watching Bard worry over his pieces.

Never looking away from the game, Bard absently pulled a slice from a partially-peeled orange and put it in his mouth. His brows creased together in concentration. Normally, he'd be smiling. Coming to a conclusion, he nodded to himself and moved the Viper two spaces.

Tiev pursed his mouth. Apparently, that isn't what he wanted. Firian's mouth curled up in a sardonic smile. *Good for you, Bard!*

"What's that big, ugly piece?" Firian asked, pointing to the Man looming over the other wooden game pieces.

A grin flashed over Bard's features. "It's not ugly. It's just a figure I got when I was home. It's Corso!"

"They sell Tanyu figures there?" Firian grabbed it off the board. Tiev's fingers twitched to stop him but he reconsidered.

He held the figure up to his face and spun it in his fingers. Corso wore a long Academy jacket and held two knives crossed in front of him. His bearded face looked grim and determined, with deep eyes and long hair. After the rebel loss at Carradoc, the real Corso had risen up and fought in ways that no one up to that time had been able to. His name was a rallying cry for anyone fighting for the liberation of Brithnem in the War of the Kingdom Rebels.

"He was always my favorite," Bard said.

Tiev stuck his neck out to look more closely at the figure. "My mom would tell stories about him when I was a kid." The contented haze of memory crossed his features.

Firian flexed his jaw. He'd heard the stories too, from schoolmates. Disjointed stories. Sometimes Corso could lead a fleet of a thousand ships, sometimes he could fly across the plain from the Charúnin Thôr to the capital, sometimes he just carved a bloody swath in the war, so fearsome that none could touch him. Firian's favorite story was about the time he got captured and taken to the arena to be killed, but then he made a knife from the meat bone they gave him and killed four guards. He escaped and freed all the animals and prisoners, who helped him storm the palace in one of the decisive battles of the war.

Tanyu had changed since then. Firian wished they fought physically more often, but that wasn't the way anymore. Since the Tanyu had hidden the Academy, they hadn't kept large standing armies. They relied on mental warfare and individual missions now.

"I'd pretend to be him sometimes," Bard continued. "Well, I

wanted to, but Jac always took that one. But then I got to be a Tanyu. Weird, huh?"

Firian couldn't help but agree. Everything he heard about Bard's older brother actually reminded him of himself, much more suited to the Academy than Bard was.

"So, were you Fern or Zhelan?" Tiev laughed. Love interest or villain?

"No!" Bard cried. And then, more quietly, "Neither, not most of the time."

Firian snickered at the image, but Bard didn't laugh with them.

Tiev took the figure of Corso and put it back on the board, lazily moving another piece.

After watching Tiev's move, Bard shot a glance at Firian. They both saw it. He could use Soldier's Pass to win in the next move. Almost imperceptibly, Firian nodded. *Do it.* This time, Bard was quick. His fingers flashed over the game and he sat back satisfied.

It took Tiev a moment to realize Bard had won. His smile faded. "Okay," he said, taking in the loss.

Bard angled up to stand. "Better luck next time, yeah?" he said, popping up his eyebrows.

"Yeah." Tiev wasn't happy. He stood up in a motion so smooth it made Firian jealous. "That was good. I'll see you later," he said, waving a cursory hand at both of them.

"Yeah, all right." Bard gave a little nod, squatting back down to clean up the pieces. The measured way he did it confirmed that something was bothering him. One at a time. Firian grabbed the pair of Vipers to help. After an agitated breath, Bard stole a glance at him. "Did you hear that Enderin was attacked?"

Firian's pieces froze in midair on their way to the bag. That would explain why Bard returned early from his last trip home.

Bard cast his eyes back down to the board. "I don't... I just hope..." He cleared his throat. "I don't think anything's happened to them," he murmured, chewing his lip. Bard came from a family so big that it had taken a year before Firian could keep them all straight. "Do you think—"

"No!" Firian cried. "Of course not."

Silence followed. Game pieces clattered into the bag.

"But what if—"

"That didn't happen."

"How do you know?" Bard asked, his voice louder now. "Why do you think they took me away so soon? Why couldn't I have stayed unless it was dangerous?"

"They're all fine."

Bard clenched his fist around the figure of Corso. "Jac was going into the army anyway."

"Look, you don't even know if anything bad's happened." Firian's chest tightened. *Maybe they wouldn't tell him. They didn't tell me.* His secret built like fire inside him until he burned with it. His heart pounded heavily and the ache in his arms spread over the rest of his body.

Bard's forehead scrunched downward in concern. He always read him better than other people could.

Firian settled his shoulders. It might have been a shrug. "You know why—" He tried again. "You know why *I* haven't left the Academy?"

"Why?"

Why am I even talking about this? "Because..." He blew out a long breath to steady himself. "Because my whole family was killed in a fire." He twitched his head as though hair had fallen in his face.

Shock and sympathy filled Bard's eyes. "Oh, Fir... I'm so sorry!" He sat back from his crouch to the floor, ready to listen.

Firian stood up and waved a dismissive hand, like someone shooing a fly. His mouth felt dry. "Yeah. Well." He wasn't going to talk about his feelings. But Bard would find out about his family eventually—it might as well be now. It had to be now, when the secret burned him like acid. His roommate was the safest person to tell. And he had to tell someone.

Bard's tears glistened on his lower lid.

Tanyu never cried. *Tanyu never cried.*

But suddenly, Brett's death, the punishment, it all caught in his throat. Blood rushed to his face and a sob broke from him. He tried to stop but it was all he could do to suck air into his hot lungs. Gasping for breath, he crouched on the floor, howling, all snot and tears. People in the hall could hear, but he couldn't stop himself. He wept until he felt he was going to be sick.

Hiccupping to silence, he subsided to a profound calm. Thoroughly ashamed of himself, he sat up. Fifteen-year-olds—Tanyu!—never cried, no matter what.

Bard, with red, puffy eyes, handed him a towel. He leaned his fist on his mouth. "It's okay," he said softly. He meant the crying, not the death. Firian knew that. Death—Brett's death—would never be okay.

Numbly, Firian took the towel and rubbed it over his wet face. He took a breath in through the nose, deep in the lungs, and out through his mouth. He had no more words.

Bard seemed to understand. And Firian knew that Bard would never tell anyone about this.

Together they sat in silence until the light in the room started to fade to orange.

11

___

KIRIA

Late the next afternoon, suitably beautiful, Kiria invited Tanis to walk with her through the grounds. She told Candrae and Vayci, her two serving girls, that they could stay behind. He had eased off his armor—*oh my goodness!*—and accepted her invitation.

She didn't know why she was so excited when he agreed to walk with her. Could he even say no to a Kepress? She doubted it. Be that as it may, he was here now, walking close beside her along the pathways behind the palace, and she felt the thrill of it down her spine. The training grounds were out of the way, so they had a little while to walk before they even reached the Amiran Academy. It felt like they were alone.

"Don't you have servants or something? Do they always let you take walks like this by yourself?" he asked, a glimmer in his eye.

He knows I shouldn't be out here. But she was a Kepress; he couldn't get her in trouble.

Probably.

"I do this sometimes," she said. Technically, she wasn't supposed to, but she managed to get out now and then. She was always careful. "I like to come out and look at the ocean or the new flowers."

The newest was some kind of lavender lily that she liked very much. It almost looked like the laird flower on the flag. Patches of them lined the far end of the field where they were walking.

"You know, you should have a guard with you," he said.

"I know, but..."

"I can be your guard." He ran a hand through his long hair.

Her heart skipped. This was silly. Now that she had his attention, what was she supposed to do with it? She probably looked like a fish, wide-eyed and gaping.

His touch sent a shock through her hand. He eased his fingers through hers and held her hand close. Breathing was complicated. She managed to smile encouragingly at him. At least, that's how she hoped he would take it.

The dome of the Amiran Academy was getting closer. *I have to go back.* The thought hit her hard and it was worse because she should have thought of it sooner. Showing her Ability to one person didn't seem so bad—judging from how the night was going, it wasn't bad at all—but waltzing back into the palace grounds where hundreds of Amir lived and worked wasn't smart.

"I'm surprised I never noticed you before," Tanis said, squeezing her hand, which was getting sweaty.

"It's okay," Kiria said. She wouldn't have noticed herself either. "You know why I look this way now?" She lowered her voice, even though no one else was around. "I have an Ability. It's Original Beauty." Anyone with eyes could already tell, but she felt a thrill as she told him.

He chuckled, half to himself. "No wonder," he said. "Did you just find out?"

He seemed eager to learn more, but they were getting too

close to the palace. *Why can't I just stay beautiful?* "Yes, let me show you," she said, although it didn't seem right to ruin the moment. "I *have* to change because not everyone knows yet. And you can't tell anyone!"

"Okay, okay, if you're sure." He let go of her hand and stepped back, as though she would burst into flame.

She didn't want to close her eyes with his stunning blue ones looking back at her. Who wanted to look *worse* in front of someone so gorgeous? But it had to be done.

Before opening her eyes again, she heaved a sigh. "So there you go!" she said, trying to sound more lighthearted than she felt.

He looked over her whole body, clearly masking disappointment. "Yeah, I'm happy you got your Ability," he said. "You can switch back, right?"

"Of course." She nodded.

A crooked smile crossed his features. "So I can't tell anybody?"

"No! No, no. I have some matters to discuss before officially revealing it." Why was her tone so formal all the sudden? "But I'm glad I showed you." She gave him a little smile.

He nodded, his glance darting toward the far gate.

"I think I might come by tomorrow to watch the training again." She fought for a second to catch his eye. "I'll be beautiful again. It's just that here... so close to the palace..."

"Do you want to walk again?"

The question stung. *Don't you?* she wanted to ask. She had shown him far more than was wise, just so he would be impressed and like her. She'd abandoned some of her good sense just to know what it felt like to be wanted. And now he acted as though he wasn't attracted to her at all.

She shoved down her hurt feelings. Maybe he didn't mean anything by it. "Let's do it."

Spurred by the churning in her stomach, she grabbed Tanis' hand and led him out of sight of the Amiran Academy, into a grove of shady trees. She closed her eyes again and a moment later was beautiful.

Tanis broke into a grin. "Okay, I'll be waiting," he said. Before he left, he kissed her softly on the cheek.

"SO I DON'T HAVE AN ABILITY," said Jori over the noise of people, stretching out in his chair in a leisurely way. "Everything I do is an Ability."

Atael smacked him on the chest, making him double over in his chair. "He's just jealous," he told Kiria.

Jori huffed with scorn as Kiria smiled. "Keep your voices down," she said. "I don't think everyone is supposed to hear us talking about it."

About a hundred brilliantly dressed people meandered around the circular stone courtyard behind the palace. Among them were two of the Keepers, Cúron and Merian. They couldn't stay long because they had called an emergency session in the Main. Torith had attacked Enderin, the main city in the northern region of Phlaxtin, and they had to decide how much help to send their ally to the north. The island of Torith was mostly peaceful, her mother had explained to her that morning, but years ago an enormous coalition of pirates set up their base on the eastern side and ran it as their own country. These mercenaries raided and terrorized both the big island north of Torith and now the continent. They had to be stopped.

The straightness of her mother's back was the only hint of her stress. Cúron didn't betray any at all. Aylmor, Atty and Jori's father, was away on business near the base of the Charúnin

Thôr mountains, where the range met the ocean directly north of Brithnem.

The grounds looked amazing from here—winding paths, rolling lawns, the forest, the hedges. A few chairs and benches strategically littered the flagstone but most of the people chose to stand and talk. The two huge wings of the castle flanked them on either side, soaring up past the trees. Long, shimmering blue flags waved limply in the breeze along the peak of the roof.

Every few months or so the Keepers would host a gathering like this one, inviting merchants and wealthy businessmen, fishermen and maids. It was a way to maintain morale among the people. If someone were lucky enough to be noticed and chosen for one of these exclusive parties, that person could brag about it for years. Kiria and the Calthwaites didn't find the atmosphere quite so intoxicating (with the possible exception of Jori, whom Kiria suspected of sneaking a glass of ale or two while she and Atty had been talking).

"Why not?" Jori asked loudly.

Atty leaned over to his brother from the opposite side. "You're an ass," he muttered.

"I haven't shown the people yet," Kiria whispered. "I will, but don't go telling everyone ahead of time."

Kiria put a finger to her lips as little Kader, who was six now, climbed into one of the shady seats next to them, pretending to be grown-up and interested in their conversation. He tugged at his buttoned, embroidered vest.

Jori watched Kader, who wiggled with boredom after only a moment of silence. "I think it's dumb that Atty gets to be Keeper."

She shushed him. Jori was so fun when he wasn't in one of his moods. Why did he have to be in a mood today? "Stop acting stupid. You know it has to be this way," she said. Younger siblings never inherited the throne. "Besides, that won't be for a while." Their parents were both relatively young. Younger than Cúron, anyway.

Launching himself off the seat, Kader ran off, weaving between the legs of the adults. He was too young to sit still for long. In moments his nurse caught up with him and brought him inside.

Atty nodded thoughtfully, looking away from them.

"See, Atty doesn't even want it," Jori goaded him.

"Shut up, *Jori*," he said sharply, looking at them again, slightly embarrassed. "Of course I do."

To be honest, Kiria was a little nervous for Atty. He didn't do very well in his studies, and Jori had always been more charismatic. Whenever becoming a Keeper came up, Atty would lift his head and say he wanted to be just like his father. Those might even be little hairs on his chin.

"Of course he does," she affirmed. "We'll do it together." She didn't know much more than he did about running a country, but they would help each other.

"My idea's more fun," Jori said, eyeing a plate of smoked fish as it went by. Part of her believed him.

Guards milled around the many party guests. Since the guest selection was all but random, they posted extra guards to make sure that the Keepers and their families were safe. Kiria found herself scanning the faces beneath the helmets. Was that a trainee she had seen earlier? *Are all the trainees here?*

Sitting made her antsy, so she stood up. "Do you want to get some food?" The parties might be boring, but the food always tasted amazing. Ten or twelve extra cooks were brought in just to help prepare the food for these events, nearly doubling the number of kitchen servants.

The boys had already leapt to their feet. "That looks good," said Jori, going for the tray of fish.

"Kepron Atael! And Kepress Kiria!" someone cried delightedly. A large woman came into view, mouth gaping, eyes popping. Her dress wasn't quite as fine as most of the others. Her eyes were a little glazed over too. "To think...! Just to think I'm meeting the future Keepers of Brithnem! I am honored!"

"Oh." Atty looked lost.

"How nice," Kiria said, trying to recover from Atty's fumble. "It's lovely to meet you." She offered her hand to the woman politely as her eyes strayed once again toward the guards. There he was, across the garden! "You must excuse me."

Somehow she extricated herself from the enthusiastic woman and wedged her way through the crowd to get to Tanis. They couldn't talk for long—he was on duty—but she had to say hello.

When she reached where he was, she pretended to be nonchalant. Her parents were at this party, and the Calthwaite boys might notice. "Hello," she whispered. Her dress restricted her breathing more than she remembered.

His helmet shone in the sunshine, like his hair and his eyes. His lips pursed in an expression of utmost seriousness. He kept his hand on the hilt of his sword where it hung by his side. He nodded to her. "My Kepress."

The words sounded so good coming from him. "I think you're doing a good job," she said. "This is good practice for the real thing."

He flashed her a quick smile. "So... you still haven't told anybody yet?"

She wilted a little, burying her hands in the folds of her skirt. "No. But I will, though."

"It's okay. You'll tell them soon."

She got just a little closer to him. "It's our secret," she whispered. Her breath fogged the shoulder of his armor.

"You're still coming tomorrow, right?"

She flushed, pleased. "Yes, I'll be there." The Keepers and

their advisors would be in meetings all day tomorrow because of the attack, but she wasn't required to go to the Main with them yet, not until she was eighteen.

"Beauty is not for the beautiful." The line from the Sacred Scroll popped into her head. Hadn't Daelon said something like that? Or was it her mother?

Her Ability wasn't just for her, but for others.

She could be beautiful just for him.

TOGETHER THEY SAT against the wall that enclosed the palace grounds. The setting sun shone in their faces as it set over the Kheltor Ocean, bleaching Tanis' hair white gold. Kiria wanted to reach up and touch the strands as they curled at his shoulder. She wouldn't have to reach far. They sat very close.

"Where does your family come from?" she asked.

"My family are all farmers," Tanis said, leaning his head back lazily. "We live on the outer edge, growing crops." The outer edge was far to walk every day. Even on a horse, it usually took at least an hour to get to the palace from the outer edge, just outside the city wall. Kiria had only been there two or three times. The land gave farmers more room for their crops. They were still officially part of Brithnem, though they were separated.

He turned to look at her. "But I'm glad I got in this program. Farming isn't very fun."

"Why not?"

Tanis shrugged and picked one blade of grass. Two.

"Do you come all that way every day?" she asked, smoothing her light blue dress.

"It's worth it." He smiled with gleaming teeth, lolling his head in her direction.

Her stomach clenched, and she edged her fingers closer to his. "Really?" she asked, pretending this was normal. She half-smiled back.

"Yes. I got to meet you." His hand closed the gap between them and rested on top of hers.

She sighed happily and looked ahead. The green field in front of them sloped gently down to the gardens, the dome of the Amiran Academy, the towering palace. It all glittered in the sunlight. Even the breeze playing with their hair and the fabric of their clothes felt warm and magical.

He was already looking at her, taking her in, when she looked back at him. "You look pretty tonight."

The words were music. "Yeah, what else do you like about me?" she teased.

He laughed. "What do you like about *me?*"

"You first."

He looked up, his forehead creasing in thought for a little while. "You're smart," he began, "and sweet... and sneaky!" He drew his legs in and crossed them, a deep breath rising in his chest that almost seemed like relief.

She couldn't stop the smile lifting at the sides of her mouth. "And you" – she crossed her legs and faced him – "are... cute" – she blushed – "and strong and nice." The somewhat uncomfortable yet warm thrill she felt with him intoxicated her. She was slowly getting used to the fluttery feeling.

He squeezed her hand reassuringly and brushed his blond hair out of his face with the other. "I wish other people could see what I see," he said.

It took her a moment to understand his meaning. "You mean... the Ability?"

"Yeah."

She smiled, lowering her head. "But you would still like me without it. Right?"

"Of course, yeah," he said, taking her other hand. "Of course I would. But you have to show other people sometime."

"Maybe I won't," she said, just to be contrary.

"Yes, you will. You wouldn't want to be ugly forever when you could be so beautiful." He reached up to touch her cheek.

She recoiled. The words hit her like a battering ram. "Ugly?"

"That's not what I meant."

"That's what you said." She pulled her hands away.

"But that's not what I meant," he protested.

"If I didn't look like this" – her breath hitched – "I'd still be... smart."

"Of course you would," he said, reaching for her hands again, a hint of exasperation in his face.

She shook her head, her eyes getting hotter. She had to leave before he saw her cry. "No, you wouldn't like me." A tear trailed down her face as she stood up.

"Wait," he said, standing too. His brow furrowed, that golden hair tumbling in his face. "I didn't mean what I said."

She set her jaw. After backing away a few steps, she closed her eyes and changed back to her usual self. "Yes, you did," she said and ran back to the palace.

PART III

MASTER (AGE 18)

12

KIRIA

Kiria and Jori went out of the palace to escape their guards, though guilt threaded through Kiria as she did so. Her guards had to be getting worried with all the time she spent sneaking off. Maybe it was unfair to them, but she wanted to be alone with somebody who wouldn't expect anything from her and wouldn't talk about anything serious. Jori was her best bet. And she wouldn't be gone long.

He ambled along beside her down the gravel paths of the garden, hands in his pockets. Far away, the splash of waves floated up from the coast. The air smelled like water. She lost herself in the smell, the touch of the cool air on her face. As she breathed in, her shoulders began to loosen. Here there were no responsibilities, no decisions about whether to lead with her Beauty or not, no people to treat her differently depending on what she chose. No one to disappoint.

The weight of one day becoming Keeper pressed more heavily every day. In just a few days she would turn eighteen and be expected to attend every session, begin her formal apprenticeship, as it were. She couldn't even live up to her Beauty. It presented her as far better than she was inside. How would she live up to a kingdom full of expectations? Her chest tightened again.

Jori's unbuttoned embroidered vest flapped as he turned toward her. "Kiria, you need a snack? A drink? You look sad."

Wonderful. Already her plan wasn't working. "You know you shouldn't drink," she said. They were seventeen, old enough to drink, but Jori tended to overindulge.

He waggled his head, noncommittal. "Sometimes that makes it more fun."

Smiling, she smacked him lightly on the arm. "You say such ridiculous things!"

"Right, though?" he said, raising both eyebrows until they almost reached the wavy dark hair falling over his forehead. "You know I'm right."

She smirked.

"Come on, I'll get you something," he said. "Nothing a drink can't fix."

"No! No... It's okay. I'm fine." But his offer had managed to cheer her up.

He shrugged. "Suit yourself. Just trying to help a friend in need," he said, winking at her.

She looked up at the churning gray sky. "Do you want to head inside?" She pulled her cloak tighter around her. It staved off the cold and covered her body like a shapeless blanket, which fit her mood.

"Sure," he said, following her gaze. "I like rain, though."

"Jori! They'll know we snuck outside. Besides, I'm sure someone will miss us if we're out much longer."

"They probably already do. Don't you like being missed? And anyway, if we're found out here, their relief will make up for everything."

"I'm glad you're not the oldest," she said, laughing. "You'd make the worst Keeper I've ever seen."

"Ah, well," he said, smiling. "Do you still want to go inside?"

Muffled thunder rumbled around them. "Yes. We can't have somebody worried. Mother will kill me if she found me out here with nobody but you."

"Afraid of what she'd say?" His gray eyes teased her.

"I don't have any protection and we're at war." None of the frontiers were close to the palace—the real conflict took place far away—but it was still better to be safe.

"I can't protect you?" he said, cocking an eyebrow.

"You know what I mean. Not really." He attempted to steer her away from the palace. "You can be so difficult," she added, steering them back.

"Thank goodness!" he said. "Imagine how boring life would be if I was easy to be around."

She laughed in spite of herself. "You're absurd."

"I know. Might as well be."

A large drop of water landed on her face. "Come on! It's starting to rain," she said, breaking into a jog as they neared the castle.

"I told you I like rain," he said again, refusing to follow at her speed.

"Jori!"

Once inside, she tried to shake the water off her clothes, but it had soaked in. "I really shouldn't do that so often. Candrae and Vayci will be so worried."

"Oh well," he replied, popping his shoulders up and down to resettle his wet coat. "I think Sen and Wyat actually like it when I'm gone. It gives them a chance to do what they want for once." Those were his servants, the sons of Atael's tutor.

"Stop getting water on me," she said, shooing the drops away with her hand.

He shook his head like a dog in answer and droplets went flying everywhere from the tips of his dark brown hair. "What do you mean 'so often'? We don't run around like we used to as kids." He smiled impishly. "Have you been sneaking off?"

There was that word again. The one Tanis had used when she was fifteen, and then again a couple weeks ago when she finally found someone else and thought she would try again. This time, it'd been a soldier. Anton seemed different. But in the end, he didn't care about her either. She was a political stepping stone, a beautiful face, and nothing more. She had only managed to be alone with him once before he was sent to the field. They hadn't so much as kissed before she realized the kind of person he was.

Was she really that sneaky? Apparently not, since Jori had caught on. She lowered her voice to a whisper. "No." But her heartbeat betrayed her lie, and she tried never to lie. "Okay, yes, just a little."

"Oh, tell me!"

"Shh! It doesn't matter."

"A *boy*, then," he said, coming closer to hear. "Have you finally had a crush? Atty will be so sad."

The truth balled up like pain inside her.

When she didn't protest his comment about Atty, he looked fractionally more concerned. "Who wouldn't like a Kepress?" he asked in an uncharacteristically soothing way.

"It doesn't matter," she repeated, not looking at him. "I have bigger things to worry about..." *Like learning to lead the nation, like the war, like choosing whether or not to show the whole country my Ability...*

"Let's not worry about them," he said, and then fell easily back into his usual laid-back attitude. "That's what I try to do at all costs. Worrying doesn't help anybody. Sen and Wyat will make sure I eat." Those poor serving boys. Jori always had been a handful.

"Nobody needs to tell you that," she said.

"There you go. I'll live another day. It's a whole lot easier when you let things go." He sailed a hand off into the imaginary distance.

I'll live another day. Maybe she had been carrying too much on her shoulders. She wasn't a Keeper yet.

She shot a glance down the hallway back to her room where her serving girls and guards were probably wondering where she had gone. "Okay," she said. "How about that drink?"

THE NEXT DAY, accompanied by her longsuffering maids, Kiria walked up to the door and knocked. The guards ignored her. The door swung open heavily and Jori looked out. "Oh, it's you," he said, opening it wider to let them enter.

As usual, Candrae remained at the door and Sen, Jori's servant, came inside with Vayci. One servant inside, one servant outside.

Jori grinned and sank indolently into a chair. "What brings you here? I was just about to get some food."

Too many thoughts hounded her, and she had to talk to somebody. Maybe Jori was a bad idea. He took nothing seriously. "Don't let me keep you," she said.

He smiled knowingly at her. "Well, if you didn't come for anything specific, can I get you something?" He rose from his chair and went over to a small cabinet in the wall. "They don't allow me to keep much in here," he said, "but I have a little bread and wine, if you want some."

She breathed out a short laugh. "You don't have to act like I'm a stranger," she said, coming over and taking a sugared slice of dried orange from the cabinet. She smiled, popping the candy into her mouth.

He pulled the wine and two glasses out of the cabinet and

closed it with his elbow. After setting them down on a small table by his seat, he pulled an upholstered chair over so it was across from his own and gestured for her to sit down. "I guess you're right," he said, sinking down again, "it's almost brunch anyway. No use spoiling our appetites."

"None at all." She swallowed the candy and sat down. "Pass me a glass."

"Certainly, my lady," he said, pouring them both some from the bottle.

She reached over as he passed her the glass half full of dark wine. "Thanks, Jori."

"Hard day?" He looked at her over the rim of the glass as he drank.

"Not really."

"Then what's the matter?"

"Oh..." She shrugged. "I think I've decided to reveal my Ability to the public soon, but I don't feel ready." For a split second, she had considered leading as she had always looked, but that option was silly compared to the other. The people expected greatness in their leaders, and Beauty would help them see that. Even if she already felt a little resentful because of it.

"You seem ready to me," he replied, mouth full of bread.

"You're such a liar, Jori! I think I'll be ready when I have to be but... it... I wish I were more ready now. I used to look forward to being a Keeper." Her own words surprised her.

"I'm sure you'll do fine. You don't have to be a Keeper now. I know I'd much rather lie around here doing nothing and be *almost* famous while I do it." He threw back his head and finished his wine in a gulp.

"Sounds good," she said honestly. The people of Brithnem couldn't judge her for taking time for herself, could they? "I could never picture you in the Main anyway."

"I have been there, you know," he said seriously, nodding his head.

"Really?" she teased.

"Yes, my father's made me go a few times," he said. "And I roamed around it as a kid. You might remember. So I do know how it tends to function, though most people wouldn't think it."

When they were all kids—Kiria and Atty and Jori—the Main had seemed so immense and dark, a hall of kings and princesses, solemn judgments and dances. These illusions were only partly true, she learned as she grew up. "I'll wager Kader goes in there too when no one is watching," she said.

"How old is he now?"

"Just turned nine, and he already likes to go to meetings and order people around."

Jori barked out a humorless laugh. "Now *he's* one I would bet on to be a good Keeper."

"The First Line, what can you expect?"

"That doesn't mean anything." He scoffed. "Oldest child... Just because his last name's Calthwaite doesn't mean he has to be boring and responsible."

She raised her eyebrows. "You're not, anyway."

"Those Ariocs, though," he said wistfully, gazing at the ceiling.

She leaned over and hit him on the shoulder. "I can have fun," she said.

He hummed thoughtfully, clearly cooking up a test of her words. Something glinted in his eye as he looked at her. "There's music in the front lawn tonight," he said. "It's for the people, but we can still go." His gaze drifted lazily to the ceiling again.

Tonight. She squinted, trying to look impish, despite the reality that more obligations crowded her schedule. Being irresponsible sounded so freeing.

"I have a lesson with Daelon," she finally said.

"And you said you could have fun." Jori stood up, cracked his neck, and smoothed his collar. Then he offered her his arm.

She took it and they swept out of the room together, their servants trailing behind. Despite running off to escape her maids now and then, she did what she was supposed to: she attended sessions in the Main (even boring ones) and she tried to pay attention during lessons. Ever since she could remember, she had always looked forward to being a Keeper... until lately. The idea of the people judging her for her looks or decisions gave her directionless anger. Her pace slowed.

"So, music?" he prompted.

"I'll decide later," she said. Skipping a lesson was a bigger step than she had taken. It was a crossroad, and she wasn't sure she was prepared for it.

They turned the corner into the huge hallway that led from the Third Keeper's wing to the front of the palace. Guards and portraits and potted trees rushed by on either side of them as they walked.

"You know how much I love later," Jori said in an undertone as he gave a guard a familiar nod. "But now is always better."

Like a closing door, the moment she would succeed her mother as Keeper threatened her, ready to shut off any possibility of relaxation and cheer. She almost felt the weight of that responsibility already. Would it be so bad to find out what a little rebellion felt like first?

She shook off the stress like a physical thing and turned to Jori.

"Let's do it," she said.

13

FIRIAN

THE ACADEMY DIDN'T HEAT many fires. Some students from wealthy families wore fur-lined coats they had picked up on a visit home. Firian could have worn his Academy-issued black coat, but the cold made him feel more alive. It kept his senses sharp and muscles tense. He was almost glad he didn't have a comfortable overcoat.

It had been a little over three years since he'd heard about his family's death, so the thought didn't bother him like it used to. Well, it still bothered him, but it didn't sting anymore. The pain had dulled.

Now he had other things to worry about. He bit down hard as he passed the hall master's room, swearing to himself. What was Tiev doing that the Masters liked so much? He couldn't figure it out. Tiev seemed only a little better than average, and yet here he was—the hall master. He didn't deserve that level of respect, especially not when Firian did everything he could to earn more.

Firian reached the courtyard and jogged to his first class. Impatiently, he sat down across from Master Belik, ready to go. Belik sat in uncomfortable silence for a few moments. It was long enough for Firian to realize his muscles still ached from the night before when he stayed up late doing training exercises. The last pose he had held for two hundred breaths left his side burning. The extra work he had done early that morning hadn't helped the soreness. He bit the inside of his lip as the Master peered at him over his glasses with a familiar, scrutinizing gaze. Why couldn't the Master see all his work, his progress? At this point, he should know that Firian wasn't a child anymore. He needed to be promoted to Defender. If he could jump or swim or fight to get that blue-stoned ring, he would already have it.

"Firian," he said, "something's bothering you. What is it?"

"Master Belik..." He hesitated. "How do I get better?"

A half-smile cracked the older man's features. "Better at what?"

"Faster. Smarter. Better at fighting. Better at the Unreal!" Firian burst out. Each word deflated the pressure that had built up in his chest.

"What do you think I'm teaching you?"

"No. You are—but... How do I get better faster?"

The Master raised an eyebrow.

"I'll do anything."

Belik's eyes became suddenly intense. "Anything?" he asked in a low voice.

Firian nodded, but the way he repeated the word brimmed with hidden motives, secret knowledge, as though he'd have to give his soul.

Belik fell back into his normal mode. "The faster you want to learn, the more you have to be willing to endure. Pain forces us to be better." He laid a hand, perhaps unconsciously, on his bad leg. "Test yourself. But be careful. Remember, the better you are, the more danger you're in of believing yourself to be dead or injured." His eyes flickered to the white scars on Firian's hands.

"I've been training myself, working out all the time..."

Belik snorted. "What do we do here, Firian?"

Taken aback, he answered, "Train for war—defense."

"And how do we do that?"

"...Mental warfare."

Belik's eyes shone. "*Mental* warfare. There you go. You have to get tougher in your mind."

"But—"

"But you're good for your age?" Belik snapped. "No one becomes the best by being good at something. You become the best by sacrificing everything else." He stared into Firian's face. "Are you ready to do that?"

"Yes," Firian answered, no hesitation.

"Then show me."

TÁNUIL WAS COVERED IN ICY, glittering snow. Huge icicles dangled off the houses like liquid diamonds. A fresh layer of snow dusted over even new footprints.

Belik's words still echoed in Firian's ears. *You become the best by sacrificing everything else.* This town day could not have come at a worse time. The Academy required students to take time off periodically, to renew their energy and focus for the coming days. Firian usually looked forward to a little time off, but he wanted to practice today. To push himself.

He wanted to bleed.

It was so cold that Bard's nose and ears looked frozen and red, and he kept shivering as they walked together to the Old Pub. Firian welcomed the slicing wind as it cut across them, but he kept seeing Bard shoot him concerned looks. If he'd had an extra coat, he was sure Bard would have offered it to him. As it was, even the black Academy coat he had on didn't seem to help.

The sign above the low door simply read OLD PUB:

KIEGAN, PROPRIETOR. Firian had learned early on that Kiegan wasn't really the proprietor. It was just a tradition to leave his name there. The Old Pub was one of the only remaining buildings left from the original settlement of Tánuil. In World Events, he'd learned that Kiegan had been a friend of the legendary General Brishen, one of the heroes of the War of the Kingdom Rebels. He, along with Shane and Mari Calthwaite, whose descendants were the Keepers of Brithnem, had stopped here on the road to Carradoc. So the sign stayed as it was.

The two of them hurried inside. Even though there only a few people, the small room seemed crowded. The air was muggy and thick with a chilling draft. A few rough-hewn chairs were strewn about the room, all taken, and there were stools lining the chunky wooden counter. All the surfaces in Kiegan's old house had worn thin and dull from use.

Bard rubbed his running nose and puffed out a breath that formed ice clouds in the air.

Firian jostled his way to the counter. "Two ciders!" he shouted over the noise to the real proprietor, Hyrum, a haggard-looking man with thin hair and dark, rough skin like unsoftened leather.

Firian turned to Bard and held out his palm for a token.

Moments later they managed to find two empty seats in a corner where most people didn't like to sit. The draft, the tight space, and the grimy windows didn't make it appealing. Good thing the hot cider came right away. It would warm him up and not dull his brain.

Bard sipped his with relish. "You know, those are made in Enderin," he said, tipping his chin toward a carved sconce on the wall. The dark, sealed wood had been carved with a branching tree.

Firian did know. Bard never lost an opportunity to point out Endrian work.

"There's a place by the tanner's that does carvings like that. I wonder if Samson's dad carved that one..."

"I doubt it." Firian ran his finger over the mug handle. "I'm sure that's been on the wall since the Calthwaites."

"Maybe you're right. And how would they get it here?" He popped his eyebrows up. There was hardly any trading in or out of Tánuil, and the border patrollers dealt with what little got through. Bard huffed a laugh through his nose. "It *is* from Enderin, though. Yeah, it wouldn't be Samson. His family hasn't traveled since his daughter died anyway." He paused as the memory hit him. "She was little." When he looked up, his face lightened and he waved. "Tiev!"

A jolt ran through Firian's body. Too late to stop Bard from calling him over. Seeing Tiev's smug face, his perfect hair, made the drink in his stomach sour.

Tiev, bundled in his coat, wove his way through the crowd and stood across from Firian. His desert complexion looked strangely pale in the cold. He shook the wetness from his hair and a drop landed in Firian's cider.

Firian ground his teeth, rounding his shoulders around the mug.

"Hey, Tiev," Bard said, grinning. "I didn't know you had a town day too."

"Just a few hours." He had to speak loudly so they could hear him over the cacophony of voices. He didn't need to bother. "Why'd you choose this spot?"

Why'd you choose to come over?

"Last place open," Bard said.

Tiev cast his narrow eyes to the grimy window. "Everyone's getting an ale."

"Or a cider," said Bard, as a shiver racked him again.

Tiev nodded. "I have an ale coming." He flattened his hand

on the scored little table, showing off his dark blue Defender ring. He preened like a village girl in that thing.

Firian let out a breath through his nose. So he wasn't just planning to harass them for a moment, but to stay for a while. Perfect.

Even Bard eyed the ring with something like awe. "It's good. It's so cold today!"

"I hope it comes fast. I have a lot to do. Could use the warmth before I go."

Bard nodded, but Firian picked his teeth with his tongue.

They sat for a few moments in tense silence.

"You know," said Bard, "now that you mention it, I need to finish packing actually. Get a couple things before I go home." He quickly gulped the rest of the steaming cider.

Firian cast him a look. Bard stood and wrapped his jacket close.

"I'm going to go, Fir. You coming?"

Firian glanced at his mug. "I'll finish my drink first. Go ahead."

Bard nodded. "I'll see you later, Tiev?"

Of course you'll see him later—he's our hall master. He didn't understand why Bard was so nice to him. Tiev deserved none of it.

With Bard gone, Tiev turned to Firian. "So, I hope you haven't been sneaking out at night." His tone was light, but he smiled and twisted the dark Defender ring on his finger as he waited for an answer. They had snuck out together plenty of times when he was a Learner, but this had an air of threat to it— not friendly at all.

"What?" Firian snapped, casting him a black look.

Tiev's lips twisted in another smile.

He likes this power over me.

He leaned forward to speak again, but Hyrum interrupted

with a mug of ale plunked between them. Tiev pulled it toward him. "I don't want to kick you off my floor, you know," he said. "I have always wondered how one becomes a Sentry, though."

Only truly disgraced Tanyu ever became Sentries. They all knew that. It was an inhuman punishment—no creativity, no freedom, only intense focus on the boundaries they needed to build. Yes, Sentries were essential in times of war so that no one could harm a sleeping Tanyu through his or her dreams. But it was the worst fate one of them could suffer.

How dare he threaten me?

Firian's face felt hot despite the cold and his next words exploded from him. "Just because you have a gory ring doesn't mean you're any better than I am!"

Tiev's eyes dilated and his mouth twitched downward.

Good. Firian tried to hide his deep breath.

"Actually, it does," Tiev said, stopping to smirk, "and I was thinking about setting up a proficiency test. A few of the Masters suggested it."

Here was his chance to prove himself to Belik. He wouldn't just pass the test. He'd crush Tiev, and prove that if anybody deserved to be a Defender, he did. "I'd be ready right now." He paused, then said in a low voice, "I could kill you in the Unreal if I wanted to."

"I'll give you one thing," said Tiev, fighting to keep his voice steady. "You're brave to speak to a Defender that way. I've spoken personally to the Tanyuin Head. I could get you kicked out of the Academy."

Firian took in Tiev's perfect hair, thin eyes, heavy coat, Defender ring... But his hands had only one scar. Firian stretched his jaw and peered into Tiev's face. "Try."

14

KIRIA

TWO WEEKS LATER, the day came.

Kiria smoothed her long dress again and touched her hair. The tailor had brought a large looking glass down at her request, so she could check herself one last time as she waited in the side hallway that opened into the Main. She wore a floor-length dress of deep red, with gold tracery that flowed like water down the neckline and bodice, twisting around the waist in royal symbols, and down to the end of the short train. The skirt was full but simple, not too gathered or fluffed.

Looking herself up and down, she straightened her shoulders, stood tall. Every movement she made didn't seem to fit the radiant image before her. She made her form less perfect when she wasn't graceful or elegant, when her expression wasn't serene or joyful. The look on her face was just too human. Her Beauty was too beautiful to fit into.

She cleared her throat. Regardless of how she felt, the people of the Western Kingdom wanted their leaders to be the best, and this was part of what she had to offer. Over the past couple days, her feelings had alternated between excitement—who didn't want to look ravishingly beautiful?—and crippling insecurity.

With Beauty she felt naked, as though there were nothing left to reveal. The surprise was ruined. Kiria Arioc was a hollow thing.

Only her serving girls stood with her, but she could hear crowds of happy voices seeping through the thick door to the Main. The wild thought crossed her mind that she could still go back to being plain. Almost no one had seen her like this yet. She could hide in the comfort of invisibility. *No, this is for the people, not for me... at least, not completely for me.* Besides, this late birthday party existed to reveal her to the world. She felt sick.

"Vayci," she whispered, leaning toward her serving girl's dark head. Vayci was as tall as she was now. "Find Jori and Atty for me and bring them here."

Vayci obliged and, minutes later, she slipped back through the door with the two brothers, both dapper in their leather vests and embroidered jackets. Kiria tried to peek through the momentary crack in the door, but it didn't reveal much but warm yellow light. Once the door closed, she shot out questions like demands. "What's it like out there? Are there many people yet?"

Instead of answering, Jori's eyes widened. "Look at you," he said. Atty didn't speak, but held the hilt of his ceremonial sword uncomfortably.

Kiria's face washed hot. Even around the Calthwaite boys, she didn't usually reveal her Ability like this. And it was a particularly nice dress. "Thank you," she said shortly. "I haven't been announced yet. I have to know what's going on." Nervously, she rearranged the gold bracelets on her wrists and checked her dangling gold earrings.

"The room's filling up," Jori said idly. "Lots of people here to see you in all your glory."

"The Keepers aren't here yet," Atty added. "But a couple ambassadors came, I think."

Jori shrugged. "The most interesting thing out there is the food."

"Food!" she cried. Remembering that it existed gave her great comfort. "Would you get me something?" She laid a hand on her churning stomach.

"Get her something," Atty said.

After hesitating a moment, Jori squeezed himself out the door. Chatter and glasses tinkling amplified through the crack in the door. The sound muted again when it shut behind him.

Atty swallowed visibly. "You shouldn't be nervous," he said.

Awkward silence followed. The girls stood at attention, but she didn't have anything for them to do.

Happily, Jori soon emerged with a glazed tart in one hand and wine in the other. Kiria snatched the tart from him and stuffed it all in her mouth at once. It did nothing to ease her stomach but it took her mind off her nerves for a moment. "Mmm," she hummed, rubbing her fingers together to get rid of the crumbs. "Thank you."

Lively string music began in the next room. One of her favorite songs. She closed her eyes and breathed once.

"Ready?" Atty asked.

Jori leaned toward her, smiling. "Ready as she'll ever be, right?"

She felt too sick to answer.

The music suddenly stopped and a voice announced something. At first, she thought Amir Chetana was announcing her and she felt bile rising in her throat before realizing that the voice had named Cúron and her mother. Aylmor couldn't come because he was somewhere near the Charúnin Thôr mountains once again for a political meeting.

"We've got to get back," Atty said apologetically.

"That's okay," she managed.

The Calthwaites both cast encouraging looks her way as they went out.

Alone with her girls again, she turned feverishly to Candrae, intending to ask her to fix her hair. Was it perfect? Of course it was. There was no use asking. She was beautiful.

It was only seconds now. *Good. Less waiting. ...When will they play that music?* She centered herself toward the door. It would open inward to present her. She just needed to stand and be beautiful, walk in, sit down, wait a moment, wander, talk amiably, dance, eat, and leave. That was it—

The door opened, washing her with light. "...Kepress, Lady Kiria—" was all she heard. Her name resounded in her head like a bell. Nine musicians played music off to the left against the wall but all other human sounds hushed. All the partitions had been removed, making the room huge. It was awash with bright flowing fabric and perfumes. Normal sessions in the Main only took up about a quarter of the space. She'd forgotten how big the room could become, with its vaulted ceiling. Everything was heady and alive, done up perfectly.

Slowly, she walked into the room. Loud gasps echoed through the room as scores of faces watched her. Before she even reached her seat at the foot of the Keepers' dais, whispers filled the space. Amir, soldiers, citizens, servants, noble families all leaned confidentially to talk low in each other's ears. Bold men tried to catch her gaze, their intentions clear. Other people, with flushed faces and misty eyes, watched her silently. The shock and reverence and excitement were all for her. Surreal.

By the time she smoothly made her way past the Keepers to her seat facing them below, she felt exhausted. After bowing to them respectfully, she sat down. An odd mixture of blue-hot pride and crippling embarrassment alternated in her body. If only she could hide and observe everyone's reactions.

She closed her eyes a moment. Maybe things would come into focus again. Her limbs felt heavy and her eyes tired as she sat there, wilting, relaxing. The initial shock was over. Short, painful, but it was over. The ball, however, was not. The players started up a lively dancing tune and she sensed exhaled breath and movement as the people began to talk and choose partners again.

"Kiria?"

She snapped out of her daze. Jori, dressed to the nines, offered her his arm. A few grumpy-looking men stood just behind him as though they'd just been pushed to the side. "Would you consent to dance with me?" he asked.

"'Would I consent?'" she repeated, rising and linking her arm around the soft fabric of his dress coat. "What way is that to ask someone?"

"*You're* the Kepress, especially now," he pointed out. "*I'm* just someone's brother." He squinted and whirled her onto the best spot on the floor, in front of the musicians, as he'd done last week when they had disguised themselves and snuck into the city for a party. "Almost famous."

"Notorious," she said, smiling. Talking to someone relieved some pressure, but she still felt everyone's eyes following her every move.

The tip of her shoe caught the dance floor and she stumbled forward a little. A hundred eyes widened. Jori laughed, stepping away from a man who let go of his dance partner to offer Kiria a hand, and simplified the dance. "Thank you," she said under her breath.

He smiled disarmingly and stumbled forward too. "Didn't know you could even trip looking like that."

"I'm still the same," she said. An ambassador's daughter sneered with her friend on the edge of the dance floor. Kiria lowered her eyes. The gold encircling her wrists glowed against her skin.

She looked up again at Jori, who raised his eyebrows disbelievingly.

"I am," she insisted.

He spun her again before replying. "You might be the same, but now you'll have to look out for yourself. Just look at you!"

She automatically scanned the curved walls where the guards held their positions. "Jori, if you say anything like that again..."

"It was an attempt at a compliment."

The music began to shift. In the pause between pieces, Kiria heard her name whispered by about eight voices around the room. She caught the eye of a middle-aged man who was dancing near her. He promptly turned back to his wife, pretending never to have seen her.

Maybe revealing her Beauty was a mistake. Everything she did seemed wrong, wooden and false when so many people were watching her. She tried to ignore them. "'You'll have to look out for yourself...'" she mimicked. "Poor excuse for a compliment. Should I be afraid of you too?"

"Oh yes," he said, escorting her off the dance floor and back to her seat. "I will have you for my wife now, because I saw you once in a nice dress." He leaned confidentially toward her. "If you need rescuing from someone who *actually* thinks that, let me know. Wink at me or something. I'll probably come help you. If I don't, then know that I'm laughing, right over there." He pointed to the table with sparkling wine and headed toward it.

She shook her head, glad that somebody could take her mind off her nerves and remind her that the world would not end tonight.

"These people have never seen anyone as beautiful as you," her father said behind her. She hadn't even heard her parents approach. They stood behind her in full Brithnem finery—all light blue, dark purple, and silver. The thought struck her that she should have worn those colors instead. After all, wasn't she supposed to serve the people of the Western Kingdom? Instead she chose the colors she thought would show off her Beauty. She swallowed down her embarrassment, her inadequacy, so no one would see.

"How are you doing, dear?" her mother asked.

"Very well, thank you," she replied, aware once again of all the eyes on her. Her folded hands gave away her nervousness, didn't they? *How does Mother hold her hands as she sits?*

Her mother smiled at a few of the dignitaries who hovered near them. "Jorrim was the first to ask you to dance," she observed.

"Of course he was. I don't know who else I'd want to dance with first. I get the feeling they don't even believe it's me."

"I'm sure they know it's you, Kiria," said her father. "Shall we dance the next, since everyone else is too afraid to ask you?" Her father rarely danced.

She smiled and accepted his offer. Plenty of others waited on the fringes for their chance, but she'd rather dance with her father.

Years ago, generals and soldiers all danced before campaigns, a last taste of joy before months of darkness and pain. But those days were over. Even the war with the Torithians felt far removed. Lately, she hadn't even thought about it.

"You're doing well, I think," her father said quietly. Even as he took her hand in the formal dancing position, his eyes darted around the room. Ever the military man, concerned with security. His thick eyebrows twitched down a couple of times as he saw something he didn't like.

"I'm doing better now," she said honestly.

He gave a half-smile. "Ready to lead a kingdom."

She swallowed. *Not quite.* But his eyes softened at the edges when he looked at her, so he thought she could do it. A well of thankfulness bubbled up. "When the time comes," she said.

"You'll make the Arioc name proud." Although others had talked down to her over the years, her father never had. Now, he saw her as strong and capable. That confidence radiated from him. Her father had never feared women in power. After all, he had married her mother and taken her name, a unique situation in a country where people either took their husband's last names or didn't have surnames altogether.

Their dance was short but meaningful. As the last note sang out, the room erupted in clapping, though she couldn't have been very graceful.

Her mother's wild face caught her attention. "Rhet!" Her hushed tone was urgent as she called them over.

They hurried to her.

Daelon stood next to her, his face pale. Kiria's stomach clenched. Something was wrong.

Her mother stood on the dais step and bent over to speak in an undertone. "Kiria, do you know where Atael and Jorrim are?"

Daelon touched her mother respectfully on the shoulder and cast a look across the room. "There they are, my Keeper." Without waiting longer, he rushed over to them—at least, that's as quickly as Kiria had ever seen him go.

"Rhet, I need to talk to you." In a flash, her mother had ushered her father away from her.

Cold with fear, she practically jogged to catch up with Daelon. If she reached him in time, she could overhear his news.

Atty and Jori were both talking casually to one of the guests, a military strategist named Petra. Kiria had always found her more approachable than most of the other high-ranking soldiers. "Excuse me, madam," Daelon cut in, "but I must speak with Kepron Atael immediately."

She'd never seen him look so serious. Often he was stern,

but never this upset. He fairly dragged Atty off, with Jori in tow. A few people began to notice the disturbance.

"Excuse me," Kiria said, moving away from someone who had come up to talk to her. *This dress...* Why had she ever liked it? She couldn't move fast enough.

People, maybe well-meaning, blocked her path, as she watched the three of them disappear through the carved doors.

She spun around to catch her parents. Maybe she could get them to tell her what they knew. But she knew her mother's body language well. She wasn't ready to talk.

The only thing to do was to follow Daelon and the Calthwaites out into the hall.

As soon as she slid between the huge wooden doors, shutting out the sounds of the ball, she spotted Daelon walking briskly down the hall away from her, his feet clipping the floor.

"Daelon!" she cried, a loud, empty sound.

He turned around. Even at that distance, his face looked strained and pale. "What is it, my Kepress?" he asked.

"Where are Att... Atael and Jorrim?" Only their formal names seemed to fit the moment.

"Unavailable."

"What do you mean?" They were always available. Jori made himself so available that they had spent the last six months having fun, going to parties, and escaping the responsibilities of the palace far more often than they should have. "Is everything all right?"

He didn't respond but stood awhile, considering. His eyes softened. "Why don't you go back to the party?" he finally said.

Her breathing tightened. "What happened?" *Not something terrible. Please.*

After pausing for a few moments in indecision, he strode toward her.

"Would you like to sit down, Kepress?" he said, motioning to the built-in bench against the wall.

She needed no argument; her legs felt shaky with apprehension. It had to be something serious to rattle Daelon this way.

He sat down next to her and ran his hands over his face that normally looked so young. "This will be announced very soon," he began solemnly, "so don't tell anyone. Not a soul."

She nodded, frowning.

"There has been... an accident."

"Who?" she cut in, but even as she said the word, she knew.

"Keeper Aylmor has been killed," he said very softly. Atty and Jori's father.

"Oh no! What happened?" she cried, swallowing against the rock in her throat.

"The report said that he was thrown from his horse. There was no pain." He cleared his throat. "Remember that you can't tell anyone."

"I won't. You know me." She let out an unsteady breath. Too many thoughts assaulted her at once. She had to go comfort them, but she was too shaken from the news. Better if she composed herself first. *Third Keeper gone.* "Then there's no... Wait! Atty's not ready to lead the country!" Her voice broke a little.

"He is a bit inexperienced," the Amir agreed. "But we will probably have the coronation ceremony before the new moon."

"Coronation..." It was too much to take in all at once.

"Unfortunately, I have to go tell the other advisors the news. It just arrived by messenger." He got up to leave.

"Okay."

Aylmor had been such a staple in her life. It never occurred to her that this would actually happen. Of course Atty would one day become the Keeper of Brithnem, but that was *one day*, not *now*. Not in the face of tragedy. But then, tragedy always preceded the crowning of a new monarch. One had to fall for the next to rise. Too suddenly, her friend was one of the most important leaders in the world.

She sat alone on the bench, shoulders heavy, and felt her Beauty seeping back to normalcy.

15

———

FIRIAN

With Bard gone to visit his family in Enderin, a visit that was sure to be brief, considering the conflict there, Firian had the room to himself. He could invite a girl over, but he wasn't in the mood. It had been too long since he had been alone with his thoughts. He dropped to the floor and started doing pushups. After all the practice, his muscles barely felt the strain.

"Isn't your Defender giving tests now?" The deep voice belonged to Master Makai, the man who had brought him to the Academy all those years ago.

Firian's joints suddenly felt wooden and cold. He sat up on his knees. "What?" he snapped, before adding an apologetic "...Master."

"I was told that Defender Tiev is giving his first tests now," Makai replied, seemingly unaffected by Firian's tone. "He should have told *you*, at least, Kess." Apparently, the whole Academy knew about the competition that had grown between the two of them lately.

"He's testing now?"

"Yes, now. Better hurry."

Firian fought the urge to run. At least Tiev wouldn't get the pleasure of seeing him rush to be on time to his little meeting, panting in the doorway like somebody begging to be forgiven for his tardiness. As far as he was concerned, Tiev could wait for him forever, except that he'd miss the chance to outdo him and prove his superiority.

Eventually he arrived at the meeting room for his floor, the one Erron had used for his tests. Each hall had one on the far end: a larger, open room used for gatherings, announcements, and testing. It looked like everybody else had already arrived. Boys overflowed out of the room, all craning their necks over the rest of the crowd, trying to see. Firian raised an eyebrow. What could they want to see? From the outside, testing normally looked like two people sitting and facing each other with their eyes closed—nothing great to look at. His curiosity took over. Obviously, something out of the ordinary was happening. Discreetly, he glanced over the other people's heads to the two chairs in the middle of the room.

"Out of the way!" Master Belik roared as he arrived. He looked haggard with suppressed excitement. Firian and the others automatically clamored to the side, creating a path for him.

The break in the sea of people allowed Firian to see what was happening. Tiev sat in one seat, with a look of perfect concentration on his face, and Rian sat in the other, sweating and twitching as though somebody were hitting him repeatedly.

"*Move!*" cried the Master again, though no one was in his way. "Tiev!"

Tiev snapped open his eyes and Rian slumped off his chair to the floor. He lay there, limp. The crowd at the door closed again, but Firian could just make out Tiev's face. The blood drained out of it as he glanced first at the unconscious form of Rian, then at Master Belik.

Belik toed Rian with his shoe, then sighed. "Gelir," he said to Tiev in a low voice. "This isn't a war." He jerked his head toward Rian. "He's alive, but if I find that you've 'tested' others like you tested him…"

"I didn't—"

"Shut up! And don't use all your Talent at once."

There was a very awkward silence while everyone waited for the Master to leave, but he didn't. Tiev seemed unsure whether to call up the next person, especially with Rian still lying by the chair.

"Well?" Belik prompted.

"Kess!" Tiev blurted. "Firian Kess!"

Firian felt numb. What just happened? Was Tiev *that* good?

Firian muscled his way through the crowd and sat calmly in the seat, making sure his feet didn't touch the prostrate form of Rian, which nobody had bothered to move. He pursed his mouth as he looked straight into Tiev's eyes. *You don't need to hold back on me.*

Tiev cleared his throat quietly. "Ready?" he whispered.

The crowd went very quiet. Firian lifted a corner of his mouth. "As long as you are."

"Hall master's choice."

They both closed their eyes. Firian let himself sink into nothingness.

There were no doors in the spotless paneled room. The walls shot upward and upward until they vanished, yielding to a thin prick of light hardly visible above. Circular windows formed an endless pattern, curling upward along the walls, allowing some sunlight to enter.

Firian stood at one end of the room, intense and calculating, with his legs slightly spread apart and his hands behind his back. Tiev stood in the same position opposite him.

"Do you see it?" Tiev asked customarily.

"Of course. Your choice," Firian added with a shrug, clenching his teeth in his mouth. He breathed the musty air, loving the possibilities sparking in his mind like flint.

A little smirk spread over Tiev's face.

To think that I was ever friends with this sniveling...

He calmed himself down. It was just a test, even if it was being administered by someone his own age.

"Can we start?" Firian asked, bringing his hands slowly to his sides.

"Sure." Two identical knives appeared in Tiev's hands and he twirled them expertly.

Please.

It was easy to look intimidating in the Unreal, but it was just that—Unreal.

Hard leather formed under Firian's palms. Whips in hand, he ran at Tiev, who started running along the circumference of the room. With superhuman speed, Firian ran in front of him.

Enough on the ground. He rose up so he was above the Defender. It took a moment for Tiev to realize where Firian was, and then he flew to meet him.

Setting his teeth, Firian mussed Tiev's perfect hair hard as he rose up beside him. Tiev's only answer was to jab his knives at him, but Firian flew out of the way.

This is all you have? It was almost laughable. Or it would be, if it weren't so insulting.

Master Asoka had told them once to be like water in the Unreal—liquid, solid, or gas. It didn't matter which, as long as it fit the situation. Every time Tiev knifed him, he pretended to be water and just let it go through him. Here he was immortal.

Bending his thought entirely on Tiev, he imagined no knives, no weapons of any kind in his opponent's hand. The endeavor was successful: Tiev's knives dissolved. In his instant of opportunity, his whips dissolved into blue smoke, leaving his hand in a tight fist. *What next?* Stars. Throwing stars. Shooting up in the air, he felt the cold bite of metal in his closed hand. Throwing feverishly, two stars at a time, he saw them sink deep into the paneling, always where Tiev had been a moment before. Then... a hit! Tiev recoiled in pain. Wild joy rose up in Firian, and he was almost ashamed of it.

He had won!

The rest of the stars melted into the air like smoke.

But just as the real world started to enter his mind and he could feel the open air of the meeting room, he felt himself being dragged back.

What?

That had never happened before. Tiev stood in the middle of the room again, and Firian got in the starting position to fight, still confused.

A blazing light began to pulse brighter and brighter around Tiev, spinning into him. *What?* he thought again. *This can't be real.*

After a few seconds, Firian had to look away. Watching Tiev was like looking straight at the noon sun, especially in that dim room. Whatever was happening made Firian nauseated. Something was wrong.

Firian's Academy coat whipped in front of his body as a gale swept past him from behind. He squinted forward again through his wildly blowing hair, trying to adjust his eyes enough to look. All the light and all the wind were sucked into Tiev with an energy that Firian had never witnessed before—like the energy of two or three Masters at once.

His mouth went thick and dry.

Here was power.

All the energy penned up in Tiev exploded out with fierce brightness and swept Firian off his feet. He hit his head hard against the wall as he fell, skidding.

"Time's up," said a faint voice, probably from the real world.

Painfully, he opened his eyes. So did Tiev. Once his eyes adjusted to the dark room—when did it become so dark?—Tiev said one word. "Difficult?"

Firian felt cold sweat dry on the backs of his hands. "Not at all," he lied, still shaken.

IT SEEMED quiet without Bard moving around and talking in his sleep. Firian lay in bed with his hands behind his head, staring at the plywood of the bunk above him. The testing a few days ago was still bothering him. In fact, it was almost all he thought about. Where had the power come from? It couldn't have been Tiev. It *couldn't*.

Everyone else, however, thought that it had been. The story had spread over the whole Academy with amazing speed. People asked Rian about his experience in almost every class. He'd recovered quickly after Firian's test was over and since then everyone had been curious about what had really happened to him. At first, he'd seemed a little resentful to bring up the subject but, after he got more attention than ever before, he started relating the incident to everyone who would listen. Predictably, his stories had gotten wilder and wilder with each telling. No one understood fully what had happened and Firian refused to give any details about his own experience, though he was asked almost as often as Rian.

Meanwhile, people treated Tiev like a prodigy or a god. People feared him, spoke about him in whispers, and argued about the significance of his Talent. Even the Masters were beginning to treat him almost like an equal. Firian's stomach felt sick and frozen whenever he thought of the possibility of Tiev being promoted to Master. Many people talked about the chance it would happen. Others followed Tiev as though he alone held the secret to being the perfect Tanyu. In the minds of almost everyone at the Academy, Tiev was in a class by himself and that caused many to revere him.

Firian pursed his lips together in the darkness. He knew he worked harder than any other student his age, including Tiev, whatever everyone else may think. As it was, he only slept four hours a night. It didn't really matter to him that he had to practice his skills in the dark cold of early morning much of the time. He'd always liked the cold season better anyway. It made him feel more alive.

He took a deep breath and sat up at the edge of his bunk. Closing his eyes, he concentrated hard on visualizing different objects, on visualizing himself as towering, as tiny, as air, as fire itself... *Fire! Is that how he did it?*

"Stop losing focus," he muttered to himself.

He was fire—all flame, but not consumed. Consum*ing*. That was it.

Powerful bright light. Burning. Power.

He lay down again as he became fire in his mind. It was abstract, but not much different than the lessons he'd been given on becoming like water, able to shift. They were both just natural elements. He would probably learn this stuff as a Defender anyway, or even later on that year.

The flames danced before him. Changing. Shifting. Burning. Flickering...

Firian was alone in a dark room. He felt cold and could only see about two feet ahead of him. Walking cautiously ahead, he found a blank wall, so he turned. After maybe five minutes, he found another wall, identical to the one he just left. Weaving his way around the new wall, he found more. These walls obviously formed some sort of maze. Without knowing why, he felt strongly that the answer to all of his problems waited in the middle and he needed to find it. He broke into a run toward what he knew instinctively was the center of the maze. It grew colder every minute. His clothes did nothing to fight off the icy chill that now bit on every side. Soon, the cold surpassed ordinary winter cold and starting gnawing inside him. He felt as though he were freezing to death. His fingers felt too fat to bend and his face was a mass of pain. *Need to finish* ... All of his answers were waiting.

He ran harder. The walls rose up closer together. Everywhere he went, there they were. Desperation set in. He was close to panic.

A cold wind blew past him. The fear that shook him wasn't enough to make him stop. He trudged ahead and a weak glow emerged from where the wind had blown. Now he could see more than one wall at a time. The center was close. His limbs moved as though he were wading through syrup.

He turned a corner. There it was.

A little wood fire burned sickly pale in the center of the maze and a huddle of people crouched around it. Firian could have cried with joy. He wasn't going to freeze and die in that meaningless maze. He must have laughed or gasped with relief because everyone around the fire turned to look at him.

Suddenly ashamed, he felt naked beneath their stares. None of the people said a word. After a moment or two, he almost wanted to sneak back into the maze to avoid them. The worst thing was that they *knew* him. Firian's breathing became thin and shallow.

"Stop looking at me," he breathed, turning away.

When he finally had the courage to look back, he saw the features of those who stared at him.

"Father?" he whispered. "Bard? Master Jovan?" He scanned a whole line of familiar faces until he lighted on one. His throat caught. "Brett."

Forgetting his fear, he threw himself around his sister's neck and broke down crying. She felt stiff in his arms, but his joy couldn't be stifled by a little thing like that. "Brett. I thought...." He shook his head into her shoulder.

When he pulled away from her, she said his name with such an odd expression that some of his apprehension returned. "What's wrong?" he asked.

"Get away from her," said his father's voice.

A creepy feeling crawled in his stomach at his tone of voice. It was as if he'd walked into a congregation of the dead. "I didn't..." he began to protest. "I just... It was cold."

A joyless laugh. "Worthless," someone muttered.

Firian bristled. "I'm a Tanyu," he said.

"He's not worth it," Master Belik broke in. "We let him in out of pity."

Master Jovan nodded his assent.

His mother didn't say anything, but he felt her sad eyes boring into him. She seemed on the verge of despairing tears and somehow all of it was his fault. Bitter disappointment etched deep into her lined features. He couldn't help her.

"Stop it," he said quietly, shaking.

"We knew you'd never amount to anything," his father said.

"Stop!" Firian said, with more force.

"What? Because *you* want us to? Just shut up," said Tiev cruelly. "No one cares what you say. Do us a favor and kill yourself so we don't have to worry about you anymore."

Firian's throat had closed so tightly he could barely breathe.

"Get away from me," Brett said softly at his side. "I can't stand it anymore."

Tears rimmed his eyes. Even Brett.

"You'll always be worthless, Firian," said someone, or it could have been all of them.

"*Stop!*" he yelled as loudly as he could.

The word echoed around the little room as Firian jolted awake. Pale rays of first light eked through the heavy curtains of his room. His chest rose and fell with heaving breaths. It took a moment for everything to spiral into silence again.

Time for more practice.

16

———

KIRIA

CANDRAE, the little serving girl, put another pearl-tipped pin into Kiria's hair. Kiria tapped her foot distractedly, screwing up her nose as she looked as herself in the glass, her head framed by Candrae's voluminous blonde hair. Hopefully her Beauty wouldn't distract anyone from the gravity of the ceremony.

"How much time do we have?" she asked.

"About twenty minutes, my Kepress."

"Right. Okay." She didn't know why she was so nervous. This was the time for Atty to be nervous, not her. But this proved that one day it would be her turn. Just because she'd never seen a coronation before didn't mean they never happened. She would be a Keeper of Brithnem too, just like Atty. "We have to get in place," she said, standing to her feet. She wasn't tall, but Candrae still had to reach up in order to keep the pin from falling out when she moved. "Vayci! Are you almost ready?" she called.

Frantically, her other serving girl emerged from the adjoining room, still holding one shoe in her hand. The servants' dresses weren't nearly as nice as hers, but they were still beautiful in a way: plain, in rich colors, with a thin decorative belt around the waist. Vayci had even tied Candrae's hair in knots before they went to bed the night before so that it would curl in the morning, and Candrae had helped Vayci with the swirling designs on her head. Kiria's silky blue dress reached down to the floor. It was almost impossible to walk because of the length, let alone the elaborate shoes she wore with it.

"We have to get to the Main," Kiria said.

Vayci nodded and put her shoe on awkwardly before standing up.

Seeing them both in their nice things watching and waiting for her made her suddenly proud of them. Usually she didn't think about them at all, but they were brought up to serve her and were doing it so well. They never complained or hesitated. It was people like these two girls that made the whole Western Kingdom work properly. "You both look lovely," she told them, smiling.

They blushed and ran to open the door for her. She swept through it and into the common area, where her parents were waiting with all six of their attendants—guards, ladies-in-waiting, and her Amiran advisor Chetana. She'd never seen her mother look so amazingly beautiful. Merian, her mother, had always had natural beauty—an outdoor kind that was best left untampered-with—but today she wore a green dress with diamond studs and diamonds in her ears. Even her father was transformed. He wore several rings that he usually kept stowed away, and he wore his best vest, with gold thread throughout it and a dark blue coat. Normally they didn't go out in all this finery, but this was a special occasion: part Aylmor's funeral, part Atael's coronation celebration.

"Are you ready, Kiria?" her mother asked.

She sucked in a breath and nodded.

Her mother took her father's arm and promenaded with him down into the wide hall that led down to the Main. Kiria had trouble keeping up because of her tall shoes, but somehow all eleven of them managed to make the long walk to the Main without making fools of themselves. Well, of course her mother and father wouldn't make fools of themselves, but she was glad that she hadn't.

A low murmur of voices came from inside the room and low lights flickered through the crack in the door. Four guards stood outside the room. They all instantly recognized them and moved aside.

The First Keeper, Aylmor's relatives, the Amir, nobles, and servants all crowded into the large room, standing mainly toward the edges of the room where dark purple fabric covered the multi-paned windows. Except for the dim lighting and serious occasion, it seemed nothing like a funeral. Everyone looked stunning, sipping cold drinks and talking in huddles. The chairs had been taken away, at least for the moment, as they did for parties.

Kiria saw almost everyone bow their heads respectfully as her family entered. Keepers didn't require any elaborate form of deference, as long as some kind of deference existed.

Kiria scanned the room for Jori. He was leaning against the opposite wall, looking sullen until someone came up to talk to him. His grin came easily until the person walked away again. He kept picking at the sleeves of his maroon tunic and glancing uneasily around the room. She almost went over to stand by him before remembering that she couldn't leave her family during the ceremony. So she tried to get his attention instead, looking intently at his face in order to catch his eye, waving discreetly. He refused to notice any of it.

Atty, on the other hand, was nowhere to be seen. But that was no surprise.

Nearby, to her family's right, stood Cúron with Kader and his wife, Varinna. Cúron's particularly splendid robe matched Kiria's dress, all light blue, one of the official colors of Brithnem. It complimented his short gray beard and hair that fell to his collar. Varinna looked like a queen in purple, with her hair done up in twists like a crown.

Her mother and father made quiet, polite conversation with Cúron and his family for several minutes. Having two Keeper families speak to each other made Jori look even more separate and dejected. He had no one left but Atty. Again, Kiria wished she could go over to him.

Daelon appeared and stood beside her. He winked and she knew it was just to make her feel better. Winking was inappropriate at a gathering like this, but not so much that people would comment.

Soon Cúron walked up onto the dais where the Keepers' chairs were and stood there alone, facing the crowd. Everyone quieted and turned to the front of the room. "Keepers, Amir, and people of Brithnem," he began in a loud voice, "we have come here today to honor the Third Line of Keepers. The descendants of Caedmon, the son of Shane and Mari Calthwaite, have served this country well through all its trials and successes. Today we witness the future and remember the past." He acknowledged his Amiran advisor standing just below him to the left. "Parohim."

Parohim strode up the steps. He was tall and thin, rather gray, and he wore the traditional coat with a high neck. Without any preamble, he began a recitation from the Sacred Scroll.

"Forever shall you worship God. In whatever you do, worship Him.

For not only the race of Khelê shall be called the Chosen Ones, but you also, as their descendants, may partake of their glory. In days of wickedness you were ignorant and evil, but now a great good is restored to you and God speaks among you once more. Be wise, there-fore, and follow no other words but those of God. If you do not chase after other gods and invent them for yourself, He shall remain present among His people. Then you shall all be as the Khelê, seeing God's goodness in the ways that He chooses you for Himself.

Forever shall you worship God. In whatever you do, worship Him."

Kiria mouthed the familiar passage as the advisor proclaimed it. All her life, she'd seen those words written along the walls of the Main, reminding the Keepers of their duty to God. They spoke of the time when the race of the Kingdom Dwellers had decided to follow a false god, giving it the name of the only God. To draw their attention rightfully back to himself, God had sent them children who looked nothing like them. The people misunderstood and thought they had been cursed. In the panic that followed, a leader (the Kingdom's first king) rose up and declared that they should kill all the strange-looking children. They even created ceremonies for these killings, and did it all in the name of God, who in his wisdom engineered ways for many of the innocent children to escape. Those people grew up and formed an army that attacked the Kingdom, which was built in the very spot that Brithnem was now, and were called the Khelê—God's chosen people. At the time, only a few Kingdom Dwellers saw the justice in what the Khelê were doing. Among them were Shane and Mari Calthwaite, who converted and were the first to willingly ally themselves with the Khelê. They were heroes, and their children began the three royal Lines of Brithnem.

Parohim stepped down from the platform. "Aylmor Calthwaite fulfilled his duty to God and to the Western Kingdom and now the Holy One has taken him, leaving his son, Atael Calthwaite, to serve in his stead."

Then there was a dead silence. A rasping breath came from somewhere, loud in the quiet. Cúron walked off the dais and back to his family, his feet hitting the floor softly.

The heavy door at the side creaked open, the same one she had stood behind, waiting to reveal her Beauty. No servant had opened it, but a figure in rags appeared, standing out in stark contrast to the overwhelming finery around him. His hair was uncombed and his feet had no shoes. He didn't raise his eyes to meet the dozens of pairs transfixed on him. His dress was worse than a servant's.

The figure wove through the crowd and approached Cúron. A large circle formed around the two of them as the man in rags dropped to his knees and pulled out a wet strip of cloth from his belt and ran it over the ruler's feet. Once he had finished, Cúron said, "Thank you." The man nodded.

Then he moved on to one of Jori's servants, named Sen, and proceeded to do the exact same thing. "Thus will I serve my country; thus will I serve my God," said the man, lifting his head.

It was Atael. Kiria had never seen him look so ragged and drawn.

"Bring a robe for his back," said Cúron.

"Bring shoes for his feet," said Merian.

A pause.

"Bring a crown for his head," said Jori finally, "that he may represent our Third Line." He shifted slightly to stand upright. Kiria understood that the next of kin was supposed to say this line; normally that would be his mother, but Ladima had died when they were very young.

At Jori's words, the Third Line's Amiran advisor and Atael's two servants left the room.

Kiria leaned over to her mother. "Isn't he supposed to wash your feet?" she breathed. It seemed odd that Cúron was the only Keeper who was part of the ceremony.

Merian held up a hand. *Impatient? Irritated?* Hopefully that meant she would give an explanation later.

In moments the servants returned with the robe and shoes, and the Amir with the crown.

"Approach the throne, servant of Brithnem," said Atty's advisor, Reynard. Atty obeyed him and stood in front of his throne. His advisor followed him onto the platform. A servant came up quickly and put a thick robe around his shoulders while another bent down to strap shoes to his feet. Once the two servants stepped down, Cúron and Merian of the First and Second Lines took their seats at the front. They had never looked so splendid as far as she remembered, but she couldn't look away from Atty long. He set his face very seriously as he stood there in a poor man's tunic and a Keeper's robe. It all struck her as a game—they were all playacting, speaking in turn when their parts came. If not for the look on Atty's face she may really have believed that this was all an elaborate joke. But this was no joke. This was how someone became a Keeper. A wave of nausea hit her suddenly. One day this would be her ceremony.

"What do you swear?" asked the Amir holding the crown.

Kiria mouthed the words with him, words she had learned since childhood. "I swear to serve my country, the Western Kingdom, and its capital, Brithnem, to the best of my ability, to guide her through war and peace, freedom and judgment, with wisdom and integrity, for as long as I live." He said the words softly and clearly, with almost no lisp. The words shifted something inside Kiria. She felt breathless and small and yet completely, finally, secure. These were the words she'd forgotten. These were the words that meant everything.

The Amir turned to the other seated Keepers. "Do you accept Atael Calthwaite as the heir to this Line and consequently to this throne?" he asked.

"I do," Cúron and her mother stated.

"And do you, people of Brithnem?" he addressed the crowd.

"We do," came the murmur of dozens of voices.

The Amir turned back to Atty. "Please be seated, my Kepron." Atty sat in the throne they had played on as children.

Reynard took a deep breath, probably for effect. "We now call you Atael Calthwaite, Third Keeper of Brithnem." And he slowly placed the crown on Atty's mussed hair. It fell into place there like a door sealed shut.

The Amir came off the platform and bowed before the new Keeper. One by one the people began to fall on one knee before him, starting with the servants, then the guests, the Amir, and finally the Keepers' families including Kiria. Then applause erupted as he stood, a Keeper of Brithnem.

Once the clapping had died down, his two servants came up to him and escorted him from the room. Everyone else followed. Kiria came to her feet as her family rose and ushered her out.

Kiria tried to see Atty, her friend, but he was soon lost in the crowd. She had expected the ceremony to be longer. It really was nothing more than a formality, establishing something that was true to begin with.

Heirs to the throne of Brithnem served the country with their lives.

Lately she had forgotten. She'd let simple insecurity shake her resolve. No more. Let people say what they wanted about her looks, her youth, her femininity, her inexperience. She felt something harden within her. *I swear to serve my country, the Western Kingdom, and its capital, Brithnem, to the best of my ability, to guide her through war and peace...*

17

———

FIRIAN

BARD SNORTED IN HIS SLEEP. "Where's the... lace?" he muttered. "I lost... tuft of lace...." He rolled over. "Really? I thought... brush had it... Maybe..."

Town day... Knuckling his eyes, Firian rolled off the bed and started getting dressed. Despite Bard's being gone for a few days, he was still used to these lively one-sided conversations.

"Stop... jumping," Bard murmured under his breath.

"I'm not," Firian whispered, absently scratching the back of his neck. The whole room still smelled of the cinnamon that Bard's mother had packed with his clothes. It was pretty, like a woman's perfume, which Firian liked on girls but not in their little space, where it felt stifling.

"Lace..."

Dressed and ready, Firian stood and smacked Bard on the arm. "Get up!" he said loudly. "It's a town day."

"S'early..." Bard slurred with his back to him.

"I'm going now," he said.

Bard sniffed as he rolled over and peered at Firian with puffy eyes. "Fine," he sighed and cleared his throat. "I'll come. Give us a minute."

"Still can't find that tuft of lace, can you?" he said.

"What?" Bard grunted. "What are you talking about?"

"Just a moment ago—in your sleep."

He groaned. "Don't tell anyone."

Grinning, Firian said, "Why would I want to do that?"

Bard threw his pillow at him and collapsed again from the effort.

Leaving the sounds of discontented muttering behind him, Firian headed toward the washroom at the end of the hall.

The door swished over a thin film of water as he entered. Tiev, Shiro, and their lanky friend Braden were the only ones there. Tiev hardly traveled alone these days. All his newfound friends followed him wherever he went. Firian ignored them and went to the nearest sink to splash his face with the cold water. It was fiercely refreshing. He slicked the wetness off with his hands and flicked it at the sink, eyeing Tiev, who eyed him back.

"You're up early," Firian told him, giving in to the temptation to poke at the bear.

"So are you."

"You're not practicing on a town day, are you?" Firian continued idly.

"What's that to you?" Tiev asked, scooping up some water in his hand and splashing it on the back of his neck.

"Just, if you were..." He shrugged.

"What?"

"You don't feel like you *need* to practice this early on an off day, do you?" Firian was satisfied when Tiev bit his lip in agitation. Apparently he'd hit a nerve.

Shiro and Braden tried not to look interested in what was happening between the two of them, but they weren't doing a very good job.

"I'm not!" Tiev exclaimed.

"Hm. Lately you've just seemed… more motivated than usual."

Tiev straightened. "I'm not afraid of you, Firian," he said angrily. "Remember the test day."

When Firian set his mouth a little tighter in response, Shiro sniggered. Firian shot him a black look. Why had he started this row in the first place? "Right! I remember. Good job attacking Learners during a test."

"At least I *could*," Tiev replied coolly.

"You had no idea what you were doing." It had to be true. Firian smiled a little.

Shiro and Braden stopped pretending to wash up. Tiev colored slightly and narrowed his eyes. "I knew exactly what I was doing." He set his jaw forward.

"That would explain the terrified look on your face."

Tiev stepped forward violently. "Shut up, Firian! If you want to be nearly killed again today—"

"What time?" Firian shouted, his voice echoing off the damp walls. He was startled by the vehemence of his own voice. His hands had become fists at his sides.

A glint of apprehension flashed in Tiev's eyes for a moment. Firian fought back a smirk of triumph. Then Tiev said, "Why not now?"

Of course he would suggest that. No Masters to judge. "Afraid someone will see?" Firian taunted.

Tiev waved a cursory hand at his two friends watching them. "Everybody *saw* the last time!"

"Fine!" Firian walked over to the tubs lining the side of the room and sat on the edge of one. Close enough to a chair. He turned to the two onlookers. "Watch. When he starts twitching and begging to be let out, just leave him there. I'm sure he's *Talented* enough to save himself. And I'll make sure I don't kill him. He just needs a lesson after all—"

One side of his face exploded in pain. He couldn't see. Reeling, he stood to his feet. "You gory—"

Tiev glared at him, shaking out the pain in his hand. Blinded with rage, Firian jumped on him, swinging both fists at his face. They scrabbled frantically over the wet floor, punching, kicking, grabbing. Firian vaguely heard Shiro and Braden, and then others, crying, "Fight! Fight!" His fury didn't allow him to think of anything but hurting Tiev. He'd gotten the position that Firian rightly deserved; he'd mocked him for the last time.

Finally he got on top of Tiev enough to sit on his chest and pin down his arms with his knees. With Tiev helpless to defend himself, Firian punched at his head. Even when his fists hurt, he kept going.

Breathing heavily, he realized that Tiev wasn't fighting back anymore, but had gone slack. Slowly, Firian stood to his feet. Blood trickled a red trail from Tiev's nose into the water pooling on the floor.

Firian sniffed. His nose was bleeding too. He ran the back of his hand across his face. He hardly knew what to think, looking down at Tiev's still body. It didn't register.

He was suddenly aware of a small crowd of boys all crammed into the little washroom. Some grudgingly exchanged coins and others bent down, trying to revive Tiev, splashing water on his face and lifting him awkwardly off the ground. He groaned and twitched a finger.

Numb, unsure of what to do, Firian just left the washroom with people talking in his wake.

As he walked back down the hall, he realized that his clothes were soaked and sticking to him. He took a deep breath. *Served him right... He started it. Somebody needed to show him to mind his own gory business.* Bitter satisfaction thrilled through him. He was better after all—as long as the Masters didn't find out. Maybe they wouldn't care, but Tiev was their special little boy now. They'd probably all go running to help him as soon as they found out.

"Why are you all wet?" Bard asked, walking toward him in the hallway. When he got closer, he squinted at his face and stained hands. "What were you *doing*?"

"Oh. Tiev..." he answered vaguely.

Bard's eyes popped. "*Really?* Firian!"

A corner of his mouth lifted to see Bard so concerned. Tiev would live. "See him. He's still in there," he said, jabbing his thumb at the washroom, which was so crowded by now that boys overflowed out the door. Firian shrugged.

Bard didn't reply. He just looked at Firian, stunned. Red-faced with concern, he moved stiffly toward the washroom, as if he were being drawn there against his will.

From the sounds of people yelling, it seemed that Tiev was conscious again. Somebody was trying to get him back to his room.

By the time Firian returned to his own room, freezing cold and dripping, he decided that the sooner he got into town, the better. He threw on some dry clothes and got the water out of his hair by sopping it with some of Bard's clothes.

He was a Defender, said a voice in his head. It sounded a lot like Bard.

Damn idiot too.

The Masters will find out, Firian.

They... they would want us to sort it out ourselves.

Careful or they'll throw you out...

Firian shook himself.

He felt cold again and grabbed his jacket. He wouldn't be thrown out. Of course not. The Academy needed as many people as they could get since the Talent was so rare now. A stupid thing like this wouldn't get someone thrown out...

HYRUM'S large hand drummed once on the counter with black-rimmed nails. He made no move to get the ales they had just ordered. "Master Jovan needs to talk to you," he said, his eyes darting between Firian and Bard, gauging their reactions.

Firian blinked. "When?" Was he so predictable that Jovan could give Hyrum the message and know it would get to him?

"Right now."

Bard looked at him, worry radiating from him. Firian didn't look back, but ran both his hands distractedly through his hair. "Did he say why?"

Hyrum shook his head, not sorry that he had no more to offer. Sometimes people of Tánuil liked to see Tanyu squirm.

Without another word, Firian turned away back to the Academy. He had the distinct feeling that he was in trouble.

He broke into a run until he reached the doors of the Academy. Jovan would probably be in his classroom about now. He never took town days. Other Masters rarely did, but Firian realized that he had never seen Jovan in Tánuil at all.

Upon reaching the Master's door, he tried to remember whether or not the he was teaching a class.

"Come in," Jovan's deep voice said from inside.

Firian hadn't even knocked.

He opened the door and saw the large room empty save for two people: Master Jovan and Tiev, who was sporting a black eye, bruised chin, and several cuts. It looked as though he'd washed up as well as he could though—his hair was perfect again. Tiev glared at him through red eyes as he came in.

Master Jovan let them both stand there in excruciating silence while he merely looked at them with his hands behind his back. His hard-set face made it impossible to tell what he was thinking. The quiet crackled.

"So, I hear," began Master Jovan, in a deadly subdued voice, "that you two have been fighting. Is that correct?"

They both nodded, trying not to look at each other.

"Speak when I ask you a question!" he barked, taking his hands from behind his back.

"Yes, Master Jovan," they said in unison.

"Normally this would not be a problem," he continued. "It happens. Just let it be. *But*—this case is different. Kess" – he started involuntarily at the sound of his name – "are you aware that Tiev is a Defender?"

"Yes, Master Jovan."

"And that you are merely a Learner."

He gritted his teeth. It was just as he thought. The Masters were stepping in to help their favorite boy. He forced down shame and disappointment, stood up a little straighter, and said, "I was aware, Master Jovan."

"Gelir," he said, addressing Tiev, as he addressed everyone, by last name, "were you also aware of this distinction?"

Firian was glad to see that he seemed nervous too. "Yes, Master Jovan."

"Then what the gore were you thinking?"

It struck Firian how even a big room like this seemed too small for Jovan. He and his presence took up the whole room and left Firian feeling stifled.

When neither of his victims answered, the Master said, "Apparently you both need to learn something about the distinction of rank. You want to be equal. Very well. Kess, you move in with Tiev for a week and see how that suits you."

Tiev's mouth fell open. Then his jaw worked furiously but he wisely held his tongue.

Firian went numb. Live with Tiev for a week? That would be torture.

He tried to rationalize. *He'll be taking different classes and I'm out all the time too. We won't even have to see each other more than a minute or two a day...*

It didn't help much.

"Don't stand there gaping like idiots," said Jovan. "Move your things. Now."

18

___

KIRIA

Kiria's serving girls watched her pace outside the doors of the Main. They'd given up on following her from one end of the hall to the other. Sometimes she would stop, listening, but she could hear nothing through the impenetrable doors. It seemed childish to press her ear against the door with the guards watching. She could tell her pacing irritated them enough.

"My Kepress," said one guard, finally. Guards almost never began conversations with Keepers or their families, so it proved just how exasperated he was. "May I ask what it is you'd like to know?"

"Nothing," she said quickly. The session should be out soon anyway and she knew very well that the guards couldn't tell her what they discussed in there, or how Atty was doing in his first session. If she had arrived on time, she wouldn't have been in this position. No one short of a Keeper could come into the middle of a session in the Main—not even a Kepress who had been required to attend.

Tight-lipped, the guard looked straight ahead as she continued to pace, sit, stand, listen, pace again....

When the latch finally clicked and the small crowd streamed

out of the Main, everyone was relieved. Uniforms, armor, robes... "Atty!" she called out when she saw him, then realized how informal that sounded. "Atael." But his real name sounded strange on her tongue—too formal.

Completely surrounded by people, he didn't hear her. She cocked her jaw in frustration. Then she saw a tall regal figure.

"Mother!" she called.

Her mother did hear her and came over, breaking away from the crowd. "What is it, Kiria?" she asked, looking serious and drawn.

"How was Atty?" Kiria whispered.

"He handled it very well. His advisor spoke more than he did, but that's normal for the first time. Everyone has to adjust after such a big change. But he's young. He'll be all right. He seems to have a rather good grasp on politics. Now I have to discuss some things with Cúron."

"But..." She still had questions, but her mother had already rejoined the crowd flowing out of the hall. Despondently, she watched the rest of the people go by. Who else could she ask?

Short, curly hair bobbed above the crowd as Chetana, her mother's Amiran advisor, walked by just a few feet away. She would know. She attended all the sessions, and she was Daelon's mother, even though they didn't look alike. Kiria could never tell who was related in Khelê families.

Kiria ran up to her, but stopped short. Chetana, not the most approachable person, was exceptionally tall, dark-skinned, and carried herself with a rigid military bearing. Kiria only came up to her graceful neck, so Chetana's far-away, Amiran gaze usually skimmed the top of her head and soared past her to more important matters.

"Amir Chetana?" she began.

She looked down at her. "Yes, my Kepress?" Her face was stoic—no... upset, though not at her.

"How did Atael do on his first day?"

Chetana's hardened face thawed into a smile, punctuated by her lace septum ring. "He's new," she replied. "He's…" Her voice drifted off, unsure.

"Tell me, please." As a Kepress, she didn't need to add "please" but it never hurt to be polite.

More people came out of the Main, but the wide hallway didn't become any louder. Everyone's brows furrowed or eyes widened, deep in thought.

"What's wrong?" Kiria insisted.

"Nothing is wrong." Seeing that she wouldn't accept that answer and go away, Chetana lowered her voice and continued. "The Torithians attacked our outpost, so our allies think we should send more troops. Many more."

Poor Atty didn't have an easy first day. "Do you think we should?" Kiria asked.

"Cúron elected to send soldiers, but your mother thought we should wait and see."

She didn't answer the question. "What about Atty?"

"He didn't say very much," she replied. "But I think he agrees with Cúron."

"Do they need us?" It felt like a naïve question, and Kiria hated feeling stupid.

"I've already said enough," said Chetana, firmly but kindly.

The air felt stuffy and close. Now Atty had to choose whether to risk the war or risk more Kingdom lives. If only she had gone to the session herself to support him. Heaven only knew how much help a new Keeper needed to lead well. At least she had Chetana and Daelon to help prepare her.

KIRIA'S first chance to speak with Atty face to face since the coronation came when he fell ill.

One of the two guards outside his door drew his shoulders back before looking straight ahead. "Keeper Atael is sick and will not take any visitors, My Kepress."

"He'll let me in," she insisted. "Ask him."

The guards looked at each other and came to a wordless agreement. One of the guards went into the room while the other stared as she tried to see through the crack in the door. She looked back at him and she assured him, "He'll let me in."

When the guard came out of the room, his expression hadn't changed. "My Kepress is allowed to enter for a short time," he announced, a flicker of disappointment dashing over his face.

She raised an eyebrow at the guards as she passed them and entered. To her irritation, two more guards already stood inside by the door. She should have guessed. That was the system arranged for her mother on most days, but Atty had always been different, just like her—famous, learning, waiting.

Atty lay in his huge four-poster bed, looking specter pale, his face framed by stringy hair. His Keeper room seemed to swallow him, it was so big.

"Atty! How are you?" she asked, rushing up to him.

He smiled faintly. "Look at me," he said, gesturing down at the covers. His black Keeper tattoo reaching out from beneath his sleeve seemed to sit on top of the white skin on his hand. Kiria's stomach dropped. It was exactly like Aylmor's. "But I'm doing all right."

"I haven't seen you in ages!"

"I know. I've been busy. I've seen you in the Main, though." He nodded slightly in encouragement.

She tilted her head from shoulder to shoulder. "I'm trying to be responsible. It gets a little boring after a while though."

He blew a laugh. "Try going to every session." He settled his big shoulders on the pillow.

"Good point." Atty disliked politics more than she did. Her trick was to focus on the parts she cared about, where she felt she could make a difference when she was older. She sat down next to him and leaned over. "I brought you something," she said quietly, taking a few small sweets out of her cloak pocket and stuffing them under the cover. "I figured they wouldn't let you have these since you're sick."

Without hesitation, he made his face blank as if nothing had happened. A holdover from their younger days.

"So how is it being a Keeper?" she asked in a normal tone.

"Busy," he answered, and coughed.

"You've been Keeper for a couple months, though. What's it like?"

He paused, thinking. "To tell the truth, it's hard. For one thing, people never leave you alone." He indicated the guards with his eyes.

"But you had that before. Is there anything that really changes?"

"People expect you to be perfect, to *be* the Third Line..." He paused and looked down at the covers. "I don't know how Father did it. He always—" He stopped to clear his throat. "He always seemed to know what he was doing. But you can't make a mistake. That's the hardest thing." His voice sounded thick as it started to slur.

Perfect. That was comforting. She sighed and a wisp of mousy hair floated up.

"You'll do great, though," he said, catching her worry. That sent him coughing for a while, deep coughs from his lungs.

"Are you sure you're all right?" Kiria asked, now worried for a different reason.

He nodded, unable to catch his breath. A guard approached

him with a glass of water, and then he bent down to tell him something in his ear. Atty nodded again.

The door opened and Jori appeared, wearing tall gray boots and an embroidered purple jacket, almost as though he were going to a party. He probably was.

Catching the fact that Atty couldn't speak at the moment, Jori turned to Kiria. "So how does he look? Any better?"

"He's all right," Kiria replied confidently.

"Made a big announcement yesterday, didn't you?" Jori said to Atty. Kiria couldn't read his tone. Jori rarely talked politics, so maybe it was a personal announcement.

Atty's breathing finally calmed. "Yes."

Before he could continue, Jori burst out, "He suggested that Amir get a vote in the Main."

If Kiria had been drinking water, she would have spit it out. "What? A *vote*?" She turned to Atty.

"Just half a vote," he said. "Cúron suggested it, and I think it's a good idea."

"They already advise us, and they do it exceptionally well," Kiria said. "If the Amir get a vote, others will want one too."

Part of her regretted saying the words the moment she spoke them. It wasn't that she didn't trust Daelon or Chetana, but she knew that giving them all a vote would start a chain reaction of consequences that Atty couldn't anticipate. If the Amir got a vote, then the military, the noble families, maybe even the Tanyu would want one too. The bond between the Western Kingdom and the Tanyu wasn't as strong as it had once been, but she would be surprised if they didn't claim their old alliance to gain more power in the Kingdom. In name, they were still the last line of defense, the elite fighters Keepers could summon in times of crisis. But the Tanyu were warriors—practically mercenaries for hire—and the Amir religious scholars and advisors.

She and Atty had been trained from birth to know and foster

the people groups, treaties, alliances, geography, economy, and culture of Brithnem. Not every well-meaning person could lead a country. She even doubted her own ability at times.

The Kingdom's system of three monarchs had worked for a long time. Why did he want to change it? Why did *Cúron* want to change it? The idea didn't sit well with her at all.

"Your mother shot him down," said Jori carelessly, sitting on the opposite side of the bed. His eyes wandered to the lump under the covers by Atty's left elbow.

"But we're still debating it," said Atty. "I think it's a good idea." He almost looked ashamed.

Kiria held her tongue. She'd already given him her reaction.

Jori pulled one of the sweets out from under the blanket and popped it in his mouth. Atty set his drawn lips flat in annoyance but didn't correct him.

"Oooh!" Jori shivered pleasurably, chewing the sweet. "Just imagine what the Tanyu will think when they find out."

19

———

FIRIAN

BARD SLID onto the bench next to Firian in the community dining room. "What did they do to you?" he asked. "Why weren't you in the room last night?"

"I have to stay in Tiev's room until the end of the week," Firian muttered, not looking up from his food. Last night was awful. Neither of them had breached the icy silence. People were constantly knocking and coming in and going out, asking for things, playing a game of Indisfate... Even Rian came and knocked his drink over Firian's blanket on the floor, obviously in a ploy to get on Tiev's good side. The result was a clammy, miserable night and he didn't want to talk about it.

"Because of the fight?" Bard continued, ripping a small loaf of bread and shoving a bite in his mouth.

Firian nodded.

Bard swallowed. "Have you heard anything more about Enderin?" he asked anxiously, leaning in a little so he wouldn't be heard. The war wasn't going well.

"No. They'll probably say something about it in World Events tomorrow."

Bard sighed and went back to eating.

Kaori, a Charäkhni boy from their hall sitting on the bench behind Firian, leaned backward to speak to him. "So, you and Tiev got in a scrape yesterday," he said.

Firian didn't respond. Whenever Kaori spoke, it seemed like he was talking too much.

"I heard you knocked him cold."

"Yeah, I did."

Kaori laughed. "What made you do it?"

"Nothing."

"Well, obviously it was some—"

"Nothing! Shut up and eat," said Firian, grouchier than ever.

"You're acting like they called *katah* on you," Kaori muttered.

"Ha ha," he replied tonelessly.

Katah was considered a Tanyuin death sentence. It was a focused connection forged between two people. Tanyu, usually women, trained in the art of *katah* learned how to focus unrelentingly on their target, seducing him into believing that their lives were linked, that they *needed* each other. Eventually, the victim, often a high-ranking general or strategist, couldn't tell the difference between imagination and reality when the Tanyu was there because he wanted her to be real, to be present. At that point, the Master could kill the target easily in the Unreal. Belief became reality.

"Wish I'd've been there."

"I'll bet."

"Nice eye, by the way."

"Sure." Firian hunkered over his food again and wouldn't look back at him.

Just then, Master Belik came to stand beside the table. Firian looked up, confused. Belik never ate lunch at that time, especially not with Learners. He felt Bard shrink at his side.

"Firian," the Master said curtly, "our classes are canceled for the next three days."

His eye throbbed and his heart pounded heavily. "Why?" He couldn't help himself.

"They will resume the day after that. I have business."

He opened his mouth to protest, but revised his response. "As you would have it, Master Belik."

"In four days, then." And Belik turned and left with many curious eyes trailing after him.

Bard waited until the Master was gone before he spoke. "What was *that* about?" he said.

Firian shrugged. "Maybe he has Retrieval work."

"Then why would he come all this way to tell you about it?"

Firian had been wondering the same thing.

"Maybe somebody really important got Lost!" put in Kaori, who had heard the whole thing.

"Like the Head," said Rian, who sat next to Kaori at the other table. Kaori's eyes rounded.

Bard gave a very incredulous look. "That's... no."

"Of course not," said Firian. Though that wouldn't be so bad. The Head had made many bad decisions since he'd been here. When Firian had first arrived, Master Jairon had seemed friendly, almost like a grandfather, but now that he had spent more time talking to other Tanyu and people in the village, very few actually liked his leadership.

But this whole conversation was ridiculous. Belik could be gone for a number of reasons. He probably couldn't get someone to send the message for him so he came himself. It was a little weird, but not reason enough to suppose that the Tanyuin Head had gotten Lost in the Unreal. That news would get out no matter how much everybody tried to keep it secret. "It's probably somebody unimportant," he said. "He does this kind of thing sometimes."

But despite Firian's logic, the rest of lunch was taken up with radical hypotheses about Belik's appearance.

Tap, tap, tap.

Firian looked up from visualizing the scenarios for Strategy homework. Tiev wasn't in the room at the moment, which was the whole reason for Firian's choosing to use the space. He sighed. It was probably one of Tiev's friends or stupid admirers at the door, as usual. He lay back down on his stomach on the floor mat.

Tap, tap, tap. Tap, tap.

"Who is it?" he snapped. Maybe refusing entry outright was a better tactic with this person than simply ignoring him.

"...Just delivering something," replied a rather high-pitched voice.

"For who?"

"Defender Tiev Gelir." The boy spoke as though he were reading the name.

"Leave it at the door," Firian instructed.

"Well... as you would have it, Defender," he said hastily. There was a dull thud and the sound of retreating footsteps. Firian waited until the sound faded completely before opening the door and pulling the small package inside. Wrapped simply in brown paper, it had good weight to it. *Who's delivering something to Tiev? Defenders don't just get packages out of nowhere...* He shook it but it felt solid. Then he noticed a few words drawn on the corner of the paper:

To Defender Tiev Gelir.

It was a pleasure meeting you today. I hear your future is bright. Perhaps this will make it brighter.

Amir Murali

– Keep the gift a secret.

Firian's mind spun. *An Amir in the Academy? Sending Tiev a gift?* The situation seemed absurd, but slowly, it started to made sense. It gave Belik a reason to cancel classes, and if anyone were to receive a secret gift from the Amir it might be Tiev, the Academy's precious prodigy boy.

He glanced up at the light leaking through the curtains. Tiev probably wasn't due back for several minutes.

Leaping to his feet, he put the package under his arm and left the room, practically jogging back to his own.

From the top bed, Bard jerked around to see who it was. "Firian?"

Firian closed the door behind him. "Come here," he said, holding out the package.

Bard jumped lightly onto the ground to see it. "What is it?"

"Something for Tiev" – he lowered his voice – "from an Amir."

Bard's mouth grew slack. "Tiev knows an *Amir*?" he hissed.

Firian shrugged. "Looks that way. I think there's one in the Academy."

"That's why Belik...!"

Firian nodded.

Wide-eyed, Bard let out a breath, trying to process everything. "Have you seen him?"

"No, but there's a note..." He pointed to the scrawled writing. Bard turned his head sideways to read it. A few moments later, he looked up.

"Wicked," he pronounced.

"Mmm hm." Firian began tearing at the paper.

"Wait, Fir! You're opening it?"

"Of course. You thought I just wanted you to read the nice note before giving it back?"

"...No."

"Tiev doesn't even know about this. He wasn't there when it was delivered." He ripped the last of the paper off. In his hands sat a rather large book with a plain tan cover. His heart sank. *That's it?*

Bard stared at it in awe. "What does it say?" he whispered.

"I don't know." He flipped it open to the first page. There was no title. He flipped through more pages until he reached the end. Pages of small, neat writing followed elaborately illustrated letters. This book was carefully, even reverently, done. "Of course!" he said. "What gift would an Amir give? This is a copy of the Sacred Scroll! They love this thing."

"Can I see it?"

He handed it over.

Bard turned the book over in his hands, opened to a random page and read a sentence with his eyes. "That's amazing," he said. "I'll bet only the Head has one of these."

"Probably." Firian took the book back. These words held even more importance than the Tanyuin Academy to some people. And he didn't even know what they said. There was no debate in his mind. He was keeping it. Tiev would never know it was gone.

At the thought of Tiev, he cursed to himself. Gathering the book in his arms, he pulled open his dresser drawer and shoved it inside, under his clothes. "I've got to go," he told Bard on his way out.

He could sense a protest, and he didn't want to hear it.

Stalking back down the hall, he prayed that Tiev wasn't there already. He couldn't handle the arrogant questions he was sure to get. If he could just fall asleep—or at least pretend to sleep—first, then sharing the same space would be a bit more bearable.

He edged his fingers around the door as he creaked it open. Success! Tiev wasn't back yet. He stripped off his shirt and crawled into his bed on the floor.

Seconds later, the door opened again. They had just missed each other. Not bad timing. Firian kept his eyes shut. Brief shuffling meant that Tiev was getting in bed too, and wouldn't bother him. Even better.

Tap. Tap, tap, tap, tap.

"Go away, Rian! I'm sleeping!" Tiev called out.

The knocking abruptly stopped.

Tiev sighed and gave a stretching yawn. *Here it comes.*

"An Amir came to visit today," he whispered.

Firian didn't respond.

"Have you ever met one?"

Silence.

Tiev soldiered on. "Master Belik took me to meet him in the Head's office."

He must know that using Belik's name would rattle him. Those should have been Firian's rewards. He fought to keep his breathing even.

"This is all confidential, so they'll have your head if you tell anyone. Thought you might be interested."

Firian breathed through gritted teeth.

He could almost hear the smile in Tiev's next words, "G'night."

Firian lay for an hour with his mind spinning before he opened his eyes in the darkness. Tiev was snoring softly on his bed. He should've expected him to crow about his meeting, but the gallingly innocent way he'd said it reached the end of Firian's patience.

He *couldn't* stay another night.

Getting up softly, he left the room and went down to his own. He always woke up earlier than Tiev, so he wouldn't be missed. As long as no one saw him coming of his usual room, no one would know the difference.

He slipped inside. Not tired, he lit a candle. Orange-gray shadows leapt up on the wall, waving and flickering. Bard slept so hard that the light wouldn't wake him.

Firian bit the inside of his lip. Being angry with Tiev would do nothing but hurt him, unless he decided to turn it into motivation.

It was never too late for a little mental training.

Yanking out the dresser drawer, he rifled around for the book under his clothes. There it was. He cleared a space on the floor littered with clothes and wrappers and in the dim lamplight began to read. *Not like an Amir*, he assured himself. He still knew that defense was more important than the words of this book, but memorizing sections of the Sacred Scroll would give him more elite knowledge. When *he* met an Amir, he would know how they think, what advice they would give before they gave it, and God knew what else. He would strip their power with their own words. And if he found that it wasn't useful, he would just stop reading.

I hear your future is bright. Perhaps this will make it brighter.

He mouthed the words soundlessly as his eyes scanned the page. Sitting cross-legged on the floor, with the sounds of Bard murmuring above him, he shoved back the dark hair falling in front of his face. Concentrating hard on the words, he tried to memorize as fast as he read. The words slipped through like water, but he caught some of them. The burning of his focus, sheer force of will, would imprint the words in his mind.

The book began by speaking mainly of God and what He did among His people, called the Khelê, the main people group that the Tanyu had been set up to protect. Firian had learned about all that in World Events. Many of his classmates were Khelê. The Talent ran more strongly through that bloodline.

When their race began, they were a completely mishmashed band of people who had survived a racial purging in Brithnem. They built a fortress named Carradoc in Shifra, a swamp that wasn't far from Tánuil, and that was where they took the name "Khelê." Master Ardal, who taught World

Events, said that meant "the divine human race" in an older language.

Apparently, the people of the Kingdom were tyrannical, controlling the lives of its people. The Khelê claimed that God had called *them* His chosen, instead of the Kingdom Dwellers, and launched a minority campaign against the Kingdom. After a bloody war, they managed to kill the evil king.

Somewhere around that time, the Exmorei was founded to defend the people and study the Sacred Scroll, which had been revealed to the Khelê only a year or two before. Later the Exmorei split into the Tanyu, who believed that defending the people was most important, and the Amir, who only studied the Scroll.

The Tanyuin mission had changed since those times, but their divine appointment and elite status as defenders had not. How could Amir not see that the Scroll was dead, history? Time had moved beyond it. But even the Keepers of the Western Kingdom were still guided by its principles.

What Tanyu has this advantage? Firian reminded himself, shifting on the floor as he hunched over the book. *The Head might have a copy, but he would be the only one.*

An image of himself sitting in *that* chair rose before him, almost spiritual. It glowed inside him. In the semi-darkness, he smiled. He would memorize the whole damn book if he had to. Anything that gave him an edge above Tiev, who now seemed smaller—the first step in a staircase to the top of the Academy.

A WEEK SPENT in Tiev's room convinced Firian firmly of one thing.

They had prodded each other in their minds, of course. There, Tiev was still maddeningly cocky. Carefully, Firian observed his methods, how he practiced, what he did to be so powerful. His thought processes—at least as many as Firian could observe without getting caught—were only a little above average.

Unless there was a deep seed of unlimited Talent that he just couldn't see, there was nothing special about Tiev at all.

"Firian, stop!" Tiev snapped, glaring at him across a blank mindfield. The setting dissolved. "Go back to your own damn business!"

Firian clenched his teeth to stop a knee-jerk reply. Instead, he paraphrased the Scroll: "*'Strength is not just for the strong.'* I was hoping to learn something." He gave him a half-smile. He couldn't help it.

Tiev shook his head. "You do it again and I'll hurt you."

"Oh, okay. In *that* case...." He raised an eyebrow. They both knew Tiev couldn't make good on his threat. But Firian let him rant. It seemed to give him a fleeting sense of power.

The problem was, he *did* have power. *Why? Why did the Masters promote him and not me?*

The question bubbled up in his gut as he walked to his lesson, but he had to be careful. He didn't want his prison sentence doubled.

In Belik's little room, Firian faced the Master as they ran through drills. Firian ploughed through them with the force of a sprinter.

"Good," said Belik. "Again."

They went back to a scenario Firian had learned about in Strategy the day before. *"What if your opponent changes the location? Can you reorient yourself fast enough to believe and not believe?"* That was one of Master Asoka's favorite phrases: "believe and not believe."

Belik changed the background at a dizzying pace. Different countries, settings, sizes. One place was even upside down.

Firian continued to attack. For this drill, he couldn't change his weapon, but had to focus on what he could do given the new environment. All he had was a sword. Firian flew, reappeared, sank through the floor, ran forward, sword flashing...

"Enough," Belik said calmly. They both opened their eyes. Belik's face was impassive. *Does nothing impress him?* "That's good."

"I don't want to be good!" Firian cried, surprising himself.

Belik's eyes widened, curious. "Then what do you want?" he asked.

"I want to be the best."

Belik smiled with closed lips, a private smile. He wiped his glasses on his trousers and put them back on.

Surely he could see well enough into Firian's mind to know the question burning there. Tiev's face wouldn't leave him. "How long do you think it will take before I am promoted to Defender?" he asked.

"A couple of years. If you're lucky, two."

"Tiev got promoted when he was my age."

"You are not Tiev," the Master said decidedly, raising both eyebrows. "You know how to get better. Double your efforts if you're concerned."

Firian smiled. Belik didn't say that Tiev was better, and he would have if it were true.

"What?" Belik said, looking intently at him.

"Nothing."

"Is something funny?"

"No, Master Belik." He deadened his eyes and let his face fall back into a stoic position. He took a deep breath. "Nothing's funny."

Belik crossed his arms. "So you've finally figured it out, have you?"

Firian's heart leapt. He wasn't imagining it!

"Gore," Belik muttered, almost to himself. "I was wondering how long it would take." His eyes shot up to meet Firian's. "You were getting lazy." His stony face cracked into a smile. Behind the glasses, his eyes shone brightly. "And look how hard you practice now."

Firian didn't dare respond. They'd promoted Tiev to get *him* to work harder?

"Tiev's an idiot," Belik breathed.

"Then how...?" The question half-escaped him before he could stop it. *What about the burst of energy during the hall test?*

Belik tapped his own chest with a blunt finger. "Now that you know how to work hard, I can tell you. More people should have figured it out, but even... others... took the promotion seriously." He laughed once, sarcastic. Running his tongue over his bottom lip distractedly, he said, "Tiev never should have met the Amir. Or the Head. It all got out of hand. At least you finally got there."

Relief, confusion, anger, and pride all swirled through Firian's body. His emotions culminated in a single word. "Why?"

The Master weighed his answer, leaning back in his chair. "You've got something," he said. He opened his mouth again, reconsidered, closed it. "Don't waste it."

20

FIRIAN

Does a man want influence? Does a man want power? Greatness is found in service and majesty in love. Remember a heritage of evil but a future of hope. This is the history that can be for every man. Therefore, do not exalt yourself above another. Rather, lift up your brother to see what you too have been given.

Firian had to read the passage four times to commit it to memory. It was getting late, so he jumped to his feet from where he had been lying on the floor and found a flint among the clutter on the dresser. He lit two candles and lay back down, flipping lazily to the second page of the Scroll. It was blank, but he had sealed a note on it with wax. The seal was already starting to chip off in soft, jagged edges. He waited until the wax from one of the candles was hot and clear enough to drip over it.

Congratulations. I knew you could do it! Now you'll be a warrior —a Tanyu—one of the bravest and smartest people in the world! I love you. I won't forget you. He didn't know why he had kept it. He wasn't sentimental like Bard. It just reminded him of who he was and who he could have been—nothing. He had fulfilled the vision that he'd set out for himself when he arrived. With Tiev and others trying to convince him otherwise, the note convinced him that his younger self would approve of his present one.

After pouring the hot wax over the sides of the note and blowing on it until it hardened, he closed the book and shoved it back in the drawer.

Without a knock, the door slammed open. Master Jovan stood huge in the doorway. Firian leapt up and stood straight.

"Come with me, Kess."

Heart pounding, Firian followed him as he strode quickly down the hall toward the stairs. They passed Bard coming back to the room. He stood almost flat against the wall as he saw them coming. His face creased anxiously and he looked to Firian for an explanation, but he didn't have one to give.

Heavily, Master Jovan descended the steps. Instead of turning left to the courtyard, he turned right, toward the wooden double doors leading out to Tánuil. Jovan opened the front door with one massive hand and led him outside.

An early evening wind cut dryly through the trees. It made Firian glad he had brought a shirt and shoes. The sky was still light blue in the west, but it quickly drained dark without the sun. They passed carts, shopkeepers heading home for the night, and wives lighting lanterns outside their doors.

Images flipped before Firian's mind. *Scroll... practice... class... I did visit Maya...* Nothing merited punishment, since he hadn't been caught visiting anyone or reading the Scroll, if that was an offense.

Jovan turned onto the path that led to the unused house that Firian passed sometimes when he met girls secretly. The stifling silence and unnatural combination of two parts of his life almost stole Firian's breath.

Firian followed Jovan inside the house. Embers from a large fireplace glowed brightly, but there was still barely enough smoky orange light to see by. A rough-hewn table with a bottle on it and two chairs sat off to one side. One of the chairs had a footstool. On the floor was a wooden box with parchment in it. A polished bronze ewer hung on the wall along with three swords of different makes and sizes; a bright stuffed bird and an urn made of blue stone glittered in the firelight. Through an open door on the left, Firian saw a cot sitting on the hardwood floor and an immense shield inlaid with gold and pearls leaned in a corner. There were no windows.

"Close the door," the Master growled.

Firian obeyed.

"Sit."

He sat. Jovan did not.

"I see you think you have Talent. Others think the same. Do you have more Talent than Defender Tiev?" The Master fixed him with a glare, forcing up his scarred forehead to open his eyes wider.

Back to this, are we? Still, it was a loaded question. Anything he said would probably get him in trouble, so why not say the truth? "Yes, Master Jovan."

Jovan didn't move for a moment, then he hummed deeply and walked toward the room with the cot. Instead of going inside, he reached in around the corner and pulled out an amber drinking glass. He picked up the bottle on the table by Firian and poured its dark contents into the glass. "Then have something to drink," he said, offering it to Firian.

Firian took the cup. Jovan hadn't poured himself any. Still, he knew better than to ask what it was.

"Drink!" Jovan ordered.

Firian had no choice. It tasted like ale. It could even have been from the Old Pub. Jovan stood looming silent before him, so Firian just drank obediently and waited.

FIRIAN WOKE up in chilly darkness. Small rocks dug into his back and arms as he rolled over. Squinting into the dark, he made out black trunks rising around him. Pine needles rasped, but otherwise there was no sound. His head felt heavy and his thoughts ran sluggish. Had he fallen asleep there? *Did I get drunk or something?* He didn't often have alcohol, preferring a clear mind, and he only remembered having one drink in front of Master Jovan...

Master Jovan! He must have put him here. But why? *I said I was better than Tiev.*

Shivers ran up and down the skin of Firian's back. He wasn't kicked out of the Academy, was he? Bard's voice rang in his head —all the warnings, all the ways to get kicked out, all the things he shouldn't have done.

Fighting with Tiev wouldn't be enough to merit...

No. There was only a small number of Tanyu in the world and he was one of the rising champions—or at least he was good enough to fight in a war if they needed him. And they'd already given him a punishment for that fight. Unless they'd learned about his Scroll, he couldn't imagine anything he'd done since to get kicked out. His heart thumped dangerously and he ran his hands over his arms to warm them.

Then he felt something attached to his left forearm with rough string. Yanking it off, he found it was a small, folded piece of parchment. He unfolded it and held it an inch before his face, but it only looked gray. Something was written on it. He bared his teeth. The darkness maddened him, crushed him.

He had to see.

Looking up, the moonless stars were too dim. He'd have to make a fire. He remembered putting a piece of flint in his pocket earlier that day. He felt in his pockets for what he had. Nothing. Master Jovan must have taken everything out. He swallowed on a dry mouth and blindly began to dig a shallow pit with his fingernails to put dry brush into.

Within ten minutes he'd built a little fire. Instinctively, he kept it low in case someone unwanted should find him. He grabbed the parchment and held it near the flame.

Come back after two weeks. Train until then.

His relief made him realize how hard he'd been breathing. Even his hands had been shaking.

It's only training. He wasn't kicked out.

This must be a physical survival test. He blew out a breath. A wilderness test showed that the Masters acknowledged his ability to the point of considering him for a physical mission.

Between his panic and the aftereffects of the drug, sleep pressed down heavily on him. So he ran his fingers through his hair to get the dirt off, burned the note, covered the fire, and went back to sleep until the sun rose.

It was Firian's third night in the wilderness. He lay on his back by a smokeless fire. Deep heat seeped over his right side but his left was dark and blue and cold. Since no bears or tree cats had appeared for the last two nights, he wasn't as concerned about them as he had been. After all, he'd had no idea where he was at first. Peering up through the black web of pine needles, he saw dotted blue and white stars. He blinked his cold eyes. The fire died down slowly to glowing black and gold embers.

This wasn't so bad, even without much food. Physical training with Jovan was harder. In fact, the time alone allowed him to exercise both his mind and his body as much as he liked. Sinking into nothing, he leisurely searched around in his mind. Before reaching far, he felt the faint buzz of Sentries.

His eyes snapped open. That was odd. The Sentries weren't

guarding him, but they were blocking someone's access to the Unreal close by. Slowly, he sat up and squinted into the space between the gray trunks. He couldn't see far. Feeling again in his mind, he hit something.

He tensed. Something was very close.

A rattle of dead pine needles and he was on his feet. He had no weapons. He took a steady breath. Should he build up the fire so he could see or would that alert the person to his presence? *Safer to let it be.* He peered harder into the darkness, slowly making his way away from the spot.

Someone wrapped a thick, hairy arm around his neck from behind. Without a thought, Firian jerked his elbow up into the man's nose. The man cried in surprise and yanked his arm back. Firian pivoted to see a stolid, husky man with thinning hair that looked black in the dimness. Blood from his nose ran down his hands as he bent over in pain. The bone hadn't gone all the way into his brain.

Firian's legs suddenly buckled. Another man had kicked him hard in the back of the knees with a boot. He crumpled in pain. Regaining himself, Firian grabbed savagely at the man's legs to bring him down but he couldn't reach, so he jumped back up again, ignoring the jabbing pain in his legs.

Five more large men jumped within the reach of the ember-light. Three gripped knives in their right hands. Firian struck out madly, rolled, broke a man's finger to kick the knife away. He hurled himself toward the knife. Hitting the ground, he grabbed a rock to toss behind him in a man's face. *Where's the gory knife?* He felt madly in the darkness, fingers scrabbling over loose dirt.

But then they were all on top of him, smothering. He couldn't breathe, struggled to move, mouth open, too hot, gasping, no air...

He tried blindly to pry himself out from underneath them all but they held him down harder the more he struggled. His flattened, ragged lungs burned, sucking at air that wouldn't come.

Now? he pleaded. *But I'm not a Master... not respected... I was never...*

"TANYU!" a man yelled from close above him, grating into his ear. Firian was lying on his back with his hands bound underneath him. Piercing pain cut into his wrists.

He pried his eyelids open but couldn't see anything beyond the slightly darker figures of the men standing above him. Breathing shallow, he felt something slide sideways down his face. Spit.

"Walk!" One of them dug his boot into Firian's side.

They already knew he was awake. If he resisted, they'd beat him, and neither would get what they wanted. He couldn't fight this many from his back, so he trundled up onto his feet. From behind him, a man grabbed the end of the rope tying his wrists. Firian writhed his hands, trying to ease the pain of the sharp cords. Pebbles and dirt fell out of the deep grooves in his skin. It was useless.

Mind over body. The mind makes what is and is not. Firian only used his physical senses enough to see where to step. The rest of his powers retreated into the Unreal. His attackers, who didn't speak, even among themselves, had set up a rudimentary Sentry on his mind, but he broke it without a second thought. They must have known it, but still they didn't say anything or retaliate.

He threw himself into the Unreal until the sound of a horse pulled him out.

He came to himself among five large horses. Three of the men mounted silently. He clenched his swollen hands as his captor led him to one of the horses. They were going to drag him.

Almost automatically, he flung himself backward onto the ground, biting back a yell as he landed on his hands. The man holding the rope flew on top of him. Firian put up his knee and caught him in the gut. His captor wheezed forcefully and rolled to the side, still clutching the end of the line.

The three who had already mounted jumped off again and attacked. From his back, Firian kicked the shortest man in the jaw. His teeth cracked together as he stumbled backward. A horse screamed and reared.

Someone pulled Firian's hair from the roots and yanked his head back. With a metallic ring a blade lay across Firian's straining neck. "Be still or die."

Firian's knees fell to the ground.

"Now stand."

He stood slowly.

Four panting men glowered around him. One of them couldn't resist slicing his arm lightly with a dagger.

Firian gritted his teeth in a closed mouth. The motion moved a tendon in his neck against the dagger.

"Tanyu can run, can't they? We'll see. Otherwise you'll be going backward."

The man holding his slack rope walked deliberately to one of the horses and tied him tightly to the baggage on the saddle. Once he found the knot strong enough, he came back to Firian with a savage light in his eyes.

Firian's muscles went taut. The dagger nicked his skin as his neck muscles contracted. If he only knew why they wanted him, he'd know how soon they intended to kill him. The man's stare left little room for doubt that they ultimately did intend to kill him.

Firian heard another scrape of metal on metal. *Is it now?* He struggled to think of a counterattack.

"Stop! Don't touch him!" a man cried to his left.

"I said not yet," hissed the man with the rope.

A knife was sheathed.

Not yet.

"Where's the Academy?"

Firian only sat up to preserve whatever dignity he had left.

Blood streamed from his nose and his head pounded, crashing in his ears. His shins and knees were ripped and swollen from the run and now his feet were asleep because of how tightly they had bound his ankles once they finally stopped riding. Rocks pierced his back when he spun to the ground, unable to keep upright for a moment. One shoulder was dislocated and his entire body ached from bruises.

He swallowed and tasted blood like copper.

A man he'd heard called Den brought out a bowl of water and held it in the light of a single candle, just out of his reach. Firian stared disdainfully, too tired to do anything else.

"I'm not thirsty." Even the lie felt thick, but satisfying enough to keep his spirit up for another moment. At least they wouldn't have the victory of seeing him beg.

"Where's the Academy? We already know the area, and all we need is you to confirm it. You aren't helping anyone by keeping the secret. There is no secret. You're only making a gory fool of yourself."

Firian had no reason to tell them where it was. The Academy was his life, all that he had worked for. Everything and everyone he cared about was there. If he betrayed it, he might as well kill himself. So he just shut his eyes again and began to sink into the comfort of the Unreal, but even that didn't block out all of the pain. There was too much of it. But it helped.

Someone struck him.

"Where is the Academy?"

He had to choose some dying words, some battle cry to sum up his life. Urgency pressured him even in the Unreal, where he was suspended in darkness like an ocean.

The Academy will never be taken. I choose death.

I will tell you nothing, because I'm Firian Kess, the Tanyu.

A man screamed, a hideous sound.

Firian's swollen eyes sprang open. The room—or... cave?—was too dark to see much of what was happening, but he could make out that all the men who had gathered around him had scrambled to their feet, facing the blackness. One lay face down on the ground. Then another.

"Come with me," whispered someone behind him, who grabbed Firian's wrists and sliced the twine off them and off his ankles. The voice seemed familiar.

Firian leapt to his feet and immediately collapsed. After a second of red darkness, he climbed to his feet again.

"You can walk," said his helper in the darkness. "Follow me."

He could hardly see the moving figure in front of him, but he stumbled and followed. He didn't care if it was a trap.

After they had gone some distance, out of the cave and into the forest, the man guiding him began to talk to him, steadily asking simple questions.

"What's your name?"

Firian didn't answer. He wasn't in an answering mood.

"I'm here to help you. What forest is this?"

"Esmeroth."

"Who are the three Keepers of Brithnem?"

"Cúron, Merian, and Atael."

"What's your name?"

"Firian Kess, a Tanyu of the Academy," he said. He knew it was a fit of dying eloquence, but he didn't care. He'd earned those words.

"How did you get here?"

Firian told him a very simple version of the story, and then ran out of breath and couldn't speak for another five minutes.

When did I lose my shoes? The sky was gray and the air was cool with dawn. The green tree moss stood out in sharp relief against the trunks. It was almost peaceful.

The man led him to a large horse. Firian didn't have much experience with riding horses, but happily he didn't have to know what he was doing. His guide helped him up behind him and galloped away.

Scenery passed hazily by him—gray pillars of trees and whirring stones and grasses. *Wish I could ride by myself,* he thought. But it didn't seem to matter very much after a few minutes. He wouldn't have had the strength even if he had been given his own horse.

Other riders rode up alongside them. Since they didn't attack, Firian assumed they were friendly.

Slowly, slowly, everything went black.

A VOICE SPOKE. Firian felt as though he were under a great depth of water, hearing someone above the surface. "Fir? Firian?"

His whole body ached, destroying any will to move or respond.

"Firian?" He finally recognized Bard's voice, full of bottled panic.

His breath became hot as something obscured his mouth. A hand? Dimly, he realized that Bard was checking to see if he was still alive. Firian moved his head just a little. That should confirm his test.

A few seconds later, the light touch of a blanket fell across him. It fell on bare skin in unexpected places. His clothes must have torn.

"Do you want me to stay with you?" Bard asked, the words getting louder as Firian's consciousness surged toward the surface.

He wished it wouldn't. With consciousness came pain. "Yes." Only the hiss of the final letter whistled between his teeth. When he tried to open his eyes, he found that one was swollen shut. He could only see the bottom of the bunk above him. Easing his eye closed, he prayed for sleep. Bard would leave soon, maybe get a doctor.

A creaking door. Many muted footsteps. The sense of new nearness.

"He'll be fine." A cursory statement to Bard. The voice sounded like Belik's.

Someone, neither Belik nor Bard, moved the blanket away and lifted Firian's heavy arm. Some kind of rough fabric had been tied around his bicep. A stabbing pain screamed through his shoulder as his arm was raised higher. Firian twisted convulsively away. The strong hands placed his arm back down on the mattress.

"Any broken bones?" Belik again.

"Not from what I can see. His shoulder is dislocated. Bruises. Lacerations." He felt expert hands probing along his other arm, his abdomen, his legs. Firian gasped as the man found all the deep bruises. "No broken bones. He should remain in bed for at least three days, and I doubt he'll be ready for any kind of physical training for twelve to fourteen days after that."

Firian hated being useless, but he had no energy to protest. He knew his body wouldn't let him stand, much less train.

"Good. Thank you, doctor," Belik said.

"I'll come back today to dress the wounds."

"What happened to him?" Bard asked quietly. Firian had almost forgotten he was there.

"Just be glad it didn't happen to you," said Belik.

Even hazy, blind, and in pain, Firian knew vaguely that he hadn't answered the question.

More footsteps, now retreating. The feather's-weight of the blanket draped over him again, and he fell asleep almost instantly.

21

KIRIA

After Daelon's lesson, Kiria went up to the second floor of the Amiran Academy, to the holy place. More often over the past few weeks, she had come to say prayers. A Keeper's main duty was to God, after all. The Amir advised them so they didn't forget his words. Atty's coronation reminded her of the privilege and responsibility of being a Keeper. She hadn't missed a session since Atty's first.

She rounded the last corner of the claustrophobic stone staircase and stepped into the upper room. Smaller religious ceremonies occurred there. Once a year, on Dedication Day, all the Keepers and their families fasted all day and came into this space at nightfall. She remembered that, as a child, she was struck by the somber mood in the palace that day as they considered the seriousness of straying from God's will. But the night was about mercy, rebirth, rededication. The celebration took place on the day Mon Párinath was completed, the palace built on the ruins of the first. A new piece of music was written each year for the occasion and Brithnem's most talented musicians performed it in that upper room.

Normally, the Amir preserved an attitude of silence there,

and could come and go as they pleased. Young Amiran students often sat there for hours, memorizing the Sacred Scroll, chanting it to themselves under their breath. On certain days, anyone from Brithnem was welcome to come and pray.

She gazed up at the vaulted ceiling, painted blue, a darker blue than the color on the flag. Strips of gold outlined the architectural segments of the dome. It almost looked like a diagram of the night sky.

As soon as she got back to the palace, she would study her lesson. Rather than dry information, the lessons now seemed like a way to whet her mind like a knife. The more she learned, the more she could rule with wisdom and justice, and fulfill the oath she would make in the Main one day. The Scroll, the laws, they were like advisors or friends that would prevent her from making mistakes.

Finally, she had found her purpose. When she was a little girl, she had wanted to be Keeper. Now, she knew what it would take, and she welcomed the challenge.

Sneaking away with Jori had lost its luster. Now it left her feeling hollow and guilty. But it was hard to explain to him that she didn't want to shirk her responsibilities. Still, he seemed to understand why she didn't spend as much time with him.

She murmured a prayer and stood in reverent silence for a moment before turning to leave. The holy place was so peaceful. Why didn't she spend more time there?

Everyone could only reach the second floor by one of two tiny spiral staircases accessible only from outside. The first floor was reserved for Amiran study cells and bedchambers. There was no access to the holy place from inside either of those. She went down the staircase and breathed in the fresh air.

Peace seemed to follow her into the light outside. At this moment, her Beauty seemed more integrated into who she was. It was always better when it began inside.

She passed several servants and Amir, all of whom turned to watch her, as she wandered dreamily toward the ocean. It churned and crashed a rhythm in the far distance. From the edge of the palace grounds, she had the best view of the bay.

She squinted. That was odd. There were more ships moored than usual. She looked them over carefully, but she didn't recognize many of them. They didn't look like they came from Brithnem or Phlaxtin or any of the other nations that sometimes traded with them.

Whose ships are those?

A muted shout filtered up from the port. Another. Her heart beat faster. The note of urgency in those shouts sent a shock through her fingers.

She needed to find someone. At best, there was a disturbance at the harbor. At worst...

She broke into a run back toward the castle. "There's an attack!" she shouted. "Attack at the harbor!"

Something slammed into her shoulder. She pitched backward, pivoting as she fell. The ground rose up and crashed into her chest, her cheek.

Confused, she looked up and saw a thick arrow sticking out of her. She felt sick. She couldn't breathe, and then her breath came too fast. Her hands started shaking, but she still couldn't scream. Pain started forcing gorge up her throat.

She saw the next one coming. It arched toward the sun and rushed at her, whistling in the air, getting bigger and bigger. She kicked back to avoid it, but it pierced the meat of her thigh, pinning her to the ground at an odd angle.

Her vision narrowed to a blackening circle. Warm liquid from her shoulder flowed across her neck onto the ground.

Above her, eyes appeared, red-rimmed and frantic. Daelon's face.

"Kiria! My God!" He knelt next to her and started tearing her skirt. She dimly wondered what he was doing. He tore the dress all the way up to her hip and she felt his hands on the upper part of her leg. His touch had never made her uncomfortable before, but she cringed now. Something tightened over her upper thigh. Fabric. A tourniquet.

Her voice came back in a sobbing scream.

Daelon took her hand. "You're going to be all right," he said. "You'll be all right. Hold on. Kiria, hold on. They're coming."

And he began to pray.

22

FIRIAN

FIRIAN COULD SEE his breath in clouds as he stretched out his legs and leaned back in his chair in World Events class. His injuries had healed, although he still had scars on his shins. He'd passed the "training" and, apparently pleased with his loyalty, the Masters gave him even more work to do. Now he rode horses regularly. He and Bard had been trying to figure out what his mission would be, but the scenarios felt limitless.

Pretending to suppress a quick yawn, he shut his eyes and briefly found Maya in the Unreal to wink at her. She smiled at him from across the room. A little warmth filled his core. He sat forward and refocused on the lesson.

"This morning," said Master Ardal, "the Kepress Kiria Arioc was brutally attacked by a band of Torithians who managed to get onto the grounds of the palace, Mon Párinath. The details are still unclear, but our sources say she'll probably live. Some say that a Tanyu ought to have been there to keep her safe, but it has been many years since Tanyu were stationed in Brithnem." His straight nose wrinkled. "The Keepers prefer the help of the Amir, who clearly were not able to help her, although she was reportedly near their living quarters at the time. Many of the threats on the Keepers have been directed at her and the heir to the First Line specifically. The Torithians apparently view them as the weakest links in the lines of succession. This event, of course, seriously affects our relations with the Western Kingdom."

Interesting. I wonder what Brithnem's move will be now.

As he tried to catch the Master's eye to see if his mission would be related to this attack, his mind whirled with possibilities. Perhaps they'd send more troops to the battlefront? Get more aggressive? Suggest that Tanyu fight in their war? Firian would do all three, if he were a Keeper of the Western Kingdom, one of the only titles more prestigious than a Tanyu. He would make them pay for harming her.

Weren't the Tanyu supposed to protect Brithnem? Yet they hadn't gotten involved in their war against the Torithians. Maybe he didn't know the Kepress, but he knew Bard, and wished he could protect his homeland from those pirates.

And why did the Torithians target Kiria Arioc specifically? It made better strategic sense to get rid of Atael, who was new and had no battle experience or heir.

But Master Ardal simply shifted to the next bit of news and the rest of the class gave no hint that they'd get to see war action any time soon.

Belik's class was next. After saying goodbye to Maya in one of the side hallways, he headed to the familiar blank room, clapping his hands against his legs to warm them.

Belik's door was open when he arrived and the Master was standing. With something like nervous energy, he shifted his weight when he saw Firian.

"We did it," he said in a husky voice.

Something in his tone made Firian stop short. "What?"

"I got you a mission."

The words echoed around his head, seductive. He turned

them over and looked at all sides. Firian's hands nearly shook with excitement and his heart pounded thickly. *A mission.* Belik look on with pride as he puzzled out his meaning. "What is the mission? Master Belik?" He hastily added the proper title he too often left off. He knew he was ready for a mission, but he'd thought Belik wouldn't allow him to go until he could reach the Second Level of the Unreal or something equally impossible.

Belik's eyes sparkled. "The Kepress was attacked this morning. Torithians."

Firian nodded, almost afraid to break the silence.

"The Keepers called for someone to keep her safe, so we're sending you to Brithnem."

A confusing mix of exhilaration and disappointment filled him. He wanted to fight, to go into the enemy's territory and save someone, or kill someone. He hadn't thought about following a princess around. But her life *was* in danger. And it was a great honor. Master Jovan had been a bodyguard to the King of Charäkhnem for several years. At least the danger suggested some action, didn't it?

"So—a bodyguard?"

"Firian," Belik said, lowering his chin and his voice in warning, "I had to convince the Head to choose you. This task puts you in a prime position, if you do it right."

"When do I leave?"

"Tomorrow," he said simply. "We need time to get supplies together. Master Gerand will go too."

The *katah* teacher? "Do I need her?" Firian asked. A chaperone was an affront to his independence.

"The Master'll speak to the Keepers when you get there, as I understand," he explained, then raised an eyebrow. "Of course you need her. Don't doubt a Master, especially me. If you do, you're not fit for this."

"As you would have it, Master Belik."

The Master nodded and then cast him a softer glance. "You want a drink tonight, Defender?"

"Yes," Firian answered, too abruptly.

Defender. He couldn't help but smile. It was about damn time. Masters couldn't look down on him from such a height and Tiev couldn't look down on him at all.

"I'll see you then. Go to your room and prepare for the journey."

All his trials up to that point had been deliberate to get him here, to be an emissary for the Academy, recognized as one of the best up and coming Tanyuin warriors. He wanted to shout with joy, but instead calmly bowed his head and left the room.

Later that night Master Belik and Firian went to the Old Pub. The Master immediately demanded two large dark ales of Hyrum, the proprietor, and sat down at a little table in the corner. As the Master cleaned his glasses between fingers of his black shirt, Firian thought the place looked a little too cramped and grimy to house Belik. For all their stealth, Tanyu had an enormous presence.

"I knew you'd be good for a mission once you shut up and practiced," Belik said, breaking the silence. A smile laced his words but not his stoic mouth. "Maybe even good for more."

"Thank you, Master Belik," said Firian. Not every Defender had drinks with Masters, so he knew to be as respectful as possible.

The ale appeared and they each took a mug. Belik didn't offer any more conversation (or explanation of "more") but only sat drinking thoughtfully. His small, dark eyes seemed to recede into him.

Since Firian didn't know what to say, he remained quiet as well. At least this drink was more enjoyable than Master Jovan's had been.

Belik flicked two rough fingers at Hyrum without turning his eyes. The proprietor, who had been rubbing down the tables with a greasy rag, returned behind the counter to fetch the order.

Belik spoke again. "We'll tell you what to do when you're there," he said. "I'll be watching your progress. Hopefully they'll let you out of sight of the palace." He spat the last words with surprising vitriol. Some old grievance. "They know we can get the job done, but they don't trust Tanyu like they used to." He finished his tankard in one long swig. Hyrum clanked the next two ales down on the table.

"As you would have it," Firian replied. Now wasn't the time for all his questions, so he'd have to be selective. Perhaps he should cast a broad net. "Is there anything else I should know?" he asked, unsure of how much others in the pub should hear but wanting to get as much information as he could.

"No," Belik said. He took another long sip, then his eyes slowly turned outward again and he looked Firian meaningfully in the face. "You deserve this mission, Firian, after how you... handled things," he said, continuing to look at him, as though he expected a reply.

Master Belik had not mentioned Firian's three tortuous nights before except to commend him vaguely once or twice. Pride swelled in him. "Thank you," he said. He flexed his feet up and down under the table.

Without mental training to talk about, they ran out of topics and spent most of the night in silence. Firian drank three mugs and Belik drank five. Neither even began to slur. Firian couldn't afford to have his head ache on the first morning of his mission.

Afterward, Master Belik led him to the blacksmith's where they picked up a long knife and a belt with a sheath. Firian wrapped it around himself and tested out the blade. Learners couldn't carry more than a small boot knife, so Firian had never had anything larger, though Jovan had taught him the skills.

They walked back together along the dark road to the Academy looming in the distance like a black cliff of rock. At the walkway to the main doors, Belik stopped and turned to him. In the darkness, he looked like a living shadow. Firian stood at attention.

After a pause, he said, "Remember to do anything we tell you."

The Master had turned to him so deliberately, he had expected something more profound. This was common sense. "Of course, Master Belik."

Lightening his grim manner slightly, Belik added, "I hear the girl is beautiful."

Firian imagined rather than saw his knowing glance. Belik was no fool and knew Firian better than most people. He knew that Firian had been sneaking off with girls for years. Firian grunted noncommittally in reply.

"Enjoy yourself," Belik continued, "but don't get caught up. Always focus on the mission. We already have your supplies. Be ready to leave with the sun." With that, Belik left Firian to return to the Academy alone. The Master turned off the road to his house. It was odd to see him going into a house.

As Firian walked back through the Academy, with its huge stone pillars and staircases, high-roofed ceiling and fountain, his thoughts refused to settle but seemed to fly around in fragments that made it difficult to believe that his time had actually come. Only last night, he had known nothing of his mission, and now he knew what he had been working toward all this time.

But now he knew. His mission, although shrunken now that it was finite, held great importance. It also held the potential for more. Firian hadn't been working in the dark, solitary hours of the morning and night for years just to protect a princess. No, this was a mere stepping stone, but a crucial one.

If they had only given him more than one day to prepare, he

could have told Tiev... Maybe his sudden disappearance would work just as well.

He topped the stairs and walked down to his room. Bard was asleep when he entered, already snuffling to himself with one arm slung over the edge of the bed. He would tell him about it in the morning. Now that he had the mission he had waited for, the room looked more comfortable than it had in a long time.

23

KIRIA

She heard someone say, "No one can see the Kepress."

"Who is it?" Kiria asked. After staying in her room for a week, alone except for the doctor and visits from her parents, she was anxious to see someone else. She was too weak to be very good company, but hours without human voices grated on her. It felt as though no one else existed. The silence gave her too much time to focus on the pain.

The guard didn't seem to have heard her. "Who is it?" she asked again.

"Amir Daelon," he replied.

Images flooded over her against her will. Searing pain and the look of panic in his face. She was struggling in her own blood with the thick arrow standing upright in her shoulder, he was ripping her dress, applying a tourniquet, and praying... She remembered hearing him pray before she lost consciousness.

She hadn't spoken to him since. "Please let him in."

"My orders do not permit me."

"Whose orders?"

He ignored her.

"The Keepers?" she snapped. Never had she felt so helpless.

Just as she was beginning to feel she could be a strong leader, she was cut down and everyone started treating her like a helpless child. Rage and disappointment filled her. "May I at least see him? Can you open the door?"

To this, the guard reluctantly consented. The heavy door swung open to reveal Daelon, immaculate in his high-necked robe. He bowed his head. "My Kepress," he began. "You seem much improved." His eyes, darkened with bags, rested on the sling holding her shoulder in place.

"Of course, especially since the last time you saw me," she said, shifting. Burning pain flashed along her left arm. Her voice sounded loud and dry after such a long silence.

"Has the Second Keeper informed you that we have sent for a Tanyuin bodyguard?" he said, very formally.

"She has," she said. She wished they could just use one of the palace guards instead, since the Tanyu were such a touchy subject with both Daelon and his mother Chetana. There was some bitterness there, bad blood. She didn't want to stir up any old wounds.

He released a breath. "My Kepress, when I found you..."

"Don't," she cut him off. "Let's not talk about it."

He looked at the ground. In the slit of his eyes, she saw tears. If he hadn't come just at that moment... Without warning, tears welled up in her eyes too, hot and stinging. They shared a thick silence.

"It's too quiet here," she said. "I'd like you to come and talk to me sometimes."

"It's true that only one voice is wearisome," he said with a small smile. She recognized the line from the Scroll. "I'd be glad to keep you company. I could resume our lessons." The thought seemed to cheer him up.

She nodded, but the attack had dampened her enthusiasm.

As she'd lain in bed the past few days, there were times

when she felt ready to hobble into the Main and become a Keeper that very minute. She'd proven her mettle, her survivor spirit. But, other times, anxiety choked her mind, sending it spiraling into darkness and fear. She couldn't know the right decision to make. Even as a Keeper, she wouldn't wield real power. Cúron would take care of everything, and the Amir too—thanks to Atty. Every halting step she took would please some and anger others. She could never be sure that she was making the right choice. The very thought made her feel trapped...

And then she would breathe.

"The Second Keeper, Merian Arioc," one of the door guards announced, as her mother appeared at the open door. And she wasn't alone. Chetana was with her, striding purposefully by her side up to Kiria's bed. It always amazed Kiria that Chetana and Daelon were related. She was martial; he was academic. She was dark-skinned; he was much lighter. They both were smart and composed, proud of the Amir and the Khelê, but that was the extent of the similarity Kiria could see.

Her mother swept to the side of the bed and knelt down. "Kiria, how are you feeling this morning?"

"A little better."

Her mother took her right hand and kissed it. "I'm so glad! Our troops killed or chased off the last Torithians this morning. They won't come to our harbor anymore." She smiled as though that were the end of it, the soothing end of a fairy tale.

Standing by her son, Chetana chimed in. "But there is still a threat to you."

Daelon looked at his mother in surprise.

Another threat? The idea made Kiria feel sick. She moved her injured leg a fractional amount, trying it out. The burning pain made her grit her teeth.

Her mother chastised the Amir with a look, as though the pain had been her fault, but Chetana didn't flinch. Even a

Keeper couldn't intimidate her. "Our sources say that there might be someone inside the palace, so we've doubled your guards."

"Yes," her mother said quickly. "We have six guards outside your room now, so you're perfectly safe. And I already told you that we've called for a personal bodyguard, who will be here in less than two weeks."

"But why are they targeting me?" It seemed odd that the Torithians weren't threatening everyone in the palace.

Her mother cast her eyes to the far end of the room, clearly uncomfortable. "They haven't said, but it must have to do with your Beauty. I don't see any other reason."

Chetana nodded her agreement. She had a military background, so she would probably understand their rationale. "It would end the Second Line, the female line, and they would have your legendary Beauty to do with as they wanted. It's a first step." She said the words with perfect composure.

Her throat tightened. "Do they think I'm weak?" It felt strange having everyone croon over her, guarding her, reassuring her, looking at her. The last thing Kiria wanted was pity, so she sat up, trying not to flinch with the pain. She'd bring up her thoughts about the Tanyu now, even with the Amir here. It wasn't appealing to have someone else fussing over her. "I'm not sure I want a bodyguard. We can use guards from the palace, can't we? Until the threat is dealt with?"

"She has a point," said Chetana. "We have excellent guards here. Even I have some experience—"

"The Tanyu are the best warriors in the world," her mother explained, looking only at her, as though Kiria hadn't heard it before. "And we need all the guards here at the palace for the war, now that it has come to our shores..." She looked abstracted for a moment. "A Tanyu can protect you single-handedly as you move to a safe location."

"Wait, I'm leaving the palace?" Kiria cried.

"It's only temporary," said her mother. "I don't want you to leave either, but it's the best choice for now. As soon as we eliminate the threat, you'll come home." She smiled weakly.

"My Keeper," Chetana prompted. Her face was like thunder, restrained and angry. "Do we know which Tanyu is coming to take away your daughter?" The question was pointed.

Her mother clearly didn't appreciate her advisor's tone, but she didn't correct her. "Yes, I know the name."

Daelon paled as he waited. His demeanor made him seem many years younger. Why should he be so anxious?

Her mother's hesitation showed that she knew the names wouldn't be well received. Kiria's stomach twisted. Chetana and her mother were rarely at such odds.

"They are Defender Kess and... Master Gerand."

"Gerand! You know you can't trust my sister!" Chetana burst out. But Daelon loosened his shoulders, clearly relieved.

"Chetana!" her mother snapped, rising to her feet, suddenly a Keeper. "The Tanyu won't let anything happen to my daughter. They have sworn to protect us. I know that the Amir and Tanyu have a rocky history, but you have to put your prejudice aside."

Their history had been more than rocky if Daelon's lessons were right. He lived by a code of scrupulous honesty, so Kiria had no reason to doubt him. The two groups worked together at times, but individuals within both organizations perpetuated an ever-growing feud. She'd even heard rumors of a militant Amiran group whose main target were Tanyu, although that was hard to picture. The opposite was much easier to conceive. Maybe that was just a rumor.

Chetana drew herself up. "It isn't—"

"I know your feelings about Master Gerand. She will not be the one taking Kiria alone. *Defender Kess* will be her bodyguard, and I assume you have nothing against him!"

Chetana's eyes flashed, but she said nothing.

Her mother turned back to Kiria. "All we want is to keep you safe," she said. "And we're doing that the best way we know how."

Kiria nodded. If she had doubts before, Chetana's reaction made them worse. But it was true—Tanyu really were supposed to be the best—so she would have to trust her mother and the others who made the decision to send for them. Honestly, she was curious to meet Defender Kess, the man who could stir up such radically different reactions.

24

FIRIAN

THE JOURNEY to Brithnem passed silently and uneventfully. They stayed off the main roads and bypassed towns whenever possible. Twice Master Gerand sent Firian into a village to buy food and supplies, but otherwise they fled from the sight of people like fugitives. The fewer people recognized them, the better. They could blend in if they wanted to, hide in a crowd, as long as no one knew their faces. That was a helpful ability to have on a mission like this.

The mountains harbored no ghosts; the road hid no robbers. Yet they set up a watch rotation at night regardless.

Now, almost three weeks later, they had to be getting close to Brithnem.

He pictured the map he had studied right before he left. They must be riding through the forest called Á Quihilmar—an old name that meant "Of Gray." Several passages in the Scroll referenced it. Bored, he tried to remember some of them, but they wouldn't come. The monotony of this trip was getting to him. Still, he knew that this forest meant they were getting close.

His horse nickered and tossed his head. The trees thinned. Firian caught a whiff of salt on the air and sat up straighter.

The trees ended and he saw, far away, the falling sun glinting on the surface of the sea. It shone like metal, blazing where it melded with the sky. Black against the shining ocean, thick turrets rose high above the small buildings clustering around it, spreading out evenly beyond the wall around the city. Raewhith could fit inside the city walls many times. And this was the city that had called for him.

Gerand rode up next to him and nodded toward Brithnem. For a glorious second, he had forgotten about her, and the gesture irritated him. Firian put up with Gerand's arrogance all the way over the mountains and he didn't want to have it interrupt this moment now. He turned away from her and looked back at the city.

They rode through stretches of farmland before they reached the wall. It soared above them, ancient, but without the primal power of the Academy. This wall had seen war, but it was still light, almost graceful. Firian was surprised no one had conquered it.

They trotted up to what looked like the main gate, since it was the biggest and had the most elaborate metal designs. Six men stood guard. Two of them came forward as they approached.

"State your business with Brithnem," one said.

Gerand answered, "We are Tanyu of the Academy. My name is Master Gerand, and this is Defender Firian Kess. Your Keepers summoned us to come to Mon Párinath as soon as possible on a matter of security."

One of the four guards remaining at the gate whispered to his neighbor.

"Very well," said the first guard. "We've been expecting you."

Four men hauled open the great gate for them. Firian kicked his horse with his heel, and she lumbered forward. The cobblestone road leading up to the wall continued into the city. The simple stone houses lining the roads reminded him of Tánuil. In the distance, the palace rose, majestic.

A man in a blue-gray robe came down the street toward them. "Welcome to Brithnem," he said loudly. "I am Amir Parohim, advisor to the First Keeper." *An Amir.* He looked about the same as Firian had pictured. His long, high-collared robes wouldn't allow him to run; his face was pale, creased with study, not with work; his hands were the same, long and pale, without callouses. His slicked-back hair reminded him of boys in Tánuil when they courted a girl for the first time.

Parohim turned to Master Gerand. "You must be Amir Chetana's sister." His face was not as carefree as his voice.

Gerand's sister is an Amir? The revelation made Firian uncomfortable, though he couldn't pinpoint why.

"I am," she said shortly. "Shall we go to the palace?"

Parohim ignored her, turning instead to Firian. "Is this your first time in Brithnem, Defender Kess?"

"Yes, it is," Firian said.

"Then let's walk to Mon Párinath together," said the Amir, gesturing to a woman who stood nearby. They all dismounted and she led the horses to a stable attached to the city wall. "They'll be well taken care of," Parohim said, leading them along one of the streets to the right.

The city was alive with people talking, trading, walking, washing, and even singing. All of them looked so strange to him. For years, Firian had recognized almost everyone around him. Now he saw no familiar face. It encouraged him to think that if he didn't recognize them, they wouldn't recognize him. Still, wasn't this supposed to be a secret mission? Did everyone in Brithnem need to see them? Firian knew they were conspicuous in Academy black. Parohim led them down the middle of the road, exposed to everyone's view, forcing them to move around carts.

One came up the road toward them, and Firian shuffled to the side to avoid it. Suddenly he felt young again, and bile churned in his stomach. He wasn't that pathetic little boy anymore, cringing at the sound of his father's voice. This wasn't Raewhith. It was one of the most powerful nations in the world, and its leaders wanted him, Firian, to protect their princess.

He looked back at the palace, visible from everywhere, and threw back his shoulders. He clenched and unclenched his hands as he walked.

About twenty minutes later, they reached what seemed to be a great arena. Gold leaf sparkled in patches on the crumbling stone. Large flags, light blue and dark purple rimmed with silver with a flower in the center, flapped on the walls. Parohim led them in through a dark corridor.

"Why are you taking us here?" Master Gerand demanded.

"I want to show you some of the glories of Brithnem," he said.

They came out into a large open oval, with benches rising up in tiers around the sides. In the center rose a crowd of statues in a tight circle facing outward.

In a reverent voice, Parohim explained who they were. There were Shane and Mari Calthwaite and their four children, ancestors of the current Keepers. There was General Brishen, the Khelê war hero who led Shane and Mari and a small band to fight for God's people against the evil king who created the Kingdom.

Firian listened impatiently. He already knew some of the quotations that Parohim recited from the Scroll. Master Gerand tapped her foot as the Amir continued to explain. She probably had never read the entire Scroll, much less memorized portions of it.

A while later Parohim lifted his dry face to the sky. "I'm

afraid it's getting late," he said without a hint of apology. "We ought to go to the palace now."

Through many twisting streets he led them until Firian approached Master Gerand and expressed his doubts with a look. She shook her head dismissively. Parohim was no threat. The long tour through the city still made him uneasy. Too many people had seen them.

The air grew thicker with the mist and flavor of the sea. Then, finally, the palace. It had three huge wings: one in front, and two thrust back into the grounds. Flags waved from turrets that rose victoriously above the city. Over the doors and windows, relief sculptures depicted historical scenes or flower patterns or lines from the Scroll. Firian saw no immediate evidence of a threat.

Parohim led them along the wall until they were well to the side of the palace, rather than the front, and let them in by a small door made of dark wood and intricately worked iron that led to the gardens.

"You will stay in the Amiran quarters," Parohim explained, gesturing toward it. The round, domed building was attractive in the extensive gardens, almost like a huge ornament. It had little of the Academy's ancient, forbidding mass. This was a place to study in peace, a place to stay in times of war, a quiet place. Pillars created a colonnade. All the way along the outside rim of the building hung burning lamps.

Round, white lanterns. Firian squinted at them. They were blown glass. He had completely forgotten about his class, his early vocation, and those glass balls that Raewhith always sent to Brithnem. Seeing them here was surreal. He closed his open mouth.

Although the sun was setting, darkness hadn't crept in yet. The ghost-lanterns staved off the dark.

Servants conducted Firian to his room while Master Gerand discussed details with Brithnem's officials. Firian's room had thick carpet and was much bigger than the room he shared with Bard at the Academy. On the wall hung an old tapestry of a ship called the *Paladin* approaching land. He looked for a picture of the Second Line, but there was none. He'd just have to wait to meet the Kepress in person. Across from the tapestry was a small window. The way the warm yellow light streamed in made him feel much younger. Light had come through his window the same way in Raewhith. Academy light seemed different—purposeful, not so flippant with its wasted beauty.

Firian hadn't expected to recognize so many things here. It was almost like going home, and he wasn't sure he liked the familiarity.

He looked down at the cloth wrapped around his arm, staunching the cut he'd accidentally given himself while practicing the Unreal on the road. *Believe and not believe.* That was the life he wanted, power and respect. The cloth looked very similar to the one he'd worn years ago. Black was the standard Academy color, but a scrap of black around the wrist meant mourning.

He shouldn't be thinking like this. He wasn't sentimental. And he shouldn't be, especially now.

Unable to stay still, he checked that everything was in his bag. Nothing lost. Surely he could walk around outside without someone stopping him. The palace and its Amiran Academy were walled in, and he was a Tanyu.

He slipped out and walked along the colonnade. Dusk had washed the rounded walls in dark gray. Far away, he heard the cries of birds and the splash of waves. Busy servants maintenanced the gardens, snipping and watering.

Just in front of him an Amir emerged from his room. They quickly sized each other up, recognizing the outfits instantly. Every Amir seemed to wear the same bluish-gray cloak with the stiff collar reaching around their neck. This one was younger than Parohim, but his exact age was hard to pin down. They were the same height, but Firian could take him down easily if he needed to.

"Hello," Firian said, forcing a smile. It was always better to give a good first impression.

"Are you the Tanyu that the Keepers requested?" The Amir closed the door behind him.

The words sounded good coming out of the man's mouth. "I am. My name's Firian Kess."

"I'm the Kepress's tutor, Daelon."

One name. Must be Khelê.

"What brings you outside?" Daelon asked. His gaze showed marked distrust.

"Just some fresh air."

"I thought you would be eager to settle in after a long day of traveling."

"I don't get tired easily."

There was an awkward pause.

Firian had never been alone with an Amir. As much as he disagreed with them, this was an opportunity. And this man was the Kepress's personal tutor. "So, what is the Kepress learning now? Maybe I can encourage her in her lessons." *When she's away.* The unspoken words hung frostily in the air.

"That's private information," said Daelon.

"The Scroll? I assume that's part of it."

The Amir's eyes narrowed as though Firian had insulted someone close to him. "Of course it is. The Scroll teaches us all wisdom."

"I only asked because I have great respect for the Scroll." It wasn't hard to guess how to get on an Amir's good side.

Daelon sucked his teeth. "I haven't met many Tanyu with that view. Have you read it?"

"I have. It's very interesting." Seeing Daelon's skepticism, he added, "We have a few copies at the Academy."

Daelon's face began to thaw. He lifted his chin and his eyes softened with amusement, but his voice became an instructor's. "*For as long as I speak, I will speak the praise of God. For as long as I hear—*" He stopped and waited. It was a famous passage, a test.

"*—I will heed God's wisdom,*" Firian finished. "I think that's it." *Heed* sounded fancy. The word was something like that, at least.

"It is, it is!" Daelon said with the sparkling joy of a teacher. An encouraging smile lit up his face. "The Kepress will be glad to know you've read it."

It was always about the Scroll. But it could only do so much; otherwise, why would they have called for people who could actually take care of her? "Good," he replied. "How is she feeling?"

"She's doing much better now. The doctor says she's well enough to travel." A shadow darkened his face again at the thought.

Is he interested in her, or is he just concerned?

Firian smiled. "That's good. I look forward to meeting her. Is there a specific time...?"

"No. No," Daelon said. "I was just about to announce your arrival to her now. Will you be the only bodyguard? I know you came with some others." He laid slight stress on the last two words, enough to tell Firian that he knew more than he said.

"I am the only one." Gerand was welcome to leave immediately, as far as he was concerned. Even being reminded of her sent him into a glowering mood. As though he needed to be babysat... But he wanted to meet the princess, so he arranged his face to look neutral. "Would it be too much to ask to meet her now?"

This way he could be rid of Master Gerand looking over his shoulder. Besides, he was curious about how beautiful she really was. The tales were legendary.

Daelon looked over his face again, searching for something, maybe an ulterior motive. Firian gazed back innocently. Daelon turned away and walked toward the palace. "Come with me," he said. "I'll ask her if she wants to meet you."

25

KIRIA

THERE WAS a session going on in the Main, but Kiria wasn't there. Her shoulder and anxiety were acting up, so she asked to be excused.

She was waiting for Jori, whom she had seen more often in the last couple weeks than she had for months before that. She could use some of his levity right now.

The sling was almost a novelty at first, but now it annoyed her. She wondered how people without maids dressed themselves if they were injured. As she sat in front of the mirror, she tried shifting her arm but she couldn't find a comfortable position.

The door opened. "Hello, darling," Jori said lightly, coming in. "I thought you'd be in here." A guard closed the door after him.

"I'm always in here," she said, looking at herself as Candrae did her hair. Her Beauty was comforting. When she was upset, she experimented with new fashions. In fact, that was the only time she tried them.

He eyed her new hairstyle appreciatively. "You know, you're late for the Main."

She groaned with guilt. "Don't even say that. I know. I'll go back soon. I just…"

"Here." He saved her from having to explain her feelings by settling a glass in front of her. "Let's forget about the Main."

Part of the reason he always redirected the conversation was his jealousy for Atty's position. He never said it outright, but she knew. His eyes crinkled and his jaw flexed when Atty brought up the important decisions Keepers got to make. But Atty also envied Jori's easy charm. No one had everything.

"All right," she said, picking up the glass with her good hand. He poured something into it. She took a burning sip.

He poured some for himself and downed half of it in one gulp.

"You're going to hurt yourself," she laughed, loosening the pins Candrae was trying to hold in place. "That's all right, Candrae," she said, dismissing her.

Jori pulled up a chair and clinked his glass against hers. After taking a pointedly smaller sip, he said, "Speaking of, how's the arm?"

"I think I can take the sling off soon. Thank goodness!" She couldn't play her instruments with it on, and baths were painful as she struggled to hold her arm in one position.

"Ah!" he exclaimed, topping off with more. "That's my girl! Always moving forward. It'll be a shame to take care of yourself again." His eyes twinkled.

She knew trying to make him talk seriously about the attack would be useless. Jori didn't want to think about it in those terms. To him, everything was all right. So she gave a little hum and retreated to her drink.

"Are you planning to go to an event this evening?" he asked, eyeing her nice outfit and half-done hair.

"No. I was just trying something out."

"Shame no one gets to see."

She smiled. When he complimented her Beauty, it felt different. He had always had a breezy way of complimenting her, no matter what she looked like, so it didn't feel fake like some of the others. "You're seeing," she said, and held out her glass for more.

A knock on the door made her jump. Daelon came in. His gaze swept over the two of them with their drinks and his face became unreadable. For some reason, Kiria felt a little ashamed. "My Kepress, I'm sorry to interrupt, but your bodyguard would like to meet you," he said. She was about to dismiss the idea when he added, "He's waiting just outside."

She twisted her mouth to the side. She was in no mood to meet a grim Tanyu that would remind her of the danger she lived in. But she nodded. She had to meet him sometime. "Just give me a moment, Daelon."

He nodded once and went back out the door.

Jori should have known to excuse himself, but he didn't. He was curious.

Kiria set down her glass. "Turn around," she told him. For some reason, she hated using her Ability in front of anyone but her serving girls. It exposed her, like changing clothes.

Her mother, Chetana, and guards had told her not to reveal her Ability to the Tanyu. It was a kind of compromise her mother made to settle their worries. Besides, they said her plain face would act as a sort of disguise when they left the palace—better for avoiding attention.

A tingling sensation and she was plain again. "Okay," she announced so Jori would know it was safe to turn around, and Daelon would know he could bring in the bodyguard.

After a soft snick of the lock, Daelon entered with the Tanyu—a handsome young man about her own age, lean but muscular. He strode in confidently, right beside Daelon, not behind. In her experience, Tanyu never liked to be second. He wore a long-sleeve black shirt and dark pants tucked into dirty boots. He hadn't cleaned up before meeting her, so he must have just arrived. His dark hair and eyebrows contrasted strikingly with his light skin. Like every Tanyu she'd met, his moves were calculated and powerful.

She had expected someone older, who would hover around her invisibly, detached from everything but his duty. This man looked right into her eyes, almost as though he were trying to communicate with her, but she couldn't read his face. She suddenly felt ugly and it bothered her. Her sling must make her look so helpless, and she hated to be helpless.

"My Kepress, this is Firian Kess, the bodyguard that the Keepers ordered."

She'd heard that name before. Daelon had taught it to her. *Firian, just like Mari's nephew in the story.*

Daelon turned to the Tanyu, who bristled at the introduction. She wondered why. "Defender Kess, this is Kiria Arioc, heir to the Second Line, Kepress of Brithnem and the Western Kingdom." He gave her title much more weight than his, slowing down the words as though he wanted to impress their importance on the Tanyu.

Firian made a small bow from the waist. Some of his disheveled hair fell into his face. He looked up at her and smiled a little as he bowed. She couldn't remember ever having seen a Tanyu smile.

She set her jaw hard. Firian was already trying to get on her good side, but it suddenly irritated her and she didn't know why. "Pleased to meet you," she said, sensing Jori's excitement as he stood beside her.

"You as well, Kepress," Firian replied. The words were just formal enough, but skirted the edge of casual.

Kiria had known Daelon long enough to know that he was annoyed, although his face betrayed nothing. He always wanted people to show her the utmost respect. "Defender Kess will accompany you when you leave in a couple days. I'm sure he'll do his work admirably." His eyes flashed to the floor as he paused. "We don't want to keep you," he said, beginning to back toward the door.

"Why don't you stay a little?" Jori chimed in. The words were obviously aimed at the Tanyu, not Daelon.

Firian glanced back at the Amir, a question.

Daelon paused. "Only if the Kepress agrees."

Kiria had never cared for Tanyu—they were so hardened and proud—but Jori seemed so happy with his huge smile that she didn't contradict him. He had never been able to spend time with a Tanyu, only admire them from afar. "Of course he can join us for a while," she said. "You can come pick him up in an hour."

Jori was already pulling up another chair, almost giddy with excitement. "Come, come!" he said, presenting the seat with a theatrical gesture.

"You don't have to stay if you don't want to," Kiria said quietly.

"No, I'll stay." Firian came forward easily and sat down with them as Daelon excused himself from the room. She trusted Daelon in most things, but he did have a bias against the Tanyu. To be honest, maybe she did too.

"Firian Kess?" Jori said, settling into the chair closest to hers. "Fresh from the Academy. I think you're the youngest Tanyu I've ever seen."

Firian's deep-set eyes sparkled a little at the compliment. "Do you see many here?" he asked.

"An ambassador comes once a year, but that's about it. Do you care for a drink?" Jori plucked the bottle and two glasses from where they had been sitting. He didn't have a third glass, so how he thought he could offer, Kiria didn't know.

She and Jori could share drinks together in her room, laugh

and pass the time, but it felt strange to have Firian with them. They didn't know him. All in all, she didn't feel like herself, dressed up, hair half done, arm in a sling, drinking in her room with Jori and a stranger. She was better than that. Though she sometimes wanted to forget, she was the heir to a throne of Brithnem. Shouldn't he meet her in a formal capacity first? They were skipping steps. She would (she realized) be alone with Firian at some point, but to spend such relaxed time with him now didn't feel right.

She stepped in, addressing Firian. "This is Jorrim Calthwaite," she said, knowing the last name would register with him.

"Jori. Third Keeper's brother," her friend clarified, handing her the half-empty glass she had set down earlier.

Firian nodded. He didn't seem awed by either of their ranks.

Jori offered to pass Firian the bottle. Thankfully, he gestured that he didn't want any.

"So I've wondered," Jori said, twisting around to put the bottle back on the vanity counter, "what do you do all the way out there at the Academy?"

"I can't say." One side of his mouth lifted in a smile.

"That's what they all say." Jori took a drink. "But I'm sure you can tell us something. Do they hang you up by your ankles, or pit you against each other in boxing matches? We only hear little pieces, and I've always wanted to know."

He was teasing, but Kiria colored. "I'm sure they don't do either of those things," she said.

"Just know that we can offer the greatest security," Firian said, setting his hands on his knees. They were calloused with many light scars. She wondered how he got them.

"Well, I hope so," said Jori. "That's why you're here. We can't let this happen again." He lifted his chin at Kiria's sling. "You have to take care of our girl." He smiled at Firian, but his eyes were serious.

She sighed through her nose, running her finger along the base of the glass. "It *won't* happen again," she said. Even without a bodyguard, she could be more careful, and be just fine. She shifted in her seat. "I'm not afraid of the Torithians, and I don't want to be away for very long."

"Then I'll just make sure you're safe, and we'll return to the palace as soon as possible," Firian said.

"Good, because everything I know is here, and it feels terrible to be taken away just because I'm being targeted!" The words gushed out of her. To her, the bodyguard embodied her unfamiliar situation. It wasn't that she disliked him, but his presence put her in a testy mood. "Honestly, I wish you didn't need to be here. But we'll get through it."

Firian leaned forward on his elbows. "We will," he said earnestly, although the last reminder had been for herself.

She was a little taken aback by the intensity with which he looked at her.

"I wish I could go with you." Jori ran his fingers through his hair, practically pulling at the roots. He wasn't kidding.

"I'm sure you do," Kiria said, suddenly laughing. "I doubt it'll be very fun, though." She turned to Firian. "Do you know where we're going?"

"The Keepers are discussing that now," he said, a shadow falling over his face. "They'll tell us both in the morning."

26

FIRIAN

FIRIAN RETURNED to his room that night deep in thought. So far, many parts of the mission had been disappointing, but spending time with the princess and the Third Keeper's brother was a welcome break from Gerand's company. The princess wasn't as beautiful as everyone said. Frankly, her reputation of extreme beauty was a little baffling. He saw servants better looking than she was. But she was powerful, so it didn't matter.

Her friend Jori, more than anyone else so far, seemed to respect Tanyu. And he didn't respect very much. It was odd that more people didn't seem impressed. Of course, he had mostly met Amir and they tended not to like the Academy.

He had barely entered his room when he heard a knock. Without waiting for an answer, Master Gerand entered, the lines on her face deeper than when he had seen her last. "Here you are," she said, as though she had found a little boy. "The Keepers have asked to meet you. Come with me." She turned without seeing if he followed.

His fists turned numb with anger. At least no one else had been there to see how she treated him.

He had no choice but to chase after her. No matter how he felt, he couldn't be late to meet the Keepers of Brithnem.

Cúron, Merian, and Aylmor. He had memorized their names in school. He knew that Aylmor's son, Atael, was the Third Keeper now, but the sing-song voice in Firian's head still said the father's name. And Kiria would become the Second someday.

Gerand and Firian rushed through the gardens through one of the palace's back entrances. Daelon had taken him through a different entrance before. This one opened into an enormous hallway, all but abandoned except for a few guards who seemed to expect them. At least, Firian hoped so. *No wonder the Torithians chose to attack near the palace.* Deep rugs stretched over the spacious floor, and tall potted trees and portraits lined the walls. The palace was a glassmaker's dream—so many intricate panes forming patterns on the windows.

Gerand led them both to the left, where wooden doors as tall as two stories rose to the ceiling. Intricate carvings covered the entire face of them, probably depicting historical scenes, though none of them registered in Firian's memory.

The Master halted in front of the four guards that stood at attention beside the huge doors. "Master Gerand and Defender Kess," she said in a clear voice. "The Keepers are expecting us."

The soldiers recognized the names and cracked the door open enough to admit them. The space inside was round, with four large statues staggered across the circumference—three men and one woman. The vaulted roof went higher than the Academy's. Three thrones stood in the middle of a floor mosaic on a little raised platform. Before the thrones stood a small knot of people.

A guard conducted the two of them to the group in the center. Firian saw Cúron immediately. He had to be the bearded one wearing sweeping blue robes with long gray hair and flashing blue eyes. His every movement was royal.

If it had not been for the understated crowns on the two others, he wouldn't have been able to pick them out. Merian, Kiria's mother, was taller than her daughter, and frankly more beautiful, but she had little of the commanding presence Firian expected from a leader. Her expression, though strained in concern, settled into a look of calm distraction. Atael looked even more out of place. He resembled his brother, but his features were less refined, clumsier. He had a redder complexion and bigger bones, although he wasn't taller. He gave the impression that his clothes had been misbuttoned.

Besides the Keepers, there were several others—guards and Amir, by the look of it. He only recognized Parohim. Judging by the look of hatred on Gerand's face, she recognized someone else in the group too.

Cúron moved toward them with the expansive gesture of a benefactor. "We're so glad you've arrived!" he said. "Master Gerand and Defender Kess, welcome." He cast a tiny look at a dark-skinned woman standing by Merian.

The guard beside Firian introduced the three Keepers but said nothing of the others.

Merian stepped forward, covertly looking Firian up and down. "We're glad you could come for this temporary measure," she said. "We have agreed that you and my daughter Kiria will go to Carradoc until we have assessed the danger here at the palace."

The fortress of Carradoc featured in many parts of the Scroll. Firian should have guessed that's where they would send him. "I'm honored to be able to protect her," he said, bowing. Now was not the time to give these leaders any doubts about him.

The tall, dark woman pursed her lips, obviously unhappy. The more Firian looked at her, the more he got the impression he'd seen her before.

Cúron addressed the woman. "Only Defender Kess will go with the Kepress, and soon the danger will have passed."

The woman's face, severe and proud, punctuated with a septum ring, remained impassive. She kept casting distrustful looks at Gerand. Even though the two looked very different, this had to be Gerand's sister.

The Master turned to Firian, maybe to get away from the woman's gaze. "You will leave tomorrow and as soon as the threat is eliminated, their Watchman will inform you."

Firian had never had the chance to hear from a Watchman, so that would be interesting. He wondered if it was just an Amir with the Talent. *Probably.*

"Have you met Kiria?" Atael finally said something.

Before he could answer, Merian replied, "No, not yet. Could someone conduct us to a place where we could all meet?"

The dark-skinned woman spoke up. "I don't think Master Gerand needs to meet the Kepress," she said pointedly. Her whole manner reminded Firian of a Tanyu, but she wore the high-collared robes of an Amir. "Defender Kess will meet her by himself."

Firian felt the heat of Gerand's anger like a physical presence.

"I'll have someone introduce them tomorrow morning," Merian said, playing the peacemaker. "And now, I'm sure you're tired from your journey and would like to go back to your rooms." She nodded at a guard.

"Yes," Cúron said, booming, final. "We thank you for coming. The Defender will meet the Kepress tomorrow and they'll begin their journey to Carradoc." The guard took the hint and ushered Gerand and Firian out of the room.

27

KIRIA

THAT NIGHT, Kiria shuffled around her room with Candrae and Vayci, quietly packing. She set an extra pair of shoes by the pack lying open on her bed. Would she need more than two pairs? That might be too much.

She bit her lip. She had no idea how long she would be gone, and the whole situation put her stomach in knots. Hopefully she would arrive in Carradoc—that part excited her, at least—and then turn around to come home. *Strange that they chose a safe place so far away...* Surely it wouldn't take long to find the mole inside the castle.

She pointed at a pair of beige pants. "Bring those over," she told Vayci. Those would be good for traveling. She probably shouldn't bring any of her nice dresses. Even the thought made her blush. No wonder she wasn't ready to lead. Who would think to bring royal dresses on such a long clandestine trip? She might as well not hide her Beauty.

Yes, she would bring mostly pants. That would help her to ride horses more easily and walk over rough terrain. Her Tanyuin bodyguard had more experience, but she was determined to keep up even with her healing leg.

Her bedroom door opened and the guard announced her mother and father. Kiria turned to say hello and felt an unexpected lump in her throat. She tried to swallow it down but it wouldn't budge. Her mother's eyes softened when she saw her standing in front of the half-packed bag.

"Kiria," she began, but Kiria was already in her arms with tears stinging her eyes. Her father reached over and stroked her hair. *Why am I crying?* she thought. *I'm stronger than this.* Kiria knuckled her eyes with her good hand and stood up straight.

Her mother patted her arm. "I just met your bodyguard," she said. "Chetana's sister was there too. I'm not sure why she came after the first negotiation." Her eyebrows furrowed. "Only Defender Kess will be going with you in the morning." She caught Kiria's eye. "I'll do everything I can to make sure you come home as soon as possible."

"We'll miss you while you're gone," her father added. Something in his tone suggested more than he said.

She furrowed her eyebrows. "I'll miss you too," she said. Even though she'd been spending less time with them lately, the idea of going so far away made her sad. She and mother didn't always agree, but her parents both loved her. She wished there was something she could do to make them proud.

"Oh!" her mother cried and wrapped her up again in a hug. Kiria's face only came to the beading on her neckline, now pressed against her cheek.

"Remember not to show your Ability to the young man," her father said.

She couldn't forget even if she wanted to. "I'll remember."

"And stay safe," said her mother, rubbing her back gently. "The girls will help you pack and then you'll be all ready to go in the morning." Her mother had a habit of saying obvious things like that, but now, with the windows dark and a journey with a stranger ahead of her, Kiria didn't mind. Her parents' love filled her like a warm cup of tea.

"Make sure you get that threat," Kiria said, separating from her mother. "And don't let Cúron do all the work." She couldn't help adding that last part.

"Oh, Kiria, of course I won't," her mother said like someone who'd ripped off an old scab.

"It's too bad," her father said. "I know you've wanted to see Carradoc. It's a beautiful place." Because he was a general, he had been there a couple of times. "But I'm afraid we'll have to bring you back before you reach it."

Amused, Kiria nodded, torn between wanting to see the fortress and hoping he was right.

"We'll let you get back to your packing," he said, putting his hand on her mother's shoulder.

She reached up to hold it as she looked down at Kiria one last time. "It won't be long," she said. "And the bodyguard seems like he'll do a good job."

Her father gave a look that said he'd better. "Let's go," he said gently.

"Good night, Kiria!" said her mother as they both went out.

"Good night," she called after them. "Ah!" She turned to her serving girls. "I'll be so glad when this is over."

Candrae gave a ghost of a smile. Both of her girls had always served her nearly in silence as all the servants did, waiting to be asked before interjecting an opinion. Kiria liked to hear what they thought, but they respected her position too much to speak first.

"What do you think would go with these pants?" she asked, coming back to mull over her outfits.

Vayci raised her head to speak when another knock sounded at the door.

Kiria made an exasperated sound as the door opened again. "Oh, it's you!"

"That's a way to say hello," Atty said as he came in hesitantly. He looked thin and pale compared to the last time she had seen him. His brown hair curled around his bronze crown. "I just came to say goodbye."

"I'm sorry to be leaving you like this," she said. Even though they didn't spend the same time together that they did as children, she knew he valued her support, especially now that he was a Keeper.

He waved the apology away. "It's not your choice. I know you would stay if you could. I wish you could stay." His eyes strayed to the bed. "Getting ready?"

Another obvious question. "Yes. Just about there."

Knock knock knock. *Again?* One of her guards cracked the door open and announced Jorrim Calthwaite and Firian Kess.

She would never finish packing. "Let them in." Maybe Jori wanted to say goodbye again, too.

The two of them sauntered in, Jori looking proud to be with a Tanyu. He stopped when he saw Atty. "Oh, I didn't know you'd be here," he said. "All saying goodbye, I guess?"

Atty nodded.

"Well, that's not why I'm here," Jori went on, turning deliberately to Kiria. "Since it's your last night here, I thought we'd have a bit of fun. Since you're here, Atty, you can join."

Atty's mouth lifted in an offended smile.

"You've met Firian?" Jori asked off-handedly.

"We've met," Atty said.

Firian nodded in agreement.

"So, what do you have in mind? I do have to get ready..." Kiria said. It did sound better to have fun with her friends than continue worrying about tomorrow.

"Oh, it won't take long." Jori walked forward. "We're going to sneak into the Main."

Atty made a face. "We have guards posted all the time now. Should we really sneak around the palace, especially considering...?" He gestured to Kiria.

"I could do it," she said.

"I don't think it's a great idea," Atty said.

"Then if we can't get into the Main, we could go somewhere else." Jori jabbed a thumb toward Firian. "He can keep us safe. No worries." He flashed a smile.

It did sound fun, a throwback to their younger days, before the war had any effect on them. "As long as we aren't gone too long." She ducked to catch Atty's line of sight. "You should come with us. It'll be fun!"

"We won't be caught." Atty said it like a warning.

"No," Jori said lightly. "We have a Tanyu."

Firian hadn't spoken yet. Maybe he disapproved of sneaking around. It wasn't exactly the best idea for someone whose life was in jeopardy. "You'll come with us, right?" she asked him.

"Sure. You can do anything you want," he replied.

"That's it then!" Jori rubbed his hands together. "Serving quarters? Kitchen? Garden?"

"Not the garden," Kiria said. Too many memories.

"Kitchen," said Atty.

Jori smiled at his brother. "Midnight snack? I like it."

It really did feel like old times. Minus the bodyguard, of course, but he was starting to do a better job of being invisible.

"Do we have to wait?" Kiria asked. In the past, they had waited until all the adults went to bed. Based on the traffic her room had seen this evening, none of them had turned in for the night.

"What if we didn't?" Jori said. "Make it more exciting."

"Unless we're caught," said Atty.

"Doesn't being a Keeper have any perks? I'm sure you can go to the kitchen and eat whenever you want. Don't be boring."

Kiria looked at Firian. "Do you think you can get us around the guards even if everyone isn't sleeping?"

His deep eyes regarded her seriously, and the question felt childish. Still, this could be a good test of his skills, and she hoped he had a sense of fun sometimes. It would make traveling with him easier.

"Of course I can," Firian said.

"See, there!" Jori raised his hands as though that settled the matter. "We'll go where we want, grab a snack, and be right back." He winked at the serving girls. Candrae blushed.

Atty set his mouth in a line, tired of his brother's antics.

The humor of the situation struck her. What a miss-matched group! A Keeper, his brother, an heir, and a bodyguard they had all just met, sneaking around Mon Párinath like a troop of children. She couldn't stifle a laugh.

"See there," said Jori, setting a hand on her good shoulder. "This is just what you needed. Everyone's been far too serious." He clapped his hands. "Everyone ready to go?"

Kiria and Atty nodded. Firian didn't respond, but he had the Tanyuin quality of looking ready at all times. He ran his thumb over his jawline.

Jori led the way, although Kiria thought Firian should go first. She wanted to know what he was made of. Did he walk cat-like, aware of everything, invisible when he wanted to go unnoticed? She wouldn't be surprised, based on what she'd seen of him, but this was a good test.

They passed the guards outside her door, who let them all pass without comment. If Kiria had been alone, they probably would have stopped her, but here she was with a Keeper and a Tanyu. Jori nodded jovially at them.

Firian bent down to speak quietly to Jori. "It looks like we won't have a problem. Who is it you want to avoid?"

Jori shushed him. "It's all in fun," he said.

Firian remained alert, but clearly didn't appreciate the response.

It was true. They could go almost anywhere they wanted if they were all together. Eating from the kitchens was bad form, but not forbidden. They could even go up to the Watchman Tower if they wanted to, although no one was supposed to disturb the person meditating up there.

They walked along the edges of the hallway, making sure to step on the rugs to dampen any sound. Kiria saw the Tanyu's shoulders relax. Maybe he was disappointed in the lack of danger. He had seemed more excited back in her room.

The main kitchen was in the front section of the palace. The four of them slipped through the archway that led downstairs. Kiria's mouth started watering at the smell of baking bread. A snack was a good idea. Jori's plans weren't always the best—she had to vet them, even before the coronation when they would sneak into the city together—but she appreciated this one.

At the bottom of the stairs, the kitchen felt humid and warm. It was like easing into a bath. A few staff stopped bustling around the room and looked at them, wide-eyed.

"My Keeper," said one, addressing Atty since he had the highest title. They all dipped a little bow. "How may we serve you?"

Jori gave Kiria an almost imperceptible little wink before he stepped forward. "We smelled your cooking and couldn't resist coming down," he said, moving toward a young female baker.

"Thank you," she replied, her eyes widening.

"I've always wanted to know how you make such wonderful things. Could you show us the ovens, the mixers...?" He started to walk with her to the far end of the kitchens.

Kiria realized what he was doing. She nudged Firian, who bent down to hear her. "Take some things for us while they're distracted," she breathed into his ear.

She hoped he heard her because he didn't respond. He only stood up straight when she finished giving instructions.

"Oh yes," she chimed in, walking forward. "I want to see too."

Atty still didn't see what was so exciting about the ovens, so Kiria leaned toward him. "He'll pick up some food," she whispered. "They won't mind."

Atty mouthed "okay" and they all went back for a little tour. The kitchen staff seemed perplexed by their visit, but they were clearly proud of their work. Kiria actually learned a few things.

A few minutes later, they said goodbye, thanked everyone, and left. Kiria felt a little bad about tricking them. It was a small thing, and she knew the staff wouldn't mind—they might not even be surprised, with Jori in the group—but she still felt a pang of guilt.

When they reached the top of the steps, Firian strode away, forcing everyone else to catch up. He went straight through the garden doors and took a sharp right, hugging the exterior wall of the palace so closely that they had to squeeze past hedges. Kiria fought to keep her arm in the right position as she shuffled sideways behind the plants. They scratched her good arm lightly and she wondered if spiders lived in those bushes. She couldn't see the webs very well because the sun was going down. There was enough light to see, but not much. *Where is he going?* It seemed odd that Firian was suddenly taking control. Jori nearly skipped with excitement.

Suddenly, Firian halted beside a large window far from any door. He reached above his head, shoulders straining, and pulled himself up to see through the window. Apparently the view satisfied him, because he let himself fall lightly back to the ground. Businesslike, he began pulling things out of his pockets —bread, sweets, oranges. Kiria held out her hand to take something. She had no idea there were so many places to hide things. His shirt was form-fitting. How had he gotten anything in there?

Even Atty looked excited now as he held snacks and waited to see what Firian would do.

Again, the Tanyu reached up to the window ledge, but this time he pulled himself all the way up so he could stand on the narrow, rocky strip. He arched backward enough to survey the whole window. Then he leaned against it and started feeling each panel, reaching blindly with his fingers. Kiria heard a lower one scrape. Firian smiled and crouched down, gently pushing that panel in with both hands. It gave. Her breath caught, but he caught the top edge of it before it fell. He turned the glass panel sideways and eased it through the hole, hanging on to hand it down to Atty, who took it and set it down against the castle wall.

"Make sure you put that back," Kiria said, fascinated.

Atty agreed. "Yeah, you can't leave it open."

Firian didn't answer. He just jumped through the opening, landed on the ground, and then leaned out again. He extended his hand. They were all going through the window.

Kiria made a face. She should have expected this from the moment Firian stopped at that odd place along the wall, but she was so curious about what he was going to do that she didn't realize it meant her climbing through a window with a sling.

"The Kepress first," Firian said, stretching his hand toward her. "Help her up," he told the others.

They all handed their food to Jori. Atty laced his big fingers together to make a step. She took a deep breath and put her foot on his hands. The window wasn't very high, just enough to be inconvenient.

The thought crossed her mind that she should have worn pants today too. Dresses made it harder to climb. She reached up and took his hand. Atty lifted her foot and Firian pulled her up, squeezing her hand, so that she could rest her good elbow on the ledge.

"I'm going to lift you," Firian said, letting go of her hand, reaching down, and holding her just below her ribcage. She opened her mouth to protest, but then she realized it was the only way she could do this. Stones from the palace wall scraped her skin as he dragged her up and through the opening. She swung her legs over and landed beside him in the darkened room. He let go of her and stuck his head out to check on Jori and Atty. Her waist was probably bruised, he had held her so tightly.

Firian handed food backward to her. She had to cradle it in her arm to hold it all.

Atty appeared next, crawling through the missing pane, then Jori. Even the softest sound echoed. Kiria spun around to look. They were in the Main.

"Just like old times," Jori said, a little out of breath.

Firian smirked. "You should post a guard out there," he said.

28

FIRIAN

FIRIAN FORGOT TO put the windowpane back in after the four of them left the Main the night before. Hopefully that would teach them to put a guard outside. At least the Kepress and her friends seemed impressed by what he could do. That was the main thing. And he'd had a surprisingly fun time outsmarting the soldiers.

They left in the gray of the morning. Fog from the ocean blanketed the city in ghostly white. Cloudy shapes of buildings and, far off, the dark smudge of the city wall made Brithnem magical. He'd never seen a city look so beautiful.

As they walked silently through the mist, the cool, wet fog on his skin energized him. He finally felt alive.

Master Gerand was gone. It was just him and the princess now. His mission had truly begun. If any threat came, he was the only line of defense. No backup, no teacher, no supervisor.

Kiria rode silently by his side. He carried both of their packs since her arm still rested in a sling. Her face was hard to read, uncomplaining but unhappy. Maybe determined was the best way to describe it.

Frankly, she had disappointed him at first. On the long

journey to Brithnem, he had lain awake at night picturing his mission as dangerous and even glamorous: combating enemies with a beautiful girl at his side, who was either his or his to be won. The reality of the mission so far paled in comparison. She wasn't hideously ugly by any means, just a bit plain. But the reports of her great beauty had been bald lies, all of them. Maybe they were designed to tempt him into accepting the mission. But that was impossible. Who in their right mind would refuse an opportunity like this? Even if she had been too ugly to show her face, he still would have come.

But his original daydreams aside, last night had shown him that the attack hadn't made her timid at least. She'd kept up with the rest of them and even seemed more confident than the Keeper Atael. He appreciated that. And the men at the palace certainly seemed to care about her. Maybe it was just her position as their Kepress, but there could be something more that inspired their loyalty. He would watch for it.

She looked up at the sky, squinting so hard that her whole face looked comically angry. "How long will it take us to get there?" she asked.

"It depends on how quickly we go," he said. "It should be less than two weeks."

She pushed the hair out of her face. "I'd like to go as quickly as possible."

"We have to take care of your leg." He had already noticed her wincing when she thought he wasn't looking.

"I've always wanted to see Carradoc, and I'm sure they'll catch the threat soon."

Firian secretly hoped they wouldn't. If they caught the threat inside the palace, the Watchman would call for him and his mission would be over. He had to be useful first. "When can you take off the sling?" he asked, returning to the topic of her injuries.

"Just a few days." A smile flashed across her face. "I can't wait."

He grunted. In her place, he would feel the same way.

She pointed to the left. Through the mist, he could just make out a large, empty plaza with a statue in the middle—maybe a fountain. "That's one of my favorite places in Brithnem. I've only been there a couple times, but it's beautiful. Daelon showed me. It's a statue of my great-grandmother and the other Keepers. They look so amazing!" She strained to see better through the fog, sitting higher on her saddle.

"Maybe they'll make a statue of you," Firian said.

Her forehead wrinkled in thought. "Maybe," she conceded. It seemed she wanted to say more, but she fell quiet.

The horses' hooves clopped in the silence.

THEIR FIRST REST stop was an old Exmorei outpost. Tanyu had commandeered it after the order split into two groups: Tanyu and Amir. Made of rough, dark stones, the outpost looked a bit like a little Academy, about the size of his house in Raewhith. There were four rooms, the largest in front, kitchen beyond, and two smaller rooms across from each other on the side, where they would sleep. Beyond it grew a garden overgrown with mint and stunted strawberry plants. Enough to eat for dinner.

Firian set up the horses outside, scanning the forest for the best entry points. Even with the slitted windows, the outpost presented some problems. Master Gerand might have been wrong when she suggested this place. A skilled attacker could come through the thatched roof, and a boot could break the lock on the front door.

The fog had burned off long since, but the deep shadows kept him from seeing very far. He squinted into the forest. Some of the trees had leaves instead of needles and he heard running water nearby. Nothing else seemed to move.

Easy enough. Firian slapped his horse and went inside, where it smelled moldy. Kiria was already busy preparing the cot in one of the smaller rooms.

"I thought we'd be camping," she said as he walked in.

"Not tonight."

"So we will later." It was a question.

Of course. "We'll have to," he said.

She quirked her mouth. Was she excited or disappointed? "I've never camped before."

"It's not so bad." He smiled.

"It actually sounds kind of fun," she said, smoothing out her bedroll with her good hand.

He just nodded. She really wasn't as plain as he had first thought. His first impression—that she was far less beautiful than the reports had said—had been premature, maybe. In his surprise he hadn't noticed that she had a decent figure and bright, intelligent eyes.

"Do you need anything?" he asked. Maids always helped her, Amir taught her, Keepers probably scheduled her days. Living rough would be good for her, but it couldn't hurt to get on her good side.

"Where will you be?" she asked after a pause.

"Front room." He could observe everything that went on from there. "I have some food when you're ready."

She nodded and turned back to her cot. He had no idea what else she wanted to set up. It all looked finished to him. Maybe she expected art to appear on the walls. But she looked busy, so he left and rolled out a blanket on the wooden floor of the main room.

Soon she emerged for the food he'd mentioned. She strolled up to him, but there was a fragility to her ease, as though she were covering up her real worry. "Hello," she said, looking around for a place to sit. There wasn't one. "What did you bring?"

He gestured to the floor. "There's a garden out back," he said. She didn't understand.

"We'll eat food from there." He sat down cross-legged on the floor.

She eased herself down. It hadn't occurred to him that sitting this way might hurt her. "I think I got sunburned," she said, settling into a more comfortable position. She pressed the tip of her finger to her skin. When she lifted it up, her skin flashed white and then red.

"That's going to happen." He didn't notice burns anymore, if he still got them. He spent enough time outside to tan. Tentatively, she poked her arm again. It was just a sunburn, nothing to be upset about. "I'll get something for it in the morning," he said.

"Thank you."

He was used to getting up early anyway. Hopefully, she wouldn't sleep too long after the long day's ride. Maybe she was used to sleeping in every day. *What is a princess's schedule?* All the awkward dead space in their conversations started to grate on him. He had forgotten to be charming, too focused on the intoxication of freedom. Now that they were out of the palace, and away from Master Gerand, he should get to know her, and get her to know him as well.

In several short years, she would be a Keeper, one of the most powerful leaders in the world. And here she was at his disposal. Just the two of them, alone. He scooted closer to her.

"It doesn't look too bad," he said, touching her arm.

She flinched at his touch and her eyes hardened. "Do we still need to pick food from the garden?" she asked, matter-of-fact.

Annoyed, he bit the inside of his lip. "I have some of it here," he said, stretching backward to gather what he had collected when he was outside with the horses. He'd laid it by the kitchen area. They would supplement the strawberries and mint with bread they'd brought from the palace. It would go bad in another day anyway.

He would have to try another tactic. "Have you ever been this far from Brithnem before?" he asked, rubbing the dirt off the strawberries before handing them to her one by one.

"A couple times, yes." She spoke in a more business-like tone, taking the strawberries, but still inspecting each one. "I've been to Charäkhnem, and I took a boat to Phlaxtin once."

"What was Charäkhnem like?" There weren't many Charäkhni at the Academy. Kaori and Tesni, a girl with hair and skin the color of sand, were the only ones he knew for sure. Tiev and Shiro lived farther east.

"I mostly remember the zoo, and that the trip was kind of awful. You have to go over the Salt Fields. There's not much to see for miles and miles, but the city itself is very interesting." She balanced the strawberries carefully on her knee, not looking at him.

"The zoo?" he asked.

"Yes, Shear Ganesha has a whole collection of animals that he keeps on the palace grounds. I loved them when I was little. I used to draw them all the time." She bit into one small strawberry. Her face announced it was sour. Princesses were so delicate. "Where have you been?" she asked.

He paused. He hadn't been anywhere. "I've been training at the Academy since I was very young," he said. "That kind of focus doesn't allow for much traveling."

She eyed him. "So is this your first time away?"

"To Brithnem, yes." Hopefully she wouldn't see through him to the truth. Was it so bad that he had never traveled?

"I'm glad you got to see it," she said. "The Tanyu who come

never seem to appreciate it. They're always so stern and stoic, but the city is beautiful. They should be impressed." She got the same look in her face that she had gazing toward the statue of the Keepers they had passed on their way out.

"You love the city," he murmured, passing her another strawberry. "That's good, since you'll be in charge someday."

"Not in charge," she said, and then checked herself as though she had said too much.

"What do you mean?" he asked, edging closer. How could the Keeper of Brithnem not be in charge? He had learned their names since childhood as some of the most powerful people in the world. Even Raewhith skirted the Western Kingdom's huge domain.

The air buzzed with a secret.

She edged away. "Nothing. It doesn't matter. Yes, I'll be the Keeper someday," she said. She chewed another strawberry. This time she didn't make a face.

"What do you mean?" he insisted. "Who's in charge if it isn't you?"

"Of course I'll be in charge, and that's not your concern, Defender Kess," she said, separating them with the name, as though a Tanyu were beneath her.

"You can call me Firian."

She hummed in acknowledgement and focused on her dinner. He broke a small loaf of bread in half and handed her a piece. It wouldn't be long before he would break down her walls. The princess had her secrets on the surface, not buried deep like so many Tanyu. Warriors were hard to crack; Kiria wouldn't be. Yesterday, in the Main, he had seen her blush. And it wasn't for Jori or Atael or Daelon. It was for him.

29
——————

KIRIA

Kiria woke to the sound of irregular thumping in the other room. Her heart pounded fast and she tried to sit up. An attacker wouldn't be making so much noise, would he?

Groaning, she realized how sore her neck and back felt. It had only been one day, and already she missed her bed. Yesterday had felt like an adventure, leaving early, alone with a stranger. It helped that the Tanyu was handsome, but that also made her a little nervous for some reason. That feeling had begun to wear off by the end of the day, but then he had touched her. It was innocent enough, but he should have asked first. Part of his job was to make her feel comfortable. He, clearly, felt comfortable around her despite her title, but she wasn't sure about him.

Firian wasn't one for conversation, so she had to find some way to stay positive and energetic today. She wouldn't be away long, but even a short stint away from the palace wore on her.

The thumping continued. *What is that sound?* She eased herself up, careful with her bad arm. Rubbing the sleep out of her eyes, she came out of her room.

Firian had already packed his bedroll and set it by the door, ready to go. He stretched out in the middle of the room, shirtless, doing some kind of exercise. Balancing on the balls of his feet, he pushed off with his hands, landed, and eased his straightened body down again. It didn't look like he was exerting himself very much, although the muscles in his shoulders and back moved and strained with each motion.

When he saw her, he jumped to his feet. She realized she had been staring.

He dusted off his hands, clapping them together. "Did I wake you up?" he asked. He didn't seem very concerned.

She shrugged, looking away. The sunlight already shone through the windows, so it was probably time they left anyway.

"I didn't realize I would wake you up." He went to the door and fished out something from his pack. It was a plant. He held it out to her. "Here. I found it this morning. You can put it on your sunburn."

She had forgotten about the sunburn. Why didn't he put on a shirt? She glanced down at her arms. They weren't nearly as red today as they had been last night. "Thank you," she said as she took it from him. "I'll get ready to go." Quickly, she turned around and headed back to her room.

When she closed the door, she stared at the plant in her hand. How was she supposed to put this on her sunburn? The leaves looked too small to cover it. She might look foolish trying to get out any sap or juice. She patted her skin with it experimentally a few times. The leaves were cool, but that was all the relief the plant seemed to offer. With a fingernail, she pealed back the skin of one of the leaves, hoping to find answers. The pulp looked wet underneath, so she pressed the opened leaf to her arm instead. It left a slimy gel that actually was very soothing.

She covered the whole sunburn with the stuff and turned to the task of getting dressed to go. With Candrae and Vayci, this step was easy. They always dressed her in the morning. She had been especially grateful for them since the attack.

It took her a long time to get on her travel gear, tenderly avoiding the fresh scar on her leg and keeping her left elbow at an angle. But she refused to ask for help. Finally, she finished and came out.

Firian, now with his black shirt on, had more strawberries for her. She set her pack by his at the door and ate her breakfast standing.

"Are you going to work out every morning?" she asked between bites. "We're already riding a long way." She flexed her foot and the movement sent an ache all the way up her thigh.

He smiled. An image of Tanis flashed before her mind, self-assured, entitled, and part of her was disgusted. "I can be quieter," he said.

For some reason, she felt annoyed. "I just don't see why you need to do it at all."

"I want to protect you. And I want to be the best. I've always practiced this way."

"Aren't you already the best? Why would they send anyone else to be my bodyguard?" It struck her again how young he was. Every other Tanyu she had seen looked at least ten years older than Firian. Did they think she would be more comfortable with someone her own age? Or did the Tanyu not respect Brithnem as much as she thought?

"I am the best," he said simply.

"But you're so young."

He popped a strawberry into his mouth. "Yes, I am."

She decided to drop the conversation. His arrogance irritated her. "So, are we leaving?" she asked.

"I'll saddle the horses," he replied, heading out the door.

<hr>

SHE TOOK off her sling two days later and stretched her elbow thoughtfully, feeling for discomfort. The wounds on her shoulder and leg still felt tender, but now she could function. She packed the sling away, grateful to be rid of it.

As the day dragged on, again mostly in silence—that seemed to be Firian's natural state—her shoulder ached more and more. Maybe taking off her sling was a bad idea.

She watched the slow rocking of the horses as they picked their way over the rocks of the foothills. Dark clouds came in. She looked up and one huge raindrop fell on her face, narrowly missing her eye. She blinked the water out.

"It's starting to rain," she said. "Should we find a place to stay?"

Firian didn't respond right away. It was just the early afternoon, much earlier than they had stopped any other day. But today her arm ached, she was tired, and the sky looked ready for a downpour. She wouldn't mind settling in early.

"If that's what you would like," Firian said, slowing his horse to speak to her more easily.

"It is. Do you know of a place close by?" she said, pulling her hood over her head as the raindrops began to fall more steadily.

"I'm sure I can find something."

She pursed her lips. Firian was handy in situations like this, but even he didn't know where they could go. Getting caught in the rain at the palace was one thing; she could always go inside. Here, the elements could dominate them. She kicked her horse lightly to hurry.

Cold wind whipped through the trees, over the rocks, and across her shivering body. She held her hood together with one hand and rode with the other. The blackened sky let out a faint thunder roar.

"Do you see anything?" she asked above the sound of the wind.

"There's probably something up here," he said, pointing vaguely over a shallow ridge. The land dipped down to cliffs rising on the right.

Water began pouring down in torrents, blowing in their eyes. In seconds, she was drenched. The poor horse, soaked through, had to clop through puddles. There wasn't so much as a cabin over the ridge.

Kiria lowered her head as they kept on, the lightning getting closer. Piercing pain in her shoulder made her let go of the coat's hood. She couldn't hold on anymore. Compared to the discomfort she felt hanging on to the hood, letting her arm rest was a relief, even though rain poured freely over her head. The horse steamed as it trod through thickening mud.

Firian seemed relatively unaffected. He rode high, didn't put up his hood, and kept swinging his head to look for a place to stay. His black figure got dimmer in the darkness.

What would her mother think of this? Was this any way to keep her safe? Thunder boomed. The reminder her that she could be struck by lightning at any moment made her flinch. A few weeks ago, she wouldn't have been as afraid, but now she felt like a target, so high up on that horse with the lightning igniting the sky.

As time wore on, she started to accept the misery. The rain mixed with her running nose. Every few minutes, she slicked wet strands of mousy hair from her face so she could see. When was Firian going to stop?

Then he pointed ahead, sure of himself. Kiria's heart leapt. *Finally, finally!* She urged her horse to go faster, bobbing in the saddle. It couldn't pick up the pace, but at least there was a roof ahead.

Ahead of them, through darkening trees whose leaves spilled steady streams of water, was a shack. It hardly deserved a better name, but at that moment, she didn't care. It was tucked into a thick part of the forest, maybe a trapper's cabin. As soon as she got close enough, she heaved her way off the horse, hopping awkwardly on her bad leg. Firian ran up splashing and took the reins from her. She handed them over and ran inside, head ducked down.

She reached the doorway panting. The dry cabin was tiny but so much warmer and safer than outside. She never thought she'd be so thankful to see one drafty little room. Cold water drained from her sleeves into her hands. A puddle already pooled on the floor beneath her.

Leaning her head back out the doorway, she squeezed out her hair. Even though she was cold, she should probably take off her coat too and wring it out before she made the whole place sopping wet. She unbuttoned the front, but the wet cloth stuck to her as she tried to peel the coat off her arms.

Firian rushed in behind her with the bags and strode right into the room, his heavy black coat leaving a thick film of water leaking across the little floor.

"What are you doing?" she snapped. She hadn't meant for her tone to be so sharp.

"What?" He spun around and glared at her.

"You're getting the floor wet!"

He raised his dark eyebrows in surprise. "I hadn't noticed." And he hadn't cared either, judging from his expression.

"We're going to sleep here, right?" she asked pointedly, still struggling with her sleeve.

Firian came over and pulled her arm through. Stabbing pain shot down from her shoulder and she gasped.

Firian stepped back. "Did I do something wrong?" Barely restrained irritation showed through his voice. His eyes flashed darkly and rivulets of water ran from his hair into his face.

"My shoulder," she explained, easing carefully out of the other sleeve. "I just took the sling off today."

A tense silence filled the little space.

"I found us some shelter. You should be glad," he said, turning away from her. "We'll stay here tonight." With that, he knelt down by the packs and fished inside.

Her chest twisted angrily. She felt the retort bubbling up inside her before it came out. "Why are you so arrogant?"

He stood up more calmly than she would have expected, a flint from his pack in one hand. Taking a calculated breath, he faced her. "And why are you so entitled?"

"I'm not entitled!" she cried, shocked that he insulted her. "I just—"

"I don't control the weather. I found a place to stay, and you're complaining that I get the floor wet." His low tone almost scared her. His lip almost imperceptibly started to curl.

"It's better to keep it dry if we can," she said. She still believed that was the best way. Let him try to intimidate her. She had stood up to greater powers than he.

Her heart beat hard as he gave her a pointed look. The rain roared outside. He turned away and began to light the two torches hung just inside the door. Once they were lit, he reached past her and closed the door.

An odd relief flooded her heart as she took one side of the room and he took the other. At least they had rest now.

Deep, flickering shadows coiled over the walls. Monstrous shadows followed them whenever they moved. They reminded her that she wasn't outside in the rain, so she almost welcomed them as friends. *I'm not entitled. Right?* She shoved her hand inside her pack to feel for drier clothes. Something at the bottom didn't feel soaked. It might even be dry. *I don't expect Keeper treatment. I've been keeping up despite my injuries, and I've been traveling without using my Ability or bringing my serving girls or guards. We've barely eaten anything. And I've been in pain. How dare he accuse me of being entitled?* She started steaming again, and glared at him out of the corner of her eye. This was the first time she'd done anything like this. She hadn't trained as a warrior for years, and she was still doing pretty well. His expectations were too high.

He shook off his long coat and peeled off the shirt underneath. She turned back to her pack. He needed to learn how to act in front of a Kepress, but maybe now wasn't the time to tell him. She busied herself digging out the dry clothes at the bottom of her bag. A pair of brown pants and a shirt came out as she tugged. Her nightgown was sopping. If she didn't pull them out of the bag and lay them out, they would just stay that way, so she took out almost everything and started to lay the clothes flat. She hung a shirt on each sconce.

"You really don't like rain, do you?"

She looked back at Firian, still shirtless, who watched her with amusement in his eyes. A few of the small, white scars that laced his hands covered his strong chest.

"Put on a shirt," she said, not answering his ridiculous question. "And turn around, please. Or you can go outside. I want to dry off before I go to sleep."

"It's too early to sleep," he said, facing the wall.

She hurriedly changed into the dry clothes, watching him the entire time. When she was done, she said, "I really don't think I'm entitled. I've been doing a good job so far."

Firian turned around. "All my clothes are wet," he explained carelessly. "I'm not putting them on."

He wasn't going to obey her? "I'm a Kepress," she began.

"I know." His tone shifted from harsh to mischievous. "Do I

make you uncomfortable?" He knew exactly how good looking he was.

Heat rushed to her cheeks. And he didn't make her that uncomfortable. Why did her face have to make him think otherwise? "No," she snapped. "But when I ask you to do something..."

"I have to obey you?" He wasn't taking her seriously.

"Yes," she said coldly. She was used to people underestimating her or her mother, but it was always done in subtle ways. She could work around that, rise above it. She'd practiced for years. But this blatant disrespect was something new. A chill replaced the heat in her face. "Yes, you do. *We* hired *you*."

"To do what you couldn't do for yourself. Tanyu *earn* their respect."

"We should never have hired you!" she cried. "Our own guards could have done this. Chetana was right." Firian had seemed different at first, when he spent time with them in the Main, but he was just as egotistical as every other Tanyu she'd met. So self-assured that even Keepers didn't deserve their full attention.

His face reddened. "Wait until somebody attacks. You'll see why they called for me."

The rage of their argument subsided into the sound of the rain.

She realized she was out of breath.

His voice rose just above a whisper. "I've practiced every day for seven years. You won't question me." He was so sure that she shivered, almost afraid.

She narrowed her eyes. Defending her position meant more than defending herself. Leaders of Brithnem deserved esteem, no matter who sat on the thrones. She suddenly wished she weren't alone. "I will if you need to be questioned." She drew herself up to her full height, still not higher than his chin. "Firian," she said, leaving out his title, "whatever you think about me, I still outrank you. And you've sworn to protect me, so you'll do that without question." She set her mouth in a hard line. Her heart beat heavily in her chest.

He licked his lips, considering how to respond. After a while, he nodded, ending the discussion. But he still didn't reach for a new shirt as he laid out his bedroll as far against the opposite wall as it could go.

***

Kiria watched as Firian moved a Bird across the board.

"So that's... Overbridge?"

He smiled, his stoic face creasing. "Yes."

This was the second straight day of the downpour. It didn't make sense to try to travel in this weather, so they were stuck in the little trapper's cabin. At least, that's what Kiria had decided to call it. They both had woken up feeling frosty toward each other, but that got so boring after a while that she finally broke the silence. Indisfate had come up and he spoke as though he needed to explain what that was. So she got the brilliant idea to have him teach her. It was a matter of an hour to gather enough matching stones, leaves, and other small items to imitate an Indisfate board.

Kiria kept back her smile, pretending to struggle with her next move. She picked up a Falcon, hesitated, put it down. Taking the Man two spaces forward would throw Firian off.

His smile faded as he realized what she had done. "You learn quickly," he said, a hint of uncertainty in his tone. His eyebrows beetled. Clearly, he wasn't used to being beaten.

She burst out laughing. "I've known how to play for ages," she said. "I just wanted you to teach me."

He raised one eyebrow. "Why?"

"So I could see that look on your face. It was worth it." Her giggles subsided. Maybe all this was childish, but how else were they supposed to pass the time? "Did you grow up knowing how to play?"

He paused, looking suddenly thoughtful. "No. I learned after I got to the Academy."

She drew up her knees and hugged them to her chest. "How long have you been at the Academy? You're the youngest Tanyu I've ever seen. What are you? Eighteen?"

He tilted his head down and looked straight into her eyes. For a second, she felt uncomfortable. "I got in when I was eleven," he finally said.

"That's really young."

"Yeah." A touch of a smile passed his lips.

"What did they teach you when you first got there? Indisfate? I knew people who really wanted to get in, so they would want to know." It was all for the best that Jori and Atty didn't get invited.

"You can't tell anyone." He touched her to punctuate his point. The room felt warmer than it had though the fire was dying.

She nodded at him. She wouldn't tell.

"Everyone who gets in needs to have the Ability and strength for it," he began.

"Okay," she prompted.

"They teach you how to use the Ability to go... into the Unreal."

"That sounds fake."

He pursed his lips, indignant. "It isn't."

A crackling silence passed between them. She was only kidding. Why did he have to take everything so seriously?

He started again. "They show you how to control your Ability, how to strategize, how to kill if you need to."

"When you were eleven?" She looked down, thinking. "When I was eleven, they were teaching me geography and music and the Scroll. Killing only came up in history, not in real life. Until the Torithians attacked, of course." When she looked up, he was studying her. "So... what's the Unreal?" That actually did sound vaguely familiar. Maybe Chetana or Daelon had brought it up at some point.

"Close your eyes," he said.

"What?" She wouldn't close her eyes alone with him. He wasn't a guard. He was serious and deadly and cocksure. And they were sitting so close.

"Do it." He demonstrated, keeping his own eyes closed.

Hesitantly, she did it. "Okay."

"Now," he said soothingly, "clear your mind."

Every attempt brought up more thoughts—her mother, tomorrow's food, the new bandage she needed, where they were going—*where are we going?*

"Are you doing it?"

"I'm not sure. Where are we going next?"

"Focus."

"No, I should know where we're going." She opened her eyes. His were still closed.

"If you try this, I'll tell you," he said.

She chewed the inside of her lip for a few seconds, and then closed her eyes again. Still, thoughts bombarded her—what else was north? The mountains, Enderin, Shifra—the difficult passage in her music. Blood. Her arm had been sliced. Firian's intense eyes.

"How do I clear my mind?" she asked.

"Nothing."

"Excuse me?"

"Think of nothing."

"I can't do that."

At least she knew they were going to Shifra. The picture had always looked lovely. Green swampland with guardian trees rising from the shallow water and overshadowing the paths. Wooden walkways still crisscrossed the marsh on the way to the fortress of Carradoc. But the part that sounded so beautiful in the old stories were the lanterns. The round lanterns at the palace were meant to echo them, but the originals shone many different colors. A celebration of color, casting festival light glowing over the walkways as she walked serenely over them. Fireflies rose over the water, twinkling. The smell of the trees filled the humid air with musk. Old yet fresh. A fish splashed gently in the water as she walked by.

And almost ran into Firian. His wide eyes were glowing.

She opened her eyes. Firian was looking straight in her face, as he had done in her imagination. His breathing was excited and an enthralled smile played on the edges of his mouth. "You have the Talent!" he said.

"What?"

"You have the Talent," he repeated. "Has no one told you?"

"No..."

"Did you see me?" He grinned, happier than she had ever seen him.

She nodded. "Yes. What does that mean?"

"Could you see me clearly?"

"Pretty clear."

"How did nobody know about this?" he said, almost to himself.

She bent down to catch his eyeline. "Hey, what does this mean?"

"You can go in the Unreal. I can see you there."

She scrunched her eyebrows together. She wasn't sure she wanted him to be able to see her in her imagination. "Are you saying you can read my thoughts?" she asked, a little disgusted.

"Not exactly." He stood up, clearly still processing the new information. "I'm going to tend to the horses," he said.

"Wait! You'll explain later?" she said, standing up and dusting herself off. *What a time to go out to the horses!*

"I'll explain later." He pulled on his coat and went outside into the rain.

30

FIRIAN

FIRIAN CAST his mind back into the little cabin as he stood by the horses, the soft rain falling less torrentially than before. Kiria would appreciate that the weather was clearing up. They might be able to get in a few miles before the end of the day.

He patted his horse's flank absently. His mind hit a slight buzz, but nothing constant. It was no wonder he hadn't noticed it.

She had the Talent.

As he stood in the rain, he smiled. The Academy would love this information. But he had only left Gerand a few days ago—he had no desire to get more instructions. For now, he would keep this to himself, a juicy secret. The Academy already had plenty of those. He just had to decide what he would do with it. Would it be stupid to train her? She had power, but she wasn't part of the Academy. *What would Bard say?* He would probably say they should all be friends, and that Firian should contact the Academy for permission first. He wasn't doing that.

Kiria in the Unreal. Even though it had only been a couple days, he did already miss being surrounded by people with the Talent. Until today, she had bored him a little. Her power enticed him, but her company offered very little. With extra possibilities, the trip wouldn't feel as mundane. Besides, he could be a good teacher.

The horses had banded together under a clump of trees. They looked uncomfortable, but they weren't in need of anything. He couldn't stall any longer.

He creaked open the door to the cabin and went inside. Kiria was cleaning up the game of Indisfate, carefully storing the pieces for another day.

"So, if I have the Talent," she said without introduction, "then I can do everything you can do?"

"I suppose so," he replied. What exactly did she think he could do?

"Why couldn't you teach me?"

He looked up into her earnest eyes. The firelight from the torches glowed on her face. Even though she wasn't very pretty, there was something that was alive about her. It gave her some beauty where she had none. And Brithnem and the Academy were supposed to be allies, after all. "Of course I could teach you," he said.

She smiled, full teeth. "Good. It'll give me something to do." After a moment, her mouth twitched again in a private smile as she said, "Jori will be so jealous. Atty too. They've always wondered what you do there in the Tanyuin Academy. They're royal, so they didn't have a chance to try out for it. They had to stay in Brithnem," she explained.

"But you'll get to find out," Firian said.

Kiria looked at Firian warmly, as though they were co-conspirators. Apparently she didn't mind his arrogance so much now. This felt more like it did back at the palace. Part of her loved adventure, and he would feed that side.

"Let's start," she said. "As long as you can be civil. I don't have to do anything I don't want to."

He sucked his teeth and reminded himself that this was a princess. If he indulged her, good things might happen. He'd had to do that with other girls he'd been with. It was worth it in the short term. "Okay," he said. "Sit down." There were no chairs, so they sat across from each other as they had while they played the game. "Close your eyes," he told her. That was the way that Belik always started his lessons. "The way it works—" He paused. It felt illegal to teach the inner workings of the Academy to an outsider. "Swear you won't tell anyone what I'm teaching you," he said abruptly.

Her eyes popped open, one eyebrow lifted. "Sure," she said, looking amused at how serious he was.

"Swear."

She twisted her lips to the side, but consented. "I swear."

"Good. Now close your eyes. Now think of nothing."

"I still have no idea what you mean by that," she said.

"Just don't think—no color, an empty space..." he chanted, hoping this was worthwhile after all. In his mind, he pictured Bard as vividly as he could: small, tan skin, black eyes, wild black hair, concerned expression, quick smile... "Tell me when you see something," he said.

The quiet stretched for such a long time that he wondered if she would ever see it. Maybe this whole thing was a waste of time.

Finally, "There's a person," she said slowly.

A chill ran through him. She did have it. "Good. Describe him for me," he said.

"He's... he's... wait, he's getting clearer. I don't think I know him. He looks like he sees something but it worries him. Short black hair. He's wearing all black, too. Is he a Tanyu?" she said.

The success was so heady it surprised him. "That's right," he said. "That's... someone I know from the Academy."

"He looks nice," she stated, as though that defied expectation.

He ignored her comment. "That's the basic idea behind using the Talent. That's what starts everything. That way you can see what I see. Later, we can both visualize into the same place. Does that make sense?"

"I didn't realize it was so simple."

"All right, now you picture something and I'll tell you what it is. It works both ways. Make sure I've never seen it before," he added.

Instantly, he could see a domed room made of sandstone, the edges segmented into cages. Only pieces of it appeared at one time. He had to swing around to catch the details, which came into focus piecemeal. A bird squawked loudly from somewhere. Behind one set of bars, a cat-like creature about knee-high with a long nose and dusty stripes bared its teeth at him. *The zoo in Charäkhnem.*

"Ambitious for a first try!" he said. "It's the zoo. There's a cat and a bird."

The vision disappeared, so he assumed she had opened her eyes again. He quickly tried to sense any other minds that might be near their cabin but all was quiet. He couldn't let his guard down completely for this.

Back in the real world, he looked back at her and smiled. Belik's excitement over Firian's victories made more sense now. It was easier to see why he hungered for Firian's success, through any means possible. Looking at Kiria, he knew how Belik felt.

Kiria smiled back, glowing with pride. "That's what I was picturing!" she said.

"I know, I know." Automatically, he reached out to touch her, but pulled his hand back. "You'll get better at picturing different things, and seeing what I see."

"That's amazing..." She looked off to the side, musing. "But how does any of that help you be a warrior?"

"Watch this. Picture it again."

He dove back into the zoo scene, focusing specifically on the desert cat. Its slender tail balanced behind it as it walked forward to the bars. Triangular ears perked toward him. He filled in detail: velvety texture, glint of wetness in the black eyes, small paws slicked wet by licking. Reaching his hand into the cage, he caught the creature's attention. It regarded him warily before striking with sharp teeth that sank into his finger. He hissed and drew his hand back.

Swimming back to reality's surface, he held his hand out to Kiria. Blood dripped from the finger. "All it takes is belief."

She creased her forehead in surprise, staring at the blood.

He smirked at her concern. "There are lots of different ways to hurt somebody," he said. Maybe that's where he should draw the line with her. She didn't need to know how to fight. "But there's no time to go over all of those today. The rain is letting up, so we should pack up to leave soon."

"That was a short lesson," she said, catching onto his evasiveness. She didn't move from her position on the floor.

"Have to leave you wanting more," he replied, getting to his feet. Bending over her, he gave her another smile, hoping that would be enough. Honestly, he wanted more too. He wanted to see how her mind worked. And there would be time for that, he reminded himself.

THEY ONLY GOT a couple hours of riding in that day. The paths were mucky with sludge and the rocks were too slick for the horses to get over easily. They were getting close to the most treacherous part of the journey, going through the mountains.

Firian remembered the passes that he had taken to get to Brith-nem, and didn't look forward to traversing them with someone unused to travel.

Kiria skipped out of the little shack, glad to be free. Almost immediately she said something about the ground smelling like artichokes. No one he knew talked like that, but he supposed she was right.

The next stop was a cave carved into the mountainside, as close as they could get without actually beginning to go over. Night fell as they went inside with the horses. The cave was big enough to house all four of them. Sounds echoed loudly, but Firian knew that the cave didn't go very far back. No enemies could attack from inside. It was a dry, strategic position where they could even build a fire without fear. Firian went to work on that immediately, gathering kindling from just outside the mouth of the cave. The larger sticks were still wet from the rain, but some smaller pieces of leaves and brush had dried.

Kiria dismounted and patted her horse gently on the face, happy for it. She whispered something to it. Probably its name. He had never considered names for the horses.

As he brought the brush back inside, Kiria laid out her bedroll. Even a few hours of riding had tired her out, apparently. Firian didn't mind. If she slept, it gave him more time to think. Their argument the day before still strained their conversations. The two of them would get along until something small turned the ankle of the discussion and brought it falling on its face. The simplest things offended her, but when she wasn't acting like a princess, she was all right. At least she tried to keep up with him and didn't complain very much.

He watched her out of the corner of his eye as he bent over the small pile of kindling, coaxing sparks out of the flint with his knife. She sat cross-legged on the bedroll, eating some rations. At times, her gaze flickered back at him.

He didn't want to give her another lesson today. He'd just stand watch over the cave most of the night, considering what to do. Little sleep didn't bother him at all.

Another few moments and she lay down to sleep, curled up, facing away from him. The trip must have exhausted her, because her breathing became deep and steady before he needed to add larger twigs to his little fire.

There wasn't much to see from the wide mouth of the cave. Even the rising moon was blocked by the mountain behind them. A blackened mass of trees was the only scenery. He turned back to Kiria's sleeping form, peaceful and innocently sensual there. Her shoulder sloped down to her waist and back up to her hip. At that moment, peace and restlessness wrestled in his chest. He missed the comfort and certainty of the Academy but he wanted to be here, the princess's sole protector. Despite her insults, she must trust him.

He worked his jaw. What was she dreaming about? He'd never gone into anyone's dreams before—well, once, for an assignment. But even Bard's colorful dreams had never interested him. He figured that if they sent him to war and he had to intimidate someone as part of a fear campaign, it wouldn't be that difficult. People's subconscious intersected with the Unreal in dreams, so even people who didn't have the Talent could potentially be vulnerable.

The temptation of the Unreal pulled at his brain like a caught thread. Maybe it wouldn't be interesting. But it would be something.

He nudged his mind in her direction. Right away he saw a section of Mon Párinath. Deeply carved double doors of dark wood stood at the end of a hall lined with exotic potted trees and a mosaic floor. Two young women stood talking by the large doors. One had a parchment clutched in her hand but she faded in an instant. The other drew his gaze and kept it prisoner.

She was the most beautiful woman he had ever seen. Her hair fell long and full on her smoothly glowing skin. The floor-length blue dress fit her perfectly, its golden edges almost necessary to adorn her strong curves. Power spoke in her features—large, focused eyes, graceful hands, a mouth that could speak truth. Truth so piercing and final that it could shatter him.

Pleasure ran through him at the thought. Who was this goddess? To hold her would surpass any petty relationship he'd had. All of them looked as hollow as eggshells now.

Oddly, the gorgeous woman moved in a familiar way, although he would remember meeting anyone who looked like that. She was beautiful in a way that women never were, or maybe never had been. Her form made him ache, but even her *soul* was beautiful. He realized he was breathing fast as he watched her talk with that other girl.

The beauty turned toward him before vanishing. A stab of recognition shot through him. As he opened his eyes, he felt winded.

Kiria? Kiria can look like that? The vision seemed like too much to imagine casually. Did women imagine themselves as devastatingly brilliant in their dreams? His chest still constricted painfully at the memory. He had never wanted anything so much, except his position at the Academy, and at this moment, even that seemed on par.

He stared fiercely at Kiria's back. It couldn't be. He'd seen a vision, just a tantalizing vision. But he couldn't go back to seeing her the same way. If that divinely attractive woman in any way reflected Kiria, he would dig that part out of her. She would share it with him.

THE NIGHT PASSED SLOWLY. Firian hardly slept, even when the

fire burned out. He'd always liked the cold, so he intentionally felt the breeze flow over him. Cold had the power to harden, to break. Heat tended to weaken.

He flexed his hands in the darkness, open and closed. He couldn't get the vision out of his mind. Maya waited for him back at the Academy—or at least she would come back to him when he returned—but she, despite her figure and her fierceness, didn't shine out like the negative image of Kiria burned into his brain.

A couple times he almost woke her, but he resisted, proud of his resolve.

As the morning sun leaked into the bare cave, she rolled onto her back. His heart gave a hard beat. She threw her arm over her eyes like Bard used to do and groaned.

"It's time to get moving," he said, surprising himself. He rarely spoke first in the morning. But now that he had her attention, he continued. "We have to get over the mountains today if we can." He almost leapt to his feet. Despite not sleeping, he didn't feel tired at all.

She brought her eyebrows together skeptically as she peeked above her arm. "We're going over the mountains in one day?" she asked, her voice husky with sleep.

"If we can," he repeated, cleaning up the fire and getting rid of its traces. He moved quickly, rushing from that to the horses, where he began to heave the saddles onto their backs.

Resigned, she grabbed her knees and sat up.

He carefully watched her stand and slowly repack her bag. Compared to the stunning woman, she moved heavily, clumsily. Her hair wasn't as thick or rich. It hung limply around her face. She wasn't ugly, but she was another eggshell person. He had to have imagined it. There was no way Kiria could have been the woman in the vision.

As soon as the horses were saddled, he jogged over and grabbed her pack.

"Thank you," she murmured, yawning. "You seem like you're in a good mood."

He tilted his head back and forth.

"I can't believe I slept so well. Did you watch all night? Did anybody come?" She looked at him with trust in her eyes.

Maybe a glimpse of the beautiful woman shone there, like sunlight on a flipped coin. Enough to give him hope. "Nobody came. There aren't many people around here," he said.

"I'm glad we're going through the mountains, then," she replied, passing him on the way to her horse. She worked her fingers through the knots in her hair. Her face showed that she wasn't used to wearing the same clothes multiple days in a row. Now she knew better than to mention it, though.

He handed her some dried fruit for breakfast. Their store had gotten a little slimy in the rain, but they couldn't be picky. Soon enough—nine days or so—they would be in Carradoc and get new food. He fished through the pack for his helping and realized their rations wouldn't last that long, not with two people. Only lone hunters and meager tribes lived in the mountains themselves. If they cut straight north instead of northeast, they could shave off a day and restock their food supplies in Raewhith.

The thought stopped him short. He hadn't seen Raewhith since he was a boy. On the bright side, no one there would recognize him as a grown man. He swallowed. *Not even my family.* They were all gone.

Now was not the time to feel sentimental. They had to go to Raewhith to replenish their food, and then they would cut east to Shifra from there. They wouldn't lose more than two days. The leaders at Brithnem seemed a little jumpy, so he would let them know about the change of plan when they got closer.

"Have you heard anything from the Watchman?" Kiria asked, nibbling on the fruit and struggling not to let disgust show on her face.

"Not yet." In fact, he'd almost completely forgotten about him. Besides a cursory check at sunrise and sunset, per their agreement, he didn't waste a thought on him. And he didn't check in last night.

How could he say what he'd seen in her dream? He looked for a way to bring it up and nothing sounded right. "Kiria, you did a good job yesterday," he said finally. Using names usually brought good results. "I'm amazed you haven't used the Talent before."

She smiled at the compliment. Her horse stamped the ground beside her. "I didn't even know I had it. It's crazy that I can do that. I thought everybody imagined things," she said, running her hand over the saddle. "You should give me another lesson today. The last one was terrible."

"What? Terrible?" *What does she mean by that?*

"It was too short."

"Oh." He leaned just a little closer, trying to hide his smirk. "You want *more* of my lessons?"

"Not like that," she said, waving him away. "It's just interesting. I want to know more about what you do."

"The Amir never told you?" he asked because they both knew the answer.

"No," she said pointedly, finishing her tiny portion and getting up on her horse.

He felt the conversation fizzle to a stop. That wasn't good. He had to know—was she or was she not the gorgeous girl in her vision? He stalled. "You know, I heard... before I came down to Brithnem... that you were very beautiful," he said, hating that he sounded unsure.

She looked at him sideways, as though reading his thoughts,

almost accusingly. Even without answering, she confirmed it. A pleasurable chill ran through his body. "We decided that I wouldn't use my Ability on this trip," she said. "It would just draw attention, so it's better that I stay this way."

He fought to keep the excitement out of his voice. "But you have the Ability to change?"

"Yes." She raised the end of the word in a question and note of caution. "But I'm not going to. Why are you suddenly so interested?"

Watching her dreams sounded creepy, so he couldn't tell her the real story. "I just thought I should know. That information is important. If I'm going to keep track of you, I need to know all the ways you can look." As the words came out, he realized how stupid they sounded.

"Really?" She raised her eyebrows and looked like she knew exactly what he really wanted. "It doesn't just happen on its own."

The memory of her Beauty burned inside him like rage. He mounted his horse to see her at eye level. "I think you should show me. The whole Kingdom has seen you that way."

"I don't want to," she said quietly but firmly.

"I'm not going to do anything to you," he said, moving his horse parallel to hers.

Still she shook her head.

The absurdity of it all hit him then. "Why do you hide these things about yourself? You're beautiful and you don't show it. You're the heir to a kingdom and you act like you have no power. You have the Talent and didn't even know. It's ridiculous! You've been given everything, and you act like it's nothing!" He realized he was standing high on the stirrups, his stomach knotted in frustration.

She blinked fast but didn't recoil.

"I came from nothing and I worked. Harder than anybody

else. I practice—I still practice!" He swept his arm over where she had slept. "I've given up sleep and comfort to be here. You sit there like a princess, expecting everything. What have you done to earn this? And why do you act like you have nothing?" The silence surged in like noise after his words. He exhaled the breath he'd been holding tight in his chest.

Kiria flushed bright red and her eyes glistened, but she didn't bite back, as though she feared the words that would come out. Something fierce lay coiled behind her expression.

His throat constricted uncomfortably. He had told the truth, but he'd ruined his chances with her. Certainly today, maybe for a very long time. What was he thinking?

She opened her mouth to speak, tasting the words beforehand. "You will not speak to me until I speak to you," she said, each word deliberate and distinct. She held up a hand as though he were about to protest. "No. You will do your job, and that is all. One day you will regret speaking to me as you just have. You have no right. I forgave you the first time, but this proves that you think yourself above an heir of Brithnem, and I will not tolerate that." With a finger, she gestured that they should begin riding.

Firian's mouth tasted like bile, but every word he had said to this girl was true. He bit his tongue until it bled, almost unaware of the pain, or thankful for it. The horses clearly felt the tension and tossed their heads uneasily, taking more than once to get over obstacles. The frustration cooled his bones, running like iron through his veins.

He had no words to speak. That should please her.

31
____

KIRIA

Gray light, just enough to see by, streamed into the outpost. Kiria grated her eyes open. The tension between her and Firian these past two days had made her jumpy and anxious. Every noise sounded like an enemy. All news was bad news. Anger radiated like heat off Firian even as he rode.

Alone with her thoughts, she listened as Firian's words hurdled down familiar tracks in her mind. He never should have said those things. The memory made her so angry she could cry. Tanyu would see that as weakness, though, so she swallowed tears down into bitterness. *You act like you have nothing.* He'd spat the words, so angry that she was given everything *he* wanted. That she wanted the same things, but she got them without working as hard. His arrogance made more sense now, but she couldn't excuse it.

The small, round outpost had two floors, so she had taken the second and he the first. Quiet thuds rose up from the first floor. He was practicing again, doing some kind of exercise.

She closed her eyes. If not for hunger, she doubted she would ever go downstairs. If only Jori or her mother could be here. Firian didn't scare her as much as he should, she realized.

He could hurt her easily if he wanted to. If he did, though, the Keepers would kill him. She had absolutely no doubt.

Why do you act like you have no power?

She chewed her lip. That line had grown on her mind. Easing herself up, she looked around the little circular room. Wooden floors, stone walls, two embrasures in place of windows. And a staircase leading down. Firian was arrogant and wrong about a lot of things, but something about that line hit her strangely. Maybe it was true. What had she done with all her power? As a child, she anticipated being the Keeper, but she lost that fire when she grew up. It had all happened so slowly. Before Atty's coronation, she had done everything she could to forget she was an heir at all. There would always be time... and then there wasn't.

She winced as she stood up on her bad leg. Her back ached in a dozen places and a crick twinged in her neck. Traveling wasn't very fun, but she would be tougher at the end of it. And she was starting to realize that that's what she wanted. A Keeper shouldn't be soft. She should be able to battle injustice, weather storms, mete out wisdom, rise as a symbol of hope for a nation, never to be crushed.

From now on, if Firian was awake, so was she.

She stood up and stretched. Her bouts of anxiety wouldn't keep her from becoming the Keeper she dreamed of being. During these in-between hours she could practice visualizing things in the Unreal, exercise like Firian did, quote the Scroll to keep it fresh in her mind, or start thinking seriously about what she wanted to change about Brithnem when she was its leader. Darkness provided plenty of opportunity.

But it was still early, and her limbs felt tired. If she went downstairs, she couldn't sit and relax, not with Firian watching.

It's good for me. This is good for me, she told herself. Hopefully that was true.

Slowly, she packed her bedroll and slung it over her shoulder as she headed down the stairs. Firian sat on the ground doing sit-ups, covered in a light sheen of sweat. Small scars shone white on the ridges of his abs.

When she came in, he didn't stop. They just gave each other a piercing look. Firian's eyes flashed with suspicion but not anger. His dark eyebrows came together and his concentration redoubled. Maybe the icy attitude had thawed a little on both sides overnight.

She slumped her pack by the door next to his. Automatically, she checked her hands. Still plain.

A little self-conscious, she sat on the floor and began to stretch her bad leg. Her movement was so much easier than his, but it was all she could manage at this hour. She leaned down and reached for her outstretched foot. Ignoring Firian, she closed her eyes. Dark sleep surged near her like the tide. That wasn't going to work. She needed something else to keep her awake. Under her breath, she murmured a passage of the Sacred Scroll that Daelon had made her memorize years ago. It was a long passage, so that should keep her focused for a while. Her lips formed the words as she felt the stretch burn up her calf to her thigh. *Careful.* The last thing she wanted was to reopen that scab-covered wound. She switched to the other leg, wrapping her hand around that foot. This actually felt good. Maybe waking up so early wouldn't be terrible.

A small shuffle meant that Firian was on his feet. She opened her eyes and saw him nibble on one of their rations. He had been taking less. Probably thought she didn't notice.

He looked down at her and held up the piece of hardtack in a question. She shrugged and nodded. He had to reach past her to get a new piece out of his bag. He smelled like musk and pine.

After he handed her the food, she said, "We don't need to leave right away."

He raised his eyebrows. She had broken the endless silence.

"I just figured that as long as you were awake, I should be up." The first bite of hardtack dried out her mouth. She kept chewing, trying to moisten the crumbs, but she had no saliva. "Are we getting close to Shifra?" she asked, clearing her throat.

Firian searched her face. "Five more days. We'll need to stop for food."

"Where?"

"Raewhith. It's a little town just north." He pointed vaguely without looking.

She hadn't heard of it. It must not be big enough to merit a place on the palace maps. Still, speaking to him without antagonism was a relief. Neither apologized, but they had moved on. "I thought we might run out," she said, swallowing the dry crumbs.

He grunted. "The rain took out half the supply."

She pursed her lips. *Shouldn't he have known to plan better?* He reached past her again to get his black shirt and stretch it over his head.

She sat, considering him. "I was thinking," she said, "shouldn't I know more about defending myself? Maybe you could show me a couple things."

She flushed, suddenly angry with herself. Firian made her uncomfortable. Did she really want him teaching her self-defense? If only she could ask someone else, but they were alone, and the Torithians still targeted her. What if Firian couldn't manage on his own? She had to know *something*. Daelon's image flashed through her mind, knowledgeable and gentle. Not the sort to teach her anything but disembodied warfare tactics. And her mother never prioritized safety as highly as she should.

"I know the emergency procedures in the palace if something goes wrong," she added quickly, "but that mostly involves hiding in safe rooms. I didn't know what to do when..." Her voice and gaze drifted off to her wounds. She hadn't meant to bring those up.

"You know I can take care of you," Firian said in typical fashion, offering his hand to pull her up.

Kiria almost rolled her eyes. She got up by herself. "Don't be like that. You know what I mean. I would feel better knowing that I could do something if anything... were to happen again. Honestly, I'm a little surprised something didn't happen earlier." The more she'd thought about it—and the attack had consumed her thoughts these past couple days—the more surprising it seemed.

"What do you mean?"

She lowered her voice, as though others stood in the next room with their ears cocked. "It wouldn't be hard to besiege the city if they came in with enough troops."

Firian blinked once, his only sign of surprise.

"Tell them when the sun comes up," she said. The Watchman would relay all her updates to the Keepers. They might all know that a siege posed a great threat, but then, if they did, no one had told her.

"Sure," said Firian, glancing at the gray light rimming the door. Dawn would come soon. The cold breath of air ushering through the room announced it. "And I can show you a couple moves." He took another bite of his dry breakfast.

She waited. He didn't move. "Why don't you show me now?" she asked, pleased that he could see she didn't mean to sit around as he served her. He hadn't done a great job of that anyway.

He shoved the rest of the hardtack in his mouth and wiped the crumbs off his hands. She smirked as he kept chewing the dry biscuit.

"Main thing is mindset," he managed through the crumbs. Irritation showed through his face, but his full mouth just made it funny. She held back a laugh. He swallowed half of what filled his mouth and tried again. "The main thing is mindset. Always be aware. Always look people in the eye."

She nodded. "Okay."

"Now, if someone comes up to attack you, there are a lot of options." He held up a hand to number his points. "You can run, get away. You can hide. You can fight back."

"How do I fight back?" Not a lot she could do against a flying arrow, but maybe she could take out an attacker close by.

"There are many ways to kill a man—"

"I don't want to kill him."

A smile played on the corners of his mouth. "What if you have to?"

"I just want to hurt him."

"You might have to kill him."

"Just show me how to stop someone."

He actually smiled at that. She squinted at him. It didn't look like a bitter smile. Was he mocking her? "Okay. I'll show you how to stop someone," he said. "There are many ways to *stop* a person. You want to focus on a couple areas, if you can. Everyone has weak points, so exploit those." He paused fractionally, maybe remembering her angry speech. "The eyes, the throat, the groin. Use anything you can to strike those. Just one should make anyone stop."

"I just punch him in the throat?" It sounded too easy.

"Or scratch his eyes. Knee him in the balls. Whatever you can," he said almost lazily.

"What if they have a knife?" A thousand scenarios floated up in her mind. What if her arms were pinned to her sides? What if two people came at her at once?

"The sun's rising," he said, turning away.

"Wait! Pretend to attack me." She needed to get at least some sense of what he was saying.

He shook his head. "Pretend to attack you? You don't want me to do that." He didn't say it out of fear. It was as though he knew that, if he did, she would get angry again. And their relationship was just starting to be bearable again.

"Here, just be careful," she said, spreading her feet to brace herself.

Before she could get out of the way, his hands shot forward and grabbed her wrists. He twisted her arms behind her back and turned her around, pinning her against the wall with his body. She felt his breath by her ear. "What would you do?" he asked.

Her insides squirmed. With a heave, she pushed back against him and he let her go. She rounded on him. "I'd... kick you where it hurts!" she said fiercely. He was right. She was fuming, and smelled faintly like pine.

"That's what you should do," he said, crossing his arms, smiling, "but I thought you wouldn't hurt me. For a real attacker, just act. Don't think. You have too much sympathy."

"At least I have some."

He paused, his smile fading. "I need to check in with the Watchman," he said, turning away briefly.

The door outside beckoned. She would rather be with the horses than with Firian right now. But she needed not to put herself in any danger, for her family's sake and for Brithnem's. Her sense of helplessness returned. Back in the palace, she could be independent, but this journey locked her in a cage, tethered to someone she didn't even like.

Happily, Firian's silent update didn't take long. The way he returned showed her that the Torithian threat still lurked in the palace and that they still had to continue. "Ready?" she asked, impatient.

"Let's go."

Outside, the horses were already saddled. Kiria didn't relish the idea of waking up even earlier, but she would if it meant matching Firian's dedication. *Eyes, throat, groin.* She could remember that. Maybe tonight she would suggest playing Indisfate instead of a lesson. She could beat him at that. Teach him not to be so cocky.

"Today," Firian announced as Kiria swept Indisfate pieces into her pack, "we'll see if you can imagine an environment that we can both be in. This can be a little difficult at first, because you have to hold the place together enough for the other to move around in it. Understand?"

She picked the hay out of the handful of rocks and pinecones that served as game pieces. Beating him at the game had put Kiria in a better mood, and he seemed glad to move on to something he knew better. "Do you want it to be any place in particular?" she asked.

"Someplace familiar is all right," he replied. "Later you can create new places, so you don't have to use memories, but it's easier if you can remember something. Just plant something unfamiliar in it—an object or a different color—so you can remind yourself it isn't real."

She nodded, trying to come up with a place. Coming up with anything besides the palace proved difficult. She missed it. Grime covered the abandoned barn where they sat, but the space was warm. She couldn't wait to return to her clean bed. But at least she had beaten Firian at something.

She could picture the arena. Statues and rows of seats rose above her. Gold burned brightly in the sunlight. She stood on hard-packed sand in the shade of the magnificent figures. The smell of the dusty barn filled her nose, and straw ends poked into her legs as she sat cross-legged on the ground. *No, it smells like hot sand and a breeze. The sun hurts my eyes.* It took a few minutes for the shelter to fade away completely and for the arena to take hard-edged shape. Once the setting stabilized, she looked around for Firian. Turning around, she found herself face to face with him.

She jumped and the image wavered. Elements vanished.

"Get it back," he said patiently and leaned back against the statue of Shane Calthwaite. He watched her, smiling slightly as she struggled to restore the image.

The arena materialized around her, complete again. "There."

"Very good," he said. "Now talk to me. You have to get used to interacting in this space. It has to be second nature."

The statue wobbled. She forced it back. "What should I talk about?"

"It doesn't matter. Just look at me and talk."

She eyed him, clear-cut in the arena. He aggravated her, but being friendly and showing some goodwill might go a long way. "Where are you from?"

He chewed his lip before answering. Always so secretive. "Raewhith," he said.

His answer sent the soaring risers to dust. "The town where we're headed?" A few seconds later the background returned.

He nodded, scratching the back of his neck.

"Is that why we're going there?" she asked.

"No. No, we just need supplies. I wasn't lying about that."

"Is your family still there?" Firian acted so independent that it was almost hard to picture him with a family.

At her question, his thoughts became so loud that her vision darkened again, oppressed by an almost audible buzzing. "No," he said.

"Where are they now?"

He picked at the foot of the statue with his fingernail.

"They're dead." His voice was small, matter-of-fact, but he didn't meet her eye.

She gasped. "I'm so sorry! I didn't know... What happened?"

"There was a fire." The two of them now stood in darkness with only the statues rising behind them. Firian's gaze flickered up to her. "Get it back," he said again, waiting.

She struggled to put the arena together again. *Why did I choose something so complicated?* The last seats, the blue of the sky, the expanse of sand, all settled into place. Firian waited for her, lost in thought. She saw Atty in his eyes. "I'm sure they'd be proud of you," she said gently.

He scoffed. An honest reaction, unedited.

"No, really," she said. There was no sense in bringing up his shortcomings now. Surely his family would be impressed by his accomplishments. "You come from a little town and now you're a Tanyu. That's impressive. Look what you taught me." She cast her eyes around the arena she loved so well.

He tipped his mouth, weighing her words.

"You could do so much good with what you have! I'm sure they'd be happy with that."

"They were never happy with me." He whispered the words almost to himself as though he couldn't hold them in. After they escaped, his face darkened.

Something twisted in her gut. Firian was usually all callous bravado, trying to cultivate a sense of mystery. But here was the truth, the pain that lay beneath. She didn't know what to say. "Well, look where you are now," she tried.

He looked up from the sand at his feet and gazed at her steadily, seriously, as though trying to find meaning in her face. He read her features like a scroll, scrutinizing them for signs of deception. His brow furrowed in concentration. To speak now would mean breaking his trust in this moment of vulnerability, but she felt uncomfortable. Maybe he wouldn't find the meaning he wanted.

His gaze dropped. A sarcastic smile spread over his face. "It's true. They never expected this."

"Did you?"

"What?"

"Did you expect this?"

He considered for a moment. "Yes, I did. I knew I could make it happen." There wasn't as much arrogance in this statement as she was used to. He just stated the truth as he saw it. Coming back to the present, he shook himself and changed the subject. "You keep talking about doing good. What will you do when you're the Keeper? Keep looking at me."

That's right—we're still practicing. "I used to think a lot about it," she confessed. "Anybody who's going to be put in that kind of position should think about it very seriously, I think. I would... Well, I've thought about making more copies of the Scroll so they wouldn't be confined to the Amiran Academy. I'm trying to work out how to improve our defenses and our alliances." She tried to gauge Firian's reaction so far. He took it all stoically. She continued, remembering some of the notes she had years ago, along with ideas she'd had just before the attack. "Some of the roads are very bad, so I'd fix those. Relations between Kingdom and Khelê are strained in some places, so I'd do my best to make peace between those groups. And there ought to be more beautiful statues and paintings because it's good to remember heroes and appreciate what we have. People will protect something they love. Those are some of my ideas." They sounded too simple when she stated them in a row like that, but many nights of thought had brought her to those conclusions. It had been a while since anyone had asked.

"That's not a bad beginning," Firian said thoughtfully.

"Beginning?" she asked. "What would *you* do?"

He just smiled.

Her own laugh surprised her. To feel comfortable enough to laugh was a relief. It made her burst out laughing harder. "What do you mean that it's not a bad beginning?" she said.

"You think too small," he said, clearly glad that they weren't talking about his past anymore. This topic made him stand taller, look bigger. She got the sense that he was flexing his arms. "You only live one time. You get *one* shot. Is that what you're going to do with it? Or do you have the courage to do what isn't safe?"

She fell through his words into a vision of herself, beautiful and admired, victoriously bringing peace, well-being, and the knowledge of God to every person in Brithnem, now celebrated as the center of all culture and learning, and as the home of the world's best warriors. Wise and well loved, her life was filled with romance and adventure. She, alone, overturned expectations by bringing wars to an end. Strong in mind and body, she made bold decisions, saving her people and enlightening the other Keepers.

The vision was vague but powerful, like strong perfume. Uneasy, she shook it off.

He looked expectantly at her.

"You didn't answer my question," she said.

"You're right. I didn't," he agreed. "Your plans aren't bad, but I prefer action to words. Maybe I'll show you someday."

She rolled her eyes. "Stop trying to be mysterious."

"I'm being honest," he replied. It seemed like he used honesty, rather than being an honest person. A moment ago, she had seen through the veneer, but it was back.

"Still, I'd like to know what you'd do," she said. "You won't ever control the Kingdom, so it's best to tell me now so I can be impressed." She quirked her mouth in a smile. "If your ideas are good enough, maybe I'll do something about them."

She stood tall, squaring her shoulders. "It's a rare opportunity."

"I prefer the surprise," he said, mouth lifting in a smirk.

"Well, you're not going—"

A soft scuffling noise bled through the Unreal. Firian's image popped like a bubble as he went back to reality. Kiria froze, her breath hitched in sudden terror. *They found me.* The arena disappeared completely until all she saw was the back of her eyelids. She focused all her energy on hearing until the barn seemed loud in the silence. The hair that had fallen in front of her ears rubbed together like dry straw, a tree creaked outside, a breeze hissed through the barn slats, bringing the pattering of blown hay with it. Firian's quick, gentle footsteps echoed. She curled further into herself, braced for what would come.

Firian laughed.

Her eyes sprang open. She didn't hear that sound often. Firian stood in the middle of the shadowy barn and pointed to the corner. A brown cat arched its back to slink through a gap below the boards. Its soft tail darted out behind it.

She exhaled. *Only a cat.* After a few more heavy breaths of relief, she grinned and put her hand over her face. She peered at Firian through her spread fingers. "It's a good thing you were here," she said.

He popped his dark eyebrows up in mock agreement. "That cat would have gotten you otherwise."

32

———

FIRIAN

FIRIAN'S MUSCLES strained as he pushed himself up. Power flowed through his arms, his back, his shoulders pinching together. Riding horses only worked out a couple muscles and left him feeling sore but not strong. The morning routine he'd had back at the Academy made him feel more like himself.

In the middle of the barn floor, Kiria rolled over and sat up, woozy from sleep. She leaned over her knees in an easy motion that reminded him of the grace he'd seen in her glorious dream. Though he might want to, he couldn't forget the burning beauty he'd witnessed. If he forced her to show him, though, he would only gain an enemy. The greater challenge was winning her trust and inspiring her to become beautiful of her own free will. And he never shied away from the greater challenge.

Eyes half-mast, Kiria struggled to sit cross-legged. She worked both hands through her long hair and muttered something to herself. Maybe she was praying. She did that sometimes.

He eased himself up slowly, precisely, to his feet.

"Good morning," she murmured.

Half his mouth lifted. "Morning," he said. She was like Bard, in love with sleep, and yet she woke up early every morning since she had committed to keeping pace with him. And her training in the Unreal was going well, as far as he could tell. At least she progressed fairly quickly. Her ideas were naïve, but she had a streak of independent thought. All her criticism at the beginning left a bad taste in his mouth, but he could learn a lot about Brithnem from her. Sometimes she surprised him with her knowledge of large-scale warfare. She didn't talk about it often, but there was an ease that made him want to lean in close. His training had been almost exclusively on individual tactics—the work of a person, not an army. But what kind of warrior was he if he didn't understand as much as she did about clashing nations?

Her head hung low, weighed down with sleep. Tangles of mousy brown hair fell into her lap. Her lips continued to move in some kind of plea or recitation. He got out a water skin and sat across from her. When he thrust it into her hands, she started and looked up, straining to see through the dimness. Blinking, she took a drink.

"Lessons this morning?" he asked.

She looked at the ground, thinking. "Just don't..." she began, but her thought trailed off.

He knew what she was thinking. As much as she liked his lessons in the Unreal, she'd gotten angry when he showed her basic self-defense, as though he should have gone easy on her. That's not how self-defense worked. Enemies wouldn't match their strength to hers. It was best for her to learn that right away. And besides, he liked the feel of her body against his. Maybe she did too.

Yes, he would prefer to teach physical than mental self-defense today. Yesterday, he had revealed too much about himself. Hardly anyone knew those things. Frankly, though, she was a good person to tell. His confession made her soften toward him, yet she didn't patronize him.

"I don't think there's enough time," she said in a husky voice, looking at the dusty light beginning to stream in. It was still ghostly gray, but she was right. He had to check in with the Watchman soon.

"Later," he said, leaving her to her water and prayers.

Maybe the Watchman would be ready now. A little early, but they were a priority, so the Watchman's mind definitely turned their way. He cast his mind south toward Brithnem. Only silence, stretching like a sea into darkness. There wasn't much to report—and he wasn't going to tell them about her Talent—so would it be terrible to miss a day?

He waited in silence. Hazily, he felt the light grow around him. Kiria's whispering made the quiet almost religious, or at least meditative. Deep in his lungs, air dragged in and out. Blood beat in his ears. Still no Watchman. Firian had practiced patience all his life, but he had none when another was supposed to come and didn't arrive on time. His mind began to buzz with suppressed fury, growing low like a mold. He wouldn't wait forever.

A flash of thought dawned so brightly that he squinted before remembering they were in the Unreal. There was no light.

He stood face to face with Brithnem's Watchman, whose wizened face, rubbed to a smoothness of deep wrinkles, now contorted with urgency. Firian was usually the first to speak, but now wasn't the time. Something was wrong. The Watchman's usually impassive eyes glinted with the whites. "Defender Kess, is My Kepress with you?" he said quickly.

"Yes," Firian said, his own eyes widening. He reached out into the Unreal, like feeling blindly with one hand, to check for dangers around the barn. Nothing.

"I have terrible news," the Watchman said. "General Rhet has been killed. Do *not* bring the Kepress back to the palace. Take her to the safety of Carradoc as planned. A full-scale search for the Torithians will continue until they are caught and executed."

Firian's face went cold. His heart beat thickly in his chest. "Yes," he said stupidly.

"You must tell the Kepress."

He licked his lips. "I will." What else could he say?

The Watchman nodded once and vanished to complete other business.

Firian let the real world in slowly, seeping back into his consciousness like blood.

It's just an assignment. Just an assignment. Just tell her.

Thankful that his back was to her, he let his eyes dart around the room. *Just say the words.* He tried to form his tongue around them, but they puffed like cotton in his mouth.

He steadied his breathing and turned around. Kiria was on her feet, watching him with suspicion. His back must have shown his tension. Stalling, he grabbed his shirt and put it on. She always wanted him to cover up. At this moment, she didn't know about her father. Her fragile peace was about to break.

"What is it?" she asked, her voice nervous.

His guts squirmed. He had to do it now. And he was usually so good at hiding things. Why couldn't he have bought himself some time, been kind to her for a while? Maybe this was better —just getting it out. This news would have soured every hour he held it inside.

He cleared his throat. Kiria turned pale, realizing how serious he was. "The Watchman" – he swallowed, out of breath – "he just said that... um, General Rhet has... been killed..."

"What?" Her face was bloodless.

He tried to say the words again, but they wouldn't come. So he only nodded.

Her body twitched, convulsing in small ways as though she was about to be sick. Shaking her head once, she tried to speak, confusion pooling in her eyes.

He nodded again, answering her unsaid protest. It was true.

With a pitched groan, her knees buckled. He almost caught her before she collapsed to the floor. Kneeling with her, he tried to set her down but she lay across his knees, as though unable to sit up. She shook violently in his arms. The first sob came in a burst, almost a scream. The sound twisted through his gut, painfully recognizable.

More violent sobs chased the first, as though the noise had admitted the truth that he was dead, had sealed his fate. Words tried to form, almost screamed out, but they died in a chaos of pain. Her hands moved in confusion, up to her mouth, down in a question. His left knee grew warm and wet with her tears. He heaved her up to a more comfortable position with her face in his shoulder.

The light grew around them as she bared her teeth, shuddering with grief. Finally, she pulled herself up to sit. "What happened?" she stammered, her chest rising and falling raggedly, convulsively.

"Torithians," he replied quietly.

A fresh gush of sobbing made her cling to him, grabbing his shoulders so hard her nails dug into his skin. She pressed her face into one shoulder as weeping rocked her again. She moved as though trapped in her own body. Unsure of what else to do, he held her close to his chest, swallowing against the rock in his throat. Tears and snot smeared the shoulder of his black shirt, and he felt her hot breath as her crying began to subside from the screams of shock to the weeping of grief.

He shifted her just enough to reach for the dagger he kept by his side. Bending his leg toward himself, he reached for his ankle and sawed off the cuff of his black pants. Sheathing the knife, he drew the fabric around one of Kiria's wrists and tied it there.

She looked at it, uncomprehending at first. She stretched her fingers and balled them back into a fist, watching the tendons in her wrist shift against the mourning bracelet. He drew her back in. She didn't protest and held him like a ledge to keep her from falling.

THEY COULDN'T TRAVEL FAR that day. Kiria was too distraught. Firian offered her his share of the food, knowing that their rations wouldn't stretch the extra day, but she refused. No appetite.

He went to check on the horses, who would be getting a long rest today. They both chomped contentedly at the grasses around the barn.

Possibilities. Belik's words from a recent lesson came to him. *Possibilities are currency. Always think of more. Death is just the end of one possibility. For better or worse, you won't see that person anymore. Without possibilities, our lives would snuff in the present moment, all the air sucked out. But there are always more.*

As soon as he walked back in, he sensed the energy in the barn had shifted. "We have to go back to Brithnem," she said sternly. The sun was high and her eyes burned red.

"We can't—"

"We *have to.* They'll target my mother next. I can't believe I was so selfish!" Tears sprang again to her eyes as she looked up at the roof. "We have to leave now."

He shook his head. "We can't leave now."

"But—"

"The Watchman told me to keep you safe. So that's what I'm doing."

"Take me back!" She demanded with the voice of a queen, eyes flashing.

"No."

She stomped toward him with fists balling at her sides, the ragged scrap of black fabric still tied around one wrist.

"I can't," he said calmly, refusing to take a step back as she charged at him. "Just think. You couldn't do any good there. If you're right, then you're just making yourself an easy target, too. Remember, your mother hired me to look out for you. She doesn't want you to come home."

Her words barely made it out. "But she's alone." Her determined steps wavered to a shuffling stop. Her gaze dropped to his feet.

"I'm sure she's surrounded by guards now," he said, trying to catch her eyeline, but she shrugged off his comment as though it meant nothing. "She's safe."

"I need to be there for her," she insisted. Their only course of action was obvious, but she kept letting her pain speak for her.

"Think about the Kingdom," he said. If she was so worried about being selfish, then this would catch her attention. "What would they do if they lost the Second Line?"

She swallowed visibly. "I can't let that happen," she said so quietly that it barely went beyond moving her lips.

"See? There."

"Chetana is with her, and Daelon," she said to herself. "And she knows I would come if I could..."

He nodded solemnly in agreement. After a moment, he asked, "Do you think you can ride today?"

She tucked her hair behind her ear, still avoiding his gaze. "That might be good. I'll go crazy if I stay here."

He felt the same way. The shadows in the drafty barn

replayed the past few hours in a relentless loop. He preferred to remain stoic, not rocked by memories.

A buzz. He snapped his head around to look behind him. Someone was very close. He dove into the Unreal, grateful that Kiria had turned away. *More news? No, it's coming from the wrong direction.*

Dark, spiky hair on a slight frame, dressed all in Academy black. He knew it as clearly as the smell of cinnamon. Bard. Firian let out a sigh of relief, but his insides clenched again with the uncertainty of why he had come. "Bard! What are you doing here?"

Bard grinned wide, a smile that split his face. "Hey, Fir!" he said. Neither one of them bothered with a background. Just the two of them floating in space.

"Wait, what are you doing here?" Firian repeated, though his stomach relaxed at Bard's happy expression.

"Just seeing how you're doing." Bard's black eyes darted down, then up. He was hiding something.

"Checking on me?" Firian asked, almost moved. The death of Kiria's father had weakened him. He pushed out his chest.

"Yeah. Well, I have to. It's for an assignment. Master Gerand got back yesterday so she's teaching *katah* again. We're supposed to practice—"

"You're declaring *katah* on me?" Firian grimaced, torn between feeling disgusted and amused. It was still a mystery why the Masters had added *katah* to Bard's schedule. He was a guy, and the word "sex" made him blush. Usually, women learned the craft and seduced opposing generals and tacticians. That's how *katah* worked.

"No, no," Bard said quickly. "It's not that. And *katah* isn't what you think." He turned his pleading gaze to Firian's face. "I need somebody to focus on, Fir. You're the only one I could think of."

Firian huffed a laugh through his nose.

"Please, Fir? You know how Master Gerand is."

He raised an eyebrow and tipped his head to the side. He really did know. Two weeks of traveling with that woman was more than enough.

"Are you coming back soon too?" Bard asked, barely masking the hope in his voice.

"I don't think so."

"Are you still with the Kepress?"

Leave it to Bard to use her accurate title the first time. "Yes, she's here."

"What's she like?" Bard had a question beneath this one: *Are you behaving yourself around her?*

It would be fun to pretend that he had struck Kiria with a wild passion for him the moment they met, but he couldn't lie. Not when the Masters might find out somehow. Kiria was too important an asset for him to mess with right now. Besides, if *she* found out, she'd hate him after all she had been through today, and she didn't need any more pain.

"She's..." Firian struggled for a word. "She's not bad. She's tougher than I thought."

Judging from Bard's expression, he hadn't expected that answer. "I wish I could meet her," he said. "It isn't the same here without you around. It feels like we're moving. The Head keeps ordering us to clear out rooms. It's weird."

Firian knit his brows. "That's strange."

"Yeah," said Bard, encouraged by Firian's interest. "But I'm sure it's much more interesting where you are. Have you seen any Torithians yet?"

"No." Firian shook his head. "I don't think we'll see any. I'm going to stock up on food and then we'll head to a safe location." The Torithians' easy window was rapidly closing. Which reminded him. "We're actually leaving now," he said.

"Okay," Bard replied, with the awkwardness of expecting the other to leave first. That meant he would keep watching him, per Master Gerand's orders. With enough focus, the kind required for *katah,* any Tanyu could sense another person's mind and even watch their thoughts to some extent, even when they weren't consciously in the Unreal together. Firian had never practiced the discipline. Did Gerand want to learn about his mission through Bard? Firian had a feeling she did. The look Bard gave him confirmed his suspicion. His friend shrugged apologetically.

Curse her.

Firian regarded Bard for a few seconds. "S'okay," he finally said.

Bard looked relieved, a little smile forming in his eyes and around his mouth.

Let Gerand look. She would find nothing to criticize.

33

FIRIAN

Now that they were over the mountains, Firian recognized this part of the woods. He had always had a pretty good idea of where they were, but now he knew every path and tree. The nearness of Raewhith settled like a weight in his chest. All at once, his situation felt surreal. He was returning to the town where he grew up, now as a Tanyuin bodyguard for the Kepress of Brithnem. He glanced at her riding beside him. She had struggled with the reality of her father's death the past few days, but their lessons in the Unreal had helped. She was coming along nicely, able to keep a strong image steady and talk to him at the same time. They stuck with safe, non-emotional subjects: her interest in music, Jori's antics, her love for fruit tarts. Even though she trusted him more now, she never brought up her Ability, and they hadn't spoken of the general.

A few low buildings peeped through the trees. Their memory smelled like dust or a familiar meal. He lifted his head to see around the little brown shops. Did he recognize anyone? Should he hide if he did?

Why am I so nervous?

They emerged by the edge of a bustling street lined with

shops. Memories piled thickly over him. To the left, just out of sight was the trade school where he had gone as a boy. To the right was the road to his house where he had grown up.

Jovan's voice came to mind. *Even when you're in the Unreal, remember where you are. Never lose your balance in the moment.* Firian fought to stay aware of the present when the past and even the Unreal washed over him like a strong current. He rotated his shoulders and cracked his neck, just to feel them.

Next to the blacksmith's was the stable. He had learned the order of the shops as he had learned his numbers: *the tailor, the fruit seller, the cooper, the blacksmith, the stable... one, two, three, four, five...* Despite his unease, their order felt correct, like puzzle pieces fitting together. Exactly as they should be.

They dismounted and led their horses to the stable. After a brief exchange with the boy on duty, the two of them set out on foot, weaving through the little crowd buying and selling.

He kept his head down and his eyes up as they edged past other shoppers. Schoolchildren peeked through the alleys between shops to watch them as they passed. Raewhith didn't get very many visitors.

"Plums! Nice juicy plums!" cried the man at the fruit stand, holding up a purple plum in three fingers, as others would hold up a prized possession. "Plums! Only one token each!" Kiria, hurrying beside him in her plain brown dress, shot him a glance, concern glinting in her eyes. He tilted his head forward to urge her to walk on, looking into her eyes. *There's nothing to get nervous about.* Fruit wouldn't last long, although Shifra wasn't far, maybe four days.

He knew an inn stood down the road on the outskirts, past the spot where his house had been. As a kid, he'd had almost no chance to go there, but he heard that travelers came to get rest, food, and drink. He wouldn't say no to any of those.

A large wagon rumbled toward them and he grabbed Kiria's arm. She looked surprised as he brought her out of its path.

Pain twisted in his chest. *I'm sorry, Brett.* He wasn't sure why he felt sorry. Maybe because he hadn't been there when she died. He couldn't save her. At least he could save Kiria.

The weight of memory kept him silent as they traced his steps from the school, up the hard-packed dirt road up the hill. Sunlight reflected the road to white as the knot of people thinned, leaving the way clear for the two of them.

"You grew up here?" Kiria said in an undertone.

"Yes," he said, feeling the absurdity of it. His world had been so small. "I was going to be a glassmaker." The word tasted like ashes, and he spat on the side of the road. A few more steps and he would see the burned house. His chest tightened.

She replied but he didn't hear what she said. The house they'd rebuilt over his old one looked remarkably similar. It was a little smaller but that was the only difference. Maybe he had expected to see smoke still rising out of its charred remains. Briefly, he realized that his former neighbors would be the most likely people in town to identify him, and that his plan was not very safe. Of course, it probably didn't matter if they knew his name. He was a Tanyu now, far beyond that worthless eleven-year-old in skill and importance. And no one would recognize Kiria this far north, especially without her Beauty.

"Are you ignoring me?" Kiria asked as they crossed the street.

The new house's chimney leaned a little to the right too. Firian dropped his voice low. "No, I'm not. It's just... Just go along with me here." He knocked on the door, hardly aware of what he was doing.

Moments later, the door opened. Blood drained his face cold.

It was his mother.

"Hello. Who are you?" she asked, eyeing them. She wiped

her hands on an apron worn to translucency. Her wispy hair now streaked gray. She had tied it in a knot behind her head but flyaways crowned her face. Her thin lips had wrinkles and her eyes were milky.

Firian closed his mouth. "I'm...." Indecision paralyzed him. "Is Mr. Kess at home?"

"No."

A baby started crying inside the house. *What does that mean?* The mystery seemed impenetrable, like a note in a song that didn't match the rest. It was just there.

"Can we come in?" Firian asked breathlessly.

His mother's gaze grew suspicious as she stared at him. "You look so much like someone I know," she finally said.

"I..."

Brett appeared at the door, holding the baby on her hip. Firian's breath caught. She was so beautiful, fully a woman now, but her face showed the same sweet spirit that defended him as a child. The baby reached for the end of Brett's long, glossy braid. Her face had filled out, and she wore a stained dress. But he saw himself in her eyes. At the sight of Firian, her mouth dropped open and her eyes rounded. "Mother," she breathed.

His mother's eyes narrowed. "Firian?" said his mother. She blinked away wetness.

"Can we come in?" he asked, with renewed urgency. He didn't want anyone else overhearing their conversation or getting a good look at them.

"Of course!" Brett said.

His mother opened the door wider. "Firian, come in, come in!"

Nothing had changed in the main room. Besides a few additions that looked like they belonged to Brett and the baby, everything was exactly as it had been, just distorted. He was bigger now, so the room was smaller. The little fireplace on the wall to the right, the table in the center of the room, the kitchen through the doorway on the left, the door to the garden straight ahead...

"Firian," said Brett, disbelieving. She handed the baby to their mother. "You've come back!"

He had no idea what to say, so he nodded and sat down. The house hadn't changed at all. It hadn't burned down. Everyone was still alive. There never had been a fire.

"Can I have a drink?" he asked. His mother went to get water from the kitchen. That was not what he had had in mind.

"It is you." A question bled through Brett's tone. She stared down at him, looking over his eyes, his hair, his clothes.

He was afraid to speak, afraid she would disappear if he broke the spell, so he just nodded again, almost holding his breath.

"Firian!" His name came out as a sob. She threw herself toward him, but checked herself. It had been so long, and he was a Tanyu. Could she touch him?

Sniffing back a tear, he stood and welcomed her into his arms. She squeezed him tight, as though he would run away if she didn't hold him down. It was surreal, surreal. His tightly closed eyes pressed out tears he couldn't stop. "We didn't know where you were," Brett said into his chest.

"I'm okay," he said. "I'm okay."

He remembered himself and let her go, and Brett's face glowed with happiness.

Their mother returned with two cups of water. Firian really was very thirsty. Looking around at the familiar room, he felt oddly disconnected from it. He was disconnected from them too. It was as though they were ghosts or figures intruding upon the Unreal. Something tightened in his chest. As he gulped down his water, he seethed. Why had the Academy told him they were dead? How could they have caused him so much pain?

"You have a baby," Firian said to Brett, feeling oddly empty. Everything felt like too much.

She laughed and said, "Yes, this is Sabir." She didn't seem old enough to have a baby. She had been so much younger when he saw her last. Seeing an opening, Brett introduced herself to Kiria, who had stood silently by the door during their reunion. "I'm Firian's sister, Brett," she prompted.

"Lovely to meet you," Kiria said, offering no more information. She hid her surprise well. He was almost impressed.

"This is my wife, Maya," he said when he had finished his water. Kiria didn't deny it. The truth could be damning, so he was glad she saw the sense in his story.

"Oh my goodness! It's wonderful to meet you," said his mother, who kept a respectful distance despite looking like she would like nothing better than to embrace her new daughter-in-law. Brett ran forward warmly and hugged Kiria with her free arm as though they were sisters.

The baby kept crying, fraying his nerves and trivializing this meeting that, for him, was monumental.

Brett caught him looking at the baby. She looked at him with eyes bright with concern. She was always the first to notice that something was wrong.

"Where's your husband?" Firian asked curtly before she could fuss over him. "Why isn't he here?"

"Gaius is fighting in the Torithian war. We expect him to come back in about three months to recuperate before returning to the front. I'm living here until then." Brett shifted the baby, the only sign that the arrangement made her uncomfortable.

Back with Father. The idea horrified him.

"How long will you be staying?" she asked.

"I'm not staying," he said, more forcefully than he intended. "In fact, we're leaving now." He took Kiria's hand. "We have to reach the Farmer's Inn."

"You can't leave now! Firian, it's been so long!" his mother cried.

Brett looked stern. "You've only just gotten here. I'm sure Father will let you borrow a horse and cart when he gets home so you can reach the inn in time if you really have to go."

"No, we have to leave now. Academy business." That should silence them.

His mother sniffed. Her eyes glazed over with bright tears. "Firian...." She had never shown this much desire to spend time with him. Maybe she regretted those years when she ignored him and thought he wouldn't amount to anything. He stood up straighter, his shoulders back. She had been wrong about him. He had amounted to something, but that didn't mean that he wanted to give in to her tears now. He almost wished he could, but that would have to be under different circumstances. At that moment he felt a little repulsed.

"We'll see each other again," he said dismissively. "Goodbye!"

"Nice to meet you all," Kiria added as they swept out the door.

Walking very quickly, he led them away from the part of town he recognized. In the new silence, he breathed deep into his chest. The baby's crying had finally stopped.

His head spun. *What just happened? Why didn't I know before?* Heavy in the stomach sat the certainty that the Academy had lied. Raewhith hadn't reported a fire. The Academy, for some gory, godforsaken reason, had pretended they were dead. Red rage filled his body. Even Kiria's presence irritated him, reminded him of his loyalty. Had Belik known about this? He'd lied to him before.

"Are you all right?" Kiria asked, breaking through his thoughts.

Firian shook his head as if he could send his doubts flying like cobwebs. "I'm fine."

"You're not fine," she said in an undertone. Her concerned look made him wonder if he had fallen into the Unreal for a moment as they walked. Shock could send a person there, make him abstracted. It was a dangerous place, to be in the Unreal without knowing it.

"Here's the inn," he muttered. They went inside the two-story wooden building that he hadn't been allowed to visit as a child. Of course, he had snuck up the hill to come here and listen to travelers' stories a few times.

The clunk of his shoes on the wooden boards echoed back those memories. Hooks for coats lined the walls just inside the door, leading through the empty entryway to the innkeeper's counter. A staircase led up to the rooms on the left and a small room crowded with round tables opened on the right. Even vacant, the entire place felt cramped, claustrophobic.

He edged his way to one of the wooden tables. Kiria followed, her expression both concerned and accusatory.

Moments later, a barman thunked two mugs of ale in front of them. Firian drank his gratefully.

"What happened back there?" Kiria asked.

He didn't answer, taking refuge in his ale.

Her eyebrows came together and she leaned her elbows on the table. She tried to meet his eyes, but he didn't take the bait. He wasn't in the mood to explain himself. "Why did you lie to me?" she said in a low voice so the barman and one grizzly-looking guest couldn't hear.

"I didn't lie to you."

Her light brown eyes flashed, even as they filled with tears. "You told me your family was dead."

"I thought they were!"

"Don't play with me," she said dangerously. Her face was red with the grief that welled just below the surface.

"I'm not. I didn't know they'd be here."

"Then why did you think...?"

Firian set his jaw in a hard line. "They told me," he muttered, taking another swig.

She slid her elbows off the table in disbelief. "Why would they do that?"

He was done answering questions. Everything still felt hollow. The memory of an hour before ambushed him unexpectedly, obtruding, making his stomach drop.

This time she accepted his silence and didn't push him for more answers. Instead, she changed the subject. "Are we staying here for the night?"

"Sure," he said, glad to move on from emotional subjects.

"We can get food here," she continued, now business-like. A much safer attitude. "And I need a bath. I've never gone this long without one."

His mouth quirked up in a half-smile. He wasn't sure why. "I'll make sure they draw one for you." He could probably use one too. Slicking his face and hair with stream water wasn't enough.

"And then off to... our destination," she said, almost letting the word slip. Even here, they couldn't say the place aloud.

He nodded once.

She said something else but he wasn't listening. Muffled scraping reverberated by the front door of the inn, but no one came inside. "Shut up," he whispered.

She scrunched her face in disgusted disbelief. "Firian, if you—"

He scraped back his chair just as the door burst open and six men piled into the tiny space. They brandished weapons as they barreled toward the princess, their bald heads glistening with sweat. Their thick necks strained forward. Light from the oil lamps glinted yellow on the knives and axe blades.

Ale sloshed everywhere as Firian yanked Kiria to her feet. "Here!" he yelled, pulling her in front of him. Picking up a chair that blocked their way to the back room, he hurled it at the Torithians. With no room to maneuver out of the way, they ducked and leaned to avoid it but it still struck one hard in the head.

Kiria almost collided with the barman, who emerged from the narrow kitchen doorway to see what was going on. She sidestepped. Firian punched the man hard in the face and then flung him around by the front of his shirt to shield them from the fighters, who shouted to each other to kill him, to cut them off, to follow them.

"Go!" he screamed at Kiria, cursing loudly to himself because he hadn't seen this coming. A few men struggled to get around the tables while the others ran back out the front door. If they didn't have men posted at the other exits, he could escape these idiots.

Kiria ran into the kitchen. Firian heaved the barman's unconscious body at the two men still hurdling toward them through the dining room, and ran to follow her. He couldn't leave her alone. The kitchen steamed with stuffy, hot air. He scanned the room. On the right, a large fire burned in an oven. Over the flames was a spit but no meat on it. Beside the fireplace someone had stacked piles of wood and a bellows. On the other side of the room, shelves held stacks of plates and mugs. Below them was a large, covered barrel of ale with a ladle sticking out.

In the back wall was a door. A way out. Firian grabbed the enormous ladle as he ran. It wasn't at all balanced like a sword, but it felt heavy enough to withstand one. And he always had the knives—large one on his belt, small one in his boot. Ahead of him, Kiria stopped at the back door. Firian flung the door open. His eyes adjusted to the bright sunlight just in time to see one of the Torithians swing his sword. His shadow filled the doorway.

Kiria screamed and covered her face.

Firian swung the ladle full-force at the man's head. Using the man's hesitation, Firian pulled him closer and slammed the door on his sword hand. Kiria gasped as the bones in his arm crunched and the man screamed in pain. The sword fell to the ground.

Firian scrambled to pick it up. Sword in one hand, ladle in the other. The door bounced back open and the brawny man, snarling like an animal in his rage, threw himself at Firian. His huge body caught Firian by surprise and he stumbled backward, slamming into the shelves. Pottery crashed around him. Gigantic hands, worn like leather, crushed Firian's windpipe. A jagged purple vein traced up the Torithian's large nose. *Broken.* The man's face, like a mask of rage, streamed red, sticky blood onto Firian's neck and chest.

A jolt and more pottery shards told him that Kiria had smashed something on the man's head, but his thick skull didn't register the pain.

Bursts of dark stars clouded Firian's eyes and he gurgled in his fight for breath. His muscles recoiled from lack of air, stiffening, the veins standing out on his skin.

He had a sword. He was an idiot! He'd practiced for moments like this. Rolling the force of his body with his arm, he thrust the sword into the man's back. Firian felt the man go rigid with shock, and he heaved the man to the floor. The Torithian fell on his back, stunned. Firian stabbed him in the neck. The quick well of blood told him he was dead.

Kiria's hands covered her mouth, her eyes grown wide. The swift crunch of gravel told him that more were coming. Two other men ran up, clenching weapons in their fists. Maybe they had been guarding the other doors. Firian took one deep breath. *Many ways to kill a man...*

"Give us the Kepress!" one barked.

"To you?" Firian bared his teeth. It could have been a grin. "No."

Provoking them worked. They swung at him but he was ready this time. He'd practiced this with Jovan a hundred times. The moment's pause allowed him to calm his mind a little, to notice where they were coming instead of striking blindly or by instinct. They both came head-on, making them easier to see.

With the ladle, he reached toward the first man and twisted the sword out of his grip with the spoon end. Using the momentum, he struck under the man's chin with his elbow, cracking his teeth together. The man couldn't see with his head tilted up by the blow. Any sword swing would be blind.

Safe in his shadow for a split second, Firian ducked in time to avoid the second swinging sword. Unwilling to hurt his partner, the second man pulled back just shy of Firian. Grabbing his chance, Firian swung at the second man's sword arm but missed, cutting a huge gash in his calf. For a second, it looked like the man would strike again, but the shock gave way to pain and he dropped to his knees, puffing moans of pain. Firian finished him quickly.

"No! Let me go!" The scream was Kiria's.

Firian spun around. The two men from the inn had made it through the kitchen to the outside. The tallest one grabbed Kiria, pinning her hands to her sides. She tried stomping on his instep but it didn't work. The other man shielded him from attack as they hauled her away. *No!*

A movement in his peripheral vision. Firian jumped away from the first man whose jaw he'd elbowed but fiery pain sliced and burned along his back. He screamed and stabbed the man in the gut before running to get Kiria. Nausea rose up, slicking sweat on his cold face, but he forced it down.

He threw the ladle at the two men retreating around the building into the woods. It hit one in the back, but didn't seem to hurt. One man stopped to face him, knowing he had to be dealt with before they could have Kiria.

One at a time. I can do one at a time. Firian paused a little farther away than he had the last time, his back still stinging. The muscular, ax-wielding Torithian weighed more than he did. He'd have to rely on speed and surprise. *To the calm mind, everything is a servant.* Anything could be a weapon.

Of course, weapons could be weapons too.

Quick as a swallow, he took the small knife from his boot. *Disadvantage—no hands free. Advantage—two weapons.*

This Torithian wasn't a fool like some of the others. He took his time while his partner got farther away.

Firian's heart beat harder in his chest, impatient. Finally, he threw the small knife, just as he had practiced digging into the flesh of trees. The man doubled over and the knife flew harmlessly over his head.

This was Firian's chance! A moment's window. Firian started forward, but the man rose with dust in his hand, acrid and stinging in Firian's face. As the man hurled toward him, Firian forced his eyes open and stupidly held his sword straight out in front of him with both hands. His lesson with Kiria came back to him just as the man got close. He parried the axe and brought his knee up hard between the man's legs.

Taking the risk, Firian sprinted past the man paralyzed with pain. He could finish him later if he had to. Right now, he had one job. He needed to get Kiria.

It didn't take him long to catch up. The tall man moved slowly. Kiria writhed and dragged her heels in the dirt as he manhandled her forward.

She and the Torithian saw him coming at the same time. Firian's mind whirled. How to get her away from him unscathed?

Kiria opened her mouth, maybe to yell for him, but shut it again. She twisted violently and started shouting, forcing the man to pay attention to her.

He could go for the Torithian's head. That way he wouldn't touch Kiria at all. The man was a giant, much taller than she was.

But he'd seen Firian coming. He could use her as a shield.

Firian hesitated. Then Kiria began to glimmer. Even the Torithian noticed. She glowed like a mirage. In seconds, the goddess he had seen in her dream stood in the arms of the tall fighter.

Firian's heart stopped.

Then he realized what she'd done. She had changed to give him an opening. The enemy's eyes burned as he looked at her, forgetting about Firian. Firian lunged at the man, cutting his head almost completely off. His sword only stopped at the spine. His limp body collapsed to the ground, almost taking her with him.

For a blazing second, Firian looked at Kiria. Her glistening hair dripped with the man's blood. He could barely breathe as he looked into her wide golden eyes. A hint of pale fear shone through her radiant skin.

A heavy breath reminded him of where he was. Behind them came the last fighter, enraged. Firian grabbed Kiria's hand. Her soft skin tingled against him. He yanked the sword free of the man's neck and bolted into the woods.

34

KIRIA

"Go, go!" Firian's voice grated.

Kiria's legs started to burn, the initial adrenaline wearing off. But she forced them to keep moving, one in front of the other, jumping over fallen branches, climbing up large rocks, forward and forward, her breath coming out ragged and her scars aching.

She paused for a second when the realization hit her that Firian wasn't wearing the packs. They had left all their supplies at the inn.

He touched her back to make her keep moving. She knew he could run faster, but he kept her in front. She twisted her head around to see whether any of the Torithians still followed. The air blew her tears cold. She hadn't realized she was crying.

No one seemed to be after them. When she looked at Firian, he seemed to think the same thing. They jogged to a stop and silently crept to a thick grove of young pine trees. He motioned for her to go inside. Prickly needles scraped her arms and legs and chest, but she didn't care. She took the opportunity for a moment's focus, enough to make herself plain again. With that change, she felt smaller, deflated, harder to see, which was a relief. Being beautiful was horrible when it came with danger. At least her plan had worked. She shut her eyes tight, shaking.

If it hadn't...

Firian came in after her. They stood chest to chest, with no space to move. Kiria strained her ears for any sound of the Torithians. Nothing. But every time they had surprised her. She kept listening until she felt that she had gone almost deaf. No sound except for a falling pine cone and their own breathing.

She arched backward to give herself enough space to rub the tears off her face with the back of her shaking hand. For a while they stayed like that, just listening.

Finally, Firian held up his free hand to indicate that she should stay while he looked out. His last two fingers bloomed black and yellow and red, the middle knuckles swollen.

She tried not to breathe as he edged past her, threading through the spindly trees into the open woods.

He wasn't gone long. He returned to her line of sight and beckoned her out of the grove. "Let's go," he said, so quietly he might have mouthed the words.

She hurried out, ready to follow him. He gave no hint of where they were going for several long minutes. Aching bruises grew along her arms and waist where that monster had touched her. The breeze revealed something wet on her forehead. She gingerly touched it with one finger. Blood.

Glancing at Firian's sword, covered in gore, she suddenly felt sick. Saliva pooled in her mouth and she had to stop walking. Her body wouldn't go any further. Her stomach churned up bile. She couldn't get air in her lungs. Her quick breaths did no good. The air wouldn't stay in. Her fingers numbed and her limbs shook. Firian got farther away, striding with sure steps, gripping his sword. Streaks of blood painted both his hands.

"Wait, wait," she said breathlessly, hoping he could hear.

He did.

She sank to her knees, completely overwhelmed.

He jogged to reach her. "Are you hurt?" he whispered urgently.

"I don't think so," she managed through the thin air.

"We just have to get over that hill," he said, pointing ahead. "Can you make it?"

The distance seemed impossible. She started crying, overcome by helplessness.

"Up, up," he said, lifting her to her feet.

She knew that they had no time for this, but the ground wavered in darkness. When she stumbled, he caught her, but he grunted when he did. "You're hurt," she said, coming back to the present. She stood, her strength returning in small waves.

Denying it, he shook his head. His dark hair was wild. "Take a deep breath," he said.

It took her a few tries, but she managed to do it.

"Just over that hill," he repeated. He linked his free arm in hers and they went as quickly and quietly as they could.

From the top of the hill she could see another village in a valley far away. She couldn't make it all that way.

"We have no horses," she murmured.

Firian looked grim. "No," he agreed.

They couldn't go back to get them. Not now that the Torithians expected them to do that.

Tears threatened again. It was too much.

Uncharacteristically tender, Firian touched her arm and said, "Here. We can stay here for the night. I'll keep watch." He still held the bloody sword in his fist.

She nodded. At least one Torithian from that group was still alive and looking for them, and there could be more. Firian had killed two in front of her. That left—what? four?—that she wasn't sure about. Had he killed them all? He must have at least incapacitated them. How had he done that all on his own? She had tried to help, but didn't have the right training. She'd done all she could think of, and it wasn't enough. Despite all his flaws, she was deeply grateful for Firian in that moment.

"Thank you," she said.

He turned around, maybe to scan for a sheltered spot. A ragged tear in his black shirt ran from his right shoulder blade down to his waist, wet with dark blood.

She gasped. If that wound ran deep, he wouldn't last the night. "You're hurt. You're bleeding!"

"I'm okay."

"Shut up!" she said. "You're not okay. Your back..."

He reached back and grimaced before his hand reached the wound. "It's not too bad," he said.

"How are you still standing?" she asked. "Sit down."

He actually did as she said, going to a hollow just out of easy view and sitting on a large rock. She understood that's where they would stay the night. Despite her nausea, she came over to him. The least she could do was make sure he was all right.

A tiny stream ran into the hollow, pooling at the bottom, hardly enough to scoop up for drinking. She untied the sash from around her waist, hating the bruises there, and dipped the end of it in the cold water. Though she was no doctor, she knew it was important to clean cuts. The sash would be long enough to bind it too.

Firian didn't need her to explain what she was doing. He set down the sword only as long as it took to pull the shirt carefully over his head. His sharp breath betrayed how much that motion hurt.

A bloody gash ran down the length of his muscular back. She fought back sickness as she looked at it. Blood covered his whole right side.

"I'm going to clean you off," she said, hovering the damp sash over his cut.

He gave a single nod of acknowledgment, bracing himself.

His skin flinched only slightly at her touch as she sopped up the flowing blood, working mechanically from the top to the bottom. The end of the sash kept getting saturated. When it did, she wrung it out in the water and started again. By the time she finished, the little stream ran pink. "I don't think it's very deep," she said, watching the blood flow out of the cut again. The gash stretched along his entire back, but at the bottom it was little more than a scratch that looked nastier than it was.

He didn't respond, his head tilted, dazed, toward the sword in his hand. He ran his finger along the crossguard.

"Here, help me bind this up," she said, pressing one end of the sash to his back and handing him the rest to wrap around the front.

He lifted his arms and passed the fabric back around to her. They passed the sash back and forth, crisscrossing his chest and back until they ran out of fabric. She tightened the end and tucked it in, hoping it would stay. The deepest part of the injury was protected now, anyway.

Heavy silence fell.

Firian fingered the hole in his shirt. The needle and thread were in the lost pack.

Kiria felt numb, remembering the attack as though it had just been a nightmare. She never thought her life would look like this.

If her mother could see her now... dirty and plain, dripping with the blood of her enemies, alone with an armed Tanyu, with no food and no place to sleep. It was good that her mother couldn't see her. She didn't need more heartache.

But at least Kiria was alive. She looked at the back of Firian's head, now eye-level, and felt a rush of warmth. All his bravado didn't matter as much anymore.

Kiria woke up screaming. Blank terror covered her body like a physical force. Her heart pounded, heavy and painful.

A hand closed over her mouth. Feverish and wild, she looked around in the dark for her attacker.

"Shh, shh!" someone said. His breath felt hot in her ear. "It's all right."

She rolled her eyes to see him. It was just Firian. She stopped screaming against his hand, so he took it away, letting her breathe. Her heart didn't slow down. Any moment now, something horrible would emerge from the darkness.

Anger mixed with her fear. This was the third night she couldn't sleep because of nightmares. Exhausted and afraid, she sat up beside Firian. Forest mold dropped softly from her back. Maybe if she acted as though she felt normal, the reality would follow.

Today they were supposed to reach Shifra. Hopefully she would feel safer in the fortress of Carradoc than she did here in the forest. Firian had chosen a spot overhung with boulders since the trees thinned out here and they needed some kind of cover. She hated the rocks suddenly, longing for someplace with a locked door and a hot bath.

She chewed her fingernail, and Firian passed her a water skin they had gotten in Imlin, the town they had seen from the hollow. The last two times this had happened, she asked for water. Now she didn't need to ask.

She sucked in a deep breath to steady herself. "Have you seen anything?" she whispered, carefully taking a drink.

"No. I think we're safe tonight," he said. They sat close enough that their hips touched. The rewrapped sash puffed a little under his blue shirt, the darkest one he could find in town. It had cost the last tokens Firian had had in his pockets.

She needed a distraction. Briefly, her mind flitted to the pen and paper he'd gotten for her along with the food and water. She had started writing down all her ideas for ruling the Kingdom, protecting it from the Torithians and improving the lives of its citizens. But keeping her mind focused on something serious felt beyond her reach. In the morning she could begin again.

She closed her eyes, trying to reach the Unreal, something new to occupy her mind. Firian always met her there. Since the attack, they had practiced multiple times a day. Though it started as more of a distraction, she could tell she was getting better at entering their shared mental space and maneuvering in it. And the more she did it, the more she liked it.

She chose an easy place, a safe place. Her room in Mon Párinath. It fitted together, piece by piece. Each piece of furniture, carpet, and item soothed her, like old friends.

Firian appeared beside her. "Practicing again?" he said, his blue eyes smiling.

She nodded solemnly, taking in the therapeutic view. "I still don't see how any of this could be used for attack," she said. Her eyes swept over the familiar objects. How could even a trained warrior hurt her here? She could go back to reality at will.

He closed the space between them until she could feel his body heat. After a silent pause that made her gut twist a little, he said, "You can do anything here."

She flushed and cast him a look. What did he mean?

"You can bend the rules of reality." Casually, he began to levitate. She backed up, eyes wide. He would have to show her how to do that. "Your ability to fight and come up with new strategies is much better here." His mouth lifted with pride, but he hesitated as though he shouldn't explain any more. But then he continued. "During war, every sunup and sundown, people with the Talent meet to fight, pitting their best against our best. That means less bloodshed, usually, and a quicker end to war.

Tanyuin minds tend to be good at strategy, so most generals and tacticians have some Talent. That gives us easy access to the top people. They often come willingly and, if not, there are other ways to get to them. Belief allows you to kill and be killed. The more you believe in the Unreal, the better you are at attacking and the more vulnerable you are at the same time."

"Do Torithian generals have it?" The mention of generals made her uncomfortable. *Is that what happened to Father?*

Firian floated down, landing lightly on the deep carpet. The fibers moved against his feet, a detail she hadn't added. "I'm not sure. We're not officially involved in your war."

She knit her brows together, knowing exactly what to write that morning. "Why not?" It was a real question, but also a challenge.

"I don't know. We should be," he said, deep anger coloring his features as he looked down at the patterned rug, but only for a moment. "If I were in charge, I would end this war. We could do it." He looked back at her. "You're not bad at strategy either."

It took her a moment to realize what he was talking about. "It was all I could think of," she muttered.

"I thought it was brilliant," he said, looking at her in a way that made her uncomfortable. His eyes burned with desire, flattering, attractive. She didn't want to like it as much as she did.

He hadn't brought it up before this. Her stomach coiled with the thought that he had seen her beautiful. Someone dangerous and powerful seeing her so exposed. No, not exposed, though it still felt like it sometimes. She looked back at him, trying not to acknowledge the invitation in his eyes. Though she felt drawn to him, his wild unpredictability stopped her from considering him as a partner. But, if she was honest, part of her was also glad he'd seen her that way.

Furtively, she checked her hands—still plain. "It was necessary." She cleared her throat. "So, is that it? Is that what you practice at the Academy?"

He shrugged one shoulder. "There are more ways to get to people. Everybody's mind touches the Unreal when they sleep."

"Is that what keeps happening to me?" she asked quietly, crossing her arms across her body. "Can they hurt me in my nightmares?"

A chill ran through her when he didn't answer right away. "No," he said slowly. "I would sense it."

"But people *can* be killed in their dreams?"

His eyes flashed regret. "Yes, but you're safe with me."

Those words would have rung boastful a few days ago, but they both felt the weight of their truth now. The memory of Firian standing guard that first night after the attack filled her face with heat. They looked at each other, suddenly serious with anticipation. Her heart started beating hard again, but not with the same kind of fear. He stepped forward, closer...

Her eyes shot open. After the lighted room, everything looked even darker, even though the sky had lightened from black to dark blue. The cool night air washed over her. "You should let the Watchman know we're safe," she said.

35

FIRIAN

So close.

Firian didn't want to check in with the Watchman. The man might tell him that they had eliminated the threat in the palace, and that the two of them could come back. Firian just needed a little more time.

Just now he had almost managed to kiss her, but she startled like a wild rabbit. What was she afraid of? He looked back at her in the space beneath the rocks, but she sat, eyes down, braiding her hair over her shoulder. The moment had passed. And yet she was tempted. He saw it in her eyes.

His mind spun with questions and the image of her terrified face, transformed into painful brilliance, came to him again. If he came back with a successful mission *and* the love of the Kepress, he could have two worlds at his disposal. Or could he? The Academy told him his family was dead, and ever since the moment he saw them alive, other lies cropped up in his memory like symptoms of a disease. The torture before the mission. Tiev's promotion.

Too early to call the Watchman, Firian looked northwest. Through those woods rose the Academy. Rage and confusion welled in his chest any time he thought about it, but he had to say something.

Reaching in his mind, he searched for Belik. It didn't take long.

When he saw the Master, Firian's arguments seemed smaller, as though he had imagined them. Belik was just the same. He couldn't have started the lie about his family.

"Master Belik."

"Firian!" The Master resettled his glasses on his nose, raising his eyebrows just a little to reveal his surprise.

They stood in a blank space. No need for ceremony.

"I heard about the attack," Belik said. "I'm glad you were able to protect the princess—"

"Kepress." It felt good to correct him.

Belik pursed his lips ironically, apparently starting to sense Firian's mood. "But I thought you could avoid being seen at all."

Firian gritted his teeth to stop himself from saying anything rash. He took a couple steadying breaths so he could match Belik's stoicism. Normally that wasn't a challenge. "I saw my family," he said, clear and matter-of-fact, watching Belik's expression. Except for a blink, it didn't change.

"Did you?" The question was careful, almost a statement.

Firian tensed. He felt strength run through his arms and back. "Yes. The Academy told me they were dead."

Belik considered. "With good reason," he said slowly. "You didn't like them and you didn't need the distraction."

A wave of dizziness flowed through him. He snarled. "How could—"

"Consider this." Calmly, Belik raised a weathered hand.

Firian's fingers gripped into a fist.

"I saw you and I saw myself." Though his voice was as steady as ever, Belik's face revealed the honesty of his words. He never spoke about his past, of which Firian had only learned bits and pieces. Was he going to now? Curiosity dulled the sharp edge of Firian's rage, and his hands relaxed just a little.

"I was like you," Belik continued. "I was good. Everybody knew it." He held up a finger. "But then I got distracted. I thought it didn't matter, thought I was better than that. I could do what I wanted." His mouth twitched. "But then it all went to hell," he said, pounding his bad leg in frustration and emphasis. "So now you know. I did what I thought was best for you."

Firian didn't say a word. Resentment mixed with pride and anger. No one had supported him and aggravated him more than Belik. No response felt right.

"Don't hold this against me or you'll put yourself and the princess in danger," Belik said. "I need you focused. I recommended you for this mission. Don't let me down."

Firian swallowed on a dry throat. He couldn't take this anymore. Without more than a curt nod, he left back to reality.

"I RECOGNIZE THIS!" Kiria said, her eyes shining as she moved closer to Firian. Their feet rasped against the stiff yellow grass of the animal track leading toward a dense, wet forest. Just ahead, huge trees hung with long, knotted, gray moss stood like gnarled old men. Water glinted through the dark trees, as though the forest stood in a marsh or lake. "It looks like the painting of Shifra we have up in the Palace." She cast Firian a smile, all her sorrows forgotten.

He wasn't surprised at her reaction. Shifra played a central role in the stories from the Scroll she'd heard thousands of times. Outcasts built Carradoc, the secret Khelê fortress, during the War of the Kingdom Rebels. In the days of the first Kingdom, its evil king killed any person he found different and therefore defective. According to the Scroll, God protected some of those persecuted people and named them his chosen race, the Khelê, "divine people." The ones who escaped from the Kingdom fled to Carradoc where they built an army to overthrow the king. Around the same time, the Scroll itself was written there. Shane and Mari Calthwaite, the non-Khelê founders of the three lines that now ruled the Kingdom, trained there.

Firian watched Kiria from the corner of his eye, a smile playing on the edges of his mouth. She practically skipped with excitement. Turning back to him, she swept her hair behind her ear. Had he ever been that innocent? Though she had power he wanted, she was pretty and pure like water. And he had set it boiling.

"*Out of Shifra will spring my chosen race,*" he said slowly, "*out of the fortress Carradoc, and those who once were abandoned will be found again, a united people. Their God will be their strength and never will they—*"

"*—vanish from the earth.*" Kiria jumped ahead and faced him, hands on hips. "That's really close," she said. Almost like a child in her excitement, she twirled around again and headed to the murky forest. Cheerfulness made her talkative. "I wonder if they still have the lanterns. I've always thought they were so beautiful. I didn't know if I'd make it to Shifra. They don't include it on the coronation tour because it's so far away."

"I'm glad you want to see it," he said. Apart from its history, the bedraggled forest wouldn't impress many people. The girl in front of him was more impressive. Her passion reminded him of the intoxicating secret she held just beneath the surface.

"I've wanted to for ages." She shook her head. "Daelon will be so jealous when I tell him about this. His family fought in the war, and he loves telling that story."

"What about the other Keepers?" Kiria didn't talk about them very much.

"My mother doesn't like traveling," she said, "but I'll tell her about it anyway. Atty'll be interested, I think." She turned back to look at him. "The Third Line is usually the one that travels, but he hasn't really done that. Cúron's probably already been here."

She tossed out the last sentence with a little resentment. *Interesting.*

As the ground started to squish beneath their feet, he could see why attacking Carradoc had been so difficult. Soon they waded through boggy grass that swallowed their shoes whole with each step. Even Kiria, despite her excitement, became momentarily disgruntled, her face scrunching.

"Here it is!" she said, louder than she should have. A rickety wooden walkway stretched like a long water snake through the swamp trees. He gave her a hand as she hoisted herself onto it. His foot splashed as he stepped up beside her.

"It's Shifra!" She clasped her hands in amazement. One sleeve fell down enough to reveal the black cloth around her wrist.

Firian blew a laugh through his nose. Her joy transfigured the gloomy swamp, elevating it by association. She hadn't been this happy their entire journey. The initial threat, her father's death, Torithians attacking in Raewhith... She hadn't had much reason to be.

The boards groaned and creaked as the two travelers walked single file along the narrow path. Great mossy trees blocked out the sun, but there were no lanterns yet.

Kiria slowed and turned to look at him. "Do you think we can reach Carradoc before nightfall?"

The pathway wound so much that Firian wasn't sure. According to the maps he'd studied, they could make it in a straight line, but this old trail twisted and doubled back constantly. No one was following them—that much was clear.

At the fortress, people waited for Kiria. Maybe they waited to congratulate him, too, for getting her there safely. He wanted to hear those words, but he wanted another night with Kiria to himself. She felt generous now, happy.

"I don't think so," he replied. "We'll find a place where the path widens out and we'll stay there. We'll find the fortress tomorrow morning."

She nodded, and then something caught her eye. "Lanterns!" she cried, pointing.

In the distance, a red light glimmered. He bowed his head to encourage her toward it. She scampered off. Just before the light, the path grew wider and sturdier, so more than two people could walk abreast. Even armed men didn't need to fear falling through a rotten board on this part of the walkway.

On either side, hanging from iron rods, glowed round lanterns of all colors. Unlike the ones hanging around the Amiran Academy in Brithnem, these weren't made of glass but dyed and woven fabric. Glass didn't belong here.

As they paced down the walkway, Kiria stopped now and then to lightly touch one of the spheres. Her hands, not used to hard labor, felt so soft. Their memory occupied Firian for a while.

Carradoc could appear any time now. They were clearly going the right way, and the path twisted less than before, heading straight for the fortress. At the next landing, Firian shouldered off the small pack they'd gotten to replace the old one.

"But we're almost there," Kiria said, backtracking to him.

He flashed her a smile. "It's farther than it looks. We'll get there in the morning." He stretched his arms behind his back, squeezing his shoulder blades together. His cut still stung. At the Academy, he wouldn't mention it. "Can you check my back?" he said. "I think it might need to be wrapped again."

"I'm sure it's fine. Are you sure we can't get there today?" She twisted a piece of her hair around her finger.

He grimaced as he pulled his blue shirt over his head. Strange to see any color but black. "Please?" he said, starting to unwrap the sash. It smelled musty, like everything else. He couldn't be certain, but he thought he saw her eyes widen. A good sign.

"You seem to be all right." She paused a moment, but he kept unraveling. With a sigh, she said, "I'll check."

He wrapped the sweaty fabric, now completely undone, around one hand and set it down in a pile. Then he turned around like an obedient child with his back to her.

Her warm breath breezed over his skin as she scrutinized the wound. "It's healing nicely," she said after a moment. "I don't think you need the sash anymore if you don't want it." She stepped back with a rattling creak.

When he turned around, she'd already started rummaging through her pack. Probably looking for pen and paper. Since they had picked it up in Imlin, she scribbled constantly. "New ideas for the Kingdom. I don't want to forget," she'd told him.

"Having an idea?" he asked, crouching beside her after throwing his shirt back on.

"I always have ideas," she replied absently, drawing out a pen from the bottom of the bag. "Why, do you want to add something?" Next came the notebook, which had cost more than he had in his pocket at the time, but he doubted she would want to know that.

"Can I?" He sat down.

She hugged the notebook to her chest, suddenly shy. "If I like your idea, I'll write it down."

"I feel like we've done this before."

"But not with this," she said, waving the pen in the air.

"End the war," he said playfully, nudging her. "Then your problems will be gone."

"Never mind. Your time's up." She turned her eyes in mock seriousness to the page.

"You know," he said, "if you weren't so frustrating, you'd be pretty wonderful."

She looked up at him, bright red.

He'd tried that line before, but this time it felt different. He said the word as he never had before, finally starting to realize what it meant. No other girl knew as much about him as Kiria did. She saw his family and helped him kill a man. Everything he had worked for led to this. Kiria, the beautiful Kepress of Brithnem, was the height of his ambition.

But it didn't feel that way now. At this moment, she meant more. He wanted to know her thoughts, to spend time with her, to touch her. Other girls had been a balm, a pastime, but Kiria offered substance.

Her brown eyes searched his as though she were trying to read his thoughts. Concern lined her small features, all bathed in orange light.

His gut squirmed. He was never uncomfortable like this. Hating his own weakness, he forced himself to meet her eyes, thoughtful in a heart-shaped face. If she hadn't been the Kepress, and hadn't possessed any of her Abilities, he'd still want to look in that face. And that power over him that she didn't know she wielded made his mouth go dry.

The silence weighed heavy. A fish splashed.

She didn't run like last time, but he held his body still as though any movement would spook her.

"You're wonderful too," she said thickly, barely above a whisper.

His heart thumped hard at the words. Slowly, he moved her hair from her shoulder, brushing his fingers against the hollow of her neck. Her pulse pounded under his fingertips. She leaned closer as he stroked her arm all the way down to her hand, hot and soft in his. He brought his face to her small one, breathing against her mouth.

A scuffle on the walkway made him look. A sturdy, red-haired woman bustled from light to light, refilling the oil. She carried a small vat that banged against her wide hip each time she stepped.

Damn. Firian exhaled in frustration just before she saw them.

Kiria sucked in a breath and pulled away. At the sight of the woman, she hopped to her feet.

"Who's there?" called the woman warily, holding a tiny spoon in one fist. Oil dripped from it onto her heavily tattooed hand.

"It's…" Kiria started, sounding a little hoarse. She cast a quick look at him as he stood and confirmed this woman was no threat with a nod. "It's… the two you were expecting."

The woman walked closer for a better look, her short steps echoing. He hated the sound and wished he could toss her into the swamp. "So it is!" she cried, giving a tight-lipped smile. "Come with me, eh?"

Firian picked up the pack and followed Kiria's eager feet. So they were close to the fortress after all.

36

KIRIA

Kiria knelt at the grave, distracted as her kneecap hit the cobblestones. Shane Calthwaite and his son Sandor (father of the Lost Line) had fought and died here. The first time Daelon told her the story, she cried. The Khelê had tucked the memorial in a corner of the enormous open courtyard of Carradoc, carving the names deep into the stone wall. Small offerings littered the ground beneath the gravestone: tokens, herbs, candles.

She touched her forehead in respect, feeling the eyes of the Khelê scrutinizing her. The question in their gazes told it all. They wondered about her Ability. After her eighteenth birthday, when she'd been publicly introduced, everyone in the Kingdom knew that she possessed overwhelming Beauty. They were waiting.

Firian just stood next to her, looking out, acting the body-guard. She caught his eye and beckoned for him to show his respects. He hesitated before quickly bowing to one knee before the memorial.

Wishing she could have a quiet moment alone with her thoughts, she cast one more look at the grave she had longed for years to see. Slowly, she stood and faced the small crowd gathered behind her. The fortress still functioned as a military barracks and training ground, but now parts of it seemed to function more like a small city. Civilian Khelê like the stout red-haired woman formed the majority of the group wanting to see the Kepress.

Her hands tingled. If wouldn't take much to change, to impress them all, to set Firian on fire... She closed her hands gently into fists. Should she? She stood for a moment in indecision as she looked at the people of Carradoc, trying to ignore her peripheral vision.

She should be enough, even without her Beauty.

But she had made this choice. The Kingdom mattered more than her personal comfort, and right now these kind people offering her refuge were looking for their Kepress. So she transformed.

Several gasped and brought their hands to their mouths. One woman began to cry quietly, overcome by the sight. Some stepped forward, some back. A few crossed their arms, defensive, self-comforting. In one way or another, every person was moved. Firian tensed beside her. She felt his hungry stare move over her body. Her breathing grew shallow.

The tension she felt built within her. The people still waited.

"Thank you for welcoming us to this place," she said. Her voice sounded small and she was shorter than almost everyone around her. Usually Cúron did this sort of thing. Kiria just greeted guests.

She glanced at Firian. He looked back before scanning the crowd again.

What am I afraid of? This is nothing.

"It's been my dream," she continued, "to visit the fortress of Carradoc since I was a little girl. My tutor at the Amiran Academy loves to tell stories of his Khelê ancestors fighting alongside the founders." She smiled and gestured to the grave. "I pray we live up to their bravery, whether we are Keepers or tradesmen, Amir or Tanyu. But now, it's getting late, so I thank you all."

Hopefully that would be enough. It was risky to mention Amir and Tanyu together, since supporters tended to favor one heavily over the other. But her little speech didn't sound too bad. The miss-matched group of soldiers and civilians nodded and shifted, still wide-eyed.

Humid darkness filled the large courtyard like water and made the bright torches hazy. Warm firelight glowed on the faces. The lazy clunk of slow wagon wheels over cobblestones magnified in the waiting stillness. After all the day's excitement, Kiria's eyes burned for sleep.

Firian touched her waist. She spun to face him. He looked meaningfully at Matthan, the man charged with showing them around, who had approached the side of the empty semi-circle where she stood by the grave. The after-image of Firian's fingers felt warm.

"You must have had a long day of travel, my Kepress," said Matthan. "Let me show you to your room."

"Yes, thank you."

Matthan led them away from the crowd though a passage as wide as a street. Maybe it was a road. Like other soldiers in the complex, Matthan wore complete metal armor up to the neck. He had light green eyes, tanned skin, and a light beard that covered some of the tattooed symbols on his face. Kiria hadn't decided on a design for her royal tattoo, but she wanted it on her back and arms, not her face.

Firian followed behind. Since their moment on the platform, they hadn't spoken. The more time passed, the more she doubted her decision to respond to him. As Matthan led them to their secure quarters, she felt his eyes on her. He wanted to figure her out, to open her up, to protect her. For all his maddening qualities, she'd be lying if she said that part of her didn't want to yield to him. Just a small part. But it was selfish to want Firian's arms around her. Nothing could come of it. He had saved her, taught her, comforted her, become a friend. But he lacked respect, and his wild ambition could bring down the Kingdom.

It wasn't that he was a Tanyu that prevented her from being with him, despite some of the prejudices in Brithnem. Tanyuin skills fascinated her. It was that he was Firian. To give into desire would show nothing but weakness. She couldn't be with him, and she shouldn't lead him to think so.

"Here we are!" Matthan opened a wooden door set into the stone. It opened onto a chamber big enough for the two of them. "This is our finest room. I'll send an additional guard to watch the door and someone will come in the morning to draw you a bath before breakfast."

A bath. Her chest ached with gratitude. "Thank you very much," she said, going inside.

Dark red blankets covered a large bed. *Is that a down pillow?* The sight brought a lump to her throat. After weeks in the wilderness, she'd almost forgotten how wonderful it was to sleep in a comfortable bed. A large blue rug covered most of the stone floor, and even amenities like a mirror and sink stood in corners, ready for use.

She sighed deeply, the beauty and comfort of the place soothing her soul. The room wasn't nearly as grand as hers in the palace, but she felt more thankful for it. Before this journey, she hadn't considered how much luxury she had. Now she did, and promised herself to be more grateful.

She fell on the bed and hugged the soft pillow. A sharp twist in her gut reminded her of the night terrors. Hopefully tonight she could sleep in peace.

Firian didn't seem tired. Did he ever sleep? She had woken up with him in the morning, but she couldn't match his stamina to stay up late at night.

"No lesson tonight," she murmured, closing her eyes.

As the door latched closed, memory fell thick between them. She opened one eye to see where he was. He didn't expect to pick up where they left off, did he?

He leaned over her to grab the other pillow. He dropped it on the floor. "Sure?" he asked.

"I need some rest." Then, after a moment, "Maybe tomorrow."

———

THE SNICK of a lock woke her. When the door opened silently on its hinges, the contrasting moonlight revealed the outline of a man in armor. The guard. It must be. What was he doing here at this hour?

She rolled her head luxuriously to the side and squinted into the thick darkness. The man didn't bring a light. Her gut twisted.

The bed sank down as Firian sat on the edge, half leaning over her. She felt his tense heat through the blankets. He put one strong hand on her leg. His other hand must have strayed to his knife, because of the slight, leathern sound of metal against the sheath.

Her breath caught in a tight ball under her ribcage. If this really were their guard, why did no one use a light? And why didn't Firian trust him? Carradoc was supposed to be safe.

Firian's voice made her jump. "State your business." The weight on her leg disappeared. He'd stood up to face the intruder.

Alone in the bed, she realized how paper-thin her nightgown was. The blankets were a welcome barrier, but not enough. Her unshod feet went cold.

"The girl—" His words strangled away into a gasp, a choke-hold. Electricity jolted through her veins. She tucked her legs in and sat up.

"Firian! Master Firian! I'm—let go!—I'm..." He coughed, able to breathe a little better. "I'm Tanyu."

"What are you doing here?" Firian growled.

"Tanyu are everywhere."

"You're not from the Academy."

"Not for a long time. I'm supposed to deliver a message."

The shuffle of feet. Firian had let him go. He was a Defender, not a Master, wasn't he?

"Who sent you?"

"Master Belik."

The hum in the air stilled. Kiria's heart beat hollow in her chest. The name didn't sound familiar, at least not in a way she could place, but something had shifted for Firian.

"What does he say?" Firian whispered through his teeth.

"Strike a light," said the other.

She hated the command but couldn't stand the darkness any longer herself. She lit the candle on the side table. Huge, bloated shadows twisted over the walls. She drew the blankets up higher. At the foot of the bed stood Firian with a knife in his hand, stiff-shouldered. He didn't spare a look for her when the light flared up. All his energy focused on the man before him. Dark eyebrows lowered over his glaring eyes. He practically vibrated with intensity.

The other man didn't cower under the attention, even though Firian had shown how effectively he could attack. His long blond hair had been tied back at the nape of his neck. He had to be ten years older than the two of them. His torso, longer than average, sat on strong, thick legs. The sharp panes of his face looked severe in profile.

"What does he say?" Firian repeated, fractionally drawing out each word.

The blond man flicked a look at Kiria and adjusted his clothes. "The Amir have been given a vote in the Main."

It passed. How could it pass?

Her eyes widened, glad at least that the conversation now veered into something she knew. Except, it didn't make sense that this Tanyu from Carradoc would know about it.

"So your situation has changed." He glanced at Firian's knife. Apparently satisfied that he wouldn't aim it at his throat, he looked again at her, turning his head completely. His rugged face looked sharp from this angle too. Something about the glint in his eye made her insides squirm. It was predatory, like an animal gloating over prey.

Firian stepped between them with his back to her.

"The Tanyu sent their request and they were denied the same vote." The blond man's voice dripped with languid confidence now. He, at least, thought his danger had passed.

Watching Firian's back, she wasn't so sure.

Pieces started clicking into place in her mind. *Atty, what have you done?*

Amir and Tanyu had never seen eye to eye. If the Amir could vote in the most powerful kingdom on the continent, the Tanyu would expect the same treatment. Why hadn't she warned Atty when she had the chance?

The man continued. "So, you're not her bodyguard anymore. You'll keep her as a hostage until we finish negotiations."

A shock ran through Kiria's veins. All of the air sucked out of the room. Was she in the Unreal? Was this a dream? She drew one bare foot over the other. The clammy cold of the toes dragged over the bridge of her foot confirmed the reality of where she was.

The knife loosened in Firian's grip and he drew it back in, twisting it in his fist. He didn't reply.

"Don't kill her or hurt her. We're still in talks. But you can have some fun."

Her mouth went dry.

"Get out of here tonight. We'll know where you are."

"How?" The first word Firian had spoken in too long. Would he really choose the corrupt Tanyu over her?

The man's cheek creased in a smile she could see around the side of Firian's neck. "That was the whole message." The man leaned over to leer at her.

Hot fury roared through her body. No one looked at a Kepress like that. If Firian wouldn't defend her, then she would do it herself.

Surprising herself, she stood. The sensation was like jumping into the ocean. "I am the Kepress of Brithnem," she said with the strength of desperation and the voice of a queen. Her gaze flickered to Firian, who half-turned. "And I order you to leave. I'm surrounded by allies here, and we're staying."

"I am a Tanyu," the man said simply.

"No," she said, fighting to keep her voice steady. "'*To the Tanyu I have given the task of protecting the people of God and their Keepers.*'" The passage flew out before she realized she was quoting.

A hint of amused annoyance passed over the man's face. He tipped his head. "Not this time." The man nodded with parting deference. "Master Firian," he said, and closed the door behind him as he left.

37

FIRIAN

THERE WAS A HORRIBLE SILENCE. Firian realized he still had the knife in his hand. It felt heavier than usual. He put it in its sheath.

Conflicting thoughts overlapped each other as Kiria stared at him, aghast. The buzz he'd felt when he entered the fortress made more sense now. At first, he had blamed the feeling on Kiria. Like an idiot, he hadn't recognized the obvious. Sentries. He knew what they felt like—he knew the difference. That meant that Tanyu were here. But why hadn't he known? And why did the Academy shield them from his mind? The messenger wore the outfit of a Carradoc soldier, not a Tanyu.

He had a feeling—not a terrible feeling, but a blank, sure feeling—that the Academy had planned all of this. In such a storm of thoughts, this fact only bothered him vaguely.

Kiria, his hostage? It had the taste of unreality. For a split second, he willed fire into his hand. In the Unreal, it would work. He looked down at his dark palm. No spark.

Belik's words came back to him: *Remember to do anything we tell you.*

He was done following demands blindly. But this put him on

the world stage. Finish this, and he would be an equal to Belik and Jovan and all those others who had controlled him for so long...

He had to obey the Academy. Suddenly he wondered what Bard would say, but he had no idea.

Kiria's glare turned slowly from a clear, defiant question to fearful uncertainty. Firian lifted his hand and she flinched.

"You heard the man," he said. His voice sounded hollow. "Get your things."

He said it more to buy a moment away from her penetrating stare than because he really wanted to say it.

But Kiria still fixed him with a fierce look, unmoving, as though the sound of his voice gave her renewed resolve. She opened her mouth. No sound came out, so she closed it again and shook her head.

Whatever else she was, she was either braver or more reckless than he would have thought to stand up to him in this moment. The Kingdom couldn't stand against the Academy. "It wasn't a question," he said, a surge of anger welling up within him. He couldn't have said why.

"If you won't protect me, I'll protect myself," she said, her voice cracking.

"Then pack your stuff."

"I won't go." The simple statement cut the bond between them. They both felt it lashing. By just a little, her eyes grew sad. And the room grew cold.

"You will," he said, his rage growing.

Her small face pleaded with him. "Firian." The way she said it sent goosebumps over his skin.

"No. We're leaving. Now." He glared, willing her to follow his order.

Finally, with measured breathing, she stooped down to put on her shoes, never taking her eyes off him.

He felt like cursing and strode forward to grab their packs. Every shape in the darkness mocked him.

A scuffle of feet.

Kiria bolted for the door, grasping madly for the handle. With a lunge, he grabbed her, pinning her arms at her sides. She shrank from his touch as he dragged her from the door.

"Help, somebody! Help—" He clasped his hand over her mouth. She screamed hot in his hand, but no sound would reach outside the room.

"Shh, shh!" he hissed in her ear. Her nearness oddly soothed him. "They said move, then wait. That's all," he said, each word slow and distinct. "I won't hurt you."

Her wild eyes looked back in his. When she stopped screaming, he released her to speak. "You don't have to do this," she said quietly. Her heart beat fast in her chest. "The Keepers will kill you if you don't bring me home."

They can try. "I don't want to hurt you," he said, avoiding her gaze. "If you run away, there are Torithians. I'll still take care of you."

Her lip curled.

"You can't try this again. If you do, I'll know." He turned her around to face him, still holding her at arm's length. Although she looked him defiantly in the face, her hair fell disheveled and she looked distraught. That stupid messenger had ruined all he'd built with her and left him with far more questions than answers. He didn't want to threaten her. Experimentally, he let her go.

She didn't bolt, but walked back to her shoes with her head so high, it was as though she'd commanded him to let her go and, by the force of her authority, he had obeyed. At the very least, she acted the noble prisoner.

He ran a hand through his hair. *Gore.* What was he going to do now?

WATER AND MUD made slogging forward difficult. He couldn't run in water up to his hips, and she certainly couldn't with the water rising to her waist. Maybe this route was a mistake. But once people realized the Kepress and her bodyguard were missing, the first place they'd check would be the walkways—the only easy way through the swamp. This was the only other option.

Radiating anger, Kiria didn't speak. Maybe she'd never been so covered in mud.

"Nothing's changed," Firian said.

"Don't be an idiot," she shot back. "Of course it has."

His face flushed with rage.

Something slimy swam by. She jumped and whirled on him as though it were his fault. The movement was almost graceful.

They continued and sloshed around opposite sides of a massive, gray-barked tree.

You know I don't have a choice. But the words wouldn't come out. Mud and anger made him sullen.

Unbidden, Master Belik appeared in his mind as clearly as if he stood in front of him, an unreadable face in an unreadable room. He looked hard at Firian.

"Don't go to Archer's Point," he said.

"Hello," Firian said pointedly.

"Don't be a child. Archer's Point has more Kingdom allies than Carradoc. Until we have this sorted out, you'll need to stay away from populated areas." Belik spoke as though reading from a list.

"Why didn't you let me know this way? Why did you send that fool? He was surrounded!" Firian pointed furiously behind him into the darkness.

"*I* didn't send him," Belik said. "But I understand it. The princess needed the fear of God put into her."

Firian's eyes narrowed. He spat a curse. "You're just breaking all ties with the Kingdom, then." *And putting a target on me.*

"Not if they do what we say."

Firian looked into the familiar face of his Master, the one he had trusted. How much of this plan had he engineered? And now he threw Firian to the wolves. Why? Because he thought he could handle himself, or that he was expendable? "You knew about this," he said, accusation dripping from every word.

The Master ignored the comment. "The Head made me your contact. It makes sense."

"No," Firian said, "you *knew* this would happen."

"It was always a possibility," Belik admitted. He took off his glasses and rubbed them clean on his shirt. A disarming gesture, unnecessary in the Unreal. Old habits. "Firian, trust me. Stay out of sight and nothing will happen to you."

"I can handle the city."

Belik settled his glasses on his face again. "Not when Brithnem starts sending troops. Even the best can't defeat fifty people at once."

Firian tried to picture it. It almost made him wish he had the chance. It would loosen the tight knot of anger in his stomach.

"No, you couldn't," Belik continued, as though reading his mind. "For now, don't kill the girl. I know you probably wouldn't want to anyway," he said, lifting his eyebrows a fraction, their message clear. Belik's insinuation only aggravated him. "But you might have to kill her eventually, a few weeks maybe. We'll let you know when."

Kill her. His body felt electric. "But it would be more useful to keep her alive—" he sputtered.

"We're not catering to your—"

"I mean she has the Talent," Firian snapped, thinking fast. "I could take her back to the Academy."

Almost imperceptibly, Belik's mouth fell open, the only sign this was completely new information. "At this point we don't need the risk," he said finally. "We know where her loyalties lie, with her family and her country. She'll probably make herself a martyr and help them. In the end we'd have to kill her anyway."

"I might... be able to change that," Firian said, his pulse quickening from the greatness of the challenge he issued himself. Belik could be right, but what if he really could sway her?

"Like I said," continued Belik, "you might have a few weeks. They'll crack. And if they don't, you'll have to eliminate her." He tilted his head down to see over his glasses, sending a warning. Surprisingly, lines of sympathy pinched the edges of his eyes. "You're overestimating yourself, Firian. If you follow what we say, the Head will promote you as soon as you get back. A Master by nineteen. Don't screw it up." He let the words simmer.

A Master by nineteen.

Despite everything, his heart leapt. Firian had fought so hard to hear those words. All his life, he'd practiced to become a Master. It was all he'd ever wanted. And, after one mission, it was within his grasp.

Surely the Kingdom would give the Tanyu more power if their Kepress was in danger. No question. They would yield, he would release her on good terms, and then he would return to the Academy a hero.

Belik rolled two fingers together thoughtfully before he continued, treading more carefully than usual, as though he felt the words needed to be said. "You have to be prepared to kill her." With that, the blank room dissolved. Murky trees and sky and Kiria seeped into focus.

Firian tasted blood. He'd bit the inside of his lip. Disgusted, he spat into the swamp. As soon as they escaped Shifra, he would rebuild what he'd had with Kiria. She'd come with him before submitting to death. But hopefully it wouldn't come to that.

"Firian." Kiria looked at him in concern, as though she sensed his abstraction as he went into the Unreal. She probably did. She'd seen it often enough. "Firian." His name got softer in her mouth. The tips of her hair swished in the water.

He looked over the dark wetland, scanning for rescue teams or dangerous creatures. When he knew they were alone, he slowed his pace.

"I know what you want," she said quietly, her demeanor no longer angry. "I know you want to be the best. But there's more than one way." She laid a hesitant hand on his arm. "Think about what your sister would say. Her husband fights on our side. There's still time to turn around. No one will know we were gone."

"And then what?" he snarled. The mention of Brett sent him into a fury. If he did what Kiria said, the Kingdom *and* the Tanyu would have his head.

Kiria grew quiet and looked away, wading with him through the gloom. Swishing water filled the hollow silence. He felt his hands at her soft throat, a knife to her chest, a knock to the head—the relentless images played in his mind. He hated each one with visceral hatred.

His chest tightened. No one asked him what he wanted. Instead, everyone thought they knew best and could use him for their purposes. Grinding his teeth, he felt blackmailed by everything he cared about.

What do *you want?* Bard would ask.

I want to be a Master. I want Kiria.

I want all of it.

38
____

KIRIA

THE ROUGH BARK scratched the inside of her arms. Firian silently wound the sash around Kiria's wrists, tying her arms behind a tree. The black cloth tied around her wrist squeezed the circulation from her hand. Cold, howling wind blew hard through the grasses. "You could turn yourself in," she said, twisting to try to see him. "I'll make sure nothing happens to you."

He scoffed. "If you wouldn't run away, I wouldn't do this," he muttered, tightening the cloth. He laid his hand over hers when he was finished. Then, louder, "You could also give Tanyu a vote."

"Not after this." She settled back, grimly looking straight ahead. Defying him gave her an odd mixture of nervousness and strength.

Tanyu hadn't helped the Western Kingdom in any tangible way until Firian came as her bodyguard. At least not in her lifetime or her mother's. They sent ambassadors to keep informed, who were little more than vain warriors flexing their strength. They kept their talents to themselves, not offering to assist even in the Torithian War.

At least the Amir had served the Western Kingdom faithfully. If one group held more claim to a vote, they did.

The light faded, leaving deep, soaking shadows under the trees. Dark blue skies between blowing black branches.

He crawled to the front of the tree, facing her. "You know it's not my choice," he said, his face very close to hers. His dark hair whipped against her face.

"Of course it is." Heat rose along her neck, but she remained resolute. There was always a choice. Hopefully Firian didn't want to be involved in making her a hostage, but either way, he had betrayed her.

He sat up and crossed his legs, their knees touching. "Kiria, you should understand. Where would you be without me?"

The selfishness of his friendship became clearer and clearer. Irritated, she pursed her mouth. "At home with my mother."

He ran a hand back through his dark hair and took a deep breath. "I mean about the Torithians. You're not like the others. You have Abilities. Two of them."

"And you have one, but look what you're doing with it." She tried to tuck her legs closer.

His lip twitched in the waning light. "I don't want to be your enemy."

"You don't want me to be your enemy," she said slowly, in a voice of steel. Hopefully he would understand. Her mother didn't need any more heartbreak, but now the Academy had made her daughter a pawn in their political game. Kiria wouldn't stand for it. Not only was it a bad idea politically to give the ruthless Tanyu power over the Kingdom, but personally too. When she returned, she would make them pay for what they had done.

For a while Firian fell silent, looking over her as though she were a castle to be taken. She tensed, preparing for his next attempt to find an entrance.

"Kiria." He leaned close but she went rigid, flinching away from him. Out of sight, her hands twisted in their bonds. No use. As he brought his face to her ear, her heart hammered painfully. "I want to protect you from the Tanyu," he whispered, as though someone would overhear, "but I can only do that if you come with me. I want you to come with me."

Another wailing gust of air swept over her, sending loose strands of her hair flying across her face, sticking to her lips, her eyes. He let the words settle before checking her response. When she didn't answer, he sighed with frustration and sat down next to her. "You have to come with me," he said.

"Where? I have to go home."

"The Academy." The idea excited him, and he turned to her, his face alight. The intensity renewed her fear. His blue eyes flitted over her. "You have the Talent, Kiria. You could become one of the most feared leaders in the world." Goosebumps rose up on his arms. "I..." His voice trailed off.

"I can't do that." It would feel like betrayal. Strangely, their journey together had toughened her will enough to defy the danger gladly.

"You like me," he said suddenly.

The statement caught her off balance. It was true. But he'd chosen not to be the good man he could be. "And you care enough about me not to hurt me," she said, treading carefully.

He paused. They sat together, bound against their will to violent demands. Barely, he nodded—an admission.

She let out the breath she'd been holding. "Firian, it doesn't have to be like this," she said gently, his friend again. "I've seen what you can be. You can be a good man." She nodded encouragingly and scraped the sash across the bark, hinting.

Firian's eyes blazed. In the dim twilight, his eyebrows twitched downward in realization. "I don't want to be good," he said. "I want more than that. I want you."

He pursed his lips to a thin line, and suddenly moved. As she pulled away and shut her eyes, he pressed a kiss to her forehead. Her eyes shot open. Then she saw him lean back again and strip off his jacket. He balled it up for a pillow and lay down just out of reach.

WITH ONE SWIFT MOTION, Firian pulled out the pin that held up her hair. It came falling down around her shoulders, until he gathered up a fistful and held it against the nape of her neck. He guided her face to his, her mouth to his. Her heart pounded.

As they kissed slowly, she drew her hands along the ridges of his ribs all the way up to his muscular chest, and then dragged her fingers down his abs. A warm, insistent ache grew in her stomach. Her knees buckled under it and she fell onto her bed. He never broke contact with her, launching forward and propping himself up on his hands. His arms closed around her waist as their kisses became sweltering, urgent. His hand moved to her leg...

Kiria woke up gasping. The dark forest spiraled back to silence as the ache died.

How could he do this? How could he attack her in her sleep? First nightmares and then attacks? Red rage blinded her. Stretching as far from the tree as she could, she kicked Firian hard. "How dare you!" she hissed.

He jolted awake, bolt upright, hair flying crazily, a knife in his hand from somewhere. Seeing her, he exhaled. "Kiria," he said, half relieved, half accusing. She could barely hear him over the wind. He lowered the knife.

Her mouth went dry. He was asleep? Could he attack someone when he was asleep? Tanyu could do a lot of things—it might be possible.

Darkness hid her deep blush. "Firian," she said, now having no idea how to proceed, "were you in... the Unreal, just now? You *can't* just..."

He looked at her in confusion for a moment, but even the darkness couldn't hide the smirk that slowly spread over his face. "No, I wasn't."

She wished she could shrink into a hole. "Oh. Okay. You know you can't..." Her last attempt failed just like the first one.

"I wouldn't," he said, tucking the knife under his jacket pillow.

Mortified, she closed her eyes and prayed for no more dreams.

After a long time, the waves of embarrassment flowed less insistently. Firian's slow breathing told her he was asleep. She couldn't remember another time when he slept while she was awake. The simple realization made her stop short. How many opportunities would she have to get away? She had no idea how far the Academy was from here. It could be days; it could be weeks.

She curled her fingers inward toward the sash, feeling along its edges. Smooth fabric and then, a thread! She rolled it between her fingers, testing its length. With a slight tear she felt but couldn't hear above the high wind, the thread unraveled as she pulled it, passing it from hand to hand as it circled around her wrists. There was still the knot to deal with, but this should loosen the rest of the binding. She kept ripping at the thread, coiling it around her fingers, dropping the useless length, picking it up again, until her arms felt cool, freed from the top of the restraint.

Facing away from her, Firian didn't move. She held her breath as her nails caught the bulk of the knot, weakened by the shredded sash. She pulled, coaxing it to come undone. One end of the sash budged, widening the circle tying her arms together.

Straining quietly, she pulled her hands one at a time out of the loop. The black cloth fell with the rest of the fabric.

Now to get away. The forest, so dark it looked burned, mocked her as she looked around for some indication of where to go. Shifra was the only place that came to mind, and she knew dimly where that was. The messenger, that double-agent, probably still lurked there, but most of the people in the fortress would support her. Hide her. Take her home.

That was it, then. She couldn't sit here deciding any longer. Carefully, carefully, she stood, distributing her weight so the twigs wouldn't crack under her feet. Her chest trembled with her jagged heartbeats. With shaking hands, she took one painstaking step and then another. And then another.

When she was out of earshot, she ran.

39

FIRIAN

ALONE WITH HIS THOUGHTS, Firian had no choice but to sprint, trying to exhaust himself out of his black mood. Despite the cold, he felt hot.

Kiria was gone.

How could this happen? She'd floated before his mind constantly as they traveled. He could sense her like the direction of the sun with his eyes closed, her fear, her resolve. But when he woke, he felt her presence getting farther and farther away.

His thighs burned as he sprinted as fast as he could through the forest where he'd grown up. He fought the urge to scream, barreling toward the field of yellow grass. It grew tall, but the sound would give her away.

Dimly, a voice shouted in his mind. He shoved away the summons. Later, after he'd caught up with her and left anyone who'd helped her escape in a bloody heap, he could face another Tanyu. Not now.

Now... there were eyes upon him that he knew. It wasn't Belik's call but Kiria's look. Like a man dying of thirst, he dove into the Unreal. The color and power of it gushed over him.

On the Unreal mountainside, Master Belik appeared, furiously working his glasses. He shouted something but Firian, his mind crammed with bloody rage, couldn't tell what he said to him. Belik stood huge before him, filling the space with his presence as though to block Kiria from view. "I said stop, you damn idiot!" he said.

"No," said Firian.

"Listen! If you stop, you can get information. There's little you can get out of the girl while she's running around with you."

This all seemed like gibberish to Firian. A mad urge to strike Master Belik surged up in him. He had to calm down. "What?" he demanded, slowing to a walk.

"They refused to surrender in exchange for the girl," said Belik, very distinctly.

Firian furrowed his forehead. That didn't seem right. *Why wouldn't they?*

"You did what you could," said Belik. "Let her go back to Brithnem. The Amir will let their guard down. You come back to the Academy." He worked his jaw. "I know you think about her. So, *think* about her. Tell us what you find out."

Firian's chest heaved with the effort of running so long. His lip curled. "I'll find her," he said.

"No, you won't." Belik took a step forward, seeming to shrink to his normal size. "You and the girl have a *katah*, or am I wrong?"

Firian blinked. He hadn't intended to declare one on her. He and Kiria *had* practiced focusing on each other for days. Even now, he sensed where she hid, saw the trees, felt her fear as though he could see everything happening. Unintentional *katah* meant weakness; using it could mean strength.

"I thought so," Belik said, a tinge of irony in his tone.

"But we didn't—"

"Maybe you should have."

Firian popped his jaw with frustration, opening his

eardrums. A *katah*-level connection could give him power since Kiria wasn't strong enough in her Talent to counteract him. If he wanted to spy on her, he could.

Belik cracked his thick neck. "For now, watch her and find out what she knows. If you follow her now, your mission will be a failure." He spoke each word distinctly. The last one lingered in the air like smoke. Firian hated the stench of it, comprised of all his mistakes and all of Belik's. A shadow seemed to fall over the Master's face.

Picking flakes of skin around his Defender ring, Firian sucked his teeth and looked down, over, anywhere for answers. His chin jutted forward, his breaths coming short.

He couldn't fail.

"As you would have it, Master Belik."

WHEN THE ACADEMY loomed above him, all dark stone, his mouth tasted sour as though he would be sick. After hurrying to get back, he found himself wishing he were anywhere else.

I'll get her back, he reminded himself. Kiria would come to him. That would shut them up.

Standing before the enormous wooden doors, he felt stripped of everything. Bitter hatred gnawed him. After all that work and anticipation... He closed his eyes and set his mouth before going in.

The fountain splashed in the courtyard, staircases rose along the walls, leading to the rooms on the upper floors. Learners formed little groups, walking to class or talking by the fountain. He rushed past them, hating it all. His eyes flickered over the faces to find Tiev, Bard—someone he'd have to respond to. A few acquaintances, but that was all. None of them Defenders.

His rage led him to the one who had orchestrated it all. When he reached Belik's door, he didn't knock.

Belik knelt next to a man lying unconscious on the floor. At the sound of the door crashing open, the Master opened his eyes in the slow, conscious way of a swimmer after he breaks the surface. In a silence that spoke louder than a shout, he slowly turned around. "You'll have to learn respect," he said. Firian had never seen him so angry. His mouth was a hard, cold line. "I would hate to have to teach it to you."

Firian was in no mood to be criticized. "Yes, Master Belik," he grated.

Belik raised his eyebrows at his tone and stood up. "I could have left you out there," he said meaningfully. The words would have had more effect under different circumstances. Belik's hand clenched. Striking the back of his chair with a sharp crash, he cried, "I should have left you out there! But I scrambled to find a reason to keep you. Direct access to the princess's mind."

"Yes, Master Belik."

"Then finish your mission and the Academy may forgive your gory stupidity!"

At the noise, the man on the floor rolled his head to the other side and his eyelids fluttered. Firian saw milky whiteness underneath.

Belik pointed at the man. "Thank your stars he wasn't Lost," he said, as though he didn't want a reason to blame Firian for anything else. Master Belik turned away from him to the man on the floor.

Firian's chest felt tight as he stormed back through the courtyard to the stairs. Eyes followed him as he rushed past. By habit, he checked the Unreal. No eyes there. Kiria was not among those watching him.

Had they counted on a connection between him and Kiria? Belik acted as if he hadn't known about her Talent, but the

Academy had lied before. At least this war wasn't Belik's idea. He didn't have that much power. The Head had to be behind it.

That coward.

Bard wasn't in the room when Firian got back. Probably all for the best. Bard would be glad to see him, and Firian couldn't say the same thing. At least not until he'd calmed down.

40

KIRIA

Gulping for air, Kiria opened her eyes. Darkness. Where was she?

Her fingers spread open into deep, soft blankets. A pillow scented with lilies and musk cradled her head, now covered in her sweaty hair. She's slept in Brithnem, in the palace, in her own bed. But she still had nightmares. The disembodied sense of panic came from Torithians, from weapons rushing through thin air, from strangers in a pub, from Firian.

What time is it? She rolled over and tried to gauge any light coming in from the window. Oddly, it looked far away. Her room was enormous. She had woken up before the sun, even before Candrae and Vayci.

They had been so happy to see her yesterday. Against protocol, they had both hugged her, laying a dark, bare head and a dainty blonde one against hers. Shocked by how thin and bedraggled she'd become, they gave her a bath and clean clothes. The bath revealed that the raised, misshapen arrow scars in her left shoulder and thigh were here to stay. Her skin had darkened and her hair lightened in the sun.

Kiria's return to the palace was a bright blur of voices hushed and shouted. Jori brought her food, Atty glowed, Daelon smiled and brewed tea.

Her mother cried and fell on her when she first saw her daughter in the hallway. Kiria cried too, deep, heaving sobs. One person couldn't welcome her back.

In the darkness, she squeezed her eyes shut. A tear leaked out, streaking down her face into her hair. She made it back safe, but so much had happened that she couldn't relax.

They had caught the Torithian on the grounds of the castle, they told her. A couple from the city who hated the Keepers' leadership had helped him gain access. For weeks he had hidden in the wine cellar and adjacent storage rooms beneath the palace. Both the Torithian murderer and the traitorous couple had been instantly put to death.

Restless, Kiria sat up and struck a candle. When she and Firian had left Carradoc, she'd forgotten to take her notebook. It was still there when she returned, hungry and caked in mud. She thought she would remember the traitor-messenger's face, but she never spotted him. Still, an armed escort of five randomly chosen soldiers marched her back to the palace. She picked them herself, hoping that she could avoid, or at least break up, a contingent loyal to the Academy.

She picked up the notebook from her side table. With her mother still recovering from grief and shock, someone needed to contribute for the Second Line. A few comments yesterday made it sound as if she hadn't been in most of the sessions since Father died.

Her pen scratched along the page until gray light dawned. A click of the door—her head shot up. Quietly, Vayci and Candrae entered the room, carrying candles. Candrae's pale eyes widened at the sight of another light and Kiria sitting up in bed.

"My Kepress," she cried, rushing over to her, "are you unwell?"

"No, I'm fine," Kiria replied, closing the notebook on her finger. "I need a drink of water."

"Of course," Vayci replied, leaving like a dark shadow.

Candrae remained by her side. "Why is my lady awake so early?" she asked softly.

Firian's hour. "I just couldn't sleep." She pushed thin hair out of her face. Her Ability didn't need to emerge again until she went to a session. For now, being plain gave her a different kind of comfort, of invisibility.

Candrae laid a comforting hand flat on the blankets beside her. "We have posted extra guards for your safety," she said, "and we will catch Defender Kess for what he did to you."

Kiria looked down and quirked her lips. Candrae put it nicely. Others, yesterday, had cursed his name, promising to rain down torture. She understood, but she couldn't join them. In fact, their threats rankled. She knew the better man he could choose to be.

Vayci returned with the water. Kiria drank it gratefully.

A warm, black shadow entered her consciousness. Surely it was nothing. She raised the cup to her lips again, seeing if the feeling would leave. It didn't.

The girls started gliding around her room, preparing it for the morning. Tentative, Kiria closed her eyes.

In the Unreal, Firian waited, a dark figure with nothing behind. He wore the same fitted black shirt as when they first met, sleeves rolled up to the elbows. His thumb drummed absently against his leg. Despite that slight tick, confidence radiated from him, as it always did. *Almost always.* She remembered the pain in his eyes when he had looked in his mother's face.

Her breathing quickened as she ran through a mass of emotions: fear, anger, relief.

He's not here. He's not here, she reminded herself.

Surrounded by guards, she had felt safe when she came back to the palace. But she was still alone in her mind.

"What are you doing here?" she snapped. When he didn't answer right away, she said, "You can't take me back."

"I know," he said calmly. His look said otherwise. He fixed his gaze and his mind on her. The space he occupied held only the two of them. No scenery, no sense of place. When he noticed her looking around, a peaceful wooded area blossomed around them, perhaps to make her feel more comfortable. "I just wanted to see you."

She responded with stony silence. That couldn't possibly be the only reason.

"I miss you."

She cut him off. "Why are you here?" she demanded, done with his flirtation.

His voice dropped to a confidential undertone. "The Academy's making things difficult for me."

"I did what I had to."

"I know," he said again. "I don't want anything from you." His voice drifted off as though he wanted to say more. His blue eyes stared into hers, willing her to understand.

She refused. "You made your choice," she said, softening just a little. "You could have helped me."

Looking down, he ran his tongue thoughtfully over the top row of teeth. She knew that something about the situation didn't feel like a choice to him.

How could his loyalty run so deep to the Academy? Could he not see that their methods undermined trust? How could they have a vote if they were willing to coerce the Kingdom into it? What else would they try to force the Keepers to do? Over the years, the Tanyu had had the chance to help the Kingdom, but they chose to remain aloof and separate. This bid for power ran false, self-serving rather than loyal.

"I am going to help you." His eyes lifted to hers, and his lips flattened in a half-smile. His damned overconfidence made her want to punch him in the arm. She drew in a breath to tell him off.

"You're glad I'm alive," he said, rushing to beat her to the words. His thumb stopped drumming as he waited for her confirmation.

She deflated. He knew it was true, so there was no sense in denying it. She let her head drop in a nod. "I am glad you're alive," she repeated, deadpan. She didn't want him dead, but she didn't want him anywhere near her either. He'd shown his character loudly at the end.

Firian smiled and crossed his arms, the muscles cording in his forearms. "And you're back safe," he continued. A step on a path to a conclusion. "Kiria, I didn't mean for all of this to happen. We can help each other now."

Iciness ran through in her veins at the suggestion. She shouldn't be talking to him. Politically, it was a terrible idea. The Kingdom had surely passed out his death warrant to every city between here and the Eradi Desert, and with good reason.

But if he was having second thoughts about the Tanyu, she could encourage him to change and not to fight against them... A precarious plan. If it succeeded, though, she would have won a major victory for the Kingdom.

Firian was stubborn, but hadn't she seen him change over the weeks they traveled together?

"I don't know," she said. "I'll take information you give me." There was no way she'd give him any more information about Brithnem than he already knew.

"Sleep on it." His eyes sparkled with the reminder that her habits had changed because of him.

To give herself more time to think, she nodded and opened her eyes. Trying to be extra quiet, Candrae and Vayci had opened the curtains. They must have thought she had fallen back asleep. Kiria squinted against the light.

If Firian came again, she wouldn't discourage him unless he tried to get information from her. If he did, she would never speak to him again. Simple as that.

She sensed the shadow, like an exhaled breath, leave her mind.

IN THE PALACE, the celebration over her return gave way to serious thoughts of war again. Kiria attended every session and she got the notes from Hada, one of the Main recorders, about what she had missed.

Her initial elation at being reunited with everyone—her mother especially who, despite her joy, looked more worn and haggard than she had ever seen her—melted slowly away into dark foreboding. She began to realize that if they did not win victory on both fronts, they would lose the Kingdom. Brithnem would cease to be the center of noble leadership, of learning, of beauty. Her beloved city would fall.

As hard as she could, Kiria tried not to feel guilty for the time lost worrying about her when she was a hostage. The Second Line had suffered. After the ultimatum came, her mother could think of nothing else. From what Kiria could piece together, someone had discouraged her from attending sessions, since her only thoughts were for her daughter. Something about a lack of clarity and impartiality. The very idea sent Kiria combing madly through more notes, determined to show the Second Line's worth every way she knew how.

"They treat me as though I cannot think," Mother burst out one day, as though to herself.

Kiria squeezed her hand softly as they walked to the Main.

"I'm sure you'll be welcome now," she replied, disturbed she had to say anything like that at all. Her mother should always be welcome. Yet this marked her first session since Kiria's danger.

Although Kiria had only been gone a few weeks, she caught guards and servants openly staring at her, their heads tracking her movement past them. It felt good to be Beautiful again. *A woman is strong when she realizes she's beautiful.* She smoothed down her dress with her free hand, the line from the Scroll resonating inside her. General Brishen had spoken the words to Mari in Carradoc—*Carradoc!*—on the night Shane fell in love with her, though Kiria grew up thinking he loved her long before that.

Kiria wore Beauty differently now, with more purpose, like armor. Since her ordeal, she felt more solid, like a white picture filled in. Her Beauty no longer covered emptiness.

As the two of them approached, guards swung open the ponderous doors. Cúron already sat on his throne and she heard Atty's footsteps shuffle over the long rug behind them.

The Ariocs entered the Main coldly. The many-paned window had been soldered shut—Kiria automatically checked every time. Daelon had already arrived, sitting in the front row. His face split into a smile when he saw them. Also in the front row sat the royal Amiran advisors: Parohim, Chetana, and Reynard, each now with a vote. So far, nothing had really changed, the advisors siding with their respective Keepers.

Searching the faces, Kiria hooked her mother's arm through her own. Did someone want the Second Line to die? Everyone knew that two Keepers would quickly lead to one. Atty would never wish that. Cúron? It seemed odd to suspect him, because he had always been an upright man, good to her, although distant and sometimes condescending. But who else could it be?

Merian strode, stately, to her seat on the dais. Moments later, Atty hurried in wearing a fur-collared Keeper's robe. Kiria settled herself between Daelon and Hada, directly below her mother's chair.

The session began with formalities. Parohim introduced the day's topics (mostly war-related again.) Kiria watched everyone's reaction to her mother's part in the proceedings and piped in with her own thoughts. Her mother barely spoke, but she had always been reserved, content for others to make most of the decisions. Passivity galled Kiria now more than ever, but she had to show as much support as she could. All in all, everything seemed normal.

And then the shadow came.

Kiria shifted in her seat, listening to Cúron's ideas about food shortages now that so many key farmers had become soldiers. Hada's scratching pen ran over the page. Trying desperately to shake off the feeling of dread creeping over her, Kiria cleared her throat, too low to be heard. Daelon noticed. Of course he would. She nodded to assure him she felt fine.

"...until they return from the front. Sublets will..."

Focus on something else. Cúron, with his commanding voice, kept airing his opinions but she found it harder and harder to concentrate. The warm shadow tickled her mind like a hair fallen on the back of her arm—unfindable but unmistakable.

If Firian watched her mind *during* sessions... Her body seized into a tight knot of frustration. She should never have been kind to him when he came the first time.

"Excuse me," she said, almost tripping over Daelon's knees as she hurried over the mosaic floor. Guards obediently pulled open the doors to let her out.

In the hallway, she pushed her hands to her face. Someone gently touched her elbow. Daelon. His blue-gray coat floated to a stop around his ankles.

"You are unwell," he said, uncharacteristically skipping her formal title. The scholarly lines on his face had deepened since the Torithians attacked her in the garden.

"No, no."

"Come. Sit," he coaxed, leading her to a bench along the wall. She relented and sat with him. "My Kepress, something's wrong."

The closest guards stayed by the massive doors, just out of earshot if she spoke low. "I can't go to any more sessions in the Main," she said, avoiding his eyes. His immediate confusion irritated her. Even though she knew that he had done nothing wrong, she was tired of feeling like a liability.

"My Kepress," he replied slowly. "Now more than ever you need to go. This is the time—"

"I'm being watched." She didn't take her eyes off the patterned rug running almost to their feet.

"Who's watching you?" he cried, brow furrowing. "We'll take care of that. Tell me who. You know we'll protect you."

"I know *you* will," she corrected him. Someone—Torithians or Tanyu or Kingdom—was targeting her Line. First the attack, then her father's death, then the hostage situation. Through it all, her mother had been gracefully but definitely shattered. Now would be the perfect time for Kiria to ease into a Keeper's responsibilities, begin to lead the people... "But it's my thoughts. My thoughts are being watched."

"Ah," he said with dawning understanding.

Kiria finally looked up. Would Daelon understand? She wasn't shying away from her duties; she was trying to do what was best for the Kingdom, even if it made her feel useless. "I'm counting on you to be at every session. Do what you must to get them to listen to you. But don't tell me anything until I can figure this out." Anger twisted like a beast inside her.

His eyes softened and she almost regretted her anger. He was her teacher, after all, and one of her best friends. She couldn't afford to alienate anybody.

"You know what I would say. I trust you," she said pointedly.

"What do you have to do to get rid of him?" he asked. So he did understand, in a way.

"I don't know," she admitted. "I'll figure something out. You don't... know what to do, do you?"

"I'm an Amir," he said, with a strange mix of pride and regret. "I don't have the Talent. But apparently you do, so remember the words of the Scroll and let me know if I can help you in any other way. If you can figure out where he is, we'll send someone there. If it helps, we'll find someone who has enough Talent to help you. Maybe the Watchman, or my mother."

Warm relief washed through her. She sighed deeply, unable to stop herself from going on. "I don't know what to do. He comes and... talks to me. I thought I could control it, but just now I felt him there. He might overhear everything. I can't risk it. He's probably hearing this." Her chest tightened with claustrophobia. She fought the urge to check the Unreal.

Daelon put his hand reassuringly on her shoulder. "Don't be afraid. There has to be a solution. I'll pray; I'll be your voice in the Main. The Second Line is safe with me."

She inhaled another deep breath. "You're right." She was still frustrated, but the choice seemed right. It felt satisfyingly like defiance. She would dedicate herself to mastering those things necessary to being a great leader. Let them try to snuff the Second Line. They would have to kill her first. "You're right."

"He's in your mind to spy on you?" Daelon asked significantly, after a pause.

And other reasons. "Well... it seems that way," she said bitterly. "He listens. It's all the same, isn't it?"

"And you know when he's there watching you? Can you do the same?"

"I usually know," she said, catching on. "I know what he's thinking sometimes, but I'm not as good as he is. He had only just begun to teach me how to use the Talent."

"You say he's probably overhearing this conversation." He chose his words carefully. She appreciated his caution, but he didn't fully understand that Firian couldn't just hear words if he wanted to, but might also see her thoughts. Still, maybe it would help. Daelon continued, "I get the feeling that he may be watching you for more than information. Don't take offense, my Kepress."

She didn't answer him, and that was answer enough.

"If that's the case," he went on, "he might come to you sometimes even when you aren't attending sessions. If he does that, see if you can make anything of it—carefully, of course." Daelon came out of his thoughts as he seemed to realize his plan could be dangerous.

"I can do that," she reassured him. In fact, the idea excited her. She could turn Firian's visits to her advantage, rather than feeling like a pawn. "I may as well make the most of this."

"Until we can find another solution," said Daelon. He seemed to think she was too enthusiastic about the idea. "Be very careful. He's double-crossed you before. You know he's dangerous."

She chewed her lip. "I do, but I'm glad I can still be useful. Don't tell the Keeper about any of this," she added. Her mother didn't need to worry about anything else just now. Let her think that Kiria stayed away from sessions out of grief or illness. If Kiria's spy work yielded any results, it would just come as a good surprise.

41

FIRIAN

One thing was clear. Firian couldn't tell Master Belik that Kiria would provide no new information. It was out of the question. The only thing to do was find some way around it.

"Which is a lie?"

"Is this another exercise?" Bard looked down from the top bunk. Dark bags puffed around his eyes.

If this practice didn't matter so much, Firian might let him sleep.

Back at the palace, Kiria had started to use her Ability again. He drank in her Beauty any time he had a spare moment. Though he was careful, she got better at sensing his presence. Like someone half-turning her head to listen, she would lean into him just enough to confirm he was there.

She didn't speak to him. But he remembered the look in her eyes in Shifra. In the golden brown, piercing gaze of her full beauty, that look could stab him through with pleasure. He watched her incessantly, craving that gaze, her attention, a respite from darkness.

In his first rage, Firian hadn't noticed the changed mood in the Academy. Now he saw that fewer people roamed the halls and courtyard. The Tanyu he did see were either quiet with a new kind of weariness, or excited with loud, hollow desperation.

Entire hallways downstairs had been designated as war zones. Retrieving the Lost kept Master Belik occupied most of the time, since few had that specialty. Firian had little contact with him besides giving the information he learned from Kiria —not a task he enjoyed. Especially now that Kiria kept herself out of the Main.

"Yes," he said. "Pay attention. I kissed Alani today. Rian got moved to Erron's regiment."

"You didn't kiss Alani," Bard said without hesitation.

Firian squinted. "Did someone tell you about Rian? I could have kissed Alani."

"No. Nobody told me. I'm just playing along, like you said. Aren't you going with Maya?"

"How did you know the answer so fast?"

"It's pretty easy, if you're paying attention." Bard was telling the truth. Hopefully Firian wasn't as transparent.

Slight emphasis on the last word revealed Bard's defensiveness. His initial happiness at Firian's return had faded since he refused to say anything about the mission. Bard seemed to take it personally, but stopped asking questions after the first day.

Firian cracked his knuckles. He tried a few more and Bard knew the answers instantly. The options must be too easy. He would try something from the mission. Let Bard figure that one out.

"I broke a man's nose with a spoon. The Keepers gave me a dagger as a gift before I left."

Bard's black eyes widened as he considered his answer. He'd never been good at hiding his curiosity.

Finally, some hesitation.

"The Keepers didn't give you a dagger."

"How can you be this gory accurate?" Firian cried, yanking Bard off the bunk.

Bard crashed to the floor, and hopped to his feet. "I'm sorry, I thought you wanted me to do this!" he snapped. The war must really have gotten to him.

"One more," Firian said. A lie.

If Bard could see through his deception, Belik could. If Belik didn't swallow the false intelligence he had to give him… He didn't want to think about it. It wasn't an option.

He dipped into the Unreal for a glance of Kiria.

"Is that her?"

Firian hurdled back into reality. Hatred choked him before he realized it was Bard. Bard, who had never done anything wrong, possibly in his whole life. Still, what business did he have looking into his thoughts?

"One more," Firian repeated. The little stone room they shared had never felt so small.

Bard crossed his arms and prompted him with his eyebrows.

No idea came to him. Bard knew almost everything Firian did. "Which one is a lie?" he said, stalling for time. The lengthening shadows mocked him. Almost time. "Enderin sent more reinforcements to the Kingdom. I stole food from the palace." He hesitated. "My mother is dead."

Before he even answered, Bard's eyes told the answer. "Fir…"

The door opened. Firian had seen the blond man before but didn't know his name. "Bard," he said, "Tiev needs you in the War Zone."

Suddenly ashen, Bard nodded once and the stranger left. His skin's pallor made his spiky black hair more startling. "Later, Firian, yeah?" he murmured.

Firian watched him go, not trusting himself to speak.

Tiev led a regiment now, but he shouldn't be able to take Bard away when Firian needed him. What good could Bard do in battle anyway? He was never a fighter. And wasn't he studying *katah*? Focused special missions, those fitted him better than combat.

Those fitted the war better than combat. The Head's decision to launch this fear campaign, killing civilians in their sleep, made Firian's stomach turn. There had to be a better way to settle this conflict.

The dark orange sun angled through the window, casting deep shadows. Belik waited for news.

Firian swallowed and slipped out of the room. Uncomfortable silence met him. Many had questions about his mission but he'd shut down every one. Only Belik knew the truth.

As he strode slowly to the staircase, the heavy pain hovering over the Academy crept into his bones. Before, pain had sparkled in service of something better, more powerful. Firian had almost longed for it, loving the power it gave him. Now it felt futile.

Several Tanyu had died in the war already, mostly in circumstances more shameful than heroic. Losing to an Amir was already embarrassing, and whispered rumors blamed the Head's mismanagement as well. All of it gave Firian a sour taste in the pit of his stomach.

He expected more from the Academy. If he were in charge, he would end the war against the Kingdom. Or if the royals refused the terms, he would fight on both fronts, mental and physical. He would bring in people who had no Talent or very little and train them to be fighters. Surrounding towns would fear the name of Tanyu absolutely; he would punish incompetent leaders. The Academy would become a place of action, not intrigue.

Belik's door.

Firian calmed his mind, emptied it. Clarity, changeable and

lucid as water, filled him. He took a deep breath and heard Belik tell him to come in.

This time Belik was alone. He wasn't Retrieving anyone; instead he sat just as he always did his plain wooden chair as though it were a throne. It felt like so long ago that Firian had taken lessons with him. Belik, however, hadn't changed like Firian had. The Master glanced inscrutably at him over his glasses. "So," he said, "what do you have for me?"

Firian stepped forward. The Master didn't stand. "The Second Keeper is distraught over the loss of her husband," Firian recited. "She hasn't been attending sessions. Kiria suspects that someone may be trying to undermine the Second Line."

"Emotional," Belik interjected.

The word briefly interrupted Firian's calm. He went on. "They are planning to have her take over the Line from her mother very soon." If only that were true. They could end the war together.

"Anything military?"

"Kiria is scheduled to go to the Main tomorrow morning to discuss war strategy, Master Belik." It could be true.

"It sounds like spying on your lover is paying off so far," the Master said, standing. "So why are you nervous?"

The room was really very small. Firian stood up straighter. "I'm not nervous. I'm anxious that this mission be successful." It sounded too much like an admission of defeat. But at least the idea was plausible.

Belik blinked slowly, almost luxuriously. "She already knows?"

Ice shot through Firian's spine. He hadn't even begun to feed Belik information. "Are you comparing her Talent with mine?" Firian demanded.

"You like her, yes?" Belik said. "Odds are that you of all

people wouldn't be content to watch her from a corner but would rather get the information in a more... intimate way. Where she could see you. Tell me I'm wrong."

"We don't talk about politics or the war," Firian protested. *We hardly speak at all.* "She thinks I come to support her, that I'm on her side. That kind of trust is hard to create." The muscles in his throat felt stifling. "I'll watch her and gather information. After a while I'm sure she'll even confide in me herself."

"Oh, I'm sure," Belik sneered. "Feed you false information, and you'll eat it too."

Firian flexed his hands open and closed. "No one else can do this job."

"You will address me as Master Belik. And yes, we have others who can do this job better than you can. She knows that you're watching her and plans to spy on you now." Suddenly his eyes seemed to turn black with dangerous rage.

Firian tensed for a fight.

"Could you be any more of a disappointment, Firian?" Belik yelled, letting out each word separately, like he was restraining himself from saying or doing something worse. "You...!" He pointed at him furiously, then stood to jab him hard in the chest with a blunt finger. "You were...!" One deep breath composed him enough to speak. "Don't go back to the girl. Someone else will take care of her. You'll go to war under Tiev."

Firian opened his mouth. Belik's quick, murderous glance was enough to let him know that he was fully aware of how much pain his order caused.

"The War Zone. Now." Belik shooed him out with a wave of his hand.

Firian burned hot and his muscles ached with sickness. Any words of protest stuck, choking, in his throat. He couldn't think without feeling poisoned by every thought.

He could see himself, just arrived at the Academy, convinced that he would grow powerful, that all would respect him, look up to him, follow his orders. He grew up before his eyes. He could see himself training, becoming more dangerous. Even Jovan didn't scowl at him. Girls were intoxicated by him, his body and ability. The Scroll was a weapon in his mouth. Few Tanyu knew how powerful those words were. Belik gave him a mission. There they were in the pub, equals. Master Gerand flashed before him and faded, leaving the two travelers, Tanyu and Kepress. Kiria was Beautiful now with a Beauty that burned his eyes. He saw it like the negative image of the sun, always before him, coloring his vision. There was his family—Brett with the baby, his mother crying, and his father not saying he was proud. A wave of sickness. And she was gone. And he was here.

He stumbled backward and caught himself against the wall with his hand. He'd found the War Zone. People began to come into the hallway and disappear quietly in different rooms. They could have been pictures for how much he noted them.

Bard, he finally thought, *is under Tiev too*. If he could find Bard, he would be in the right place. Maybe he would never have to speak to Tiev at all. He knew that thread of comfort would break, but he held onto it until he had to let go.

Unbidden, Bard appeared in his mind, as though he had been waiting to hear his name. Firian knew exactly where he was.

He walked in the large unused classroom without knocking. Motionless Tanyu filled tight-packed rows of chairs. Tiev, looking years older, stood at the front with his eyes closed as well. Bard sat toward the back, with his eyes shut tight and sweat standing out on his clammy face.

A girl named Xan woke up, coming out of the Unreal. With no word from anyone, she came over and took Firian out of the room. He had seen her sometime before but didn't know her well. She was several years older than he was, tanned and fierce-looking with her hair back in a braid.

"Master Tiev sent me to tell you what to do," she said.

He stiffened but wasn't capable of suffering much more just then.

"We are part of the intimidation force," she explained.

Dreams. No real threat. Kiria was right. He should have taken her back to the Kingdom. He had no future here.

Xan ignored the seething fury rippling off him, and continued her explanation. "We fight at night because we aren't going against anyone with real Talent. You will be assigned your target. Most of them fight back, but aren't trained. You can't let them wake up and be able to describe you. Understand?"

He nodded once, glaring blackly at her.

"You're supposed to start immediately." She opened the door and gestured toward an empty seat in the back.

He sat deliberately, setting his arms slowly on the rests and pushing his spine against the wooden back of the chair. His body was the only thing left for him to control.

He closed his eyes. Nothingness washed over him like a thick wave. He sucked it into his lungs like a man eager to drown. The relief was immense.

Then he saw Brithnem. He recognized the houses from Parohim's tour. It was an old part of town near the outer wall—nowhere near the palace, he noticed.

There was Tiev. For a moment they both remembered the last time they had been in the Unreal together, and the houses flickered into a tall round room. In the next breath, the city returned.

"Your targets," said Tiev, pointing to two houses separated in the dark by several streets. The Unreal afforded clarity denied to ordinary existence; Firian knew exactly what he meant. As clearly as he understood which men he was to kill, he also knew that they were strategically meaningless. He was part of a mind-less campaign of fear. If people began dying in their sleep, the others would panic and urge the leaders to give up this Tanyuin war.

Any drone could do this. They had no Talent to fight back with.

Tiev, who obviously had no desire to stay longer than he had to, disappeared and left Firian alone in the phantom streets.

He would rather fight than think, so he went to the first house. A young bearded man slept next to his wife. He had the sprawling look of an oncoming hangover. Numbly, Firian let nothingness come over him again to search for the man's dream.

It came slowly and hazily. Firian hated him for its indistinct-ness. He couldn't accuse the man of anything else and he needed something to fuel his anger. *No Talent at all*, he thought. The man was helpless. Victory over him wasn't anything to live for.

If the Western Kingdom had been stronger, this fear campaign might do some good, but he knew that divisions threatened to crack it from the inside. If the Academy wanted to take control of the Kingdom, Firian could do it faster than this. But he didn't want this gory war at all.

The dream materialized. The fogginess was maddening, but Firian knew suddenly that he couldn't be apathetic here. Later he would figure out exactly what to do. Now, he would be the best fighter they had. He knew how to do that even if his world was crumbling around him.

Mist floated over his vision, but he saw the bearded man, walking by the edge of a wooded cliff. Could he have made it any easier? Firian joined him, gauging his reaction. The man saw him coming from far off and a large knife appeared in his hand.

So the man had been warned about nightmares.

This man wasn't a threat. He was just a man. One who didn't deserve to die.

Something inside Firian sank. The red rage that had pulsed through him cooled. Pausing, he peered into the man's face through the murk of his dream, observing him almost clinically. What did this man have to do with this conflict? Nothing.

This wasn't what Firian signed up for. This wasn't honorable. No one would respect him for killing a defenseless civilian. Kiria would hate him for it, and he would hate himself.

Tiev and the Academy could go to hell with their instructions. If they wanted him to fight, then he'd fight someone who was actually an enemy.

He focused on the palace.

42

KIRIA

BY THE TIME it was clear what Firian was doing, Kiria had already watched him for too long. He was somewhere in the palace.

If he had been looking for her, he would already be in her mind. No, this was a military assassination.

He seemed to be by the Amiran rooms. In the darkness she saw the round lamps and the colonnade. He entered one of the rooms. Not one of the primary advisors' rooms. Not Daelon's. She didn't know whose it was.

Rather than stall to figure out the target, she bolted down the hallway toward the door. Her serving girls and ever-present guards followed behind. "A doctor! I need a doctor!" she cried. Candrae peeled off from the group to fetch one.

They ran out of the palace into the gardens and around the colonnade. "This is it!" she cried, turning the knob. The door wouldn't open. "It's bolted! Do something!"

The guards didn't require an explanation. One threw his weight against it, but the door wouldn't move. Again, and the door hardly budged.

She pounded her fists against the door. "Wake up! Wake up! Open the door! Wake up!"

A few Amir jogged around the corner at the din. Daelon's high-necked coat was unlaced in his hurry. "What's wrong, Kepress?" he demanded.

"Wake him up!" she said. "Tanyu..."

Daelon understood immediately and pulled out a key. Kiria almost fell into the darkened room. She half expected to see Firian standing there, but the little cell was empty except for the sleeping Amir. Daelon violently shook the unconscious figure on the bed. "Wake up! You're under attack!" he yelled in his ear. But the figure merely slumped out of bed onto the floor.

The Amir was dead.

IT WAS my idea to give a speech, Kiria reminded herself as she faced the sun in the ceremonial box at the arena, looking down at an enormous crowd. So many people came that they could barely fit in the arena. Every night, men and women died in their sleep, and people from all over the Western Kingdom were panicking. Someone had to commiserate with them and put their fears to rest. Kiria could do that without knowing any specific war plans at all.

Behind her stood Daelon and Chetana. Her mother's advisor looked more than ever like a general these days. Her long neck and high cheekbones gave her the aura of an immovable statue. She hadn't been idle during the Keeper's stint out of the Main. In fact, from what Kiria could gather, Chetana played a pivotal role in planning the Tanyuin War, as significant a role as the man Firian had assassinated. Daelon, who looked more like a Kingdom man than a Khelê like his mother, always preferred peace. In their own ways, they gave her courage.

Looking down, she saw faces she recognized from open sessions and servants who had come and gone during her time at the palace.

She breathed a prayer and began:

"People of Brithnem, I know that many of you have come here for comfort. I have little comfort to offer, since I also am one of you. I have experienced your pain and your anxieties. What I can offer is what has comforted me. I can think of no greater comfort than these words from the Sacred Scroll: '*Do not fear, for redemption will come to you. While you are surrounded and the shadow of your destruction overcasts your skies, salvation will come.*'"

Beneath the banister, Kiria's fingers fidgeted with the sleeve of her ocean-blue dress.

"We may be at war with the Torithians and with the Tanyu, but the people of Brithnem have always been hardy. We stand with the strength our founders had, the strength that says that we will tolerate no injustice. We are people willing to sacrifice for what is right and in the end we will be victorious."

Jori's face appeared in the crowd, uplifted with the rest. For all his flippancy, he needed comfort too.

"We stand with the strength of hope," she said, her voice rising. "Those words were spoken over our city. The strength of our soldiers may falter but not the strength of our God. When our enemies have fled in shame, we will rebuild our lives with singing."

That line reverberated inside her. When she wrote it, she had hoped it would sound poetic enough to remember but direct enough to reassure the people. If nothing else, it calmed her a little.

"I say these things not to diminish your suffering, but to remind you that it is not in vain. When we rise up with this strength, it is not we, but our enemies, who should fear."

She blinked slowly to check for Firian's presence. Deep shame and sadness filled her when she thought of him. Clearly, potential for good was not the same as goodness. *May we rise to goodness.* In the Unreal, she sensed no sign of him. Only blank haziness in that direction.

She continued. "See the beauty of this city and the people you fight for. Let it fill you with courage to defend them. These are the things that comfort me now and will continue to comfort me through this fight. Join me in looking to God and to each other in our need. At the end of this struggle we will rise again, strong in the justice of our cause and joyful because we have seen the fulfillment of our hopes."

Silence followed. Her eyes were filmy with tears.

Applause roared up from the arena, coursing around the great statues in the center. She may have reassured them with the speech, but they also reassured her with their trust. All these people believed in her and she believed in them. Her life's goal, briefly eclipsed by Firian, came back into focus. Preserving this Kingdom was worth living and dying for.

43

FIRIAN

Just outside the battle room, Firian glared into Tiev's slanted eyes. "I killed an Amir! A strategist!"

"That's why I'm not throwing you out," Tiev cried, keeping his voice low to prevent it from cracking, "but I'd rather have ten Bards who do as they're told than one gory insurgent!" His teeth flashed white in a snarl.

Firian swore at him and stalked away. He wouldn't stay to hear more abuse. Not today. Not when everything crumbled around him—everything he'd built, every relationship he had. Let Tiev try to stop him. Firian had less and less to lose.

Bard was already snoring when Firian got back to the room, even though he had only left minutes before Firian's run-in with Tiev.

Firian felt too filthy to touch anything, even the bed. With something like despair, he threw himself down anyway and gave into exhaustion.

A long night passed in fits of sweat. When morning finally came, enough to give up the fight for sleep, Firian lay on his back. Vague memories of the night before gushed over him.

When he had gone to the palace, he saw the swish of a silk

nightdress in the corner of his mind. Kiria had been very near when he killed the Amir. Why hadn't he stopped? The Amir plotted against the Tanyu, and hated them with unreasonable passion. Firian knew that as certainly as he knew the man's name: Salaar. But his gut clenched with the idea of what he'd done, and that she had seen it all. She might hate him now. Odd that, in the moment, stopping hadn't occurred to him. Rage, desperation, and frustration had thrilled through his body enough to shut off his brain.

He reached, tentatively, toward her. All he found was a soft but alarming buzz. He sat up in bed and held his aching head in his hands. His eyeballs stung and the scabs stretched along his back. How had everything come to this?

"Heard it was a tough night," said Bard quietly, jumping from his bunk to the floor. When Firian didn't answer, he continued. "Me too. They woke the guy up before I could do anything." Relief and bitterness edged his words. He shook his head and hissed a breath through his teeth. "Gore, I hate this!"

Sometimes Firian thought that almost any trade would suit Bard better than being a Tanyu.

"You know," Bard said, "what did that guy do to deserve this, hm?" He pointed at Firian with both hands as though he were one of the targets. "He's not even fighting. I've seen kiddies running around." He looked meditatively at the floor before sitting and pulling on his shoes. "I thought war would be different."

"I know. And you're right. It shouldn't be like this."

Bard shot him an amazed look. "You agree?"

"Yeah, definitely."

A moment of melancholy passed between them. There was very little they could do about it.

"So, I'm off for the day," Bard continued. "Honestly, I don't even mind. You want to get a pint?"

"Yes, I do." Firian tried Kiria again. Another buzz, different than sensing a mind in the Unreal. This humming felt persistent, unmoving, charged with pain if he got too close. The realization left him sick and breathless. He'd felt this once before. A Sentry.

He hurled himself against it. He grunted as blinding pain seared him from the inside.

"You okay?" Bard asked.

"Yeah," Firian murmured. "Let's go." Like birds of prey, his thoughts circled around the Sentry. Without Kiria, he had nothing. He felt like the desert cat in its cage. Even the sky seemed lower. How to break the Sentry...? It was just a strategic problem, like all those others in Master Asoka's class.

The answer broke over him like a wave. He would find them. Sentries were people, punished Tanyu. Funny that he had never thought of them that way. To everyone at the Academy, they were tools, threats, objects of pain. They protected warriors from getting Lost like Anewa and punished others by tearing away the right to the Unreal. But they had to be nearby. He would follow the buzz, lean into the pain even if it broke him. Then he would be free.

<hr>

PAIN PULSED in his skull as Firian wandered behind the Masters' stone houses, keeping his mind on the threshold of the Unreal. Nothing looked like it would house Sentries, just more pine woods. But the sickening buzz definitely began somewhere out there.

"You okay, Fir?" Bard's light feet crunched the pine needles as they went. His forehead creased in concern.

"I need to... find something." He rubbed his temples hard for a few seconds, but it did nothing to alleviate the pounding in his brain. Just concentrating enough to approach but not hit the incapacitating barrier gave him a headache.

"You look awful."

Firian didn't bother to send him a dirty look. He was right. Of course he looked awful.

"What are we looking for?" Bard had known Firian a long time, so he stopped prying, and began scanning the ground as though the answer would present itself.

Firian stifled a groan as the droning ache intensified. "Over there," he said, pointing to a dense clump of skinny trees. They walked together to the source of pain. Firian gritted his teeth, the world swimming in red.

Bard cocked his head and crouched down. "Look, Fir, there's something here." He swept away a layer of pine needles and dirt. A trapdoor.

That had to be it.

"That's it," Firian said, clearing his head, leaning back into reality. Relief swept over him. He hadn't noticed the sheen of sweat over his body.

"What is it?"

Firian considered a moment. Bard would figure it out soon enough. "Sentries."

Bard paled, the black freckle on the top of one ear standing out in stark relief. A curse word escaped his mouth. "Why? Firian, this..." He shook his head.

"I have to." Bard didn't need to know why.

His friend lowered his voice just above a whisper. "We could get kicked out for this."

"I know. We just won't be caught." He knelt down and yanked open the door. Dim earthen steps with only darkness beyond. He walked down. "Coming?"

"There's a reason we're not supposed to know where it is,"

Bard called out in an undertone. But Firian was already treading down the stairs. After a pause, he came too.

Bard closed the trapdoor over them, shutting out the only light. Not only was it too dark to see, but a disturbing haziness grew in Firian's mind. Feeling their way down the uneven steps, they approached the source of the painful buzz, the Sentries who blocked him from Kiria.

Dull red light dawned as they went deeper. Heat rose too, as if they were descending into a furnace.

"Firian," said Bard, from close behind him, "this is crazy. Why do you need to go down here? We should turn around." After a pause, he said, "It's—hm—isn't it? The Kepress?" In a lower voice, "Why are they blocking you?"

Oddly, Firian didn't mind the words coming from Bard as much as he would from anyone else. "It doesn't matter," he muttered. "I'll fix it."

A whisper. "What are you going to do?"

Before Firian could answer, they came around a bend into a cramped room with a large fire on the far earthen wall. It was filled with grimy men and women, all pale with the clamminess of earthworms. The darkness of their burning eyes made them seem like another kind of being altogether. Most of them had long, muddy-looking hair, but a few had haphazardly shaved their heads, even some of the women. Many had scars and burns but the ones who did looked tired, rather than in pain. Some sat, others were standing. Two of them tended the furnace. The air was filled almost visibly with the painful and disorienting buzz of Sentries.

Firian stopped short, as though he were interrupting something. It took him a moment to remember why he had come.

"Who's assigned to me?" he said thickly.

Without a word, the people turned their sunken eyes to a large man. He must have been strong once, but now he looked overgrown and flabby. Now that Firian was paying attention to him, he seemed vaguely familiar. Most of these people had once been Tanyu. The thought horrified him.

The large man nodded, a shade of curiosity on his face.

Firian walked forward. The people shrank from him as oil shrinks from water. "Take the Sentry off me," he said. In the atmosphere of mental buzz, it would be difficult to tell whether or not he did. Experimentally, he tried to reach Kiria. No, the man still blocked his way. "Stop blocking me."

The man still didn't speak. It was almost as if he couldn't.

"I will hurt you," Firian said, looking into the man's dead eyes. For all the effect it had, he may have made a comment about the weather. Bard, however, made a slight noise. Firian had almost forgotten he was there, the only other person alive in this tunnel of the dead. He kept his attention on the large man. Now that the Sentry had a face, Firian knew he could be beaten. "Take it off or I'll kill you," he said. And he would. Horrible resignation settled on him like a weight.

"You'll just be reassigned," said a woman sitting to his left. She had shoulder-length matted hair. It was almost impossible to tell how old she was. Maybe it was just the fact that she had spoken, but she seemed to have more life left in her than most of the others. He definitely had seen her before, many years ago, but he couldn't remember her name. It didn't matter.

He looked to the large man, completely indifferent to Firian's threats, who confirmed what she said.

Firian couldn't kill them all. He wouldn't, even to free his mind. The Sentries were unarmed, hopeless, and clearly abused. The Academy used them shamelessly. If he ran the Academy, he wouldn't let this go on.

I won't let this go on. Excited, he tossed a look at Bard before saying, "If I could get you out of here, would you let me go?"

The Sentries looked at him impassively. He took that as a

yes. "You!" he yelled to the furnace workers at the back. "Everybody! I can get you out. There should be no more of this."

This garnered a little more reaction. "They'll bring us back," someone said.

"I'll tell you where to go," Firian insisted. "If you all leave at once, they won't have enough Tanyu to bring you all back. We're at war. The last thing we need are people blocking access to the Unreal. We'd be better off without you." He warmed up to his new role. "I'm sorry I threatened you," he said in a burst of generosity.

"Where could they go?" Bard asked.

Firian turned around. "If they split up and go into the bigger towns around here, it will be really hard to catch them all. I think it's worth the risk, don't you?"

Bard still looked uncertain, though eager.

"Who do you know who really needs a Sentry?" Firian urged.

"The Head."

"People who would get Lost..."

"Let them get Lost. Losing one person because he has no self-control is better than losing all these people, don't you think?" He gestured around the room. He knew that Bard would give in when he took another look. These were some of the most beaten and dispirited people Firian had ever seen. If Kiria were there, she would set them free too, for the sake of basic justice. Bard couldn't hold out for long.

"You really think it's a good idea?" Bard said quietly. "We could just leave."

"No. Look at them."

Reluctantly, he did. Then his expression hardened with resolve. "Then let's do it now."

"We're going," Firian announced.

Until then the Sentries had listened to their argument blankly, as though it didn't concern them at all.

Bard pulled an old woman to her feet.

"Come with us," Firian said. "We'll get you out of here. Don't break off the shield until you've gotten a little distance away. Can you do that?"

He got no response except a look of genuine curiosity. Affirmative, then. He told them where the nearest towns were and made sure that they all knew not to stay in Tánuil. It was a quick and confused shuffle. The men left their fires and the creatures limped their way up the dark steps.

Above the trapdoor, they almost looked worse. Most of them squinted at the light, such as it was. Only one woman murmured a thank you. When over half of them emerged and headed deeper into the woods, Firian drew Bard back to town. The Sentries could take care of themselves. They needed not to get caught.

Firian waited a moment in the clean air. Then he tried the Unreal again. There she was, standing on a platform, radiant in the sun, wearing a blue dress that flowed like water over her hips and gathered gently at her bust. Her lips spoke of compassion and resolve. Servants had drawn her rich hair back in braids that circled her head. She was nervous. But not because of him.

Bard kept trying to catch Firian's eye as they took a long way back into Tánuil. Would the Sentries be all right? Would they be caught? Now that Firian had access to the Unreal again, the questions didn't seem to matter.

They stopped to have that pint before going back to the Academy. By now somebody would be checking on the Sentries and they couldn't be caught strolling back at the same moment. Besides, Bard looked like he could use a drink.

"This one's on me," said Firian, smiling as they walked into the pub.

"Yes, it is. Bard, leave." It was Master Belik, standing by the entrance.

Firian's blood froze. Bard slunk carefully away, leaving Firian alone.

"Come with me," Belik said quietly. He was shaking. Firian had never seen Belik's eyes so full of rage. An old rage kindled new and irreparable, like family betrayal, needing only a nudge into violence.

Firian obeyed.

The Master led him to the edge of town where the woods began. "Don't come back," he said.

Cotton-mouthed, Firian stood, not understanding.

On the verge of explaining, Belik returned to the safety of the words he had already said. "Don't come back."

Firian's legs took him away mechanically. He had no thought of direction. Just as Bard had predicted, he was kicked out of the Academy. He was no longer a Tanyu.

44

FIRIAN

For a long time, Firian had known what happened to people who were kicked out of the Academy. They were too much of a liability. They had to be killed.

He ran for hours without seeing anyone. His hands numbed. He opened and closed them mechanically as he went. Normally so full, his mind was blank. Only confusion and disbelief flooded in. Muttering like an insane man, he finally slowed down and started pacing back and forth. It wasn't possible. It wasn't possible.

He had failed. That was it. He had failed at his one shot to be important. He had no love and no control. He had nothing.

He sucked air in through his nose and felt the nip of the cold wind. So what if Tanyu murdered him? It didn't seem important. A hard lump rose in his throat and he swallowed frantically.

He was only passively interested in what was happening, as though his body wasn't involved at all. Almost wishing he felt more attached to what was going on, he thought that any physical sensation was better than the torture of the despair oozing up in his thoughts.

Every new thought brought new pain. Bard, the one who was there if he ever got in trouble, stayed beyond his reach now. It was only a matter of time until they brought back some of the Sentries. If the Academy didn't kill him, they would at least keep him out of the Unreal. He had just killed an Amiran strategist the other day and would no doubt be seen as a potential threat to the Academy.

Bard... He would probably never see him again.

Firian's reputation of power was shattered. He had been popular. Now no one knew him.

Belik had seen potential in him. Being disowned by Belik was one of the most painful things. Firian felt sick thinking about it. The Master, for all his bull-necked stubbornness, was one of the best Tanyu in the world, and he had taken Firian under his wing for years, and now...

What could he do now?

Ahead of him, a small stone hut. He entered it blindly and sat down on the floor, trying to concentrate. There was nothing to hold onto, as though he'd slipped down a dark hole in a dream.

But the Unreal was still there. It would always be there. No... No, it wouldn't... He just couldn't picture life beyond it. There probably wasn't life beyond it. Nothing was beyond it.

For now, he could dive in, drown. He closed his eyes.

At first only darkness filled the space. Dim gray shapes appeared, growing and shrinking confusedly, fighting each other. He shook his head, pushed the hair out of his face, took a deep breath, and tried again.

There it was. The fountain in the center courtyard, full of clear water. It was peaceful, like death, in that large courtyard that held no one but himself, the only sounds trickling and splashing. He cupped his hands and dipped them in the fountain. They came up dripping. Carefully, he poured the cold water into his mouth and wiped his face with his sleeve. His eyes strayed to the upstairs room. He had the strange feeling that Bard was in that room still, training or cleaning or sleeping. Just beyond the edges of his mind.

Kiria was still out there too. Why hadn't she come to mind first? Now that he was out of the Academy, there was no added risk in seeing her. The worst had already happened.

Unbidden, the face of the Amir rose before him. He scrunched his eyes tightly together at the memory, even in the Real, and chewed his lip. She would never agree to see him after what he did. With the persistence of despair, he searched anyway. She might ignore him but she didn't know enough of the Talent to block him.

Before he saw her, he heard music. Around her was the music of a stringed instrument, starting at a low somber hum and then delicately soaring into higher notes. She touched each one as though she were singing. The song was the deep maroon and blue and silver of his own sadness. Yes, that's what he felt—sadness. But in her hands, it was beautiful. The song ended on a silver note that hung in the air and swept past him like a spray of mist. Solemn peace flowed around him and he breathed in the silence. The Academy faded away and there was only blackness, emptiness. He took breaths in the void and he saw her, standing as she held the wooden neck of the lyra, feeling the last note and not thinking to look for him. He sat quietly for a moment looking at her.

Then she started peering around as though something was wrong. With wide eyes, she spun around to face him. "Firian!" she cried. Tears of rage welled up in her eyes, which unnerved him. Firian had only seen a dry, hard-edged rage among most of the people he had known. This was different. "How dare you show your face here? *How dare you?*"

"Wait! I... I'm not... I'm not at the Academy now." He couldn't bring himself to say it more plainly.

"Good!" she snapped. "I can't believe..."

He started to walk toward her through the darkness, but she hardened and turned away. He kept walking. She was all he had, now. She was his only hope.

"Never come here again," she said grimly, and she meant it.

"Let me tell you what happened..."

"No! Let me tell *you*." She turned toward him fiercely, red eyes alight. She wielded the instrument like a sword. Just for a moment, her authority made him feel like a child. "Salaar is dead because of you. The people of Brithnem are dying in their sleep and the ones who aren't are panicking. It doesn't matter *what* you say." Her voice rose with heartbreak. And then she breathed. "I won't listen."

He steadied himself. "I'm not... with the Academy any more—"

"I don't care."

"I will talk to you like this or while you sleep," he said, gaining momentum, "but I am not going to leave. The Academy was just using me! I *know* we shouldn't be at war. I know there's a better way than this."

"You seemed to like them well enough! You seemed just fine with their war when you were the assassin!" By just a fraction, her tone softened. "I can't trust anyone who has done what you've done."

"Let me prove it to you."

"No." There was a tiny hesitation. "I wish I could believe you, but I can't." Her raised eyebrows punctuated the statement. "I won't."

He interlaced his fingers behind his back to keep himself from reaching out to her. If he grabbed her arm, she might see it as a violent gesture. She was driftwood to a drowning man, but he had to look non-threatening.

He nodded and stepped back. That was enough for now. She had spoken to him—a small consolation—so he let her go. She shook her head at him as she slowly, slowly disappeared. He watched a wisp of her hair that waved as she cast her disapproving look, and saw her light freckles fade to nothing. Left alone in the darkness, he felt suddenly heavy and lay down to sleep.

WHEN FIRIAN WOKE UP, it was dark. Time to move. Moonlight covered the tree trunks with a luminescent film, enough to see by. He got to his feet, crunching the pine needles, and walked toward Raewhith. Refreshed after sleeping, he scanned the trees for anyone who had come after him. The evergreens provided good protection for the Academy, but also made it difficult to see if anyone was lying in wait. Everything was an opportunity and a liability. What mattered was controlling the environment.

Yesterday he wanted to die, but today was a new day.

First, he needed a weapon. His mind and strong body could go far, but only so far against someone with a knife. Since no one had come back to the Academy to warn against the dangers that awaited those who had been disowned, he knew he had to be ready for anything.

He bent down and picked up a large stick, rough and relatively straight. This would have to do for now until he could get something better.

At Raewhith he would come up with a new plan. He could always escape to a remote corner of the world for a while as he thought of some way to get back at the Academy. Or did he want back in?

Both. I want both.

His heart pounded as he pictured his lessons, his mission, the admiration of the other Tanyu... Aching, he swung the branch in his hand, feeling its weight bend powerfully outward. *All that I've done for them...* He grabbed a fistful of his hair as he pushed it back out of his face.

Deep breath. All he needed was a new plan. All was not lost yet.

Black turned to navy turned to blue, and the stars shone brightly before they winked out above the netted branches.

A head of black hair ducked behind a tree.

Shock coursed through Firian's body. Both hands on the stick, he carefully backed up to higher ground. Let them try to kill him. Shivers ran down his back and neck like spiders. Eyes watched him.

For so long that his heartbeat began to slow, nothing moved. Well then, he would go to them. With long, measured steps, he stalked carefully forward, dark against the gray of the early morning. He had killed before.

Here was the tree where he had seen the head. Were there more of them? He still felt the eyes. Like an animal, he raised his head and turned it cautiously, smelling, listening. No one, but he still felt a presence.

He flexed his hands against the branch, tensed, and swung to the other side of the pine. Nothing. The expanse near the tree was open enough that no one could have run without being seen. He glanced up. The branches were too high and thin to climb. Had he imagined it all? No, there had definitely been something. The emptiness of the forest did not calm his apprehension. If anything, he was more alert. The back of his head prickled. Out there, someone was watching him. He hadn't studied at the Academy over seven years for nothing. He knew when he wasn't alone.

After a few minutes, nothing happened, so he jogged off toward Raewhith. At his pace, he could reach it in less than a day.

Sooner than he expected, he reached the outskirts. Low, brown buildings grouped like gossiping children, ready to give him away. The open spaces between them blazed white with the sun. He would be visible from anywhere. And, since it wasn't an enormous town, surely many people would know the Kess family and be able to spot the resemblance. Besides, he was wearing Tanyuin clothes. That, at least, was something he could change.

Tracing the backwood path to the tailor, he crept up behind the building. With the sun already setting, he could simply wait until dark and then take an outfit from the shop. Maybe he could sleep there too if he got up before morning.

The tingling touch of a gaze had never fully left him, but he'd seen no sign of anyone on his way to the village. Crouched under the window, he faintly heard the murmuring of the tailor and a customer rise and fall, and the light pattering of pins in a bowl. The tailor's voice rose one last time as he bid the other man farewell. The dull thud of fabric staves being put away, the soft creak of boards as he did his final check, and then, finally, he closed the shutters and blew the candles out. Firian waited a few more minutes before he crept in, just to be sure the man didn't double back to get something.

The little store was simple, more for repairing than selling new clothes. Only a few finished pieces were strewn across the two heavy wooden tables or hanging on human-sized frames. He chose a pair of brown pants (which didn't allow for the same range of movement as the Academy-issued ones) and dark green shirt. It would have to do. Inspecting himself in the dim copper mirror, he thought he could pass for an ordinary citizen well enough. A traveler, maybe. From here, he would head to one of the surrounding villages, working his way east until he could find a safer place to stay for a while.

As a child, he had heard of some interesting places. The most he had ever traveled was on his mission with Kiria. Left on his own, he could go anywhere he wanted—the island of Torith, Phlaxtin with its silver trees, the small islands of Shee where nymphs lived, the Watchtower Mountains across the Kheltor, the night colony of Qib in the Eradi Desert...

He pulled out a large bolt of fabric from its place in the wall to use for a pillow, then grabbed both hands behind his back and stretched. Night had fallen. Maybe Kiria was asleep. He turned his mind in her direction. Nothing. That was strange. That also meant that no Tanyu was very close by, which, now that he thought of it, surprised him.

A red flush of shame washed over his face. He had gone back to his home village. The most predictable move. Ignorant moves like that had cost him his dream of the Academy.

The Unreal waited for him like a breathing beast, or like dark waves of water. The dark silence in the Unreal, despite its apparent message that the Academy hadn't discovered him yet, unsettled him. He closed his eyes to focus more intently. Maybe Kiria was asleep but not dreaming. That happened sometimes, but it was rarer than people thought. It was probably too soon to see her anyway. Her red-rimmed eyes meant that she needed time. At least, hopefully that's what that meant. She had optimistically thought he could live up to her expectations, that there was greatness in him. He had seen it in her mind, beautiful and full of light. She might have been projecting her own potential for good onto him, but he wanted to be near that affirmation.

He fell asleep thinking of her but had no dreams.

THE NEXT DAY, Firian, his belly full of a meat pie from the Raewhithian butcher, struggled not to shy away from everyone on the road. Now, when a man appeared coming toward him, he stiffened but stood up straighter as he walked, holding tightly to whatever dignity he had left. He was a Tanyu, whatever the Academy may think of him, and Tanyu shied away from no one.

The man, large and bearded, carried a heavy pack on his back but seemed cheerful. His thick legs fit into deerskin leggings and boots that were both splashed with mud. He wore a round cap on his head, and he gripped the straps of his pack with muscular arms. He had obviously been traveling for some time. As they passed each other, the man nodded to him. "Where are you headed?" he asked with a gruff but friendly voice.

"Imlin," Firian replied truthfully.

"Is that far from here?"

"No, it's just half a day's walk."

The man turned around so he could walk in step with Firian. Something clanked in his pack with every trudging step he took. He didn't seem very threatening, but Firian watched him sideways. "I bet they have an inn and alehouse?" the man said.

"I think so," said Firian, starting to realize that this man really meant to travel with him.

"Then I'm coming too. I've been without company for a long time. That is, if I may." The man looked at him with bright, questioning eyes, sparkling above his whiskers.

Firian should say no and travel alone, but it was a relief to find someone who didn't know about his stigma. "That's fine," he said.

"What's your name?" the man asked, readjusting his pack.

"Belik," Firian replied, choosing the first name that came to mind.

The stranger's eyes darkened for a moment. "I used to know someone by that name. In another life. Older than you, though. Belik, you said?"

Firian nodded.

"Strange. My name is Anewa."

45

FIRIAN

Anewa was a surprisingly chatty travel partner, and as minutes turned to hours Firian got grumpier from a lack of food and water. He cracked his neck and reached to scratch his shoulder under his shirt.

"So, it shouldn't be much further, from what you said," Anewa continued, clanking along.

"No."

"Where are you from, if you don't mind my asking? It's just that I'm interested in that name of yours, and it's good to know who you're with in times like these."

Firian realized that he didn't know where Belik was from. He grunted noncommittally, getting more uncomfortable by the minute. Why did this man ask so many questions? And why did he constantly feel like he was being watched? It was like having a fly near his face that he couldn't shoo away. A constant irritation. He inhaled slowly, took a dip in the Unreal. Hopefully Anewa would be silent long enough for him to have a little respite.

He made the Unreal space into the Eradi Desert and looked up at the stars. The moon-washed dunes surrounded him, smelling like cooling dust and a fresh-cut melon. The black night sky was speckled and splashed with light. Tipping his face upward, he let the breeze flow through his hair. This was better. Maybe he would go to the desert after all. Then he looked down.

With an impassive expression, Master Belik stood there.

Firian almost tripped as he backed away. *A sandstorm might take him by surprise.* He immediately felt one brewing, ready for his command.

"What are you doing here?" Belik asked.

"I left," Firian said.

"Where are you now?"

If Belik didn't know, he wasn't going to tell him. "Not near the Academy," he answered.

The Master ran his hand roughly over the lower half of his face. "No, I mean, where are you now?"

"On the road."

"So you can hear me?"

"Of course." These inane questions must be some trap. He watched Belik's empty hands. "Why are you here?"

"You're not on the road," he said. "You're Lost in the Unreal."

Firian snorted and shook his head. The suggestion was ridiculous. "Don't mess with me." Belik had nothing more he could take. Was he targeting Firian's sanity now too?

"I'm not," he said. "You're in the Second Level. Look around. There's no one else here. Look for your roommate or the Kepress. They can't reach you here."

It was true. Those two presences so constantly on the edges of his mind had vanished. Not even a buzz or an image. No wonder the desert was so quiet.

"You've gone beyond the first level of the Unreal."

The Second Level. Last year, Firian had tried for months to reach it, but he kept passing out when he got close from lack of air. Even he couldn't muster the concentration. Belik had had to get him out every time, like a parent saving a child trapped under a frozen pond.

Firian had never consciously entered the Second Level. Arriving at this peaceful landscape would have been a great accomplishment a few months ago, but now, realizing suddenly where he was felt like going deep under water, running out of air, lungs straining, the panic completely at odds with the strange serene environment around him.

He was alone with Belik, who had no incentive to save him. Firian's head felt stuffed with fear and his knees ran icy cold. Heart beating hard, he opened his eyes to drowning darkness. Desperately, he tried to ascend to the road between Raewhith and Imlin, but he only managed melding the two landscapes. With a shock, he remembered where he had heard of Anewa.

"Where am I, then?" he asked steadily. "Get me out."

"I will."

Firian balked at the slow significance of those words.

Belik stood confidently, with no doubt that he could save him. But he was waiting for some response. Firian couldn't read his face. It didn't seem angry. In fact, there was—maybe—a glint as he had seen in his first lesson. Yes, there was pride.

He squinted. "Why are you helping me?"

"We'll see," Belik replied brusquely, as though awakened from deep thought. "Right now, you're in a hut in the woods. You've been Lost for days."

Firian's head spun. His words sounded too far-fetched. Even now, Belik could be trying to kill him. "So, what do I do?"

"I'll go up one level and you turn your attention to me, you understand? The road from Raewhith?" He lifted a corner of his mouth to criticize the choice. "Were you with anyone?"

"Anewa."

Belik's eyes widened. "You have good senses. What did he look like?"

Firian described him.

"Toward me, not away," the Master repeated, looking sternly at him, and then his image faded into the desert sand.

Firian closed his eyes and obeyed Belik, as much from curiosity as anything else. *Toward me, not away.* At first there was nothing but stifling darkness, followed by stifling light. He jerked violently for air. Squeezed between two worlds. Panic seized him. He *was* Lost. Just as he started to drown, the light began to look like the sun. The sun on a road. He fell, gasping, onto a dirt road similar to the one he had just left.

"Good," he heard behind him. Belik. And he sounded genuinely pleased. "One more. Close your eyes."

Almost against his will, he obeyed the Master again. For all of his manipulation, there was no one better to learn from, and he had done Retrieval a long time. Besides, Firian had nothing to lose.

"You're lying down in front of a fire," he heard Belik say. "You're in a small stone hut. I'm here, making sure you don't die." There was only a touch of irony in the statement. "I'm going there. Follow me up."

Through the emptiness, the familiar presence of his Master moved away from him. Firian followed in his mind.

Firian opened his eyes. Squinting against the fire, he turned away to the darker side of the room. The light seemed oddly bright, brighter somehow than the road on which he had been traveling. He lay on an uneven stone floor, cushioned only with a thin, rough blanket. The round hut, already small, felt smaller because of Belik's gigantic figure sitting over him. Belik's face came into focus as the Master bent over to peer in his face. "You'll be all right," he said in a father's voice.

Pain gnawed Firian's stomach. When he tried to move, he felt how much strength had sapped from his muscles. Even rolling over took more effort than he expected. But pain meant reality, and often led to greater things, so he didn't complain. "Why did you do that?" he said, trying to sit up. Belik had no reason to save him.

A sigh escaped Belik's lips. "I've always liked you, boy. So I checked on you. You weren't there, and you weren't dead. So you were in the Second Level." He shrugged a large shoulder. "No one gets to the Second Level and gets back out. It's too dangerous."

"You did."

He just smiled and adjusted his glasses. "Could you do it again?"

Firian hesitated. "Yes."

"When I first saw you," said Belik, feeling expansive, "I thought you had something. You're insubordinate and Talented. If you can get to the Second Level again, I have a proposal."

This new mood made Firian suspicious. Where had all his rage gone? Anyone who could dam up and re-route his emotions that completely had frightening, enticing control. One day, Firian could be the same, but too often his feelings and opinions showed on his face.

Now, for instance, he was sure he looked dazed, flooded by the shock of being Lost—him, Lost!—and the longing to be accepted back into the Academy. He felt the two familiar presences again, but he didn't pursue them. Belik needed all of his attention. Firian sat fully upright. "A proposal," he repeated.

"Yes. We'll give this one more try." By *this*, Firian suspected he meant him.

Before diving back into the Unreal, he observed all his surroundings closely. He had to have a better grip on the Real to give himself a way out.

After going into the familiar darkness of the Unreal, he sank to a lower level of consciousness beyond it. By the time an island materialized, the journey had left Firian lightheaded. The two of them stood on a large green wedge rising out of the ocean, a slope sliced off with a knife. Firian could see other islands off in the distance and briefly wondered if this were part of the Shee or Sharb Island chains, or if it was just part of Belik's imagination. They stood together at the apex, looking down the cliff into the ocean. Even with the smell of salty grass and the surge of waves, there was an almost unnatural silence and emptiness there, as though whispering voices had just ceased.

"You're here." Belik stood beside him, looking out at the mist hovering over the gray ocean.

"Yes. Just as you said."

"And it wasn't a problem for you?"

"Not at all." The new environment just took a little longer to materialize. Nothing to worry about. He would get even more adept with time.

"Good, that's very good," he said, with a teacher's smile in his tone. "When you were younger, I thought you might be able to, given time. When you weren't fooling around."

Firian stayed silent.

"I'll have to be hard on you when you get back, of course, but you still have many supporters," he said meditatively. "Soon, the Head will still promote you."

"You won't send me back to the same assignment?"

"Under Tiev?" he scoffed. "Tiev's a fool. He has no vision at all. The Academy needs vision. Even Sias is reactionary. But you have ambition."

"Yes, I do."

Belik looked at him approvingly. They both knew he spoke the truth. "The Head is growing older," he said, "and soon he won't be capable of leading. He hasn't set up a clear successor but will have to choose someone before the spring. Without establishing that, the Academy could suffer with all those Masters vying for the position." His tone turned regretful and bitter. "I, myself, am not in the running. Past indiscretions. But you've always seen the Tanyu for what they are and the Academy for what it could be. I've looked for someone like you for a long time. I tried to prepare you for this moment, so I want to help you."

Firian felt hot with coursing blood, trying to find the trap. His breathing came ragged.

Belik sensed his hesitation and went on. "We're both tired of being used. I believe in you, Firian. If you don't muck this up, you could be next in line."

"I'll do whatever it takes," he heard his voice say, but it seemed disconnected from him. How could this be happening? It was the fulfillment of a dream. He realized he knew exactly how he would lead, what he would change. He'd played idly with those ideas for years.

Enough with being blindsided. He could end the wars against the Kingdom, get Kiria back, and shape the Academy to have the power it deserved! He felt like flying, letting the island ground plummet beneath his feet as he shot up and up through layers of cloud and light, but he had to stay rooted to the shared environment. At least until he got better at controlling the Second Level. All these thoughts would stay here, he knew. Nothing on the surface could indicate that he dreamed of becoming the next Tanyuin Head.

He beamed at Belik, eyes shining. "Let's go back to the Academy."

46

———

KIRIA

KIRIA HUFFED out a breath and set down her lyra. Firian stood like a negative image before her mind, his tall, black-clad figure white like a ghost. It didn't seem possible that he had murdered Amir Salaar. He was the same Firian she had known. His eyes seemed sincere—redder than she had ever seen them, and he sounded desperate—but she had been too quick to trust him before.

If she saw him again, she would just ignore him. Before she went to bed that night, she would have to remind herself not to entertain the thought of talking with him, even in a dream. Thoughts and actions were one.

At least now she didn't have a reason to keep watching him. If he really was kicked out of the Academy, then he could offer no new information helpful to the war. She could cut him off completely.

Quickly, she brushed the angry tears from her eyes. Daelon must have seen the gesture, because he stepped tentatively forward, his brows furrowed. His gray-blue robe swayed a little behind him. Feeling heat rising in her face, she pretended to take special care to put the bow away properly behind the neck of the instrument.

"Is My Kepress unwell?" he asked. He always became more formal when he was uncomfortable. He probably knew what was going on.

She shook her head. "No, Daelon. I'm fine. I was just thinking about the composition and... about more ways to help the Kingdom, since I can't attend the sessions." There was only a small note of bitterness in her voice. She needed to occupy her mind right away.

Morale—that's one thing I can offer. Contingency plans. Internal unity. Better war tactics. Strong Keepers...

"Bring me pen and paper," she said as the ideas came, now flowing like water. Let Firian spy. Brithnem needed her to be strong. "Right away."

"Of course, My Kepress," he replied, sweeping briskly out of the room.

She clapped her hands together as though wiping off dust. Fueled by the challenge Firian's presence presented, she felt suddenly energized. Even without the official title, now was her time to be a leader.

ATTY HAD LOST WEIGHT, and his hair lay flat, almost colorless. His splotchy eyes betrayed the fact that he wasn't sleeping. As supportive as Kiria tried to be, he struggled with being a Keeper. She tried to remember if he had ever offered an original idea in the Main. He hadn't even come up with the idea to give the Amir half a vote. That idea was Cúron's.

But he could still attend sessions. She couldn't, at least not quite yet.

"Is he there now?" Atty asked as they walked away from the great carved doors where Kiria found him exiting. Like Jori, Atty alluded to Firian with some bitterness. They had both wanted to be Tanyu and it rankled that they were now the enemy. Disillusionment always hurt.

"No," she said laconically.

"Then I can tell you something," he said, touching her arm to invite her into his suite of rooms. "I want to know what you think." Servants opened the double doors for them into a grand room with high ceilings and rugs. "Come in. I've been thinking." The door closed with a click behind them.

"What is it?" Kiria had come to give *him* information, but he seemed excited.

"He's not there?" he confirmed.

She shook her head. No, she hadn't felt Firian's presence in days.

"We need to strengthen our alliance with Charäkhnem to have any hope in these wars." The vocabulary of a Keeper, not the Atty she knew. "During the next session, I'm going to propose that I marry Shear Ganesha's daughter." He looked tired but proud, and nodded at her, anticipating her disbelief. Shear Ganesha was the king that held the pass between the mountain ranges. Kiria remembered the prince's visit well.

She knit her eyebrows together, scanning Atty's faded fur robe. Having a supporter would suit him. It might bring life back into his eyes. But only if she were kind and understanding. "Have you met her?" she asked.

"No. She's never come to the palace before."

"That's a big decision..." she began slowly, "but it could be good for us. Hm." She wasn't sure what else to say and looked down at the carpet. If he wanted to sacrifice for the Kingdom, who was she to stop him?

"Isn't that a good idea?" he prodded.

The last thing Atty needed was more responsibility. He was

still finding himself. "You know I'll support you," she said, managing to give him a smile.

He nodded again, distractedly.

"I was thinking," she began, getting to one reason she tracked him down after the last session, "what if one of the Lines leaves no heir? I'm thinking about me now. You very well might have an heir with the princess."

He smiled at the thought, and his eyes crinkled.

"Right," she continued. "My Line has been targeted more recently and I realized that there is no provision for appointing heirs that aren't in the bloodline. That's crazy!"

"Oh, I'm sure..."

"Hear me out, Atty, please. I could have died last month. I *am* the Second Line. There's no one else."

They looked into each other's eyes furtively. They both knew her mother's time was over.

Kiria cleared her throat. "We need a contingency plan. I want the ability to appoint someone after me if I don't have a daughter of my own. Just in case."

"That doesn't sound so crazy," Atty mused.

She punched him lightly in the arm. "Why would my ideas be crazy? Of course it's a good idea! That's the first one you could present to the Main. And it could be good for you too, in case the Charäkhni don't take to your idea of marrying the princess. No one else has three leaders. It's a tradition worth preserving even in desperate times." She felt her face flush with subdued excitement.

"I'm a Keeper of Brithnem," Atty replied, latching onto her comment about the princess, a little offended but passing it off as a joke. "Of course they'll like my idea. I'm a catch."

"That's not what I meant. It's just—"

"—in case. I know. I don't like to think about 'in case.'" He unclasped the ceremonial robe he had worn to the Main and swung it off his shoulders, tossing it aside onto a chair.

"You're thinking ahead too," Kiria encouraged. "It's what we're all doing. Another thing we need is more widespread education about resisting attacks in dreams, especially for the men left in the city. They seem to be the ones targeted the most. I can help with guidelines."

"Because you have the Talent." Another twinge of jealousy.

"Because I have the Talent. I also..." she lowered her voice, "have an idea where the Academy is."

Atty's eyes widened, then narrowed. "You do? No one knows where the Academy is."

"I was heading in that direction when I escaped. I don't know exactly, but it would be worth sending a few scouts to the area to investigate. They're elite fighters, but I don't think there are very many of them." She stepped into her mind. Still no Firian. *He can't hide his presence, can he?* The thought made her feel naked, but she risked continuing anyway. The words spilled out of her. "Send people over the Charúnin Thôr and check the woods west of Shifra. I could be wrong, but I think it might be there. What do we have to lose?"

A slow, lopsided smile spread over Atty's face. Finding the Academy could mean a swift victory for the Kingdom.

47

———

FIRIAN

Invigorated, Firian marched back to the Academy at a great pace, as though walking faster would get him more quickly to his goals. He couldn't remember ever having been so happy. Belik walked much more slowly behind him and was soon out of sight.

The air smelled beautifully of pine, and the gray, cloudy sky hanging low over the trees cooled him, promising rain. The soft earth yielded under his rapid feet. If Belik was right, his work was about to pay off. He couldn't wait to be back.

Striding confidently up to the main doors, he let himself into the cavernous hall and leapt up the left-hand stairs to his room two at a time. Before he reached the door, Bard came out and jumped up, catching him in a squeezing hug. Today Firian didn't mind.

"Fir!" Bard cried with a grin as Firian pushed him off. His smile melted away into a frown of fearful concern. "What are you doing here?" he whispered.

"I'm back," said Firian, opening his arms and letting them drop. "No need to explain."

But Bard apparently wanted an explanation. His dark eyes questioned him.

"Just forget about what happened. It doesn't matter." Firian pushed past him to their room, but he had nothing to drop off and he didn't want to sleep. Electricity pulsed through his body. "Do they still have you in the war?" he asked over his shoulder.

"They do, yeah. Same as before." Bard lowered his voice. "I haven't... killed anybody though. Intimidation, mostly."

Firian turned around to face him. Bard, who was nodding, certainly didn't look intimidating. Maybe to the untrained eye he could pass as a fearsome Tanyu, but he was a stickler for the rules, who drooled for his mother's cooking. "I'm sure you're doing well."

A smile flashed over Bard's face which still radiated confusion. "What's going on with you?"

Firian realized he was grinning. He wanted to go for a walk —get out some energy, see more people... "Nothing."

Bard followed him and shut the door behind them. "Why did you disappear for a few days?" He said it like someone who knew the answer but wanted to hear a different one. "Where were you, hm? I couldn't see you anywhere."

"What, are you watching me?" Firian asked, sniffing a new shirt. It smelled like cinnamon again. Bard must have been up to his old habit of putting cinnamon sticks everywhere since he left.

"I know you don't like answering questions, but something's up."

"I'm going for a walk." He pulled the black cinnamon shirt over his head, feeling the soft fabric against his body. He needed to find Maya.

Bard stood steadfastly in the doorway. Firian reached over his friend's shoulder and pushed open the door while Bard puffed air out of his nose, frustrated. After his first burst of energy, Bard had become more subdued and Firian noticed more lines on his forehead, now gray-tinged pale. His normally shining eyes were dimmed with cares beyond the worry that Firian would break the rules.

"I'll tell you later," he conceded, moving past him.

Soon, he would be able to end the war and expand the power of the Tanyu. He just couldn't let anyone know yet.

As he ran back down the stairs, he passed Belik, who had just entered the main hall and was heading slowly back to his little room down the side hallway. He flicked Firian a practiced, impassive glance over his glasses. Firian met his eyes.

The events of the past few days seemed almost dream-like. The unreality of his shifting circumstances was beginning to form a tiny crack in his happiness. If this was another move on their part...

No, he wouldn't be tossed around anymore. The Academy had lied to him and used him too often. He was better prepared now. If they tried to kick him out again, he wouldn't leave. From now on, succeeding Sais Jairon was the goal.

He had to. It was the only way to change everything.

It was the only way to make things right—to make it all worthwhile.

He paused to splash his hand in the fountain.

The huge room was uncharacteristically empty, which surprised him until he remembered that Defenders fought most of the war at night. He could deal with the war later. He ached for company. Maya's upstairs room lay at the end of the hall opposite his, where it began to curve away from the balcony overlooking the courtyard. He ran quietly up the staircase opposite his own and strode down the hall. Tesni, a Charäkhni girl with whom he had shared classes, nodded a greeting to him, but he saw no one else.

"Maya," he hissed at her closed door, darkened by the

shadow of the recessed hallway. He had not spent time with her since before going on his mission, he realized. That seemed so, so long ago. Maybe she hadn't waited for him. He knocked quietly.

Almost immediately the door opened. Her tousled hair suggested that she had been sleeping, but her heavy eyes widened when she saw Firian. "Firian, where have you—"

He wrapped his arms around her back and pulled her roughly against him for a kiss. It only took her a moment to respond. He reached his hand into her warm hair and pressed her head against his. Too long since he had tasted a woman like this. He felt a knot in his stomach begin to uncoil and relax. This was what he needed. Thought gave way to sensation, violent well-being. She leaned into him, grabbing a fistful of his shirt. She still loved him, would wait for him when he needed her, would do what he told her. Others would too.

"Master Firian Kess," Belik announced as they stepped through the doorway two weeks later to meet the Tanyuin Head.

"Our latest Master. Well done!" said Sias Jairon, standing as Firian entered the room. It was just a stone room like any of the others, not even much bigger, with a large desk toward the back wall. When Firian imagined what the Head's office must look like, he had pictured more. Still, the austerity was just what he would have chosen. The focus wasn't on luxury, but on the man himself.

Sias Jairon was smaller than Firian remembered. He looked frail, just by virtue of being human. His skin was light, almost translucent in places, and thin, blue veins branched along his temples. He kept his dirty-gray hair short. He had quick eyes with a joke in them, almost like a bookish man. A slender iron circle with a square opening at the forehead provided the only evidence of his power. Although his bones were steel, his aging flesh reeked of introversion. Stooping, but only very slightly, he sat back down.

Firian dipped his head.

"I remember meeting you," the Head continued, "when you were a boy. I saw you coming."

"You looked up at me," Firian confirmed.

"Such a fiery young boy. I'm not surprised that Master Belik" – he nodded toward him – "decided to promote you to Master."

Firian, despite himself, could hardly stifle a smile.

"The title is well deserved," Belik stepped in, "after he investigated the escape of the Sentries, and provided key information about the Kingdom's movements in the war."

Firian's gut curled. Bard still didn't know about the Sentries. He'd have to explain that he and the others tracking them down had given them a choice: swear allegiance to the Academy and be allowed to serve in Tánuil, or defy it and suffer a double burden of Sentry work, almost sure to make them brain-dead over time. Maybe Bard would think it was cruel, but it was merciful too.

The Head made a sound that wasn't a groan or a sigh—it indicated discomfort. "Yes," he mused.

Firian realized that the Head hadn't been noticeably active in organizing the movements of the war. He usually stayed in his quarters and busied himself with new recruits, a part of the job he obviously relished. Master Belik, Jovan, and others had taken over most of the war planning.

Firian sucked his teeth. How could this man be an effective leader if he wasn't directly involved in the war? He certainly had not been a visible presence during most of Firian's time at the Academy.

Belik broke the silence. "He has, I understand, more information on that front. It could be crucial to us. Firian?"

"Yes," Firian said, snapping back to attention. "I've learned that the Kingdom plans to make a physical attack on the Academy. They are sending scouts now. They don't know the exact location, but they are aware of the general area. Unless we act quickly, one of the scouts might find us."

The Head knitted his brows together and worked his jaw back and forth for a moment. His temples bulged around the modest crown. "Well done, Master Kess. I'll consider what you've said." Almost wearily, he looked down at his hands.

The Master seemed far too disturbed by the news. A Tanyu was imperturbable, strong, undefeatable. Anything but weak. All they needed was action to negate any threat.

A creak behind him meant Belik had opened the door again to go out.

Firian's breathing quickened. Then the words burst from him. "I suggest—"

"Firian!" Belik hissed.

"—we raise a larger army in case one of their scouts gets through. Even if they don't, we might not be able to maintain perfect secrecy forever. It makes sense to have more trained men ready in a standing army. Plenty of people in nearby villages would jump at the chance to serve us."

Close to his ear. "That's enough."

A warning even glittered in Jairon's eyes. "All good thoughts for another time," he said, an ironic smile twisting his mouth. "Master Belik?" With that, he waved them both out.

Silence weighed on Firian as he walked with Belik down the hallways leading back to the main courtyard. Belik's bad leg thumped an irregular beat.

A subterranean grumble, almost like an earthquake, grew in Firian's mind. He checked the Unreal. Not there. His mouth dried up. One more level. It took far more concentration to go down further. Lost, he had actually believed the Unreal was reality, so going down one more level had been intuitive. As easy as entering the Unreal on a normal day. Now that he intentionally plunged more than one level at once, and tried to walk at the same time, the effort almost gave him a headache.

When he arrived, Belik stood in a black landscape, just black. "You want him to like you, remember?" he growled.

Strangely, Firian didn't share his concern. "I don't think it matters. I think I could be the Head whether he likes me or not," he retorted with no emotion.

He knew he was right. In fact, ever since he had returned from banishment a couple weeks before, he had felt stronger, almost untouchable. A deepening well of resolve opened in Firian's chest. He lifted his chin. Even here, in the Second Level, he felt the strength alive in his body as he rarely had before. It coursed in his veins, in his arms and legs and hands—it kept him still, it made him quick. He felt it burning.

Belik examined Firian's face for a few moments. Firian could see his own distorted reflection in the Master's glasses as Belik's searching eyes stared back into his own. Barely lifting both eyebrows in surprised resignation, Belik stepped back again. He always walked with no difficulty in the Unreal.

"Maybe so," he said. His tone was uncharacteristically soft. He opened his mouth again to speak, and then closed it.

Firian swam up toward the surface. Where was the First Level? He only saw blackness. Then he remembered. He hadn't visualized anything for the First Level. This would be tricky. He held the blackness around him like a cloak and stood firmly up. Hopefully that would be enough.

He opened his eyes—he hadn't realized they were closed—and gasped as the wind of his walking blew on his face. Blurry reality came into focus around him. Belik was nowhere to be seen.

48

KIRIA

"No, no, I've got it." Kiria untangled her hair with her spread fingers. Smoothing it as she divided it into sections, she waved Candrae away. She didn't want any help. Maybe her thin hair could be braided into the same impressive design she had seen on someone else earlier that day. It was just the kind of mindless work she needed to go back over the clues to the Academy's whereabouts.

Even without dipping back into Firian's mind, she had many pieces of information she could use. The last part of their journey had been a circuitous path to the Academy. She pictured the maps she'd studied that morning. Two mountain ranges surrounded Brithnem, which was situated on the south-western coast. Charäkhnem filled the pass between them. Charúnin Thôr, the range where she and Firian had traveled, slanted down from the north and the Somul Mountains up from the south. The Academy had to be past the mountains, near the woods where she escaped. Firian seemed at home in forests. The scent of trees clung to him even in cities.

She looked at her braid bending at odd angles with pieces sticking out like a frayed knot. "Come here, Candrae," she said.

Kiria could practice on her. Candrae had long blonde hair while Vayci had none.

Candrae came forward obediently, expecting to fix the braid, but Kiria instructed her to kneel in front of her chair instead.

Only Firian could give her more accurate information, but he hadn't spoken to her since the night with her lyra. The memory made her grit her teeth. She closed her eyes for a moment, her hands piecing out Candrae's hair, and went into the Unreal. Nothing and no one appeared. She wished she had enough Talent to see through Firian's eyes at will—to steal information from him as he had from her—but she was still new at this. He wasn't thinking of her.

A knock at the door. She opened her eyes as a guard announced Jori.

"Let him in," Kiria replied, handing the unfinished braid to Candrae.

Jori ambled in, embroidered vest undone, no urgency in his movements. "Isn't this supposed to be the other way around?" he asked, seeing her fix her handmaid's hair. Candrae stumbled to her feet, embarrassed by his comment.

Kiria ignored the question. "Here," she said, leaning over to the desk and hastily scribbling a note. "Take this to Atty. He'll know what it is." She thrust it in his hand.

"Hello, Jori," he said in a high imitation of her voice. He crunched the note in his hand. "So good to see you!"

"This is serious. Make sure he gets that." She looked into his eyes and pointed to the note.

"All right." He uncrumpled the note and held it up to his face. "'Northwest from Charäkhnem. Past Shifra. Pine forest. More than one scout.' Do you two have secret meetings now? Is this a code?" He sat down on the end of her bed, pretending to scrutinize the paper.

She stood up, took the paper from him, folded it pointedly,

and handed it back. He set his mouth, apparently irritated that she hadn't liked his joke, and stuffed it in his pocket. "All right. I'll get it to him. But what's there, I wonder?" He sat up straighter. "Wait, is this where you went with…?"

"Not exactly, but I think it may be where he is now." She kept her sentences short. Who knew if Firian would appear again, spying on her thoughts?

Jori raised both eyebrows. "I'll make sure he gets it," he said, meaning Atty. "Then we can finally kill that gory traitor!"

"Well, that's not… It's not just about him. If we know where the Academy is, we can end the war." It sounded simplistic, she realized, as she sat back down and took the braid from Candrae's hand.

"We'll get him, though. Don't worry," said Jori.

Kiria focused her attention on the braid. It was much easier to braid another person's hair than her own, she thought as she folded the strands over each other. "I need pins," she muttered. Vayci hurried forward and got them out of a drawer.

"I'm sure you want to see him caught more than I do," he continued, uncharacteristically serious. "I heard four more people died in their sleep last night."

"It wasn't him," she said absently.

There was a pause. "Why do you do that? It could have been."

She shook her head. She was getting to the end of the braid. Vayci handed her a pin and showed her where to put it in. "Is everyone ready for the presentation?" Kiria asked. Tomorrow, every neighborhood block would gather in the arena for basic information on staving off mental attacks. More awareness would hopefully result in fewer casualties. She would teach part of the lesson.

"I don't have anything to do with that. I've already been briefed," he replied shortly. "Do you still care about that Tanyu?"

"No, of course not."

"Sometimes it seems like you do. He's a monster, Kiria."

"Okay," she said, exasperated. She didn't need another person telling her that. She knew better than anyone else what he was.

A buzz just beyond the edges of her consciousness made her heart drop. Should she check if he had overheard her plan?

Jori shifted his shoulders uncomfortably. "Maybe it's a good thing you aren't going to the sessions."

"Excuse me?" Kiria snapped.

"It's like you don't mind that he's there, just watching you."

"Of course I mind!" She was doing everything she could. Her mother, overwhelmed, only went to about half the meetings. Daelon spoke as often as he could in Kiria's stead. But it still felt like the Second Line was dying. It broke her heart. "Jori, I will give everything to this kingdom. *Everything.*"

Jori set his mouth in a line. She felt him surging away from her. He closed his fist on her note.

A SHEEN of sweat covered Kiria's forehead after giving her part of the presentation. She fanned herself in the cool of the arena passage. Again, she mouthed the words she had used in her lesson. They tasted dusty. Words seemed poor, but she had offered what she could.

An odd feeling crept over her. It settled in the pit of her stomach. She fanned more furiously as it became harder to breathe.

He knew.

She knew it as certainly as she had known about Amir Salaar.

Returning quickly down the passage through the arena,

Kiria called Daelon over to her. She squinted at him, her eyes still adjusting to the inside darkness. He walked in silence with other high-collared Amir, one of whom had also presented. Mental battles almost always took place either at sunrise or sunset, so he could be spared to speak during the middle of the day.

Daelon hurried over to her. "Yes, my Kepress?"

The fabric of her dress strained against the length of her strides. "Tell the Keepers and the Amir in charge of mental warfare that the Academy knows we're coming."

"You're sure?" he replied, matching her hushed tone. His eyes admitted doubt.

"Absolutely."

***

KIRIA STARED AT HER MOTHER, who was sitting in a chair by the window. Mother's long, brown hair glowed in the light, but her skin was ashen. She had missed another session, claiming a headache. Kiria hated the voice in her head that told her that was a lie. Her forehead scrunched with frustration. Her mother had to see that on her face, but she couldn't help herself.

Seeing this weakness in her mother pained her. She felt the Second Line dying by the day.

"Don't look at me like that," her mother began, lowering her voice.

Kiria took a deep breath. "Why are you giving up like this? We're in the middle of two wars and *you* can actually go to the Main."

Merian gestured for Kiria to sit down next to her, but Kiria didn't respond to the invitation. Instead, she stood, looking down at her mother from a little across the room. Merian seemed to realize that Kiria would not obey and continued, "You know it's been difficult for me these past few months…"

Kiria felt a twinge of regret. She shouldn't speak to her mother this way, especially when her disappearance caused so much of her pain. "I know," she said softly. "But the Kingdom needs a Keeper."

Her mother wilted, bobbing her head in a nod.

"Mother." Kiria walked up and put her hand on her shoulder. She swallowed a few times before speaking again. The words had grown inside her. Now ripe, they were ready to come out. "I can do it."

Dusty lines covered her mother's face as she looked up. The weighty whisper had left little room to doubt her meaning. "But Kiria…"

"I want to serve the Kingdom. We're facing wars on two fronts. I know what's at stake, and I think I can do it." Her eyes burned with passion. They *could not* lose. Not now. So many people needed justice—innocent men and women slain in their sleep, soldiers in Torith, Firian, her father…

Kiria took her hand off her shoulder, waiting for a response. Was that sadness or relief on her mother's face? "I know you've wanted this a long time," she began slowly, not meeting her daughter's gaze. Some thought seemed to crush her under its weight. Her mouth lined with grief. With deep love, she finally looked up. "You have more to give than I do."

A lump filled Kiria's throat. "I don't want to take this from you if you're not ready."

Her mother gestured for her silence. "No," she said. "I believe you can do this. Ever since you came back, I've seen the change in you. The fire."

Kiria nodded.

Her mother's eyebrows met, suddenly concerned. "Is that Tanyu still watching you?" At this point, everyone knew about

Firian's invasion of her thoughts. Happily, her mother didn't know many details.

"Yes, but not for long." One way or another, she would make sure those words were true.

Tenderly pulling her arm, Mother drew her into a chair next to hers. This time, Kiria yielded. Her mother's eyes glistened as she gazed in her daughter's face. "I missed you," she said, pushing hair away from Kiria's forehead.

Kiria's eyes prickled. "I missed you too," she whispered, "especially when I heard..."

Her mother nodded so she wouldn't have to finish the sentence.

"I just want to do the right thing," Kiria said. It was the closest thing to an apology she could muster. Hopefully her mother would understand.

A kind hand in hers told her that she did. "I'll talk to Chetana so she can prepare for your coronation."

Kiria folded her mother's hand in both of hers. "Thank you," she said, and sighed.

49

FIRIAN

No more light streamed through the little window in his room. Firian pulled off his shirt and rubbed it absently over his hair. Tomorrow morning, he would start fighting one-on-one with the best mental warriors Brithnem had. To fight made his mind and blood tense in a satisfying way. His breathing shallowed thinking about it. But he already knew that a victory would be two-edged. Kiria would know. Fighting Amir almost seemed unfair, like Masters fighting Learners. They could only struggle for so long.

And ever on the edges of his mind was the old Tanyuin Head, looking down at his unmoving hands.

"*Master* Firian!" He looked up. Bard, with his face still wet from the washroom. "I heard! So, you're not going to get one of those houses in town?"

"No need," Firian said. After they freed the Sentries, Bard seemed alight with a fresh sense of purpose. If he knew the truth, he'd be horrified.

Bard grinned and closed the door behind him. "Good for you, mate," he said. "So, you got to meet the Head and everything?"

"Yeah." He threw his shirt in the corner and sat down on the bed.

"It's about time! Everybody knew you were going to be promoted." He checked himself, remembering Firian's stint outside the Academy. "You know, except…"

"Let's not ever talk about that."

"I need to know sometime," Bard said, uncharacteristically combative. Maybe the war had changed him a little bit, made him less submissive.

"Sometime."

Bard cocked his jaw and climbed up to the top bunk.

Firian heard shuffling at the top. "I'm going into the war tomorrow," he said.

"As a warrior or a leader?" Leaders, like Tiev, organized Defenders in their subversive campaign, while warriors fought against other people with the Talent.

"Warrior," Firian answered, lying down and rubbing his hand over his face.

"Ooh."

"Yeah."

"What was the Head like? I hardly ever see him."

Firian grunted. Unreasonable anger smoldered in him. The meeting had almost felt like betrayal. Firian had given his life to the Academy, to the Tanyu, and the man in charge seemed too weak to defend it.

Kiria was smarter than he liked to admit. She could figure out the general area of the Academy without too much difficulty. If the Head did nothing more to fortify it, one of the scouts would surely find it. What then?

"Firian?" Bard's voice prompted from above.

"Oh, he was all right. He's getting old." He suddenly wished he could tell Bard about his intention to succeed Sais Jairon as Head. Better to keep it to himself for now. Bard would support him, no matter what. He needed other Masters on his side, though, so he wouldn't have to vie against too many others for power. Jovan came to mind. Balling his hand into a fist, Firian flexed his forearm in the dark. Especially after his days spent Lost, he knew he might not be able to take Jovan in a fight. They would be closely matched at least.

"Hmm." More shuffling. A deep breath. "Well, good luck tomorrow. Don't wake me up, okay, huh?"

"Okay." Firian rolled onto his side, but he couldn't sleep.

***

THE OLD MAN was obviously of Khelê descent. He had nut brown skin, reddish hair, and a short, white beard. Firian wouldn't have feared him face to face, but often the older someone was, the better they could use the Talent.

They stood on a flat, sun-baked rooftop made of stone as red as the man's hair. It felt rough under Firian's feet—the man was good at details. Above them, the sky looked as clear and hard as a gemstone. Ponderous dark mountains rose hazily in the near distance. It could have been somewhere in Charäkhnem.

"Do you see it?" the man asked.

"Yes," Firian replied.

At first the man didn't move. He just shifted his weight a bit from side to side as he stared back at him. Did he expect Firian to attack him first? Well, if that's what he wanted...

Firian gathered energy into him, felt himself expanding, growing taller. Now he was looking down on the man, who seemed unflustered by this turn of events. Firian, now huge, easily straddled the entire width of the building, with one foot on each of the far edges of the roof. *Crush him like an ant.*

As Firian lifted his foot, the man flew suddenly, impossibly, around and up into his face, wielding fire and smoke that obscured his vision. Firian swallowed a cough—none of it was real anyway—and transported himself, now normal-sized, to a nearby rooftop. He almost liked this spunky old man. *What now? Ah yes. Water.*

Firian placed his hands calmly behind his back as the man bulleted toward him, running at twice the speed of a normal man. Water. He commanded it to gush from behind him as though a tidal wave had risen above the rooftop. A pulsing wall of liquid flowed, roared, in, sweeping away dust and flags and baskets. As though he were in a glass bubble, Firian stood untouched. The man's eyes dilated in surprise. Caught off guard, he flung heavily upward with the waves. His body suddenly looked like a child's. Firian watched him for a few moments as he struggled to disbelieve his circumstances, maintain the environment, and think of a counter-move. Belik had put him through similar tests when he was younger. He had almost choked. At the memory, he twisted his mouth to one side.

This wasn't a fair fight. The hot pulse of strength didn't live in his arms anymore as it had that morning, when he had woken up hungry to battle. He could let the man live.

The waters subsided. The rooftop instantly cleared and dried again as the old man stood up in dripping clothes. He looked small now. If Firian wanted to, he could kill him. The man believed too much in the Unreal. More even than Salaar had. Strange for an Amir, or at least that's what he assumed the man was. As they looked at each other, he noticed a familiar brightness in the man's eyes. Brown skin crinkled around them, but they looked dark and shining, almost like Bard's.

They both knew in that moment that the fight was over. No needless bloodshed. Firian had won this round.

Everything dissolved and re-formed into the small plain room where Firian stood alone. He took a deep breath through his nose. Bard was onto something when he said he didn't like this war. He agreed with the premise that the Tanyu needed more power in Brithnem, but this war seemed like such an indirect way to get there.

Belik's words burned almost tangibly in his mind. Now, to gain power in the Academy, *that* was a worthwhile cause. He stretched his back, looking up at the ceiling. Who were his competitors? These fights with outsiders felt hollow—empty flexing. Even the deaths so far were no reason for glory. His real competitors were inside the Academy, the others angling for succession.

SITTING on the edge of the fountain, Firian stared at the floor, his hands clasped between his knees. Scouts came nearer every minute, and still no word of reinforcing the Academy's defenses.

Sais Jairon was too passive. Too passive where it mattered and too violent against innocents. He had war strategy turned completely on its head. If Master Jairon would not protect the Academy's interests, Firian would.

The thought had come to him last night, inevitable but surprising. He couldn't really be considering it, of course...

It took about three weeks to travel between Brithnem and the Academy. There was still time for the Head to move. But would he?

There were easier ways to get things done.

Like a man going underwater, Firian plunged into the Unreal. Down one more level. A moment of struggling to breathe and then... space opened out like a subterranean cave, cold and dark and vast. He waited. The glint of wetness glimmered on the sides of his cavern. Here and there, a drip.

Why was he even waiting here? Maybe Belik was busy. Besides, he wouldn't tell anyone about his idea. It wasn't even a real idea, more of a hypothetical situation. His breathing sped up. No, he couldn't seriously entertain the thought.

Dismissing it with a wave of his hand, as though his idea had flown toward him with new-grown wings, he kept waiting.

Was that...? It was. The dark shape of Belik slowly materialized near him.

"Progress?" he asked gruffly.

"Some, maybe. I talked to Master Jovan yesterday. He's going to give me more training." His words sounded empty, probably because his thoughts didn't fill them.

"That's not what you need."

"I think that's the only way he'll give me his support," Firian said.

Belik shrugged his head to one side. "The man does need his precious pride to be stroked. And you're right. He will probably suggest himself when the time comes."

Firian nodded, cracking his knuckles. *What am I doing?*

"Anything else?" Belik prompted, lowering his head with a look alternating between annoyance and curiosity, as though he guessed something.

"The Head still hasn't... taken my advice, has he?"

"No. I think the border patrol will take care of the scouts."

"But you saw my point?"

"I do."

They were silent for a moment. The cave dripped.

Part of him wanted Belik to read his mind so he wouldn't have to say the words that grew louder inside him. Just by proximity he should be able to hear them. Firian's blood pulsed as the certainty grew. He had to say something.

"When do you think the..." He cleared his throat. "When do you think the Academy will be ready for new leadership?"

The line of Belik's mouth softened. It could have been a smile. "It's not about when they're ready." He shook his head.

"People are never ready for change. But good leaders make it anyway."

"You think I'm ready now," Firian said in a low voice. It was a question.

"I think you're ready now."

They paused again, the realization growing like weight upon them. Could he really do it? The fulfillment of his dream, the strengthening of his Academy, the power he had always wanted, the ability to protect, to command...

"I think you're ready now," Belik repeated.

Firian looked him seriously in the eyes. "Will you help me?" he whispered. The meaning was clear.

Belik began to nod, first slowly, then with more conviction. "Yes, I will."

So it was real—his idea was real.

The face of Amir Salaar came back to him like sickness. He had died for no true purpose. He killed him only to prove that he could serve the Academy better than everyone else—that he could assassinate their enemies. Rage had fueled him so ineluctably that he hadn't considered Kiria's face, her disappointment, her anger. Where was the strategy? What had they won? Fear in the Kingdom? That was nothing. They could achieve that in other ways if necessary—if Firian thought it was necessary. There were other, truer, reasons to kill. Necessary reasons.

Change wouldn't come on its own.

Together, they would kill the Tanyuin Head.

50

FIRIAN

When Firian walked back into his room, Bard was digging through the drawers of the dresser. The distinct smell of cinnamon wafted up from them.

"Hey, Fir," he said. "Have you seen my Tanyu figure?" He held up two fingers to show how big it was. "I can't find it."

Firian smirked. "Is it with your Indisfate game?"

"No."

"I haven't seen it. Do you want me to look?"

"Yeah, check your stuff," he said, arm-deep in clothes.

Firian dropped to the floor and lowered himself to see under the bottom bunk. Dust and hair and crumbs of food layered the ground, but no wooden figure. Bard was funny about his stuff from home. So attached. Firian pushed himself up, got to his feet, and waved his blanket around once. "Not here," he announced.

"Oh, how was this morning?"

"What?" He snapped around to look at Bard.

"The fight? How'd it go?"

"Oh." That seemed like weeks ago. "I won. He didn't... die, though."

"You know, that's good," Bard said thoughtfully, scratching his head and giving up his search in the drawer. He picked up the lumps of dark clothes from the floor and shoved them back in the dresser. Pushing the drawer closed with his elbow, he turned back to Firian. "Are you all right?"

Where did that question come from? "Yeah, of course."

"You just seem a little off. You've been weird ever since you came back. Did you check the bed?"

"Uh huh."

"I wonder where it went..." He scrunched his face to the side thoughtfully before returning to his last idea. "Yeah, I know you're always thinking about something, but it's like you have all these secrets. More than usual."

Firian shrugged, figuring it was best not to speak at all. Bard, sometimes, made him feel exposed. No one else but Belik had spent so much time with him. Other people found him mysterious, but Bard knew him too well. Not that he knew everything, of course.

"Fine," Bard said. "You can keep your secrets. Maybe I'll find out sooner or later."

He would, Firian realized. This was one secret he couldn't keep in his mind. Eventually, in a day or two, the wheels of power would turn to him. Lightheadedness passed through him like a ghost and he smiled.

"What?" Bard asked suspiciously.

"Nothing." He shook his head. Waves of excitement flooded over him, alternating waves of terror, happiness, surprise... Hopefully Bard didn't see into his mind.

His ascension would be a surprise to many people. Let it be. Longing to give voice to his thoughts in the Second Level, he lay down and pretended to rest. He could barely get to the Second Level if his eyes were open. The last time he tried, he almost ran into the wall. No, better to be completely still.

He heard his name as though the sound came from underneath the earth, or inside him. Belik already waited for him. He
dove in.

"I think we should do this quickly," Firian said breathlessly,
not waiting for the other Master.

"I agree," Belik said. They stood close together. The landscape wasn't important.

"When?"

"I have two Retrievals in the morning. Damn fools," he
muttered. "Tiev's one of them."

For a moment, the surprise didn't register. There were bigger
issues at stake now. "Tomorrow, then?"

"Night."

"Right, tomorrow night," Firian said breathlessly.

"Without the Sentries, he's vulnerable. Of course, they've
brought many of them back, but I don't think they've found the
one that normally covered Sias during the night." He gave Firian
a meaningful look. Was that amusement? Reprimand? Congratulations? "He kept himself protected when he slept," he
explained.

That was common knowledge. Firian had bypassed Sentries
before, so he figured that nighttime would provide their way in.
He had a few ideas.

"This is your parade," Belik prompted.

"Right, there are a couple ways I've thought of. One of us
could get him to go to the Second Level—use some excuse—and
the other could go into his room and do it." The guard outside
Sias Jairon's door came to mind. Losing a fighting man would be
a shame. "But a better way," he continued, "I think a better way
would be to make him think he died in his sleep. It would be
tricky, but the two of us could do it, disguised, of course. The
suggestion from the lower level that his heart is slowing and
stopping, and his breathing..." He stopped and shook his head

like a dog shaking water from its fur, shocked by his own words. They burned like liquor and went to his head. He wanted more.

"It would take two of us..." Belik said. "But it could be done."

The concentration to achieve what they were talking about would be almost impossible with one. Alone, getting Lost would be inevitable. Belik's face, almost luminous with hope, seemed to search the ground for his thoughts, to gather them. Light glinted off his spectacles as he turned his head from side to side. It felt strange to count on him so heavily.

"The war will be enough of a distraction for the rest of the Tanyu. I don't think they'll interfere," Firian said. His chest rose and fell with his breath and he stretched his numbing hands. "We'll meet at midnight."

Belik hummed, his gazing turning inward for a moment. "Once it's done, the first person to claim responsibility will become the new Head. Everyone will know what happened." That someone killed him. Firian's heart felt like a heavy cord of firewood. Belik scoffed, almost to himself. "In his sleep!"

"In his sleep," Firian said, the words suddenly empty. He tried to fill them up with meaning.

"The Masters will support your nomination. Don't worry." He eyed Firian as a bird would, beetle-black pupils inhumanly focused, yet detached.

Firian nodded, more to expel his manic energy than to agree. "They always talk about needing young blood. And who else is there?" Tiev was Lost. Jovan and a couple others would put in their names, but Firian was the future of the Academy.

"Who else is there?" Belik echoed. "Just you, Kess."

***

MIDNIGHT CAME QUICKLY. Bard was used to Firian leaving in the middle of the night, so he probably wouldn't notice if he snuck out now. Firian knew he should lie in bed and do everything only in his mind, but, as he lay there, heat and chill chased each other over his body. Even pushups would be better than being immobile. Besides, it felt right to be closer to the Head when he met Belik. What if something went wrong?

He slipped into a classroom near the entrance to Master Jairon's hallway. His room was attached to the office Firian had seen, so he knew exactly where it was. As he stood in the dark, the expanse of open air washed around him, feeling more unreal than the space where they were about to fight. The quiet, too. It was as though the darkness washing against him in its cavernous silence pressed him up against the wall where he stood, listening. Blood churned in his ears. His neck bones creaked.

The sense arose that he could walk away from all of this, and yet... he couldn't. Something like fate gripped him. No, not fate. A choice. He'd made a necessary choice. One life for true, lasting change. One life in exchange for many. He was about to become the strongest Tanyu—the strongest Tanyuin Head— that anyone had ever seen. He was the one who could bring the Academy to its full glory, and give the Tanyu the esteem they truly deserved, and win Kiria's respect. He could end the war and still bring the Academy's glowing potential to light.

Didn't he want that change? Didn't he want both Kiria and the Tanyu?

Yes, I do.

He took a deep breath. Right—the Unreal. He had to meet Belik.

He sank down into himself. Belik was there, in the darkness. The Master's grim eyes glinted but he didn't speak. They both knew what to do, but the operation would be tricky. The first step was disguise. They couldn't seem to be themselves. They had to work almost exclusively in the Second Level, where they would be hidden. But to find someone else in the Second Level... someone who didn't know they were coming... Only very, very few could attempt it.

Firian almost tangibly felt Belik's mind reaching out with his toward the Tanyuin Head, cautiously but resolutely. Like a snake. Recognizing the Head's subconscious was like encountering a familiar smell. They circled it, drawing closer. There it was.

Firian's shallow breathing sounded hoarse in his ears, though he stifled the sound as much as possible. They were swimming through the Head's subconscious now. The sensation was similar to entering someone's dream, as Firian had recently done to those in Brithnem, only the shapes were less distinct. Thick fog covered everything. Dark colors swirled, and emotions swept across them like wind. Dark blue peace, red lust, black fear...

Time to emerge from the Second Level, disguised as stifling vapor, thumping like a heart—an incredibly difficult manifestation to maintain.

Firian looked at Belik, nodded, and went first. Though he had practiced water drills many times, maintaining a vapor state to suffocate the Head took all his concentration. Subtlety was the key. Slowly building, building, enveloping his dream until it turned to darkness. Just an old man asleep in bed.

Struggling to keep his form, Firian felt a sudden rush of power—Belik to help him. With the other Master, he kept his concentration. Pressure built in his head.

There, just then, he slipped, perilously close to revealing himself. Just in time Belik sent the energy he needed, as he had during Tiev's practice fight.

Sais Jairon lay sleeping, his mouth slightly open. Fighting through the headache, Firian stretched himself further, harder. Nothing in his life had been more crucial than this moment.

The fog thickened, the thumping became a heartbeat—loud blood.

How long would he have to keep this up? He was losing his grip, too much strain on the last knuckle of his mind as he climbed.

...*Help! Help!* His frantic thoughts toward Belik, his momentary loss of concentration, made the fog shimmer like a mirage.

He froze. No breath. The thumping got quieter.

The sleeping Master rolled onto his back and looked up. Straight into his eyes. "Firian?"

51

FIRIAN

Firian opened his eyes, gasping in the darkness of the classroom. His hands were shaking. What had he done? What could he do now?

He couldn't let the Head tell anyone. He couldn't let his secret out.

His entire life... all he'd endured, all he'd done, would be for nothing. He'd never do any good; he'd never change the world. He'd end up dead or back in Raewhith.

Firian moved mechanically out of the classroom. There was no choice but to finish it. This time, Belik was too far away to help. He patted his clothes, almost distractedly. He had no weapon with him but a small knife he always carried.

There are many ways to kill a man...

Jovan's words on his first day.

His legs felt heavy as they took him closer to the Master's door. It was like walking through pudding.

The knife shook in his hand. *Wait, wait... What about the guard?* He hadn't planned to kill him. But now he had no choice. The pit of his stomach grew leaden. Another life on the altar.

The guard would sense him coming. That prickle of the

Talent would reach him before he saw Firian. So Firian could use that. He had to.

Surprise was his best chance to overpower a man who was no doubt better armed than Firian. Maybe he even wore armor. Firian suddenly felt naked. His thin black shirt rubbed against bare skin, both so easy to tear. Surprise. He had to have surprise.

Rooms and hallway, all darkened except for tiny flames, floated by like something in a dream. Mutant shadows reached across the walls and ceiling, calling him into their dark ritual.

The only ideas breaking through him seemed juvenile. Would they work?

Where was his center, his stamina? He drew a slow, shaky breath into his core, where blood thrummed like a heart in his stomach.

He could do this. *I can do this.*

Around the corner from the Head's office, he stopped. Time to decide. Best just to do it. There wasn't anything supremely unusual about a Master staying up late and roaming the halls. So he would be an ordinary Master. Simplicity often succeeded when complicated plans failed.

He walked casually by. Maybe the guard wouldn't notice the turmoil in his mind, or the knife ready on the far side of his body. He didn't remember the guard's name, but he knew his face—long nose, splotchy tan birthmark on his neck. His neck.

The guard didn't issue a challenge. Firian calmed himself as much as he could, which wasn't enough, and strolled to face him. Without a word, quick as a snake, he sliced the knife upward and plunged it behind the guard's neck, where the spine meets the skull. Hot blood gushed over his hands and the guard, his sword half-unsheathed, dropped like a puppet to the ground.

Wiping his hands distractedly, mechanically, on his clothes, he stepped over the guard and passed into the office, and then opened the inner door. Sais Jairon was his main target.

Now speed was his ally. He strode in and grabbed the pillow from beneath the old man's head. Without looking at him, Firian smashed the pillow against his face, gripping the edges. When he flailed against him, Firian got on the bed and held him down with his body. Sais kicked and twisted under the blanket, scratching at Firian's arms, trying to pull the suffocating pillow off.

Although he had some strength born of panic, the Head did not continue for long. Slowly his actions subsided. The frantic breathing under Firian's legs deflated, leaving nothing but emptiness.

Firian remained rigid. Moving felt like an admission of guilt. The dead weight under him made him nauseated and confused. Firian rolled off the bed as the room tilted and spun unevenly. When he released the pillow, his hands stayed clenched in the same position. It was almost painful to open them.

His hip bumped into something metallic, sliding it forward on the side table. The iron circle, Tanyuin crown, rocked gently back and forth.

It was a sickening thought to rearrange the pillow. But he had to, he had to. He grabbed the soft edge of the pillow with one hand, smearing it red, and with the other lifted the heavy head of the Master, replacing the pillow where it had been. Did he look asleep? He looked ashen, eyes squeezed shut. Was that a normal way to sleep?

Would they know?

The idea of touching the man's face or getting his body on its side made hot bile rise up in his throat. A massive wave of chills splashed over him. He couldn't bear to stay in that room. He stumbled out. If he could make it back to his room, he would be safe. His hair was drenched with sweat so he passed his sleeve over his forehead to soak it up. The wetness on his sleeve just made him colder and clammier.

A call from deep within. He jumped. He'd forgotten all about Belik. *No. Not now.* He had to get to his room.

He was in front of his door. *How did I get here so fast? Which way did I go?* There must not have been other Masters in the halls, or else someone would have challenged him, shaking him out of his daze with a question about the dark blood on his hands and sleeves that stuck to the hair on his arms.

His heavy breathing still came in ragged gasps. The door rattled once under his shaking hand as he opened it.

Inside was only silence. Bard didn't seem to have heard the noise.

If I can just make it to bed...

He flung himself forward into the darkness.

SOMETIME IN THE middle of the night, Firian had woken up, covered in someone else's blood. He snuck to the washroom, scrubbed his hands and arms raw, almost vomited, changed his shirt, and went back to bed.

He woke up the next morning with a fever and a headache. but he went to fight anyway. The day felt like a dream—mental warfare, training with Jovan (who told him the Head had been killed in the night), meeting with Belik.

By the time he went to Belik's room, his legs trembled from work and cold. Pain pounded his head. He creaked the door open.

"What's wrong with you?" Belik asked, looking up at him.

"Nothing. Sick," Firian grunted.

They hadn't met since before the incident, even in the Unreal.

"I thought you'd lost it."

"Yeah." Firian was in no mood to talk. He sat in the chair

opposite Belik's and closed his eyes. If he wanted to talk to him, he could do it in the Unreal. He dove down into depths of clear water. One landing, two...

When Belik arrived in the same shapeless cavern where they had made the plan, his eyes were shining. "People are eager to put a new Head in place," he said. Though his tone was business-like, he shifted his weight eagerly.

"Okay."

"Have you heard anything?"

"No."

Belik blew out an exasperated breath. "Gore, Firian! Do you even hear what I'm saying to you?"

Firian looked back in his eyes deliberately. This man knew what he had done. Suddenly, he hated the power Belik held over him. "Yes."

"I've been talking to the other Masters," Belik continued. "And there is no heir apparent. I thought more discussion would gear toward you." Something in Belik's tone tried to prepare him.

Firian licked his dry lips, feeling the light leave his eyes. *Was this all for nothing?*

"You have to tell everyone what you've done, how you've saved them from tyranny, all that stuff. They'll have no choice once you take the position."

Firian felt his pulse in his Adam's apple. *Tell everyone or it will be for nothing.* He picked the skin around his new ring.

"Should I do it today?" The voice came as a whisper. Firian couldn't muster more.

Belik regarded him, looking over him as a strategist would look over a map. Suddenly, he smiled. "No regrets, Firian." He leaned closer in fatherly confidence. "Remember why it needed to be done. You've done well." The lines around Belik's eyes softened compassionately. "And you'll continue to do well. The Academy needs you, and so do I."

Then he reached out and put a heavy hand on Firian's shoulder. The simple act had more affection in it than he would have expected. How could Belik even reach him across the chasm he'd created by his murder last night? He felt adrift and hollow. Other people seemed to live across an unbreachable space. Yet Belik found him there, and still believed in him. Hadn't left him. Hadn't rejected him.

Firian nodded in acknowledgement, feeling his face grow hot. His eyes stung. He sniffed hard, trying to rid himself of his welling emotion. Belik patted him once and turned away, almost ashamed of his outburst.

The rush of the idea came back to him. Control of the Academy. Make it better. Make everything better.

He could ignore the racking chills for one day and pretend that his head didn't hurt so bad he could barely see. Mental warfare was his specialty. That was all it took. Shove it into the Unreal and carry on as though nothing had happened, as though he couldn't see his face, and his knees didn't still feel as though they were straddling a dying man struggling to be free from under the covers, and his hands weren't sweating and slipping little by little down the edges of the pillow, and he didn't hear the subterranean muffled gasps.

One day. He could pull himself together and take control of the Academy. He couldn't let it be for nothing. It had to mean something.

No regrets.

52

KIRIA

ATTY, for one, was thrilled. "I won't be alone!" he cried.

What an odd thing to say.

"You were never alone," Kiria replied. Atty did always act as though he were alone, or somehow on the outside. Yet he technically had more say than anybody, Cúron excepted. She loved Atty, but sometimes his victim attitude got under her skin. "Cúron and my mother were always there, and Jori sometimes, and all the Amir. And you're friends with Daelon, right?"

They were sitting in the dining room where they only sat for more formal occasions. Candles hung in the chandelier above the long wooden table that was clearly meant for hosting large parties. Stretching on like a garden row, a refulgent bouquet of blue and purple lilies bloomed along the center. Official announcements and arrangements often happened here before being announced in the Main, at least when it pertained directly to matters like the coronation. All of the Keepers' families were here—a small group—their advisors, and representatives from the army and palace staff. In all, about twenty sat solemnly eating their shrimp and pickled lemon.

At a nod from Kiria's mother, Amir Chetana stood up. She

had pulled half of her curly reddish hair up for this occasion, which was beautiful but made her cheekbones and dark eyes more severe. "My Keepers," she began, "I have the privilege to announce that Kiria Arioc, heir to the Second Line, will become the next Keeper of Brithnem in three days' time." This was not new information to anyone there, but applause erupted across the whole table. "Her coronation will take place in the Main at midday. All the arrangements are being made; you all have your assignments." Chetana scanned the people sitting at the table. "The rehearsal is tomorrow..."

Under his breath, Atty whispered, "It'll just be nice to have someone on my side."

"I've always been on your side," Kiria said. Even though she'd chosen a very loose dress for the occasion, the new tattoo still burned along her shoulder blades. "Maybe you should stand up for yourself if you feel nobody listens to you. You're a Keeper."

"Yes," he mused, then lowered his voice so it was barely audible. "But Cúron never listens to what I say. If I disagree, he ignores me and follows his idea."

"All Keepers get the same vote." Maybe their whispering was starting to look conspicuous. Kiria smiled across the table to look more at ease.

"I've won the vote and he still goes ahead with his plan."

"That's not how it works." She took a bite of shrimp.

"I'm telling the truth!"

Maybe he was overreacting, but she had seen Cúron charge ahead with his plans and avoid bringing them to the Main at all if he suspected there would be opposition. With everyone, there was a bit of political maneuvering if they thought it was for the good of the Kingdom. Too much, and the other two would check him. That was the strength of having three leaders. "If that's happening, why haven't the Amir said anything?"

"I don't know. Maybe they're on his side. You haven't been in the Main for a while."

She set her jaw and squinted as she looked at him.

"...Head, Sias Jairon, is dead." Chetana's voice suddenly invaded her consciousness again.

Kiria spun around in her chair. The Tanyuin Head was dead? How had she not known about that? Apparently, others around the table had the same question, because they immediately looked at her. A twinge of relief registered in some of their faces as they saw that she'd had no idea.

"He has been succeeded by Firian Kess. It is of the utmost importance that we find out his position on the war as soon as possible."

She flushed cold, then hot. Breath was hard to draw. How had she not known? How had this happened? He had said he would end the war. Was this his way of doing it? She had too many questions. They buzzed like insects, relentlessly, and made her dizzy.

Atty put a hand on her shoulder. Eyes looked back into her own as she focused on the faces around the table again. "I'll find out immediately," she told them.

THE NIGHT before her coronation came sooner than she had expected. All alone in the Main, Kiria stood beside the enormous statue of Mari. As a child she had liked this statue the most, because it showed a woman as big and strong as any of the men.

Servants had already cleared the chairs away for the ceremony. Because of the gulfs of darkness, the room looked as enormous as it had when she was young.

She saw a young man in rags wash the feet of the lowest

serving man. *"Thus will I serve my country, thus will I serve my God."* It had happened right over there. *"A robe... shoes... crown..."* So they would all call for her. She would rise and her mother would fall.

She craned her neck to look up at the statue. Mari had a sword on her hip and regal bearing. Standing up straighter, Kiria knew she would have to embody that strength for the people of Brithnem. The time had finally come—the moment she had awaited with such excitement, dread, and anticipation. Finally she could utter the words that had dogged her, pleased her, all her life: "I swear to serve my country, the Western Kingdom, and its capital, Brithnem, to the best of my ability, to guide her through war and peace, freedom and judgment, with wisdom and integrity, for as long as I live."

But first, a matter of business, of war and peace. She closed her eyes. He would be there. He hadn't been for a while, but she knew better. With her coronation the next day, he would want to make an appearance, whether to congratulate her, taunt her with his own new position... something.

She recreated the Main in her mind with its floors glossy and lanterns lit. An almost exact representation. Careful to hide her Beauty in the Unreal, she sat on the middle throne, her throne, waiting for him. Firian might be Head of the Tanyuin Academy but she was still a Keeper of Brithnem. Her power exceeded his.

Where was he? She waited a few beats, and then said, "Firian?" Her voice echoed in the empty room.

He appeared, standing on the mosaic of the First Line. Nothing about his appearance had changed. He still wore simple black clothes and boots. Wait—was that a crown? A thin metal circlet with an open square in the center sat on his head, overlapped by his dark hair. As he strode up to her, his eyes gave an almost chemical glow, unhealthy but beautiful and bright. He jumped up the stairs to the dais and stood looking down at her.

"Firian," she said coldly, diplomatically.

"Kiria."

"I hear you are the Tanyuin Head now." She had questions about his ascendency but now was not the time to ask. More important was the kind of leader he would be now that he had the position.

"I am. And you are about to be a Keeper of Brithnem." A smile curled his mouth. Was he proud of her or of himself? Maybe both.

She nodded and continued the speech she had rehearsed in her mind. "That puts us both in a position to make good on our promise to end the war." His looming over her was becoming bothersome, so she stood to face him. "I have called you to find out your official position on the war as Head of the Academy. We could start peace terms right here."

"I agree," he said. "We have your scouts" – her breath caught – "and I intend to send them to you with my terms in writing. I won't hurt them."

She set her mouth in a hard line. Of course he had terms. "What are your terms?"

"To end the war immediately."

Her tense body relaxed, but she still suspected a trap.

He wasn't finished. "And to help you in your war against the Torithians, as long as you give us some of your troops to work with, and allow us to have the Torithian prisoners of war. That's all."

"And the vote?"

"We haven't earned a vote with you yet. You know that." His mouth twisted ironically. Maybe that was a flash of regret in his blue eyes too. "And we don't need it. We're going in a different direction for now. More independent."

"The Tanyu have always been independent," she agreed. "You're not... rejecting the Kingdom, then?"

"No." His fingers flexed forward, but he drew them back again. "We're simply acknowledging that we haven't really been part of it for a long time. We're different. But we can be allies again."

She digested that idea. "And you're sending all of this in writing? With the scouts? All of them?" If he allowed them all to return, that could mean revealing the location of the Academy, and they both knew it.

"All of them," he repeated. "It's a new age for the Tanyu. We aren't going to keep our location a secret for much longer." He lowered his voice almost to a whisper, looking straight into her eyes. "I said I wanted to show you."

Her heart beat quickly and her stomach knotted. "What you would do as a leader. I remember. I'll show you, too."

They stood silently a moment. The awkwardness reminded her of how young they were—very young and very powerful. Together they had the power to make peace... or war.

She cleared her throat. "So now we're allies," she said slowly, puzzling out the risks and opportunities.

He nodded.

"I'll wait for the writing," she said.

"I know."

She almost didn't believe it. First the Tanyuin War ended—she would check the terms and make sure there were no unreasonable demands—and now a chance to end the years-long Torithian War? Her beautiful city could find peace. Her dreams could come true.

She looked back at Firian, at the throne, at the statue in the corner. For the first time, she truly felt worthy to lead.

53

FIRIAN

FIRIAN STEPPED into the Head's office, his heart thumping hard and slowly, Belik following behind. The room smelled like dusty paper and wet stone. The blank rock walls, identical to all other rooms except for the second door, provided nothing but a backdrop for power. There was a flash of that power in them, wavering like heat. Firian felt more solid and real than they were.

He stepped around to the back of the desk. Taking a deep breath, he sat in the chair. Belik stood silently before him, his expression almost obedient. Firian smiled. "Get me some official paper, and a pen."

Belik nodded, a slight smile running over his mouth, and turned to leave. As he went out the door, Bard almost ran into him but jumped to the side in time. Firian hadn't seen Bard in days. Ever since the announcement, Bard wouldn't look him in the face.

Firian waved him into the room, but he didn't come.

"The Tanyuin Head..." He ran both hands down his face in place of words, his black eyes wide.

"It's true!" As Firian stood, he flicked a glance at the other door leading to the bedroom.

His roommate leaned into the office, open-mouthed, looking from floor to ceiling, and at Firian, awestruck. His eyes searched like conscience. "Fir, I can't believe it!" he said. "How could you do it?"

For a second, Firian squirmed. *So many reasons.* "I wanted to end the war with Brithnem."

Bard eyed him skeptically. Then he shook his head.

"No, I'm doing it today."

"I'm not an idiot, Firian." Bard hardly ever used his full name. His eyes continued to roam around the room, as though searching for something that would justify his friend's decision. His gaze lighted on nothing.

He should send him away. No Tanyuin Head courted the favors of a Defender. But this was Bard, who should stick by him. "I can do good here," he said, remembering Kiria. "You can help me."

His friend still stayed like a shadow at the door, dressed head to toe in Academy black. Something like pain crossed his face. "Fir..."

"I'm serious about the war."

Bard walked forward, one hand over his mouth, his eyes welling with tears. Light shone on the bottom lids. He swallowed visibly and turned his red face away. "That would be..." He couldn't say what, because his voice broke. "Ah, Firian!" He lay flat on his back beside the desk and folded his arms over his eyes. It didn't mean forgiveness, but friendship was a possibility again.

Firian laughed through his nose. The air felt fresher.

After a moment, Firian kicked Bard in the side. Bard's supine figure suddenly seemed out of place. "Get up! You're in the Head's office."

"Right, yeah..." he said automatically, scrambling to his feet. "I can't believe it."

"Master Kess?" The earnest voice was new. A grizzled man with tan, leathery skin stood in the doorway. Firian had seen him before in Tánuil, hadn't he? Anyway, he looked familiar.

"Yes, what is it?" Firian quickly returned behind his desk.

The man looked pointedly at Bard, as though asking whether he should wait until they were finished meeting. Apparently his information could not be given in company.

"I'll talk to you later," Firian told Bard, who took the hint and left.

The man closed the door behind him with a strong, rough hand. He spoke in an urgent undertone. "We've found and captured the last of the three scouts from Brithnem. Should we execute them now?"

"No, bring them to me."

"Yes, Master Kess." The man exited the way he had come.

For now, he would send the scouts back to the Kingdom with his demands. After he helped Kiria win the war and brought Torithian fighters back to the Academy, where all the best fighters belonged, he would announce their location. No more hiding.

These next simple moves would mean the end of two wars: Tanyu and Torithian. At the end of them, Firian would have the makings of a powerful military that didn't rely solely on mental warfare, and Kiria would love him for it. His breathing quickened and a smile spread across his face.

The door opened. Belik walked heavily in and set the paper and pen flat-palmed on Firian's desk. "Don't get used to me getting you everything you want," he said, smiling.

"Can you watch the door for me? The Kingdom scouts are about to get here."

Belik grunted, but his face wasn't as hard set as it usually was. He was proud of the new Tanyuin Head, but he wouldn't say it again. "You're making quick work of this."

Firian nodded. Watching the Master follow his commands tasted sweet and sent a thrill through his bones. When he was alone, he leaned back in his chair and took a luxurious breath. He had made something of himself. That little boy in Raewhith would hardly recognize the man he was today. He, Firian Kess, could change the world. To what extent remained to be seen. Soon, everyone would know it. But for now, he'd content himself with just a few.

Leaning forward, he grabbed the pen, smiled, and started writing.

To Yanon and Lithia Kess...

ACKNOWLEDGMENTS

I started this book when I was seventeen, so I know there are many more people to thank than I'll remember here. Here's at least an incomplete list of the many, many people who helped, encouraged, and supported me in creating *Firian Rising*:

My parents, to whom this book is dedicated for so many reasons

Summer and Hannah, my amazing sisters who love me no matter what

Levi and Noah, my wonderful brothers-in-law and some of my first readers

Mary Beth, Ellen, and Jamie, my ever-supportive best friends

Mr. and Mrs. Egizi, two of my best teachers, and Dr. Jackson, one of my best professors—I wouldn't be the writer or thinker I am today without you

Ed, Debbie, and Amanda, whose writing group feedback is always so kind and helpful

Carole, Soren, Morgan, Jeff, Kim, Nate, Steve, Melissa, and the rest of the incredible teachers I get to work with—thanks for the encouragement, the history knowledge, the English lessons, and the passion to teach high-schoolers all that you love about your subjects

Quinn, Cadman, Mira, Hans, Ian, Leslie, Jeni, AC, Zach, Caitlyn, Hailey, and all my students (I wish I could name you all!) who got excited about the first chapters, created promo art, and provided me with possible fantasy names on bus rides

Katrina Arnold, my helpful editor

The great people at Damonza who designed my gorgeous cover

This list just scratches the surface of those who have impacted my life and this book for the better. Thank you so much for everything. Because of you, I can finally pursue my dream of becoming an author. Words fall short to appreciate you all.

ABOUT THE AUTHOR

Carly Stevens lives and works as an English teacher in Colorado. She plans to keep writing adventure-filled fantasy novels about courage and hope.

To find out more about upcoming projects, check out her website: https://carly-stevens.com
Her author newsletter is the best place to get an exclusive, behind-the-scenes look at Firian's world. You might even win free books for signing up!

CPSIA information can be obtained
at www.ICGtesting.com
Printed in the USA
FSHW020502251019
63380FS